Praise for the Weird

"One of my favorite book series . . . so much action, so much violence and, oh, the lust radiating off of our heroes . . . I definitely recommend this series for lovers of all things paranormal and awesome."—*USA Today*

"Robson's blend of smart-alecky wit, good old-fashioned romance, and suspenseful episodes of fighting off evil spirits form a paranormal thriller that will make pulses pound." *—Publishers Weekly*

"[With Robson's] edgy, witty and modern style of storytelling, the reader will be drawn deep into this quirky paranormal world. . . . Strong pacing, constant action and distinctive, appealing characters—including a gutsy heroine—will no doubt keep you invested."—*RT Book Reviews*

BY CECY ROBSON

The Weird Girls

A Curse Awakened (novella)

The Weird Girls (novella)

Sealed with a Curse

A Cursed Embrace

Of Flame and Promise

A Cursed Moon (novella)

Cursed by Destiny

A Cursed Bloodline

A Curse Unbroken

Of Flame and Light

The Shattered Past Series

Once Perfect

Once Loved

Once Pure

The O'Brien Family Novels

Once Kissed

Let Me

Crave Me (coming soon)

Feel Me (coming soon)

The Carolina Beach Novels

Inseverable

Eternal (coming soon)

Infinite (coming soon)

A Weird Girls Novel

Cecy Robson

DEDICATION

To Jamie and Nic, for believing in the magic.

ACKNOWLEDGMENTS

To my three babies who still think I'm great despite my not-so-great moments. Who still smile when they greet me and who find all the gore and twisted humor as funny as I do.

To my husband. Jamie, you're still the best man I know. Where would I be in publishing and in life without you?

To my agent, Nicole Resciniti, who fell in love with my Weird Girls and made this all possible.

To Lisa Filipe, my hardworking publicist who gives as much as her heart as she does her time.

To Gaele Hince, my copyeditor. You really get me, don't you?

And to my fans who die a thousand deaths along with my characters yet still beg for more. Thank you for falling in love with my heroes and finding a place for them in your hearts. Believe me when I say, I laugh (and cry) right along with you.

Chapter One

You know it's going to be a bad day when you wake up in the morning and the first word out of your mouth is "fuck."

My right arm—or should I say my *new* arm generated after my real one was chewed off by a psycho werewolf (no, this isn't a joke) —buzzes me awake. That's right, *buzzes*.

I do my best to hide my limb. Not just because it's as white as alabaster. Or because of the fluorescent blue veins that run its length. But because it's doing things I can't control, like, interfering with my magic, glowing like a light saber, and now, making noise.

I lift my head, half-asleep, wondering how a wasp's nest found its way beneath my pillow, but too exhausted to run away screaming, *yet*. If you were familiar with my life and world, you'd understand pissed off wasps in my bed wouldn't be the craziest, or scariest, thing that's ever happened to me.

My eyes narrow at the quivering pillow as my haze clears. Maybe it's because I'm tired, or maybe it's because I'm bitter as all hell, but I can't help thinking that the arm *and* the pillow are laughing at me. I pull my glowing and buzzing arm from beneath the fluffy white pillow and swear.

"Really? *Really?*" I ask it. "What's next, singing and origami?"

Apparently, my incandescent light saber arm isn't a fan of sarcasm and proceeds to flicker on and off like a twisted strobe light. I shake it hard and smack it against the mattress for all the good it does. "Knock it off," I tell it.

It's not that I think it listens, or that I manage to control it, there's simply no controlling this thing, but somehow the glowing recedes and so does the noise, and my arm resumes its "normal" death-like tone.

It quiets, no longer casting light. I should be thankful, right? I should be happy, true?

Oh, I wish.

The color is startling, and contrasts horrifically against my deep olive skin. But its eerie tone and its unpredictability aren't the only things that trouble me. There's something wrong with this limb. It doesn't belong on me. And in a way, it doesn't belong in this world.

Maybe like me, it's something that wasn't supposed to be.

I sigh and clutch it against me. It feels like my old arm, the skin soft and smooth. It moves like my old arm. I'm not limited with either fine or gross motor skills. But it's not . . . *human.*

When I lost my real arm, the Squaw Valley Pack Omega, created this new one using ancient werewolf magic. If I were a *were*, I think things would have been fine, peachy-keen, and all that good stuff. But I'm not a *were*, or human, or witch, or vampire, or anything. Not even a little bit.

My sisters and I may look human, but nothing like us has ever existed on earth. And because of it, earth's ancient magic seems to really resent helping a weird girl like me.

I used to wield fire and lightning with ease, and catch glimpses of the future. I used to be badass. I'm no longer badass, and the only things I catch now are odd glances cast my way.

"Are you the punishment for my sins?" I ask my arm.

I don't expect it to answer, but it does. Sputtering light and buzzing before abruptly ceasing its response and sinking into the mattress.

To anyone watching, this whole thing might be funny. To me . . . nothing's been funny in a long time.

For a moment, I simply stare at it. There's a part of me that wants to cry, wondering what it will start doing next. But I've already cried too long and hard for what it has cost me.

Or should I say, *who* it cost me.

I scan the room. Nothing of Gemini remains. Not his clothes, not our pictures together. I even deleted and blocked his number. For all my arm disgusts me, I never expected it to disgust him more. After all, this was the werewolf who claimed me as his mate. The same male who swore he'd love only me forever.

I suppose forever only counts so long as I didn't change, so long as I remained perfect in his eyes. But I never claimed to be perfect, even if many believed I'd looked the part.

My arm flickers and *zings*, the electrified charge is strong enough to startle me and slap any remnants of sleep away. Yeah. No way am I perfect. Not by a long shot, especially with this thing constantly mocking me and reminding me of everything wrong in my life.

A sharp rap to the door has me glancing toward my right. "Taran?" my perky sister Shayna calls. "I heard your alarm clock go off. Want some breakfast?"

I lift the bane of my existence and sigh. Alarm clock? I suppose that's one word for it.

"T?" Shayna presses. "I'm making waffles."

She semi-sings her last few words which is a very "Shayna" thing to do.

"I'll be right out," I answer.

"Cool!" she responds. "I have plenty."

It's not that I want to eat. It's that I know how worried my sisters are about me. So I sit with them when I can, and plaster on a smile when I need to, but even that's burdensome, which sucks. I don't want my time with my sisters to be a chore. I love them. But I've learned some things can't be helped.

My arm fires with its haunting glow. Case in point.

With a groan, I slip out of bed, pulling on a fresh pair of panties and a bra before heading to my bathroom to clean up. After a few swipes of mascara and some lipstick, I yank on a form-fitting red dress and shove my feet into a pair of platform pumps, doing my best to strut and not collapse back in bed. Yet even though I'm almost to the door, there's one more thing I need. Most women won't leave their homes without their cell phones. I can't leave my room without my elbow-length gloves. It helps me hide the ugly appendage and the light show that accompanies it.

But now that my arm's buzzing . . .

I pause with my hand on the doorknob. What am I going to do about this thing?

I take a breath and wrench open the door, tugging on my gloves as I walk down the hall and into our large kitchen. Shayna abandons the waffle iron when she sees me and skips forward, her ponytail bouncing behind her.

She throws her arms around me like it's been months, not hours, since she's seen me. "Hey, T!" she tells me brightly.

I pat her back, wishing I could hug her for real. But real hugs lead to my very real tears, and I can't keep doing this to my family. "Hey, princess. Wow, everything smells great."

It's the truth, yet my comment sounds phony and forced, even to me.

Her arms fall away slowly. Although she keeps her grin, I sense the worry behind it, as well as her fear. "You look hot," she tells me, punching my good arm affectionately.

No. I look acceptable. I used to spend over an hour styling my dark wavy hair and applying my makeup. Now, I do enough so I don't resign myself to sweats, watching made for TV movies, and stuffing my face with potato chips.

"Thanks," I manage with yet another forced grin. I make a show of taking in all the breakfast foods, including the freshly baked muffins. "Yum. Do you need help setting the table or anything?"

"No. It's all good."

She says nothing more which is unusual for Shayna. Either she's waiting for me to speak, or she's debating what to say. I can't take another pity party so I lift a pan filled with eggs and plate stacked with waffles and bring them to the table. "Where's your puppy?" I ask. Or in other words, where's your gigantic scary werewolf husband, Koda.

"Oh, he already ate and left. He's doing more at the Den since Celia's been needing more ah, time with Aric."

Okay, now I really grin, and so does she. Time with Aric is a mild way to describe what Celia desires from her husband.

Our youngest sister Emme walks out of the laundry room blushing, which tells me she's heard us discussing Celia. Shayna's grin quickly turns into a laugh. Emme's shyness has that effect on her.

Emme clears her throat, but not her obvious discomfort. Where Shayna has dark straight hair, Emme has soft blonde waves and fair skin that reddens the longer we take her in.

"Emme," I offer. "What's the big deal? So what if Celia's banging Aric like the lead drummer at a Fourth of July parade. They're married. It happens."

Emme holds up her hand. "Taran, please let's keep their private life private."

I reach for a glass of freshly squeezed juice. "I would if they weren't so damn loud. I swear, I thought the walls were going to come down around midnight when they—"

"Taran . . ." Emme whimpers, shaking her hands like she can't stand to hear another word.

Emme's always been so sweet and angelic. Me? Not at all. "Hey, do you suppose Celia's more flexible now, given how Aric knocked her up? As in ankles behind the head kind of flexible—"

Emme lifts a muffin with her *force* and sends it soaring. I catch it just before it rams me in the mouth. "Eat," she insists. "Just eat."

In other words, for once in your life, shut your

inappropriate trap.

Shayna takes a seat beside me, laughing her skinny ass off. Emme sits, too, in time for Celia to stagger down the back steps.

Good God. Celia's long curly hair is tousled from lack of sleep and the insane amount of sex she's had. And her eyes are glazed with a hunger that warns me not to get too close. "Is there bacon? Please tell me there's bacon," she growls as if crazed.

Her entire face beams when Emme levitates a plateful of bacon and lowers it in front of an empty seat. Like a woman possessed, Celia sits and rams about four pieces in her mouth at once. The rest of us watch her in stunned silence as she chomps them down and reaches for another few slices. She freezes when she realizes we're all gaping at her. "Sorry. Would you like some?"

Her tigress eyes replace her human ones, making it clear she's only trying to be polite. And that only an idiot would get between her and her breakfast.

"No, nope, uh-uh," the three of us answer at once.

This seems to settle her inner beast enough so Celia's human eyes once more blink back at us. I pour her a glass of juice, while Emme and Shayna carefully place plates stacked with food closer to her reach. What can I say, we don't want to be eaten.

"Are you all right?" Emme asks her quietly.

Celia slows her frantic munching. "I don't know," she admits, her husky voice trickling with concern. She lifts her T-shirt and shows us her tiny belly. "The baby's not growing."

We've noticed that, too. Her pregnancy had been unexpected given she was incapable of bearing children. But within two weeks of finding out she and Aric had conceived, her baby bump had appeared and was visible through her wedding gown.

That was two months ago. And now, despite how this baby has been prophesized to rid the world of evil, we're all pretty much freaking out that he or she isn't growing.

"But your body's changing," I insist. I don't exactly ooze optimism. In fact, I'm a *the sky is falling and the earth is swallowing us whole* kind of gal. But Celia doesn't need to hear what's wrong. My girl needs hope and that's what I give her. I point to her chest. "If your hooters don't scream you're knocked up, I don't know what does."

She glances at her girls and then back at me, the tension in her shoulders lifting slightly. "They are a lot bigger," she agrees quietly. She gathers her thoughts, appearing to want to say more despite her obvious hesitation. "And my body does feel like it's becoming something more. Maybe not outwardly, but I can feel the difference inside of me."

"What are you feeling, Ceel?" Shayna asks. "Is your magic changing?"

Celia nods. "The magic that helped me get pregnant seems to compliment mine. But my hormones are out of control." Her cheeks flush and she lowers her voice. "Poor Aric. I can't stop having sex with him. It's like every time I see him, I pounce."

Aric bounds down the steps as if called, his eyes glassy from lack of sleep and his five o'clock shadow now a full-out beard thanks to his preference to satisfy Celia's needs rather than shave. His face lights up when he sees Celia, kind of like she did at the sight of bacon.

"Yeah, poor bastard," I mutter.

"Hey, beautiful," he says to Celia, bending to kiss her lips.

She smiles against his mouth. "Hey, wolf," she answers, stroking his beard lightly.

Emme inches away when Celia's stare suggests the need for something more than breakfast. Aric, being Aric, returns that look with equal force. I start to laugh, not because of Celia and Aric, but because of Emme's response. She's glancing around at the food like she knows it's going to end up splattered across Celia's and Aric's soon-to-be naked bodies.

My laugh lodges in my throat when my right arm

jerks as if shocked. Shayna lowers her fork. "You okay, T?" she asks.

I shove my arm under the table. "Fine," I say. I reach for a glass of juice with my opposite hand, trying to stay calm. Celia and Emme didn't notice my twitch, and I don't think Aric did either, but something about me lures his attention away from Celia.

He cocks his head, his nose flaring as if his alpha wolf has latched onto something. "Taran, what's wrong?" he asks.

Celia's and Emme's attention drifts my way. Shayna rises, fear crinkling her brow.

"I'm tired," I say dismissively, feeling my pulse start to race. I push my chair out. "I should head back to bed. I didn't sleep much—"

All at once, and without warning, pain burns its way across my affected limb, curling me forward in agony. My arm whips out, sending the table and all its contents soaring with freakish speed. Plates shatter on the floor as the table imbeds with a loud bang *into* the wall, directly above where Celia sat seconds before.

I lift my head as the burn recedes, searching for her, panicked I harmed her. Tears of relief and residual pain slide down my face when I see Aric lower her to floor and far away from me. She and our sisters stare back at me stunned. But Aric? Holy shit, he's *pissed.*

"Taran, what are you doing?" he growls.

I shake my head, knowing he's angry I almost hurt Celia. "I'm not doing anything . . ."

The burn returns and so does its torment. This time, I can't bite back my screams. I stumble forward. Aric races to me. I don't see him. I only feel his body and hear the crunch of bone when my arm flails and connects with his jaw.

He crashes against the granite counter with a grunt as my arm jerks wildly and the burn increases tenfold.

My vision fades in and out and my body thrashes, the erratic movements of my limb throwing me against the wall. I collapse, my arm still beating itself against the floor with enough force to splinter and punch through the wood. I'm not thinking. I can't. Everything hurts.

No. Everything *burns*.

"Cut it off!" I scream.

Shayna reaches for a knife, elongating it with her power and manipulating it into a deadly sword. She lifts the blade above my spastic arm, her expression torn. By now I'm sobbing, and all but clawing at my face.

"*Please*," I beg her. "Cut it off!"

"I can't," Shayna chokes out. "I can't do this."

"Pin it," Celia yells. "Pin it to the floor!"

With a flick of her wrists Shayna changes the sword's position and brings the point down toward my raging hand. I barely feel the prick before the room erupts in a ghostly light and Shayna goes flying.

Emme screams as Shayna collides into the far wall. Aric and Celia are scrambling forward, but all thoughts are lost in my torture. I'm retching with how hard I'm crying and from the anguish crawling from my arm and into my chest.

Just as the burn reaches my heart and I begin to lose consciousness, a pale yellow light surrounds me. Slowly, very slowly, the heat charring my insides is replaced with a soothing chill I welcome like a draw of fresh air.

My body shudders as the coolness spreads like a cascade of water from a gentle spring. My pain eases and my cries dwindle. It takes a long time for the ache to lessen, and even longer for my vision to clear. But eventually it does.

Not that I like what I see.

Blood cakes the side of Shayna's face. She winces as the bone along her eye socket pops out and the cut above her eyebrow knits close. Bile churns my gut. If Koda hadn't passed her a portion of his werewolf essence, I would have killed her. There's no doubt based on the amount of blood coating her skin, and what her body had to do to heal her indented skull.

I cover my mouth. "Oh, my God," I gasp.

"It's okay, T," she says, as if I can't see the pain tightening her small pixie face. "It's okay."

No. Not at all, sweetie.

Aric leans forward. Being a werewolf, and that of pure blood, his inner beast had healed him faster than Shayna. That didn't mean I hadn't made rubble out of his jaw or that I hadn't hurt him.

Or that I won't do it again.

I had no control over my arm. None. Nor do I believe I have it now.

Aric realizes as much. I don't miss how he keeps Celia behind him, appearing to shield her and their child from whatever I'll unleash next.

"What happened?" he asks, his voice riddled with anger, and maybe something more.

"I don't know," I respond, my voice trembling and my body strangely weak. "I felt pain and it-it went wild."

"Your arm?" It's a question, but he's not really asking.

I nod as Emme's healing light recedes and her hands withdraw from my shoulders. Her face is unusually pale. She swallows hard, struggling to speak. "It's her fire," she says, barely above a whisper. She looks at Aric. "It's eating her alive..."

Chapter Two

After a few phone calls (by Aric), lots of growls (collectively from the wolves), and plenty of swears (from me), I go from lying drenched in sweat on the kitchen floor, to drenched in sweat as I'm escorted out of the house and toward Koda's ride.

Aric and the wolves are transporting me to the nearest mystical healer. Emme kept me from burning to bits, but she can't prevent what's happening given that my *fire* is *eating* me *alive*!

Who the hell says this shit?

It hurts to admit that my power is doing anything and everything I can't control. But to have it turn against me is the kick to the ovaries I hadn't counted on. I curl inward remembering the pain along with the helplessness that came with it.

"Do you want me to carry you?" Bren asks, keeping his voice low.

I shake my head and gather my cardigan against me when the breeze sweeping in from Lake Tahoe picks up. It's already spring and about sixty degrees. But even beneath the bright sun, I'm practically freezing despite the jeans and long-sleeved T-shirt I changed into, and the thick sweater draped around my body.

Yet this chill beats that hideous burn and reminds me that, at least for now, I'm still alive.

"I should go with you," Emme says gently.

Aric shakes his head in a way that halts her in place and keeps her from inching closer. When he's certain she won't move, he finishes typing the directions into her phone.

"I want you with Shayna," he tells her. "Give us a five-minute head start and then follow." He lifts his gaze and addresses Shayna. "Stick to the speed limit, and stay outside the compound when you reach it. If you're needed, the witches will summon you, and bring you to us."

"How will we know when we reach the compound if the wards protecting it make it invisible?" Shayna asks. She slides her hand down Koda's long midnight hair to thread her fingers with his. It's something she does when he's angry and she's trying to soothe him. And right now, hot Native American man is plenty pissed at yours truly.

Koda's thumb grazes over her knuckles answering her, all the while watching me like a ravenous wolf would a limp bunny. "The wards are strong enough to feel and warn you, baby," he says. "Just listen to Aric and keep your distance."

She drops her hand away and whips around hard enough to flick her long dark ponytail. She starts to pace, only to stop abruptly, demonstrating her frustration. She's not happy, and neither is Emme. But when it comes to all things magic, the wolves know better than us, and we know better than to question their knowledge on all things supernatural and creepy. And given that this time, I'm the supernaturally creepy one, I keep my trap shut. At least for now.

I want to flash my sisters an encouraging smile or that vixen grin they once knew so well. But I'm still trembling and weak. I'm not fooling anyone into thinking I'm fine.

I climb into the middle row of seats in back of Koda's Yukon when he tosses the keys to Aric, only for Bren to reach for my hand and pull me up. "Let's sit in the third row, kid," he tells me.

He's not really asking. My stare shifts outside where

Aric leans on the front passenger side door, keeping Celia from climbing in. They want me as far away from her as possible.

That's awesome. Really.

Koda is already in the rear waiting for me. Oh, and look, he's glaring. I more or less slump beside him and snap my seatbelt in place, but it's not until Bren lowers himself to my right that Celia is allowed in.

I've always protected my sisters. Scratch that. We've always protected each other. I never thought I'd see the day where they would need protection from me.

Aric starts the Yukon with a roar, attempting to zip past our elderly neighbor Mrs. Mancuso without incident. However, bitchy and drama-filled incidents typically surround my encounter with the old battle-axe so of course, she doesn't offer a friendly nod our way, or God forbid pretend not to notice us. She's been glaring at me since I stepped out of my house, waiting for the right time and the right way to acknowledge me. And she doesn't disappoint.

A stiff and angry middle finger waves as we pass. Mrs. Mancuso barely glances up from where she's planting her impatiens, but her fury remains intense, her response quick, and her hand gestures ridiculously agile for someone whose neck skin flaps in the wind.

"Don't worry," Bren mutters, stretching out against the seat. "She'll fix you right up."

He's not referring to Mrs. Mancuso. That doesn't mean I like the "she" he's speaking of.

Thankfully, he doesn't say "her" name. But anything with fangs, claws, and the ability to hex knows who she is. I'd like to say I'm on my way to see a doctor with distinct abilities, or maybe some kind of shaman who specializes in the "weird" that is my magic. But no, I'm headed to see Genevieve, the stunning woman who glides instead of walks, who dresses in formal maiden gowns, and who turns heads everywhere she "glides". She's better known to supernatural locals as the Lake Tahoe region's head witch.

I know her best as the head of the coven who tortured

my sister, and the slut in Disney princess clothing who tried to steal my man. Do I like her? In a word, "no". I hope she gets scabies.

Aric, to his credit, didn't freak-out and go all wolf on me following my arm turning psycho. Yet he also didn't give me a choice. "I'm taking you to Genevieve. If anyone can help you, it's her," he said, making it clear there was no point in arguing.

And trust me, I was ready to argue.

My hand pushes aside my messy hair as the large SUV barrels down the highway. But I'm so anxious, I can't keep still. Having singed off my gloves, I tug on the sleeve, trying my best to cover my hand. But those freaky white fingers and blue nail beds poke through, reminding me that I'm stuck with what I have.

I don't know if my limb was somehow angry or if it reacted to Celia's presence. I don't want it to be the latter. But if it is, I'd rather it burn me than hurt her. My sister has suffered enough. And maybe I have, too. But I don't want anyone harmed as a result of what I've become.

"So we're going to the hag squad," I mutter, the humiliation at having to swallow my pride trickling into my voice. I don't think anyone can blame me. This is the same coven that regards me as a "thief" who steals magic from the earth and who, more than once, has tried to pick a fight with me and my family.

"Yup," Bren answers, not bothering with more. He knows I can't stand them, and that the majority of the coven wouldn't bat an eye if something big and scary put a hit on me.

Speaking of big and scary. My stare lifts to meet Koda's, but it's brief. The last thing I want is his fuzzy side thinking I'm challenging him. Except for those moments when Shayna is near, Koda is about as cuddly as a Pitbull whose bone was snatched away. His body is angled to face me, glaring at my arm like it snatched said bone.

Bren scratches at his scruffy beard, appearing relaxed. I know better given he's eyeing my arm, waiting for it to go all *Paranormal Activity.*

Bren, what can I say? This wolf has been more family than friend since the day we first met him. That doesn't mean he wouldn't tear my arm off at the socket if he had to.

Koda stiffens beside me as I adjust my hand beneath my sweater. Like Bren, he's ready to "subdue" me. That was Aric's word for it. But having werewolves subdue you is the equivalent of having what remains of your ass spit out beside your severed feet.

"Problem?" he asks when I readjust my arm, his deep voice only one octave above a snarl.

"No," I say.

His nose flares and so does Bren's, trying to sniff out any lies I might be spewing. But I'm not lying, at least I don't think I am. With this limb . . . who knows what will happen.

The engine revs as the SUV accelerates up an incline and onto a small county road. Again, I push my hair away from my face, pausing when the perspiration along my brow moistens my fingers. Was it that long ago I used to be feared and not so afraid?

Koda growls beside me when I try to hide my hand again. This time I do narrow my eyes at him. "Believe it or not, I'm not trying to hurt anyone."

"Maybe, but you still managed," he reminds me.

I straighten in my seat. Shayna had washed the blood from her face and changed her clothes before he arrived. Yet he still scented traces of blood lingering on her skin. It wasn't anything anyone could see. But it was enough that he recognized his mate had been hurt, scared and had bled, and that I was the cause.

"Fuck off, Koda," Bren tells him, beating me to the punch. He keeps his tone light as he drapes an arm around me and pulls me closer, ready to act in my defense.

Aric's growls erupt from the front, despite the gentle squeeze he offers Celia's hand. "I didn't bring you two along to fight," he snaps. "You're here to ensure *everyone* stays safe."

Aric doesn't flex his alpha-ness among his friends

often, but when he does, anything in the general vicinity damn well listens.

"You heard him," Bren says, shooting Koda a smile that's about as inviting as barbed wire. "Down, boy."

I'm not afraid of Koda—never mind, he scares me shitless. Especially the way he's managing to snarl at Bren with his freaking *eyes*, a rare and impressive feat to his credit. But like Aric, I don't want any trouble, especially around Celia.

"Are you sure we shouldn't see Makawee?" I ask, keeping my voice low because it's easier to feign courage when you're not yelling, and courage is something I could really use now. It's not just Koda or how his beast appears so close to the surface that sends my heart beating out of control. It's mainly due to my situation and life being so out of control.

Aric being a *were*, and Celia, having the heightened senses her inner tigress provides, have no problem hearing me from the front. "Makawee will be away for the next few weeks," he answers, making a left at a small intersection. "We can't wait for her to return, and I'm not calling her back unless I have to." He waits, then adds, "But even though *were* magic helped regenerate your arm, your power and that from the earth played a large role. For something like this, Genevieve's our go-to in our Omega's absence."

Okay, this more than sucks. At least Makawee likes me. Vieve . . . I'm not sure exactly what she thinks. But I can guess she and her buddies like me about as much as I like them. In my defense, I've never done anything to harm them. Can't say the same in return, or that I won't attack if provoked. Hurt me once. Shame on you. Hurt those I love, I'll char you to embers and make it look like an accident.

"Where did Makawee go?" I ask, adjusting my weight against Bren.

I think it's an easy question. But he seems to take too long to answer. "Aric?" I press.

"She's on assignment in Colorado," he responds.

Celia's long hair sweeps over her shoulder as she

turns his way. Oh, yeah, he has our attention now. "What is she doing in Colorado?" she asks.

He slows as he pulls onto a dirt road leading past an old farm. "Getting the house ready for you and the baby," he answers quietly.

Here's the thing, when a baby in the supernatural world is expected, it's not so different from that of the human world, even though the human world doesn't realize the rest of us freaks exist. You pick out furniture. Paint the nursery. Play around with names. You even get a shower. But Celia is pregnant with the first child prophesized to tip the scales to the side of good and rid the world of an evil that has steadily risen since my sisters and I were "outed" to the mystical community.

So no, Makawee the Pack Omega, with more magic in an eyelash than a clown car stuffed with witches, isn't off preparing the baby's room. If she's gone for *weeks*, she's reinforcing what will be the labor and delivery room, and the baby's first home, with powerful protection spells.

Celia's hand begins to slip away from Aric's, but he holds tight, lifting it to his lips for a brief kiss. "You're safe, and so is our child," he promises. "I'm only assuring it stays that way."

She tosses me a worried glance over her shoulder, whispering something I can't hear, but Aric's response tells me enough. "We'll keep her safe. Don't worry."

My pulse has steadily increased since the moment Emme's healing light rescinded and I was "encouraged" to get into the SUV. Now it's slowing to a steady thud that rams my chest like a hammer set on puncturing a nail through my sternum. Celia is pregnant. With everything she's been through, the last thing she needs to worry about is me.

But of course, because this asshole (aka my new arm) hasn't caused enough trouble, it starts to buzz, hard enough to shake Bren and shove him away from me.

"Aric—" he begins as Koda's growls erupt like lava from a pissed off volcano.

I don't think he gets the last syllable out before the

SUV screeches to a stop and Aric yanks Celia from the front passenger seat. Blue and white light erupts like a flash of my lightning, overtaking the cabin and blinding us.

My breath catches as I see Celia, materializing like an apparition in the distance. She's wearing a loose white gown, clutching a small bundle against her. My screams release in a sob. I think she's dead, I'm sure of it, until the light drifts away in tendrils, revealing a room with thick carpet.

Vertical stripes of beige and cream line the walls. She smiles, singing softly to her little bundle as she carefully lowers herself onto a poofy floral print chair. The blanket swaddling her little one slips away as she lifts the baby over her shoulder, unveiling a head of spiky black hair and a sweet face munching on his tiny fist.

Aric steps into sight, kneeling in front of them, wearing his typical jeans and long-sleeved shirt. He lifts his hand to lightly stroke his baby's head, a sense of awe I've never seen overtaking him like a mist.

Jesus. His son looks just like him, but those eyes blinking back at me are my sister's, causing mine to sting.

Aric says something to Celia that makes her beam, despite the lack of sleep swelling their features. They're tired and physically worn. But they're *happy*. For what seems like too long they're finally happy.

I'm not sure where I am, but I'm guessing this is the stronghold the Omega is preparing. And even though I know I don't belong, I want to stay. It's peaceful, quiet, and safe, yet the perimeter surrounding it feels like a fortress of power. But as quickly as the image arrives, it dwindles away.

That's when I feel the extent of Bren's crushing weight, and exactly how hard Koda is pinning my legs. I cough, trying to breathe. It's only as the shudders from my arm rattling the three of us diminish that Bren lifts off me.

"Shit," he says, staring toward the front where the apparition took form. "Holy *shit*, what did we just see?"

I don't answer, wondering how he saw what I did.

Koda eases off me, shock spreading along the rigid angles of his sharp features. He doesn't growl, not this time.

For the first time since taking "Taran watch" he looks to where Aric is carefully leading Celia back to the SUV.

The vision, however sweet, leaves them stunned and speechless. It's not until Aric clicks his seatbelt in place that he finally speaks, but even then, it's solely to Celia, as if no one else exists. "Are those the colors you picked for the baby's room?" he asks.

"Yes," she replies, appearing almost scared to answer.

"And the chair?" he asks. "Was that something you wanted?"

She releases a breath, and likely a great deal of stress she's kept from him. "I found it on line the other night. I thought it was pretty and selected the colors based on the tones in the pattern." Her voice grows so soft, I barely catch her next few words. "I thought they would look nice together."

Aric grips the steering wheel. "Did you show your sisters?" he asks.

He's asking if he showed me, trying to gauge how probable this future is.

"I didn't show anyone, love," she answers, a slight quiver shaking her voice. "I've been afraid to have too much hope."

I've suspected as much. But to hear her say it is a whole different beast. He gathers her to him, because for all Aric is a born killer, he's nothing but heart and soft touches when it comes to my sister.

"I've been afraid, too," he admits, his voice carrying the strain of his fears.

She melts against him. I can't see her, but I know she is smiling, and maybe crying a little, too. "I think he's a boy," she tells him quietly.

"That was my guess." He glances over his shoulder, meeting my stare. "Thank you," he says.

I almost don't think he's talking to me. "For what?" I ask.

"For giving us the faith we've needed."

My heart clenches a little, but it's not related to the

hope that suddenly surrounds them. It's fear that overtakes me. This limb may have given them a glimpse of what they want. But I don't trust it. Not when it can easily take everything away from them.

Chapter Three

Aric turns the Yukon onto a wooded path partially hidden by a dense spread of trees. And FYI, Koda wasn't kidding when he said we'd feel the coven's protective wards. What could only be described as a giant wall of plastic wrap, stretches against my body, only to release with a sudden pop.

"You okay?" Aric asks when Celia shudders. "You weren't supposed to feel it, Genevieve assured me."

She brushes her arms off like she can sense something on her skin. "I always feel their magic," she says. "But it didn't hurt, and was just a minor sensation."

"Good," Bren mutters. "Cause I hate that shit. No need for Celia and baby Bren to feel it, too."

Celia laughs. "Baby Bren?" she asks, ignoring the way Aric's eyes narrow in the rearview mirror.

"Just figured you'd name him after the best wolf you know," Bren answers, grinning. "No offense, Aric."

"Fuck off," Aric growls in return.

I wish I could laugh along with Celia, but I'm absolutely loathing the way the witch's mojo scrapes against my skin. Mercifully, the prickly sensation doesn't last. But no sooner do we plow over what resembles drying and very thorny blackberry brambles than the ground evens out and the collective muscle of the coven's power kicks into overdrive.

Stacked stone pavers materialize one by one as the SUV roars ahead, creating a path. The line of trees stretch outward, widening the road. I don't want to be impressed, but I'll admit I very well am.

I've never been to Casa de Genevieve, yet I've heard her sorority sisters gush about its beauty and elegance.

"A sight to behold," one of them raved, close enough for me and my sisters to hear.

"Over a century old and brought from Massachusetts by pure will of force," another said.

And by that she meant Genevieve's awe-worthy magic. Again, meant for us to hear, and likely to warn us, too. I didn't take it too seriously before. I've clashed with the oh-so powerful Vieve more than once and managed to hold my own. But that was too long ago, when my fire and lightning could match anything she threw at me.

"Have your visions ever been visible to anyone else?" Koda asks, pulling me from my thoughts.

He's kept his gaze ahead since the vision appeared, as if waiting for another one. That doesn't mean he hasn't kept a close watch on me. "No," I respond.

"So it's related to your," he motions to my side, "Appendage."

"You mean this thing?" I ask, lifting my arm and smiling with as much warmth as Bren had. "Looks that way, big guy."

My visions are another thing that makes me weird. In the supernatural world, only soothsayers and mystical leader-types are supposed to be able to experience them. But they have better control and use magic from their packs, covens, or clans to call them forth. Mine appear at random and usually revolve around death, destruction, and exploding demon parts.

Feel free to envy me at any time. Or don't, and hang on to your sanity.

I want Aric to be right and that whatever we saw is a glimpse of all the good things to come. But honestly, I can't help thinking this arm of mine is screwing with all of us. So I'm not exactly tickled pink over what I saw. Mostly, I'm hoping it doesn't end in detonating innards, mainly ours.

I try not to react as the pavers materializing in front of

us expand and the tree line vanishes, unveiling acres upon acres of cultivated land.

Along the fields, women in long gray dresses, white bonnets and aprons, tend to the newly sprouted leaves. Anyone lucky enough to survive all the mystical booby-traps leading into this place would likely think he or she stumbled onto an Amish farm or a convent, based on the way they're dressed. But the Amish and nuns are considered quiet, modest folk who keep to themselves. Not like these women of power. Oh, no, anyone here is likely capable of torturing any man or beast who they feel wronged them.

Even from this distance, I can see their lips moving fast, chanting as they water the bundles of green leaves and tend to the soil. Whatever they're saying strengthens the earth and wards along the compound. But those plants are soaking up the magic, too, assuring they'll fortify any potion they're used in.

If I hadn't seen the witches' dark side firsthand, or had the experiences I've had with Vieve, I'd likely be impressed by their commitment and hard work. But I have, and know better than to trust them.

Weres have an alliance with the witches, and as Guardians of the Earth they share a special connection. The only connection I have is with my sisters, and every now and then with the vamps, but that's good enough for me. My sisters are my best friends. The vamps are . . . okay, self-centered, bratty, and more than a little slutty. Yet, at least the vamps have the stones to tell you to fuck off to your face as opposed to hexing you the moment you turn your back.

The road veers off in three different directions: one toward the field, another toward the woods, and another to what appears to be the rear of the compound. Aric keeps going more or less straight until the fields lined with herbs are replaced with what feels like an enchanted garden.

Rows of rose bushes in alternating shades of red, purple, and yellow blooms as large as my hand, extend outward and over the heads of the witches tending to them. These spell-wielders are a lot closer. They glance up as we pass, frowning slightly as they continue their chants.

They sense the wolves. But their frowns deepen because they also sense me and Celia. We've never been popular, and we sure aren't going to score any points today.

Celia stiffens, her claws protruding slightly before she lulls her inner kitty back to sleep. Like me, she's not a fan of the coven, nor is she thrilled by the response we evoke.

"Easy, sweetness," Aric whispers.

Celia's claws can puncture through bone, but Aric keeps his hand over hers, regardless. He doesn't want to let her go. Hell unleashed the last time he did.

"I would have liked Shayna and Emme here," she tells him.

"I know," he responds. "But I couldn't be sure what would happen on our way here. Koda and Bren were the better choices to subdue Taran."

There's that word again. But he has a point, the wolves are physically stronger. Yet Aric's choice was based on more than their combined muscle. Shayna and Emme are more polite and pc than me, but they recognize how petty the witches can be, just as Aric recognizes they would rush to my defense if the witches messed with me.

"He just didn't want the four of you getting into another mystical smack-down with the broom humpers," Bren says, pointing out the obvious. He grins. "Though it could be kind of hot."

Only because he's picturing the smack-down taking place in a pool of mud and us wearing nothing but thongs and naughty smiles. I laugh a little, but this time Celia doesn't join me. She casts me a worried glance as we round a garden and Vieve's crib comes into view.

As much as I'm trying to keep my expression neutral, I'm blown away by the yellow and white Victorian mansion straight out of the 1880's. The thing is mammoth and so ridiculously pristine it practically sparkles.

What must be Vieve's family crest is etched into every lead glass window while intricate patterns of flowers and ivy are carved into the shutters, molding, overhangs, and along the porch railing. The double, extra-wide and extra-tall, front doors are made of stained glass and brass, depicting a woman with long dark hair on one side and one with gray on the other, their hands united. The one on the left resembles Vieve, but based on the appearance of these doors, they were created long ago and decades before she was born.

Two witches march across the widow's peak three levels up, their deepening scowls appearing to interrupt their chanting. Given their positions and their tight hold over their long metal staffs, they're Genevieve's bodyguards. And because of their appointed roles, they must be among the strongest in her coven.

Instead of brooms, Volkswagen Jettas in alternating colors line a large lot to the far right. Aric, doesn't bother with the lot, parking in front of the walkway leading up to the three-story monstrosity. I'm not sure if his choice of a parking spot is a reflection of his position among the supernatural elite, or if it's something more. Whatever it is, it gives me one hell of a pause.

"Wait for me," he tells Celia, half a breath before appearing on her side to open the door.

He takes her hand as she slips out. I follow behind Bren, my attention on the witches and the way they're eyeing us. I should be happy I'm here, and that maybe Aric is right, Genevieve is who I need. But I've never wanted to need anyone, especially her. So I'm not happy, not even a little bit, the anxiety twisting my stomach, roiling it further.

Bren flings a lazy arm over my shoulder as I hop out. I try to smile at the gesture of support, despite my need to rip Aric's keys from his hand and get us the hell out of Witchville. Forget that it's already been a shit day, but the collective magic from this mystical bunch continues to claw at my skin and is seconds from biting.

Before the incident that robbed me of my arm, I would have met that magic with equal force and a whole lot of attitude. But I can't protect myself like I once did, and what's worse is, I can't protect my sister and that little one nestled inside of her.

Aric draws Celia so close his knuckles brush against her thigh. It demonstrates who she is to him and warns anyone against getting too near. I know he'll keep her safe. Not that I want him to *have* to.

"You all right?" Bren whispers in my ear, giving my shoulder a squeeze.

"Fine. Just want this over with," I answer. He's trying to be a friend, all while keeping me away from Genevieve's peeps.

Hey. Just because my magic sucks doesn't mean I won't try to use it if threatened.

The two on the roof levitate downward, the amulets perched on top of their staffs glistening with sunlight and their power.

"Aric," the one with the dark hair and olive dress says. She tilts her chin slightly his way all the while pegging me with a glare.

Yeah. Not making homecoming court around here.

"Xana," he says in a way of an answer. "Genevieve is expecting us."

"All of you?" she questions, keeping her attention on me.

"Yes," he says, his tone gaining an edge. "Not that I should have to explain myself to you."

Once more, there's that alpha muscle, and once more it flexes. She nods slightly. "My apologies," she says, like it's killing her to say it.

Her stance is rigid, struggling to keep her gaze away from Celia. Girlfriend better try real hard. She's already insulted the wolf. Don't piss him off by casting shade on his mate or giving him a reason to think you're a threat to her safety.

"Lesser Paula," she calls.

Lesser? I turn in the direction of the garden. *What the hell?*

"Coming Superior Xana!" A young witch hurries from between the rows of rose bushes, a long red braid draped over her shoulder. Her steps slow as she nears. Although she can't

26

be more than eighteen, she recognizes what the wolves are, and unlike Xana, she makes no attempt to rattle their cages.

"Yes, Superior Xana?"

The Lesser title doesn't sit well with me. But in a way, the Superior label bothers me more. "Inform our most Superior Sister Genevieve that her guests have arrived," Xana says.

Paula's eyes widen, likely thrilled to pieces to have an excuse to interact with Genevieve. She takes off in a run, eager to please, but also more than a little terrified.

"This way," Xana says.

She takes the lead while the other witch with short blonde hair and deep magenta dress guards our rear. Her glare rivals Xana's, but for some reason there's more of a sting to it. I find out quickly why.

"Hey, Christie," Bren says.

"Fuck off," she tells him.

Bren nudges me. "I guess I should have called her," he murmurs.

I don't mean to laugh but I do, earning me more popularity points with the witches sweeping down the staircase.

It's like some kind of medieval sorority. Unlike the witches chanting and sweating their asses off in the field, dressed as a mix of Amish, nuns, and freaking pilgrims, these gals are dressed in simple maiden dresses. The material they wear is cotton if I had to guess, unlike the velvet and silk numbers that Vieve always glides in. They're higher up than the field workers, but evidently not on the same level as Vieve or her guards.

I don't know who they are. But judging by their deep-set frowns they know who I am.

At least they think they do.

They pause by the steps, bowing their heads to Aric as a sign of respect. Aric acknowledges them with the barest hint of a nod, lifting his hand to circle Celia's waist. The muscles along my back grow rigid, I'm realizing he's attempting to shield her from any magic they might fling her way.

His protective instincts fire my own, causing my blue and white flames to ignite over my head with a snap, crackle, and pop.

"Easy, T," Bren murmurs in my ear. "We've got Ceel, and you, too."

I take a breath, and another one, too, trying hide the relief I feel when my surging power withdraws into my core when I pull it back. My magic, being as unstable as it's been, doesn't always obey. But I want to keep that little tidbit of knowledge far from the witches, at least for as long as I can.

My flame was triggered by my emotions, not like that's anything new. But the way it surged and how it threatened to teeter out of control was definitely unintentional. Yet it did catch the attention of the broom humpers and put them on guard. The one in the front passes her fingertips along the talisman around her neck, the green stone at its center flickering and giving a hint of her power. She's not challenging me, at least I don't think she is. Like the others she seems on guard, and maybe even a little afraid. They think I still have what it takes to mow them down. I don't mind them thinking that. It will keep them from trying something stupid. The problem is, the moment we leave Vieve's office, that's all going to change.

We're escorted down a small hall to a set of double doors. One of the guards walks through. I can't see her, but I hear her well enough. "Sister Genevieve, Aric Connor, Alpha and Leader of the Squaw Valley Den Pack is here, along with his mate, two of his Warriors, and the mate's sister."

The mate's sister, I repeat in my head. Hey, these bitches have called me much worse.

"Please show them in," Vieve's regal voice calls from a distance.

I walk in expecting Vieve in her all too perfect glory, and she doesn't disappoint. Her long dark hair is gathered in an elaborate bun, with ringlets cascading around skin so fair and flawless, no pimple would dare to disrupt that shit. Her dark blue velvet gown matches her large eyes, yet contrasts deeply against the yellow stone in the silver talisman circling her neck. I think it's intentional so anyone and everyone sees the stone, reminding them of who she is, and what she can do to them.

Like I said, I'm not surprised to see her look so good, or even to find her in a giant library standing beside a marble fireplace large enough to park a Mini Cooper in. What I am surprised is to find my ex-lover Gemini—aka the wolf who broke my heart—leaning close against her and whispering into her ear . . .

Chapter Four

Those slow deep breaths I took in the foyer, you know, the ones that calmed me down? They're doing jack shit now.

"Good morning, everyone," Vieve begins, easing away from the mere inches separating her and Gemini. "It's a pleasure to welcome you into my home." Her light and regal voice abruptly cuts off when my arm buzzes from my charging lightning and zaps Bren off me.

He stumbles away from the jolt, curling inward. "Fuck *me*," he says, his stare cutting from me to Gemini.

My vision sharpens, alerting me that my irises have gone from blue to white and signaling to all in my vicinity that no, I'm not happy, and what the hell is this shit?

"Taran," Celia begins. "Take it easy, okay?"

I'm not so much as breathing, but rather panting. "What's he doing here?" I ask. My body shudders as mini bolts of lightning release from the fingertips of my right hand, charging the air. Celia looks at me, appearing at a loss. "I asked what is *he* doing here?"

My glare cuts to Gemini. I barely catch sight of his hardening features before Aric blocks my view and steps in front of Celia. "Taran," he says, doing his best to keep the growl from his tone, but doing a pathetic job. "Gemini is my second in command and the Pack's liaison with the witches."

"Oh, I *know* who he is to the witches," I fire back.

My zombie limb shoots out, angry flames of blue and white, erupting along the length and keeping Koda in place when he races forward.

"Uh, uh, uh, big guy," I warn. "I wouldn't come near me right now."

I don't see Genevieve's guards charge me but my arm feels them. Perceiving them as a threat, it snatches the staff away from Xana, and brings it down on the blonde's hand, forcing her to drop her staff. I step on it when she dives on the floor and tries to lift it and toss the other aside. But that stone—the one that amplifies her power doesn't have to be in her hand to use it. Her eyes meet mine as she mumbles a hex, only for Celia to break free from Aric and lift blondie up by the throat.

Celia's tiger eyes replace her own as she slams her against the wall. "You will *not* curse my sister," she growls.

"Celia, put her down," Aric rumbles, placing his hands on her shoulders and attempting to ease her back.

My head whips away from them as Xana retrieves her staff and calls forth her magic. Streams of olive and silver slam against the blue and white flames my arm darts out, the collision of magic sending us soaring in opposite directions. I crash-land on my back, my arm shaking hard enough to rattle my teeth.

Gemini is suddenly there, hooking his arm beneath mine and lifting me to my feet. I wrench loose from his hold as my magic withdraws. "Don't *touch* me," I tell him, ramming my finger into his chest.

It's bad enough my own power charred my insides less than an hour ago—and forget how I'm here—essentially begging a woman I can't stand for help—only to find the man I still love with his body practically curled around hers. But to watch the way his stare falls to my sickly pale arm and for him to cringe away from its reach becomes my undoing. I swallow back the lump making my throat its bitch and storm away.

I don't know where I'm going, or even if I'll make it

to the foyer. All I know is that I can't stay with this crew.

"You can't leave, Taran," Genevieve calls to me.

Her voice is soft, calm, but I don't miss the force behind it or the way it seems to tangle around me like a thick, sticky web.

"Watch me," I snap.

I lurch forward only to be hauled back by an invisible force. Oh, neither me nor my arm like that one bit. It rumbles, shaking me hard and spiraling blue and white flames across its length. The heat is brutal, smoking like a damn torch and forcing my head away so I don't set my hair *and* face on fire.

But I refuse to admit defeat, despite that I'm sure as hell defeated.

I throw myself forward, keeping my arm out and away from me. The two steps I manage are like trudging through waist-deep glue. Again, I'm lugged back by my arm, skidding across the floor as I kick out and attempt to dig in my heels.

The muscles along my arm stretch against the bone, twisting and tugging painfully the harder I fight. But pain is something I'm used to. It makes me stubborn, surges my adrenaline, and propels me forward, something I damn well use to my advantage.

My feet stomp as my magic flares, each step echoing in harsh furious beats. I'm almost to the door. I see it, and am reaching for the knob.

Yet whatever has me isn't letting go.

My teeth clamp down, every swear word I know shooting out. The intensity of my flame builds, the heat brutal enough to bite at my skin. Sweat pours down my body, my clothes clinging against my drenched skin.

Celia calls to me, begging me to stop fighting and to give in. But my will is all I have left and I refuse to succumb.

My head jerks in Genevieve's direction. Unlike me, she's barely moving, and she sure as hell isn't sweating, swearing, or struggling. Her hands are clasped in front of her as if merely observing. Only her penetrating stare gives away her focus, her blue irises shimmering from the amount of magic it's taking to hold me.

"*Legare*," she says, inflicting every syllable with her potency.

Streams of yellow light snake from her talisman, wrapping around my arm and wrenching me viciously back. My feet leave the floor as if kicked out from under me, the motion so fast I barely register the floor rushing beneath me as I soar across the room.

I land hard on my ass, the wind knocked out of me. Before I can catch my breath I'm dragged in the direction of the fireplace. My arm spasms out of control, jolting my body as it fights to break free and regain control.

Vieve's magic winds around me, the streams of bright yellow light crisscrossing like twine, forcing my arm to obey. My arm repeatedly collides against the floor, her power bashing it until my flame is put out and all that remains is residual smoke.

As I watch, the streams of magic that crisscrossed around my arm solidify into thin straps of brown leather cord. In a perfect world, I'd lurch to my feet and demand, "Is that all you've got?" But my pseudo-perfect world vanished long ago, leaving me lying in Vieve's crib like a fried tadpole in the sun.

I don't like to admit defeat, ever. It's the one thing I hate, and why I come out swinging as hard as I do. Yet I think it's safe to say I got my ass kicked by Vieve *and* my fucking arm. If the char marks on the floor aren't proof enough, the soreness claiming every speck of my sweat-soaked body erase any lingering doubt.

My hands push against the floor in time to see the edges of an elegant blue gown sweep past me. "Let's take a seat, shall we?" Vieve calmly offers. "There is much we need to discuss."

Celia lowers herself beside me as a super-sized red wolf stalks to her side. Werebeasts may resemble their animal counterparts, but only in appearance, not size. Koda alone hovers around five-hundred pounds, and from my position on the floor, he looks even bigger than that.

"Are you okay?" Celia whispers.

I do all I can to beat back the hurt and humiliation, yet it still finds its way into my voice. "Oh, I'm just peachy," I answer.

My blatant lie earns me a growl from the giant red wolf. Celia frowns. "Stop it, Koda," she tells him. "She feels bad enough."

He ceases his growls, but maintains his glare. "Here, let me help you up," she offers.

"Celia," Aric warns when she extends her hands. "Don't touch her."

"She's not going to hurt me, Aric," she says, keeping her voice gentle, for me and his beastly side.

I'd never harm Celia, but I can't assume my arm feels the same. I force myself to my feet, wishing it didn't hurt so much and swearing because it does. I stagger when I attempt to straighten and almost fall again.

Celia hurries to steady me, but I hold out a hand, keeping her back. "I'm all right," I respond, ignoring the way my body insists this floor isn't so bad and perhaps I should lay back down before I hurl.

I push my messy and somewhat crispy hair out of my eyes, forcing the bile working its way up from my stomach back where it belongs. Of course, I don't like what I see. Vieve sits primly behind her desk in a chair that resembles more of an ancient throne than anything *Ikea* could have put together. Her guards flank her sides, their hair electrified on their ends and their skin and clothing smeared with ash.

Bren, also in his wolf form shakes off, offering me a weak tail wag to assure me he's okay in spite of his soot-covered hide. I'm not sure what the hell happened, but it was enough that his inner beast and Koda's compelled them to *change*.

Celia speaks quietly to Aric, but he keeps his focus on me. Like the others, his hair seems electrified and black smears cover his gray T-shirt. I don't understand what happened or why Vieve and Celia appear untouched. Yet as a familiar sense of unease and loss overtakes me, the need to ask is gone.

I don't see Gemini so much as feel him behind me. I turn around slowly, meaning to only steal a glance. But that's not what happens. I startle and lose my balance again when I see him and his twin wolf.

"Holy *shit*," I say, gasping.

The red T-shirt he was wearing hangs in pieces, and if I'd dumped the remains of a charcoal grill over the top of him, he wouldn't be any less coated with soot. His beast, a midnight black timber wolf with a white right paw doesn't look much better, appearing gray instead of black from the amount of ash coating his fur.

I don't know what to say, much less do. His inner wolves are naturally fierce and dominant, but of the two twins, this one is the most aggressive and reminds me as much. He hones in on my arm, baring his teeth before he leaps into Gemini's back, disappearing beneath his flesh as he unites with his human half.

I hate the response of his wolf. Domineering or not, he's never demonstrated aggression toward me. My first instinct is to rush to Gemini, to make sure he isn't hurt and that the reaction of his wolf wasn't a result of pain I'd inflicted. But then I stop, reminding myself that he no longer belongs to me nor craves my touch.

"Taran," Vieve's voice says, her tone maintaining that infuriating calmness. "Kindly take a seat."

The last thing I want to do is sit. Like before, I want to get the hell out of here. But as my attention breaks away from Gemini's and latches on to the leather ties fastened to my arm, it's clear I'm not going anywhere until Vieve allows it.

Son of a bitch and the seven dwarves. How does this happen to me?

Celia approaches me, easing away from Aric's hold around her waist. She sighs, sweeping my hair over my shoulder, her expression heartbroken. "We need to figure this out, Taran," she says. "The only way to do that is to hear Genevieve out."

She takes my hand, my good one, and leads me

forward. My muscles throb with every step and the right side of my jaw tingles when I tighten it. But after two rounds with hardwood floors, and the floor winning each time, I suppose I should be pretty sore. It's a miracle I didn't break a bone or shatter a rib.

Celia releases me to take a seat in the plush chair beside mine. There's not much room between my chair and hers, yet that doesn't stop Aric from forcing his way through and positioning himself between us.

I lower my lids as Gemini releases a harsh breath, his frustration and anger as evident as all the ash coating his tall and muscular frame. Just a year ago, his breath released in that deep profound way only in bed, when his body moved with mine and we'd spend the day and night making love. But back then I didn't have the problems I do now. Back then I was whole and he promised to always love me.

Vieve's stare flickers behind me. I'm not aware of the exchange between her and Gemini, I can't see his expression with my back to him. But I know one took place. Again my arm zings, attempting to build an electrical charge, sending everyone on high alert. Yet as quick as the power energizing it surges, it just as quickly peters out.

I keep my attention blankly ahead, past Genevieve and toward the large leaded window overlooking the enchanted garden. It's not that I'm any less freaked out than anyone here, or that I'm not shocked by the behavior of this limb. I'm simply done, emotionally and physically, but most of all spiritually. How many ways, and how many times, can a gal's ego be bitched-slapped in one day?

Again, that harsh breath releases behind me. I can almost picture Gemini rubbing his neatly trimmed goatee before he crosses his arms and his almond shaped eyes assume their ever vigilant focus. He's angry, exasperated, and maybe something else, too. Yet he's not alone.

"Is that . . . tie enough to control Taran's arm?" Celia asks.

The guards pucker their brows yet quickly lower their gazes when Aric stiffens beside me.

"There is still much the Wird sisters don't know about the mystical world," Vieve tells her guards, bowing her head slightly in Aric's direction. "I expect you to show them the patience and respect they deserve." She cuts off the one when she tries to speak. "You provoked that attack. Your role is to guard me, not to prevent someone who isn't a prisoner from leaving."

I should give Vieve credit for siding with us and against her "sisters". Never mind. I still wish her scabies.

"It's a bind, Celia," Vieve explains, smiling softly. "You can equate it to a magical straightjacket or cage to control Taran's feral arm."

Now my limb is the equivalent of a rabid creature. Awesome. Oh, and by the way, feel free to chat about me like I'm not sitting here, sweating off what's left of my ass on your chair.

Vieve purses her full lips. I'm not sure if she can read my thoughts, but if she can, it wouldn't shock me. Either way, the anger righting my posture gives plenty away, and so does the way my right hand twitches in would-be protest.

The muscles along my limb strain when the enchantment binding my arm tightens enough to limit the movement of my fingers. I'm not sure what she's doing, but I'm pretty sure it's the equivalent of having my knuckles rapped with a supernatural ruler.

My glare lifts from my hand back to Vieve. But surprise, surprise, she's not even remotely threatened by me or even mildly disturbed.

"It's not permanent," she continues. "And based on the power it took to bind it, I can't be sure how long it will last."She leans back, scrutinizing me closely. "How much control did you have?" she asks me.

My jaw tightens further. Here's the thing, pre-loss of my arm, all the power I felt, be it the charge from my lightning or flare from my fire built within my core. All I needed to stimulate either was to borrow from magic drifting in the air. Unless I was upset, then my emotions seemed to borrow it for me. Either way, it would stir or withdraw at my core.

Since this arm formed, it appears to fight me *and* my core for control. And good God, if that spark starts in my arm, my arm is going to do what it wants, choosing to disobey more times than submit.

Vieve interprets my silence as enough of a response. "So is it safe to infer you weren't the one holding the others back?" she asks.

My attention shifts to Celia, unsure what Vieve means, and more than a little freaked out to know.

Celia's large eyes search my face as she gives herself a moment to find the right words. "The energy from your arm charged the air when the fire engulfed your arm," she explains. "It forced everyone back and away from you except for me and Genevieve." She taps her finger against the armrest. "I kept my distance and stayed with Aric when I realized how little control you had."

And to keep her baby safe, she doesn't add.

"So it didn't . . . hurt you?" I ask, begging her to tell me no.

"No. Like I said, it didn't touch me or Genevieve," she assures me.

"It tried to reach me when I stepped forward," Vieve says. "But my magic was able to block the imposition." Her focus trails behind me. "*Weres* don't have that ability."

Her tone and features respond apologetically, as if pleading with everyone here to forgive me on her behalf. And doesn't that just piss me off.

I open my mouth only to quickly shut it. Anything I say will make me look more bitchy, volatile, and out of control. Not to mention make Vieve all that much more the hero who came to save the day from the evil I've become. It's a wonder there's not a cape flying behind her.

"Have your abilities ever allowed that kind of influence before?" Vieve asks.

Again, I can't bring myself to answer, feeling more like a fight dog that's been muzzled and chained than a person who should be relieved that she's not setting things on fire.

But when you're a survivor of an abusive childhood, control is everything and very much something I no longer have.

"Taran was extending her abilities beyond her fire and lightning before the incident," Celia answers for me. "Tahoe's magic somehow helped amplify her own, but she's never possessed power like this."

That soft sympathetic smile returns, making Vieve appear more innocent virgin than a woman capable of making us sprout forked tails from our asses. "With all due respect, Celia, I need to hear from Taran."

Aric leans in, keeping his voice low. "Taran, I know this is hard, but you have to cooperate. Whatever this is, it's strong and very different from anything I've seen."

"Just do as Genevieve asks," Gemini growls behind me.

He's growling in anger, something else that was a rarity when it came to me. I ram my eyes closed. That familiar hurt is eating its way through me again, and I can't allow it. No. I can't allow *him*.

"You need to leave," I say, the fury and pain I'm feeling causing my right hand to tremble. But it's the way Vieve's mojo forces its surrender that has me fighting not to scream. "I'm serious. I want you out."

"*No*," he responds with as much anger as he did the first time.

My gut burns with rage. Once again my vision sharpens as my irises turn white. But I refuse to look at him and show him how much he affects me.

"Christ," Aric mumbles, swiping his face.

"Aric," I bite out. "I don't want him here."

It's the truth, and it's not simply because Vieve's presence, or because I resemble a corpse dragged from a swampy grave, or even that I'm losing what little of me still remains. It's because I'm weak *and* look the part. I can't allow myself to be many things, and weak is one of them.

Aric isn't happy, which is no real news. I've never been his favorite person. We've clashed too many times over Celia and the way he's treated her in the past. So when he meets me with kindness, I'm not prepared, the gentle way in which he speaks to me, making me feel worse and accelerating my insecurities.

"Taran," he whispers. "You're Gemini's mate. It's beyond my ability to order him from your side."

That angry burn working its way through me morphs into agony. Of all the things he could have called me.

"And even if it was within Aric's right, I'm not going anywhere," Gemini responds, his tone laced with resentment.

"Yeah, heard that one before," I reply.

My voice is barely above a murmur, but it's enough for the wolves and my sister to hear. Aric straightens, the tension thickening the space between my back and Gemini's front enough to raise the short hairs along my neck.

"Taran," Celia pleads. "The more you cooperate, the quicker we'll reach a solution and the faster we'll leave. Please, let's work through this."

"The world is kept in perfect balance," Vieve begins, as if the werewolf behind me isn't ready to maul everything in sight. "Your old limb was sacrificed and so was the power that resided inside of it. In its place you were given a new appendage, but also something more."

"But I didn't want it," I say, emphasizing every word as I lean forward. "Any of it."

It's true. When I lost my arm, it wasn't a clean break, a smooth cut, a precise surgical removal. It was savage, *brutal*, severed viciously at the elbow by a row of long jagged fangs. I didn't have a stump. I had shards of jagged bone with torn flesh dangling from the sides. If I hadn't fastened my scarf around it like a tourniquet, I would have bled to death.

Yet despite the devastation of losing my arm, I was starting to come to terms with it. As a nurse, I knew it could have been worse, and that there were therapies and prosthetics that could eventually help me cope. I'd never be the same, but I was determined to do the best with what remained.

Gemini wasn't having it. He couldn't deal with what happened and begged the Pack Omega to help me. He wanted me whole. But he never counted on this.

Vieve raises her small brows, the motion so subtle, anyone not paying attention might miss it. "It doesn't matter what you wanted," she responds in that regal way of hers. "The fact remains that it's a part of you."

"Then get rid of it," I snap.

"I can't," she answers simply.

So *not* what I want to hear. I want her to tell me she can chop it off and bury it deep where I never have to see it, and where it can never harm another soul. She can toss whatever she manages to rip off into an active volcano for all I care. That's how desperate I am. I'd rather go through life with just one arm then have my affected arm slowly kill me or turn on someone I love.

Vieve suspects as much, I'm sure, not that she appears fazed. "*Were* magic is as old as the earth," she explains. "An ancient power such as this cannot be tamed, altered, or disposed of like trash. You must learn to harmonize the remains of your original magic with what this arm has become."

"And what has it become?" I ask, my voice trembling with increasing frustration.

"I don't know," she answers. "Whatever it is resents you as much as you seem to resent it, and that antipathy has intensified with time." She motions to Celia. "Yet it also looks to protect you and those you most care for."

"It wasn't that way this morning," Aric reminds her.

Vieve nods as if agreeing. "From what you described during our call, and from what I observed here, it inadvertently lashed out, not to harm, but in response to the bitter energy that's been building between it and Taran. Celia was simply in its path when it reacted."

"You're sure?" Aric asks.

"I am. There's nothing that leads me to believe the limb's actions were intentional until it felt threatened. First by you, then Shayna, then the others here." She pauses as if working through her thoughts. "What troubles me is that while it does appear to protect Taran, the resentment that exists between its power and hers is fueling out of control."

"No shit," I mumble.

Celia shifts in her seat, trying to draw Vieve's attention. Vieve isn't exactly "scowling' she's far too superior for that, but she is eyeing me closely, clearly unimpressed by my colorful vocabulary.

"So if Tarn accepts her limb, it will in turn accept her and her magic?" Celia asks.

Vieve shakes her head slowly. "It's not so simple to harmonize something that's been for so long distressed. This ancient magic was called forth to become her arm in exchange for the arm sacrificed."

"Balance," Aric says.

"Yes, balance," Vieve agrees. "But it was also called forth to become a part of Taran and her magic." She regards me with so much pity it takes all I have not to throw what's left of my boots at her. "It may be attached to her body, but it's clearly not a part of her, or the power residing inside of her."

"So what can we do to change that?" Aric asks.

"You can't do anything. This task falls solely on Taran." She sighs, once more feeding the pity-o-meter, before responding to me directly. "To regain control, you must accept your new arm regardless of its flaws and imperfections, make another sacrifice to even the scales, and learn to manipulate the new magic generated from your residual magic and that of ancient earth."

"How does she do that?" Celia asks, ignoring the way I stare at Vieve like she's lost her broom-straddling mind.

"The sacrifice and acceptance is her burden to carry," Vieve answers. "I can't help her with that."

"But you can help her master her magic?" Celia asks hesitantly, her attention skimming my way.

"I can," she responds.

The corners of her mouth tilt slightly, but she's not exactly smiling. No . . . good ol' Vieve is up to something

I don't know what it is, but Aric seems to. And so does Gemini by the way he groans behind me. He's not one to swear, but he does then, adding to my growing dislike of this conversation.

"Genevieve, this isn't a good idea," Aric says.

"Nor is it one I freely offer," she states, all evidence of friendship and alliance between her and Aric quickly dissolving. "This is an exchange of services between us. I'll request reimbursement when the time is right."

"I have no doubt," Aric says, his deep voice as terse as Vieve appears. His stare darts toward me. "There's no other way, no incantations, no sacred relics, nothing that can help her?"

"If there was, I would certainly take it as opposed to what I'm offering," she responds.

"And what are you offering?" I ask, this odd sense of dread pouring like tar down my throat.

Everyone quiets as Gemini steps in front of me. "She's offering to train you, to make you a witch and part of her coven.

Chapter Five

"No," I say. I'm already to my feet, the chair sliding behind me from how forcefully I stand. But my weakness remains. I wobble, clinging to the armrest to stay vertical as anger overtakes me. "No way in fuck am I doing this!"

"What choice do you have, Taran?" Vieve asks.

She doesn't exactly appear thrilled to death over the proposal, but she's not entirely disappointed either. Because however masochistic her offer is, it's also to her benefit. Aric will owe her a favor. And a favor owed from a Leader extends to his Pack and potentially every *were* he oversees and is connected to.

Gemini in a word, is enraged. He looms over me, so close I can feel that familiar body heat. It's more than he's dared to do in months, and all it took was getting my insides roasted.

Yet for all he's practically on top of me, I can't forget the small space separating him and Vieve when I arrived. The reminder has me stepping away from his reach and eyeing her closely. Okay. Maybe "eyeing" is too mild a word.

"You don't like me," she says, sounding indifferent despite the intensity behind my glare. "Or my sisters."

"I can say the same about you," I respond. I'm not yelling. I'm actually eerily quiet. But all that in your face hatred sticks to each of my words like venom.

Her angelic stare trails to Celia. "That's not true."

"You're kissing up to her now?" I ask. "Why? Because of who she's married to or what she's carrying?" I straighten to my full height. "She could have used your compassion when it mattered, back when your *sisters* tortured her to the brink of insanity."

Vieve leans back ever so slightly. She's not freaking out. Vieve doesn't do that. But she doesn't appreciate me calling her out.

"What happened when you first moved here was out of my control," she answers simply.

I purse my lips. "Hmm. I find that hard to believe, seeing you were second in command at the time."

"Taran," Gemini warns.

He steps in my line of fire. But I'm not here for him. Just like he's definitely not here for me.

I step around him, forcing myself to ignore him. "I haven't forgotten what your sisters did to her." My rage turns on Aric. "Did Celia ever tell you what happened? All of it? What they put her through?"

"No," Aric answers, his wolf appearing too close to unleashing. "Genevieve did when she became aware of who Celia is to me."

Okay. I wasn't expecting that one. Yet maybe I shouldn't be so surprised. In addition to the whole Miss Supernatural Universe vibe she gives off, Vieve is also absurdly smart. She would spin the incident to her advantage to avoid the wrath of the big, bad alpha wolf.

Aric turns to where Celia is sitting perfectly still. This is news to her. All of it.

"Those who willingly assisted Genevieve's predecessor were dealt with long ago," he tells Celia, keeping his voice quiet.

"When?" she asks, her focus fixed ahead.

"When I realized you were mine," he replies. "And before I claimed you."

In other words, within weeks of meeting. Celia

doesn't reply, and neither do I. When someone is "dealt with" in the mystical world, they don't stick around to repeat the same mistake. I wonder briefly when exactly Aric took care of business. Knowing him, it didn't take long for his wolf to demand vengeance.

"It's a different coven now, Taran," Vieve says, careful to avert her attention away from Aric and Celia. "The war between the Alliance and the Tribe helped us sort through those too weak to fight their darkness, and those we couldn't trust to remain loyal. And while it's ultimately to our benefit, it left a multitude of Lesser witches without means to hone in their power, and few Superiors to aid me."

"Are you talking about the same bunch who glare at us every time they see us?" I ask. I smile with as much warmth as I'm feeling. "You'll forgive me if I have my doubts. Won't you, Vieve?"

There's a saying about poking a sleeping snake. But this snake is wide awake and I never did mind being the stick.

"My apologies for how your magic is interpreted by those who don't understand it," she responds softly. "You and your sisters are different."

"You mean weird, right?" I ask, cutting her off.

Again there's that oh-so genial smile that makes me want to rip her lips clean off her face. "'Different' is often misinterpreted as dangerous, which is why my sisters and Lessers react as they do in your presence and that of your family," she replies.

In other words, deal with it. You're freaks, and that's how we'll treat you.

The corners of her mouth tilt, reinforcing my suspicions that perhaps she can read my thoughts. In that case, *Head bitch or not, the day's going to come when I'm going to knock you on your perfect ass, you egomaniacal man-stealing Disney Princess wannabe.*

She tilts her chin, considering me, but also appearing slightly amused. I expect her to call me out on my threat, but that's not what she says.

"Regardless of what you may think of us, you must

come to terms with how wild your magic is, and what can go wrong if you fail to gain control," she responds. "My coven and I can help you to grow, harness, and manipulate your power as we do with all witches born of magic, despite that you're not one of us. Ultimately though, our efforts will be futile if you fail to accept your appendage and make the appropriate sacrifices to even the scales."

"Yeah, you mentioned that," I reply stiffly, resenting the corner I've been shoved into.

"Very well then," she responds, barely blinking. "You'll move in with us—"

"Ah, no I won't," I say, harsh enough to cause sparks of my lightning to charge the air.

"That's not going to happen, Genevieve," Aric tells her, motioning to my side. "You bound her arm from losing control. What if that's enough and she can use it now as is?"

"At will, against another power? That's highly unlikely," Vieve says. She lowers her lids, when the blonde guard bends to whisper in her ear.

Vieve shakes her head at the same time Aric and Gemini growl a "*no*."

"What?" I ask, my attention darting between them.

"Xana is suggesting a test of sorts," Vieve responds. "Something we often do when a Superior witch from another coven seeks acceptance into ours at a higher positon. But you're not qualified."

"Don't tell me what I am, and what I'm not," I say, practically spitting the words through my teeth. Okay, mostly I'm talking to talk, given my pathetic performance seconds ago. But as out of control as I am, I'm not this little bird that needs to be shoved in a cage so it doesn't hurt itself flying.

Her stare lifts to Aric's. "If she refuses my help and acceptance into my coven, I can't command her to do anything nor order her to stand down." She motions to her guard. "What my sister suggests is your call," she tells him.

"It's not his call," I answer. "He's my brother-in-law not my keeper."

"*Aric*," Gemini growls.

Aric meets him with a level stare. "Gemini, I can't come between the two of you or your obligations to her as your mate—just like I can't influence her choices. She's family, not Pack."

"I don't want her to do this," Gemini growls, crossing that line between them as friends.

"Neither do I," Aric snarls back, his anger reducing only slightly when Celia stands and takes his hand. "But I also can't stop her."

"Quit talking about *her* like *she's* not here," I remind them, sending my arm into an aggravated fit. It settles quickly, but it's not like the motion goes unnoticed.

Celia slinks her way to my side, the distress in her features alerting me that she knows what's happening long before she speaks. "A few months ago, a witch new to the area applied for acceptance into Genevieve's coven. She was of Lesser power and asked for instruction only to go rogue weeks later. Although her power is limited, she must be accounted for."

Because rogue witches go one of two ways without a coven: dark or crazy.

Awesome. That doesn't mean I'll shy away from this fight, especially if it will get me one step closer to the control I seek. "So if I find her and bring her here, I won't have to do that chanting crap?" I ask.

Vieve surprises me by smiling despite how her peeps seem ready to cut the bind around my arm and let my fire toast me like s'mores. "Submit Savana using your residual power, and that of your arm, and you may convince me you're capable of synchronizing your magic without my coven's help" she responds.

"So no to the Sisterhood of the Traveling Broomsticks?" I clarify.

"Correct," she says, not that I think she's wild about the reference.

"What if she can't?" Aric asks. "Or what if she fails to bring back the witch?"

"Then she'll belong to me," Vieve responds, losing

her smile. "As your young *weres* belong to you."

Aric shakes his head as Gemini mutters my favorite swear word. His response gives me pause, like I mentioned he's not one to swear or swim in all this rage he has going on. It's a struggle not to meet his face or to assure him that I'll be fine. He doesn't want me, he made that clear long ago.

Instead I focus on Aric, and how his features reflect my annoyance at Vieve insinuating she'd own me.

"Taran is neither a young *were* for me to manage or a Lesser witch for you to command. She's proven herself as a formidable member of our Alliance on numerous occasions and should be treated with respect."

Vieve leans in, making it clear she's not playing around. "She's proved herself as she was. It's time for her to prove herself as she is." This time when she speaks, her attention is all on me. "If you fail, upon your return I will place you with Lesser witches who are closer to your age and also the weakest among us."

"Genevieve," Aric begins. "This is insulting to both Taran *and* me."

She motions mildly with her hand. "Would you prefer I place her with our school-aged population, who may I add, already possess more command and power than Taran? Or would you rather she be among those older yet struggling as she does? These are my terms, Aric. Take them or don't."

"She'll stay with us," Aric responds. "And she'll master her control safely. Those are *my* terms or you can forget any favors the Pack will owe you."

"You're both assuming I don't stand a chance against Hannah," I begin.

"Savana," the other guard mutters.

"*Whatever*," I respond. "Just point the way and I'll bring her in."

"I'll allow a small team of three to watch your back should you encounter other threats," Vieve replies when she catches something in Celia's features. "But Savana's capture must be achieved using your magic alone." She relaxes against her chair all-too gracefully. "Need I remind you,

you're the one who has something to prove."

"I don't need reminding," I tell her. "Heard you loud and clear the first time, Vieve."

"Don't even think about it, sweetness," Aric says, when Celia stirs beside him. "Not in your condition."

Her stare hardens she dips her chin. "I know," she says, so quietly I barely hear her.

Bren, who's been unusually closed-mouthed for him, nudges me with his big wet nose. I stroke the fur along his large head with my good hand. "It's okay, Ceel," I reply, knowing that at least for now, her days of kicking ass are over. "Bren has my back."

That much I know. Yet, the way Bren regards me and wags his tail touches me in a way I'm not prepared for. I walk carefully away when I feel my emotions begin to spiral, not bothering to say goodbye. No one stops me and no one follows me except for Bren who trots loyally beside me.

I'm not sure what to expect as I march through the house. For all I know about a dozen witches armed with eye of newt or whatever the hell are waiting to take me out in the foyer. Yet even though I can sense magic practically seeping through the walls of this ancient building, and hear voices trailing from the upstairs rooms, I don't see anyone until I step onto the wraparound porch.

What seems to be a new set of Lesser witches trail between the crops, carrying buckets of water. This group wears light tan and white pilgrim / Amish / nun outfits. Bren chuffs beside me, his frown bouncing from me to them.

"Believe me, I don't want to end up out there either," I tell him.

I fold my arms in front of me and lean against the railing, my stare latching onto the leather cord crisscrossed along my psycho arm. It's not as tight, having gradually loosened once it got my arm under control. But it's there. I feel Vieve's power skulking beneath it, ready to smack it around should it disobey.

With a defeated sigh, I return my attention to where the Lesser witches trudge through the soil. A few don't quite make it to the center of the field before having to lower their buckets and take a few needed breaths. I don't want this to be my eventual fate. It's not that I don't believe in hard work, I've worked hard all my life. It's more like I don't feel like I belong. Not that it's anything new.

"I was pretty bad in there, wasn't I?" I ask Bren.

Bren releases a small whine in affirmation, but then pokes me in the elbow with his nose, careful not to touch my affected arm or Genevieve's bind.

"Yeah, it helps," I admit. "But it's like trying to seal a gaping wound with a Sponge Bob band aid, buddy."

The door creaks open behind me, and although I feel the familiar tension, I'm still surprised when Gemini positions himself to my right. Bren, for all I'd like him to, doesn't stay. He hops down the steps, disappearing into the garden.

I hope he lifts his leg over Vieve's favorite rosebush. Hey, a real friend would.

Gemini shifts his body to face the field, neither of us speaking, at least not right away.

"How are you?" he finally asks, his deep voice rumbling and his dark eyes fixed on the field.

Being as defensive as I am, and as hurt as I've been, I want to tell him that it's none of his business, and that it hasn't been since the day he moved out. But it's because I'm still devastated over our break-up that I don't lash out.

I'm miserable, I want to say.

I miss you, my heart responds.

Why did you have to stop loving me?

Yet my mouth remains closed. I hope my emotions can follow suit and stay just as silent, except they don't. They never could settle around him.

"I don't want you to go after Savana, with or without a team," he tells me. "You should stay here and do as Genevieve asks. It's the only real chance you have to regain command over your magic."

Maybe it's because he's trying to tell me what to do that my anger returns. Or maybe it's because he mentioned his new girlfriend *and* how he expects me to bow down and give into her demands that pisses me off.

Hmm. I think it might be the latter.

I lift my chin to meet his face. "That would be like me telling you, you shouldn't be here," I respond.

He frowns. "You know my position with the witches. This is nothing new."

"I'm sure you take *many* positions with the witches," I reply, all the resentment I'm feeling lancing each word. "One head witch in particular must be very familiar with them by now."

Gemini barely blinks, his anger rivaling mine. "*You* pushed me away," he says, closing the small space between us. "Just as you did in there. Why do you think I'm the one most covered by the remains of your clashing magic? *I* was the one fighting to get to you the hardest, and the one *you* fought to keep the furthest away."

"Did I push you away?" I ask as pensively. I lift my bound arm. "Or did this?" I scoff when he withdraws from it like it could somehow bite. "It did, didn't it? Right into the healthy arms of another."

"You're so wrong," he growls.

"No. You are." I back away, whipping my hand out to stop him when he reaches for me. Of course it's my bad hand, and of course it easily keeps him from drawing closer. "Don't touch me," I tell him, my throat burning with impending tears. "You lost that privilege a long time ago."

I don't wait for his response. I barrel down the steps, passing Celia and Aric. I didn't notice them there, but it's easy to be distracted when your heart is busy breaking.

Chapter Six

I adjust my position in the front passenger seat, along with the magical equivalent of MapQuest on my lap. There's a reason you don't hear much about Kentucky. It's quiet. Almost too quiet, and the people are ridiculously nice. Too nice. I'm not saying it's a Stepford state, but I'm not used to so many people smiling my way and meaning it, unless I'm at a club and they happen to be staring at my ass. If I had to guess, I'd think the whole state was under some eerie spell. But I'll take it. I grew up in Jersey so I'm just excited that at least for the moment, no one's tried to "cut" us.

We barrel down the country road in our rental Jeep, passing another band of locals who smile and wave our way. We wave back, Bren's grin widening when a young woman in a cowboy hat, bikini top, and not much else blows him a kiss.

"It's not such a bad place. Is it?" he asks. "Nope, not so bad at all . . ."

Bren's driving because I'm too busy giving him directions and Shayna aka Hades' Chauffeur isn't allowed to drive us anywhere. It's not that she can't drive well, it's more like she can't drive slow and doesn't care if we live so long as she gets there.

Ordinarily, I'd just ask Siri. She's my girl. But apparently rogue witches don't like to leave forwarding addresses or ways to be easily found. So I'm stuck staring at a stick punctured through the center of a piece of cardboard. "N" for North, "S" for South, "E" for East, and "W" for West, are scrawled in charcoal around the perimeter of a drawn-in circle. A strand of hair the witches believe belonged to Savana is tied to the stick on one end, and wound around a pebble at the other end.

I made a mental note to avoid leaving any DNA around Vieve. You wouldn't believe the kind of shit witches can do with piece of your hair or, God forbid, a toenail.

"Bear right," I tell Bren when the pebble tilts between "N" and "E".

Koda's growls erupt from the other end of Shayna's phone. She's sitting in the rear with Emme. Bren's blasting the radio and I can still hear Koda like he's perched on my lap.

"Puppy, there's no sense in fussing," she tells him calmly.

"Fussing" she calls it. Um. No. Fussing is what babies do when they drop their favorite toys from their highchairs. Koda's sound effects are reminiscent of a wild beast tearing flesh from his prey's bones.

More growls, more snarls, and something that may or may not have been the sound of cracking molars. If he was here, I'd be running for my life. Yet Shayna, unlike the rest of us, isn't scared of Koda and is very much used to him flipping out.

He doesn't want her here with me. It's not just because of the witch we're hunting, even though no one is taking her seriously, but also because he doesn't trust my arm even with Vieve's bind. He's afraid I'll hurt her, and he's not alone. This bind maybe forcing my hand to behave, but Vieve made it clear it won't last, and when it goes, we could be in a firestorm of trouble.

The thing is, my iPhone isn't exactly overflowing with contacts I can call. Celia's out of commission due to her delicate state, and the vampires are well, slutty. And when it comes to vamps and owing them a favor, you'll always get screwed in the end and in every position possible. Vampires suck that way.

Bren was the first to offer his help. Emme volunteered in case she needed to heal me, but also because she's sweet and genuinely wants to support me. Shayna is always ready to skip into danger waving a battle axe, since that's how my perky sister rolls. But Bren and Emme don't have anyone to talk them out of joining me. And Shayna . . . let's say her fuzzier half isn't happy.

The next set of growls have her extending the phone out and away from her. "Puppy, don't fret," she says sweetly, returning her phone to her ear. "I promise to make it up to you when I come home."

She whispers something that I don't catch, but cracks Bren up. "Holy shit. That's some kinky stuff there, Shayna."

Shayna covers the phone as I glance over my shoulder. Her cheeks are pink, but there's that smile that lights up every room she enters. "He likes peanut butter," she tells him. "Most people do."

"Most like it on bread. Not on their—"

"I'm going to stop you both right there," Emme says, holding a hand out.

I crack up with Bren, despite it being Shayna's cat that's run screeching out of the bag, Emme's face is flaming red. Shayna laughs for whole different reasons, now that her scary beast is under control. She whispers into the phone, giggling when he says something I don't hear, and probably shouldn't.

"What's the matter, Emme?" Bren asks her, when her blush doesn't seem ready to leave her. "Never had peanut butter slathered on your rolls?"

I start laughing until I catch sight of Emme's face. Her skin remains just as flushed, but there's more riddling her angelic features than shyness. My smile fades as she seems to shrivel inward, trying to hide from the world.

"What about honey, baby?" Bren presses. "Ever try a little sweetness down below?"

I touch his arm when he continues to laugh, the way I

shake my head causing him to immediately quiet. Emme's not a virgin, but she's very virgin-like in her mannerisms and thoughts. We tease her because of it, and it's all in fun, but something's different this time.

His eyes cut to the rearview mirror, his thick brows knitting tight. "You okay, sweetheart?" he asks.

Emme nods, forcing that smile she's flashed way too many times, but keeping her head down. "I'm fine," she says, stammering slightly.

It's clear that she's lying. Bren doesn't have to take a whiff to know as much, yet he still does. His nostrils flare as he inhales, only for his breath to hitch. "Fuck," he mutters.

"What's wrong?" I mouth.

His humor is now long gone. "She's not doing well," he whispers.

I angle around to see her. The shadows cast by trees pass along her face as she stares out of the window and withdraws further away. Emme's our light, she always has been. So why does it seem like that light is dwindling right in front of us?

"Liam?" Bren mouths.

I shake my head, not just because I don't want him mentioning Liam's name, but because I don't think his memory is the cause. At least not this time.

Liam was one of Aric's Warriors, and a close friend to him and Gemini. He was also Koda's best friend and Emme's lover. She adored him, but she wasn't his mate. No, Liam belonged to another. So when Liam died, Emme didn't just mourn the loss of someone we all loved, she mourned what she believed she was never meant to have.

I know that feeling because I share that same sense of loss, only it's not due to Liam.

Bren nudges me with his elbow as we speed down a small highway with ancient trees on either side, their branches extending out to entwine like carefully clasped hands. He wants to know where my thoughts are headed, so he can get a stronger fix on what's wrong with Emme.

"She's lonely," I say under my breath.

He keeps his stare ahead, giving nothing away. But I know he heard me. Those heightened senses of his never miss a thing.

The next few miles are quiet, which is typical for Emme, but not for the rest of us. Even Shayna hasn't said a word since disconnecting with her not-so adorable "puppy". Like the rest of us, she's likely picked up on Emme's solemn mood.

I want to talk to her, except this isn't the time for a heart to heart. I know it, and so does everyone else.

My brows lift when something stimulates my so-called compass. "Um, go right," I say, watching the pebble angle up toward the corner.

"Right as in east?" he asks.

"More like Northeast," I answer, watching the pebble continuing to levitate.

"You sure?" He eases off the gas, appearing to take in everything ahead of us and along the deeply wooded edges. "I only see straight."

I start to insist, only for the words to seep back down my throat when the strand of hair and pebble float parallel to the paper. When we first slipped into the Jeep, it swung along the edges, tilting just enough so we'd know where to go. Now, it's tugging at the hair hard enough to snap it.

"I'm going to go with yes," I tell him, my voice trailing.

I'm not thrilled at how this little stone is acting. But when it starts to shake like it's freaking *scared*, I'm reminded how much saving the world sucks monkey ass. Peeps, this is so not a good sign.

"Bren—"

I lurch forward when he slams on the breaks, my grip instinctively tightening around the edges of the compass. I don't have to look at him to know he sees what I see. The pebble is no longer shaking, it's jerking violently. I jolt when it breaks free from the strand and soars through the partially lowered window, chipping the edge.

Bren sets the emergency brake, sniffing in the

direction the eerily rigid strand of hair is pointing. All that's there is thick brush and trees centuries old. Yet that doesn't mean I'm any less afraid.

Something is really wrong.

"Stay here," he says, opening the door and slipping out.

I lower the window the rest of the way and peer out. The slight breeze lifts my hair. It's warm, but not so warm that we needed air conditioning during the drive. Instead, we opened the windows about halfway down, allowing the aroma of blossoming flowers and trees to indulge our senses.

Yet while the now familiar scents continue to trickle into my nose, the air itself is different, stirring within it more than pollen and bits of dust from the road.

My vision sharpens, I don't realize how white my irises turn until I catch sight of my reflection in the side mirror. Christ, they're practically glowing.

"T . . . your eyes," Shayna says.

"I know," I respond, my voice appearing to drift. But neither my voice nor my reflection keep my interest. Bren does.

His back is to us and his hands are placed firmly on his hips. The breeze picks up again, sharpening everything in front of me until the scene appears like paper cut-outs layered on top of each other.

Bren's hands fall cautiously to his sides. I toss the compass on the floor and hurry out, slamming the door behind me.

The magic charging the air drags me forward like the pull of a relentless stalker. I'm not a runner, but I am in shape. Yet despite that Bren stands only a few feet away, my legs feel heavy, as if I've just reached the end of a very long race.

My pace dwindles, slowing me to a stop just beside him. "What is it?" I ask, recognizing something is very wrong.

He shakes his head, anger stirring his beast. "Nothing good," he says.

Without asking, Shayna slides into the driver's seat

and turns the Jeep to face the direction we drove in from, ensuring a quick getaway should we need one. It's a smart tactic, and one we've implemented several times throughout the years. You might notice we've been in danger once or twice.

"This isn't supposed to be a strong witch," he reminds me. "The brief Genevieve sent describes her as mediocre at best, and someone never properly schooled."

"Yeah. I read the memo," I mutter.

Shayna and Emme zip the power windows closed and hurry out, slamming the doors behind them.

I motion ahead when they reach us. "This doesn't feel like the kind of magic a mediocre witch would cast. So either Vieve was wrong, *really* wrong, or she played us."

Bren gives it some thought. "Genevieve wouldn't deliberately screw us over, we're too close to Aric and she's not stupid enough to mess with him."

"But her sisters might," I point out, remembering it was one of her guards who suggested this little bounty hunt. "Neither said anything you or the other wolves could have perceived as a lie."

Bren shakes his head. "I'm not buying it. Guarding a head witch is a position of honor, granted to those deemed most worthy. It's similar to when were beasts are selected as Warriors to guard our pureblood Leaders. Genevieve's guards wouldn't risk their status or their lives, and Genevieve would be obliged to turn them over to the Pack if they knowingly set us up."

He huffs when another breeze streams through the trees, the force harsh enough to lift my hair away from my shoulders and send his messy waves sweeping along his brow. "Either this witch has aligned herself with someone stronger, or she's not the weakling everyone thought."

I try not to react or make it about me. But it's hard to stomach that despite Savana's wimp status on the magic scale, Vieve didn't think I could take her down. That's how little she believes in my abilities. Well, maybe it's time to prove her wrong.

"You guys ready?" I ask, forcing myself to stand slightly ahead of Bren.

Shayna fumbles through her backpack and pulls out a box of toothpicks before passing the heavy pack to Emme. Emme doesn't need her hands free to kick ass, but Shayna does.

"So what's the plan, dudes?" Shayna asks. "Onward and upward?"

"Yeah," I answer, shrugging when Bren looks at me. "This isn't the good kind of magic, Bren. With all the evil set to rise, and the bad guys needing dark witches to make it happen, you know our motto: no stone left unturned, and no scaries left to chew on our insides."

He snags my elbow when I start to head for the dense brush. "If we can, I'll let you make the capture. It's the only way to keep Genevieve from sinking her teeth into you. But that thing in there—if it's as bad as I think it is—there's no bringing her home alive, got me? I'll make the kill if it comes down to it."

He doesn't think I can take her, much less kill her. And maybe he's right. But that doesn't mean we can turn our backs and pretend she's not here.

I kick at the dirt at my feet. I don't like to kill, despite what people think and despite that it's something I'm freakishly good at. I've had plenty of practice, believe me. My first kill occurred when I was just a teen, the second, moments after. It was the right thing to do given what happened. That doesn't mean I wasn't sick to my gut. I burned them with enough heat to smoke their chests, allowing them to feel every ounce of pain they caused me and my sisters. Too many followed after that, enough that I've lost count. But as much as the dead mark my bones, and stay a part of me, I'll do it again if I have to.

I meet Bren's face. "Dead or alive, we have to take care of Savana and whoever else might be helping her."

"Even if it means you get stuck serving Genevieve?" he presses.

He's not asking. He knows taking out Savana is the

right thing to do. He's just making sure we're all on the same page. "Yes," I answer. My focus drifts to my sisters. "Do what you have to do to stay safe. Don't worry about me."

It's a stupid thing to say. Of course they'll worry. For once in our lives I'm the one who needs coddling. Not that I don't absolutely hate it.

My hiking boots press into the ground as we move away from the road. They're not what I count as cute shoes. But since my cute clothes tend to end up covered with blood and smelly supernatural fluids, here I am in jeans, a long-sleeved shirt and vest, and yeah, the hiking boots.

Bren leaps over a thick section of brush, landing smoothly as I try to figure out the closest way in. "It's clear," he says. "Come on."

He means the first few feet are clear. I can't see jack over these thick brambles. I look hopelessly to Emme, wishing I didn't have to. She regards me almost apologetically, realizing what I'm asking her to do.

Emme is good at a lot of things: baking, scrapbooking, and keeping up on all our collective bills. But her aim sucks. So when she throws me over the brush with her *force*, it takes all I have not to scream. Thankfully Bren is good at catching, no matter how bad the throw.

"Christ," I mutter as he eases me down.

Shayna inherited a bit of *were* from Koda's essence. And while she'll never heal or run as fast as a *were*, he gave her enough agility to clear the thick brambles without Emme's help.

Poor Emme. Her aim isn't any better on herself. Bren has to "go long" to keep her from slamming into a tree when she launches herself forward.

Shayna and I jog ahead to where Bren is lowering Emme to the ground. He kisses her cheek, a show of affection he often demonstrates to us, but this time she doesn't welcome it like she once did. She meets his eyes, backing away slowly, as if she's afraid to step too close. Bren frowns, speaking low. Emme answers with a nod, but again steps further away from him.

Shayna doesn't seem to notice, skipping across the rugged terrain as if we're out for a stroll and not walking into some evil crap we may have to kill before it rips us apart. But I notice. Something is definitely up with Emme. I stiffen when he strokes her cheek. And son of a bitch, it may have to do with Bren!

What the hell?

I hurry forward when I realize I'm just standing there, gaping at them.

I don't think I take more than a few steps when something crunches beneath the sole of my left boot. I think it's a stick, but the sound seems off, especially since the ground is so moist. I lift my foot only to jump away.

"T, you coming?" Shayna calls when I don't move.

"T?" she asks again.

I swallow hard, hoping I'm imagining things as they run back to me.

"What's wrong?" Emme asks. Unlike Shayna who's fired up for all the action about to go down, I can sense the worry in her voice.

"Bren . . ." I begin, pointing to the spot near my feet. "Is that a, um, *toe?*"

He cocks his head. "Nah."

Emme places her hand over her heart and sighs. "Oh, good—"

"It's a thumb," he answers. He sniffs the air. "Right hand, male, and the poor bastard's been dead a long time." He looks ahead. "Yeah, this shit's not good. Call it in, Shayna, but type it. Don't use voice-to text."

"Why, dude?" Shayna asks, reaching for her phone in her back pocket.

"Because I'm not sure how well this bitch can hear, or if she has other things listening for her," he responds.

He motions ahead to a crow. It squawks twice in our direction and flutters away.

Shayna lifts her phone to show us the blank screen. "Phone's dead, kids." She quickly pockets it and places a handful of toothpicks in her palm. "I wouldn't bother,

Emme," she adds when Emme reaches for her phone. I doubt any of our phones are working."

"She's right," Bren says. He shoves his phone into the backpack Emme is carrying and peels off his white T-shirt.

"This keeps getting better and better," I mutter.

Bren strips out of his jeans, leaving only his underwear and shit-kickers on. "Em, stay behind me," he tells her. "Shayna, you've got the rear."

Which leaves me in front of Shayna and the most protected. I'll be honest, this helpless damsel in distress role does nothing for my morale.

I march ahead, forcing myself to snap out of the shock of finding some guy's thumb, push aside my fear and tap into my inner diva. I remember a little too late that my inner diva is louder and usually sashays in platform stilettos. I slow my steps, careful not to disturb the creepy things hiding in the bushes.

Let me be the first to tell you, woods are bullshit and top the scales on the scary meter, second only to graveyards. It's the reason so many horror movies are based here, and why I'm watching out for psychos with machetes lurking behind trees. But given our past experiences, where danger lurks, so do the dark ones. I've had my fill of alleyways, construction sites, abandoned structures, but especially these damn eerie woods!

With every step, the canopy of twisting branches above us tightens, darkening the forest. But it's the shift in the air that sends goose bumps skittering up my arms. Instead of warmth, the surrounding breeze grows dank and heavy. My stare darts in every direction, knowing we're no longer alone.

Something shoots out from beneath an old log, scuttling like a crab and moving so fast I barely catch sight of it. It skitters beneath a spread of thick ferns, causing the cluster of leaves to tremble as it passes, only to come to an abrupt stop.

Okay. So much for not disturbing the creepy.

I back away from it, only to slam into Bren. "Was that a spider?" I ask.

"No," he responds, his voice gathering that edge it does before he sprouts fangs.

"It wasn't?" Emme stammers, inching closer to Bren. "It moved like a spider. A *really* big spider. I mean, it had legs and everything."

"Those weren't legs," Bren mutters. He turns to Shayna. "I point, you shoot. Got me?"

Shayna's eyes narrow, demonstrating her focus. The small amount of sunlight trickling through the overhanging branches shimmers along the length of the toothpicks as she transforms them into long and deadly needles.

Bren inhales deep and closes his eyes. No one else moves. Hell, no one else breathes. His hand shoots up, pointing down and away from the line of ferns. Shayna doesn't hesitate. Her hand whips out and the needles shoot forward. Again, Bren points. Again, Shayna sends a long needle soaring, further away between a tight row of trees. The motions repeat, causing whatever it hits to scratch frantically against the earth.

"What are they?" Emme asks, barely able to get the words out.

I shake my head, unable to respond. Whatever those things are, they aren't happy about being caught. They're not just scratching, they're *clawing* at the ground, trying to break free and causing the mounds of ferns camouflaging them to shake violently. This, I may add, also does nothing for my confidence.

Bren opens his eyes slowly, releasing a satisfied breath. "Okay. You got them," he says. He frowns as he takes another whiff. "At least those close by."

"And what exactly did she get?" I force myself to ask, longing for spiders.

"I'll show you," he says, marching forward. "This way."

We follow in silence, but it's the sweat slicking his broad back that makes me want to ask if he's okay. His face doesn't give much away, but the perspiration running down his spine shows me how hard he's working to contain his beast.

The wolf inside him wants out, likely to maul whatever he senses. I almost hate that my sisters are here. Bren is protective in general, but with more of us present, there's more his beast wants to protect, making him edgy and hard to contain. Yet when we near the first of Shayna's captives, I'm glad my sisters are with me. You can even say I'm tickled pink.

Emme bumps into me when I grind to a halt. Bren stops in front the tree trunk where Shayna's needle has punctured through a hand. That's right, a *freaking* hand! Chunks of drying muscle shrivel into what remains of the wrist, but doesn't exactly hide or muffle the brittle bones clicking beneath the layers of skin.

But the disturbing imagery doesn't end there. Oh, hell no. The fingers are scrambling, circling and pressing against the trunk, desperate to get free.

"Humph," Bren says. "Just as I thought." He pulls the needle out and examines the quivering hand still trying to scramble away while I do my best not to face-plant on the forest floor.

"What is that?" I manage, doing my best not to hurl.

"A hand," Bren says.

"I know that much," I snap, fear and nausea making me irritable. "But how—I mean, *why*? Why is it moving?"

"Because it's not completely dead," he answers like I'm the stupid one.

He steps closer to us with the hand in, well, *his*. We step back because yeah, we're collectively skeeved out. As it is, the thing is losing it, shaking and squirming and making grabby motions.

"You see that?" Bren says, pointing beneath it to a dark spot on the palm.

Whatever it is flakes off and falls to the ground. "Yeah," I say because in truth, I have nothing else and it beats screaming like I very much want to.

"That's rotting skin. It's a zombie hand—not like yours, no offense."

I ram my hands on my hips. "Bren, I'm not really sure how I'm supposed to take that, but for the love of all, just keep going."

"They shouldn't be here," he says.

"What? The hands?" Shayna asks, glancing around like she's missing something.

He shakes his head. "No. Zombies." He leans back on his heels, like he didn't just say the "z" word and as if me and my girls aren't ready to haul ass back to the Jeep.

"My guess is that they're a least four close by based on the amount of hands running around and whoever the thumb belongs to. This Savana chick is up to something major. We better find her and the other body parts before they find us." He sniffs the air, frowning in the direction of a darker section of woods. "They're over there," he tells us. "This way."

Chapter Seven

"Zombies," I say, trailing behind Bren.

"Yup," he says.

He stalks forward while me and Emme more or less stumble behind him through the uneven and littered terrain. Shayna's Jack be Nimble steps make her more graceful. That doesn't mean she's any less terrified.

"Just so you know, I promised Puppy I wouldn't be eaten," she says. "Don't make a liar out of me, Bren. Koda wouldn't like that."

"And neither would I, kid," Bren adds.

For all we joke about being munched on like shredded wheat, we're not really joking. There are things in this world that crave and survive on human flesh. And if it weren't for the *weres*, witches, and the often begrudging help from the vamps, the human populace would be a virtual smorgasbord and overpopulation wouldn't be an issue.

I cross my arms in front of me. It's not that I'm cold. I'm scared. Fear is something I've gone to bed with too many times. But it hasn't been this bad in years. I glance at my arm, noting how the bind presses into my skin, keeping my limb in check like a naughty child. For a fleeting moment, I debate whether to yank off the cord. Yet as much as I fear what's lurking ahead, I fear the volatility of my arm more.

CECY ROBSON

I drop my hands to my sides and close the distance between me and Bren. "I hate to sound like a complete moron," I tell him. "But what do you mean by zombies? Are you talking *Walking Dead* zombies, as in suck on your brains type creatures?"

"Nah, that's just T.V.. They can't make us one of their own and don't eat brains." He thinks about it. "At least not the brains of fresh kills. For the most part they eat other dead things, road kill, rotting animals, you know, things like that."

As nasty as the alternative sounds, you know your world is screwed up when rotted-prey-eating zombies are happy news.

"So they won't try to kill us?" Emme asks.

"I didn't say that," Bren says. "I only said they wouldn't eat fresh brains."

"What—wait," I say, reaching for him and speaking low. "If what you're saying is true, we're going to need serious back-up. I mean zombies, *zombies*, Bren! Why haven't we heard of them before?"

His face shadows in anger. "Because they're not supposed to be here," he says. "Savana, or whoever the hell's with her, is into some really evil shit. The dead are supposed to stay that way. To raise them is illegal, and among the deadliest sins in the supernatural world."

Emme inches to our side, keeping her head low. "Celia and Aric fought them in El Salvador. But she said they were more like skeletons." She motions cautiously at the twitchy hand Bren continues to carry. "Based on the amount of flesh, it hasn't been dead that long."

"No," he agrees. "It's fairly fresh and newly exhumed which is a lot worse." He pauses as if wrestling with how much to tell us. "You know what a familiar is?"

We all nod, but I'm who responds. "Something that attends to and obeys a witch, typically an animal."

"Yeah, or in this case a person," he clarifies. "That's why it's illegal, it's like slavery, but in some ways more messed up."

He yanks the needle free from the hand and tosses

68

both aside. We may or may not have jumped as it scuttled away, and Emme may or may not have squeezed my breast when she clutched me.

"Sorry," she squeaks.

"It's okay," I say, watching the hand disappear into the shadows. "Bren, you have to tell us more than that. How do you raise something when there's no soul attached to it?"

"You can't raise a body whose soul has passed, unless that soul remains trapped in purgatory," he explains. "Or if the soul continues to roam the earth, like a ghost for example."

"So those who haven't yet crossed into heaven," Emme reasons.

"Or hell," he adds. "Which is why Savana can raise them, their souls continue to linger, unable to achieve their peace—because of either something they did, or something they think they still have left to do."

"She's preventing them from moving on by keeping what remains of their souls enslaved in these bodies?" I ask. Bren nods. "What a raging psycho."

"Yup. But it's the power behind the rage that makes her lethal," he adds. His features harden. "We have to end her reign of terror or whatever the fuck before she reassembles elsewhere and raises more dead."

"So no time for reinforcements," Shayna mumbles.

"Not if we're going to help the zombies," Bren replies. He looks at me. "Fire is the best way to break Savana's spell over them. Light them up. Make sure they burn to ash."

My lips part. "You want me to kill them?" I ask.

"No. I want you to free them. I can rip them apart, but they'll piece themselves back together if they find enough to eat. Is that what you want?" he asks.

"No," I manage, not that I needed the visual. But, I also don't want hurt something that's innocent.

Shayna senses as much and tries to help in her own Shayna-like way. "I could cut their heads off," she offers.

Bren pats her back. "And I'm counting on that, baby,

especially if they attack. But the only way to ensure they don't come back is to destroy the body completely. That means fire." He looks at me. "T, it's either that or kill Savana outright."

I nod, determined to help, but not so willing to hurt. "Okay. Let's go," I say, adding a lot of attitude to mask my growing unease.

I try to pump myself up for whatever we're going to fight, kill, or mutilate. But the forest feels eerily quiet and it takes a very long time before we see anything. Yet, it's like everything sees us.

The knots along the wrinkled trunks resemble eyes, their twisting branches appearing ready to snatch us as we pass. The leaves sweeping in the breeze tilt and stretch in our direction, attempting, it seems, to get a better look.

Bren keeps his head forward, more or less resembling any half-naked man out for a walk. But I know him, he's taking everything in, down to the aroma of the earth at our feet.

We reach a section of the forest where all life seems to have died out. There are no ferns or moss. The only green dangles from the branches of a tree perched a few feet away.

This is one of those in-your face clues that darkness is upon us. Not that it prepares me for what we encounter next.

A lake stretches out in front of us, a small island with a wood cottage sits near the center, its beach nothing more than mounds of rocks.

Bren motions to a rowboat that's seen better days. "You're kidding, right?" I ask.

I barely get the words out when the breeze picks up. I shudder from the amount of magic that strikes me. But it's that awful pull from the lake that makes me want to break away. "She's on the island," I say.

"I know. I can scent all the rotting flesh from here," he says. "My guess is she's in the process of raising more dead. We'd better get out there before there's too many to manage."

Shayna wrinkles her nose when the wind picks up again and I release another shudder. "I smell it, too. Do you think it's a bad sign that I can easily recognize the smell of decomposing bodies?"

"Yup. Yes. Uh-huh," we all mumble.

Shayna and I help Bren tip the boat and shove it forward. But as soon as we hop in, Emme shoots us forward with her *force*.

"Nice, Emme," Bren says, lifting the oars out of the water to toss inside the boat.

"I'll take them," Shayna says. She takes them from Bren's hands, transforming them into long and deadly swords with her gift.

Emme knits her small brow, focusing hard on pushing us forward. She doesn't move us in a perfect line, but she's steady in her movements, allowing Bren to keep a vigilant watch.

The cottage reminds me of the one from those old Grizzly Adams movies our foster mother used to watch with us when we were kids. It's quaint and unassuming, but maybe that's what Savana wants the locals to believe.

I'm expecting everything. You have to if you want to survive. Yet once again I'm not prepared for what I see. Bren lifts his hand, attempting to halt Emme's efforts. But she's so focused, she doesn't notice.

I cup her shoulder. "Slow down," I whisper.

She clasps her hand over her mouth, muffling her gasps and likely her screams. What I mistook for large rocks littering the beach are actually skulls, hundreds of them. Some human, some not, some . . . freshly cleaned.

"I thought you said they only eat dead animals," I say to Bren, trying to keep my voice low and steady and doing a horrible job.

"Looks to me like they've been eating each other," he says. "Savana's probably starved them and turned them into cannibals. Em turn us around." He frowns when the boat slows to a stop. "Em, we have to get out of here—"

He growls when he sees Emme sitting perfectly still. Jesus Christ in heaven, it's all I can do not to shriek. A swarm of arms in various stages of decomposition stretch out from the water, stroking her paling skin. Wet, ragged clothing hangs loose against feeble shoulders, exposing damaged muscle and flapping skin from the festering bodies. But it's their gaunt and skeletal faces, and the agony in what remains of their stares, that humanizes them and keeps me from attacking.

These *people* are walking around in anguish, forced to live, even when they died so long ago. What kind of monster does this?

"Taran, take a breath," Bren says. "I need you to stay with me, kid."

Again, my arm is shaking. Again, I feel like I'm losing control. But I'm not alone. Shayna hovers over them, her swords raised in her trembling hands. Horror traces every speck of her pixie face. Like me she sees and feels their pain.

Bren shakes his head when she steals a glance his way. "Don't," he tells her. "They're not attacking yet."

"And if they do?" I ask, biting out the words.

"Then we have a job to do," he growls. "Emme, turn the boat *around.*"

She swallows hard, trying to shake her head, but not quite managing, when a zombie pulls herself up to caress Emme's cheek.

"I *can't,*" she says. "They're holding us in place. If I try, I'm going to drag them along the bottom."

I jump when I see the row of hands along the edge of the boat and more heads poke through the surface of the water. There's a woman missing half her scalp, helping the others bring the boat closer to shore. She smiles, showing me what's left of her teeth. I think she's trying to be nice, but when a tiny snail slinks out between two spaces, I think I would have preferred a more vicious response. Those I can handle. Those I'm used to. But this . . . how are we going to get through it?

My arm is shaking me so hard, I swear I'm rattling the boat. But it's not fear I sense. Oh, hell no. It's an overwhelming need to act, lash out, and charge whatever did this to them!

"Taran, easy," Bren says.

My magic charges over my head, firing from my core.

Sparks of blue and white erupt above me, lighting the air. Like small children, the zombies point, appearing in awe of the shimmering energy.

"Emme, turn the boat around," Bren says when only mere feet remain between us and the shore.

She rams her eyes closed, lifting the boat only for it to be wrenched back down. More heads bob up. More arms. More dragging us forward. The boat jerks back and forth, Emme fighting against the collective pull of at least twenty zombies.

"Should I cut off their hands?" Shayna offers, the sorrow in her tone expressing she'd rather not do so.

"Please don't hurt them," Emme begs, tears streaming down her face. "I can feel them . . . I can feel them hurting."

Bren kicks out of his boots and peels off his underwear. I stumble out of the boat onto the stony beach, trying not to react when the brittle bones of legs and skulls crunch beneath my feet and the zombies gather around us.

Bren's massive brown wolf form lands gracefully ahead of me, growling when he turns back toward the boat. He didn't like all these zombies touching Emme, and his beast dislikes it even more.

"Easy, Bren," I mutter. For all this shit's too sick to be real, I can't shake the sadness these zombies inflict. It's the prime emotion overtaking me. That, and rage.

I reach for Emme to help her down when Shayna positions herself behind her. My right arm is shaking like a leaf beneath the wrath of a storm, but it's Emme who seems ready to keel over, her pallor a deathly white.

"I can feel them," she repeats. "Taran, I sense their pain."

Emme's healing *touch* is more than simply possessing the ability seal wounds. Her sympathetic nature enables her to find the hurt so she can fix it. But she can't fix this, which is why it's affecting her so deeply.

"It's okay, baby girl," I say—like there aren't dead

and mutilated bodies swarming us, and pretending like these poor beings aren't moaning, aren't in pain, aren't practically begging us to help them.

She grips my palm as she steps from the boat, ramming her eyes shut as more bodies surround her, stroking her like the sweet, precious gift we've always believed her to be.

"It's okay," I say, again, even though it's not. "Come on."

I keep her hand in my good one. The way I'm feeling: volatile, angry, and scared, no way am I touching her with my bad hand.

I march forward, pulling her with me. Do I want to be here? No. I want us out like yesterday. But like Bren says, we have a job to do, and that includes taking this wicked bitch down.

Smoke trickles from somewhere behind the house, the stench of whatever is burning causing my stomach to roil. But as it billows and expands into a black and broadening cloud, I know something's wrong, and that it's more than what this psycho witch is grilling.

Bren snarls as Emme's hand slips from mine. I whip back to check on my sisters, but all I see is darkness as my world slips away.

Chapter Eight

Son of a *bitch*.

I groan as I roll onto my back. I'd like to say this is the first time I've been knocked unconscious. I'd also like to say my boobs are the same size, but hey, such is my life.

Dirt. All I sense is that and dank heaviness that accompanies a . . . cave? Through the fog taking up residency along my brain, I make out a dim glow. It takes me a moment to realize it's coming from my light-saber arm. I push up on my hands, grimacing when my fingers sink into the soil. Yet it's what I see when I glance up that has me scrambling to my feet.

A lonely hand scuttles by me, chasing after a rat. Oh, but it gets better. I press my back against a dirt wall as a foot hops by, chasing after the hand, that's chasing after the rat, with a decapitated head rolling —I shit you not—merrily behind them.

It's like some kind of fucked up nursery rhyme. I don't want to know the next verse, especially not with the collection of zombies gathering from all sides. These are different from the ones who pulled us onto shore. Their grisly faces are more emaciated and their bodies are in a more advance stage of decomposing. As they shuffle toward me, pieces of their skin fall in small moist clumps.

I hold out my hand. "Stay back."

They collectively moan.

And move closer.

I grit my teeth, summoning that spark from deep in my core. The dank air seems to enclose around me, giving me a chill and snuffing out my inner heat.

Shit, shit, shit.

On wobbly legs, I slide my back against the dirt wall, my hands out. The zombies gather closer, cocking their heads, their empty sockets mesmerized by the glow of my arm. At first, I think they're simply curious. But then their short thick tongues push forward, appearing to lick what's left of their lips.

I jump when another hand scrambles by, its pinky brushing against my foot. My back presses against the dirt wall as I slide against it. I'm not sure where to go. I only know I can't stay here.

I bang my fists against the wall, trying to stimulate my fire. My left hand doesn't react, tensing uselessly. But that spark I so need triggers from my right arm, igniting flames along the path of my blue veins only to putter out.

Come on, *light.*

I punch the wall harder, the effect causing another spark.

The zombies limp forward, closing in, reaching out.

I jerk from fear and pain when a root pokes me in the back. I can't be too far from the surface. That doesn't mean I can see a way out.

I punch at the wall, the small space I managed to put between me and the zombies quickly disappearing. Come on. Come on. *Light.*

A woman with no ears tugs at my hair.

Please, light.

A boy, no more than four grips my waist.

God damn it, light!

The long dark tunnel explodes in a wash of blue and white as my arm catches fire.

I gasp from its viciousness and its sudden arrival. "Okay, thanks," I say, wishing I didn't fear it as much as I do.

The zombies have stopped, appearing stunned as their absent stares focus on the light. I think that I'm in a good spot, and that at least for now, I'm safe and can find my family.

Until the little dead boy at my waist grabs my arm and detonates to ash.

My screams echo along the dirt tunnel, the sob that follows lodging in my chest when the zombies hurtle themselves forward and knock me down. Hands reach for me, batting at my skin. I think they're trying to kill me. But it's not until my arm blows them to bits that I realize they're trying to re-die.

I push up on my legs, shoving the mounds of heavy ash away and take off running. I keep my arm out and away out of habit. Yet despite the intense heat, it's not singeing me—not like before. But like moths to a flame, the zombies stagger forward.

They're not fast, but neither am I. The stones poking through the ground make it hard to maneuver, and so does the narrowing tunnel. I'm sure I'm going the wrong way, and burying myself deeper, until I catch a small trace of sunlight in the distance.

The pitiful howls and the moans of the zombies overtake the small space. They're close. All of them. But I don't dare look back.

I try to reason that I did the merciful thing back there, and that I should just light them all up like the Fourth of July. But guilt and fear are among the most brutal emotions, second only to grief. And to see that little boy, dead or not, engulfed by my flame, tore me up.

Sweat trickles down my face. I'm hunched over, dirt raining down on me as my shoulders and head smack against the protruding roots. I stumble over a large stone, causing my knee to smack hard against another. But the space is so narrow, I don't dare stand, falling to crawl on all fours.

I see the small opening just ahead when the foot from before hops in front of me. I think it's going for my firing arm, which is thankfully choosing not to harm me, until it kicks out my other arm and makes me fall forward.

"What the hell?" I say, spitting out dirt as it hops back behind me and kicks me in the ass.

I lurch forward, swearing at it when a hand (and nothing else), snags my ankle.

I kick out, trying to shake it off as I continue to Army crawl forward and the moaning zombies gain ground.

The hand hangs tight, and the foot continues to kick, and good God, this is so not right.

I wrench my flaming arm behind me. It rattles slightly, spitting bits of blue and white flames. It's not a lot, but it's enough to light the tunnel and help me catch sight of the crowd of zombies rounding the corner. They crawl over each other like freaky babies through an alien womb, the bigger ones shoving the smaller ones down and away in their urgency to reach me.

Their flailing limbs and increasing speed cause the ceiling to crack and pepper dirt in chunks. I cough and gag, my lungs struggling to draw a clean breath as I drag myself forward. I don't want to kill them. But they want to die and possibly need to. So with a grunt, and another string of swears, I try again, digging deep until that familiar heat ignites my core in one brutal rush.

Like a bullet through a chamber, I'm propelled forward. It would be a good thing, but this tunnel doesn't go straight. It winds like serpent causing my shoulders to slam against each bend.

I scream, and so do the zombies. Me, because holy crap, I'm in pain, and the zombies in celebration of their re-deaths. It's only a guess. I can't see anything.

Smoke blinds me, burning my eyes. I dig in my feet, pushing forward as the earth caves in around me.

I keep my head down, creating a small pocket between my mouth and the ground as I claw forward. I'm certain I'm going to die when my flaming hand punches through the earth and into air.

Moist soil falls along my fingers as a cool breeze sweeps along the skin. I'm exhausted and out of breath. But knowing I'm inches from freedom helps lurch me forward. I push through, spitting out mud as the first rays of dim sunlight spread across my face.

I dangle from a hole on a side of a hill with one arm out while my chin rests against the opening. Smoke filters out from the hole. I know I should keep going. But right now all I want to do is breathe.

Nothing like a zombie hand scrambling along my shoulder and smacking me across the face to snap me out of my stupor.

"What the fuck?" I scream at it.

I try to backhand it when it smacks me again, but it skitters out of the way and latches onto my forehead, trying to shove me back into the hole. And of course, because that's not bad enough, something else grabs my right ankle, then the other. The remaining zombies haul me backward, refusing to let me escape.

There's several things wrong with this scenario: getting chased down by zombie groupies—who *want* me to kill them, being shoved back into the hole where I was almost buried alive, and getting my ass kicked by random and decrepit body parts.

Apparently, zombies don't need air. But I do, and so does my fire to work. But apparently zombies forget a lot of things like, I don't know, staying dead and basic chemistry.

By now, I'm spitting mad, kicking hard and scrambling forward. In the movies, the hero would strike one massive blow and break free. That's why movies are movies and my reality sucks big hairy rhinoceros balls.

The next five minutes consist of me inching forward, and them hauling me back, until I rather unceremoniously fall out of the hole and down a small embankment. I lay on my side, exhausted, coughing and spitting out more dirt. Zombies, bless their little shriveling hearts, don't need much rest, despite their limitations and nasty diet.

They spill out of the hole, moaning excitedly when they see me.

"Christ," I mutter, pushing myself up on my arms.

I almost keel over when I make it to my feet, raising

my arm, instinctively ready to fire. They stop a few feet away, tilting their heads with confusion as they take in my arm and fail to see so much as a flicker of flame. One of them leaves the group, limping forward and poking me in the arm. She expects the equivalent of a Dura flame. They all do. And as much as I want to bring it, it fails to appear when I summon it from my core.

I shake out my hand, trying to stir the power awake in my arm when I can't rile it from within me. The female pokes me again, her motions growing insistent. I jolt when her finger snaps off and falls at my feet, the gruesome sight inciting my arm to rouse its fire.

Like a match being struck, my arm is encapsulated with white and blue crackling flames. The zombies scramble forward, shoving each other to be the first to touch my arm. I lift it, my body trembling from my need to release the mounting power.

I should light them up like torches. Yet despite my growing need to unleash my magic, I can't bring myself to do it. As much as they scare me, they don't mean to hurt me. They simply see me as a means to end their horrible existence. So I can't just aim and release.

My eyes scan my surroundings, my stare fixing on an old dry log. It's huge, yet far down the embankment and away from the other trees. I turn in its direction, landing on my ass when my arm—not me—sends a funnel of white and blue into the log. It shatters like glass, my fire eating away at the bits of bark and drying leaves.

And my, don't the zombies lose their shit.

They race away from me and to the fire, flinging themselves in. It's a good thing, I tell myself, not that it's any easier to watch. I shake out my hand, extinguishing what remains of my fire. It gives me an excuse to turn away. But their moans . . . oh, I can't take it. I hurry down the ravine, searching for where it levels off so I can find my family.

I grip a protruding root to help me balance when I see Shayna, covered in slop and chasing after what might be a liver.

Chapter Nine

Why, yes! That is a liver my sister is chasing, said no girl, ever.

This whole thing should give me pause, and don't get me wrong, it does. But the pause isn't as long as it once would have been. With a sigh, I stomp forward, ignoring the sting to my shoulders.

Shayna, in her quest to shred the liver to pieces, doesn't see me, bringing her sword down as she chases after the rotating thing. It takes me a moment to realize where it's headed. My fire. It senses my fire and is trying to head home.

"Shayna—*Shayna!*"

Instead of stopping, or turning around, she races further away. "Shayna?" I squeak before tearing after her.

Low hanging branches skim along the top of my head. My heart is racing from the stress and lack of recovery time following my near-death in the dirt tunnel. That doesn't mean I can slow down.

"Shayna!"

I'm running fast, but she's faster and it doesn't take me long to lose her. I can't see her anywhere, but somehow she cuts around and we ram into each other.

We fall backwards, landing on our asses. She blinks back at me, her blue eyes unusually cloudy. "Taran?" she asks, as if unsure it's me.

"Yes," I answer crawling slowly toward her. "Are you all right?" I ask.

Tears streak down her cheeks, making me rush to her and cup her face. "Shayna—Jesus, what happened to you?"

"I can't see anything very well except for the zombies. I woke up in the woods almost completely blind. It's only when I started stabbing them that I could make some things out." Her voice trails. "T, I don't know what's happening."

My fingertips carefully push away the strand of hair that escaped her ponytail. "This is spell, Shayna. Meant to mess with your mind. Savana wants you to see her zombies to scare you. It worked, didn't it?"

She nods slowly, only to jerk when the liver rolls to a stop in front of her. "Don't," I tell her when she tries to stab it. "It's searching for my fire."

While she keeps what remains of her focus on the liver, her voice picks up a little. "You made fire?"

"Yeah. The zombies, or whatever remains of them, are flinging themselves into it, trying to free themselves from Savana."

She points to the liver with the tip of her sword. "So then why is this thing rolling around?"

I think about it. "Not to sound like a prick, but in its defense, it doesn't have eyes."

"I'll give you that," she responds, grimacing.

"Come on," I say, taking her hand and pulling her up with me. "I say we find Savana and light her shit up."

She nods, allowing me to lead her forward. Like some twisted pet, the nasty and dirt-coated liver follows behind us.

Son of a bitch. I don't remember Superman having to deal with this shit.

I'm not sure where to go until I see more billowing smoke overtake the sky. "Damn it."

"What's wrong?" Shayna asks, tightening her grip on her sword.

"It's Savana. I think she knows we're free and is casting another spell."

There is no grace to our steps as I drag Shayna along, and as we reach the edge of the woods, I yank her to the ground.

The liver proceeds ahead, the zombie it belongs to bending forward to lift it and shove it back into his cavernous torso. I barely see him, too busy gaping at the woman with long blonde hair and narrow face storming forward.

Based on the photo we were given, I recognize her as Savana. She's pretty, stunning even. But there's nothing beautiful about what she does or what she holds in her hand.

She lifts her staff. It's gold in color, but instead of housing a stone, a small skull is fixed to the center. She brings it down hard on a zombie tending to the fire.

I cringe at the sound of crunching bone when the zombie's head caves inward. The poor thing falls at Savana's feet, her spikey ice blonde hair smearing with black blood. She cowers, curling inward and moaning like she's crying.

My hand twitches and heat singes my core. "Taran . . ." Shayna begins. "I can feel your fire."

Instead of stopping, Savana lifts her staff again and brings it down on the zombie's back, making her howl in agony.

Again Savana strikes. The zombie shrivels inward, covering her head as another blow cracks her skull.

"Taran," Shayna warns. "It's building."

She doesn't know what's happening, but it's too late to explain. My arm darts out, a funnel of blue and white streaming forward. It just misses Savana, colliding into her house and erupting it in a giant fireball. The force of the blast resonates in a massive heat wave, pitching us back. I fall on my injured shoulder, ignoring the jolts of pain and leaping to my feet.

Once more, my fury gave my residual magic all the power it needed. I race onto the beach of drying bones, the small hairs on my arms and neck raised from the hot, electrified air. My fire hadn't been the only power to stir. Currents of charged energy course from my core, sending bolts of lightning spilling from my fingertips.

I'm determined to end this bitch but the collection of skeletons littering the beach slow my pace, altering my steps to resemble quick stumbles forward. Savana rises, pushing aside the pieces of smoldering house covering her.

Rage darkens her eyes as she watches her zombies pitch themselves into the burning house. Yet when only mere feet separate us, she looks at me and smiles.

"*Leone!*" she screams.

The earth trembles. Cracks web along the soil, out and around Savana, the force of the shaking ground sending me sprawling on my knees. My hands strike the ground, knocking out the charge of lightning as five giant gray lions break through the earth and attack.

Bren, in his brown wolf form appears behind the first lion, taking him down before he can touch me. But he's only one wolf and there are more of them than there are of us. I fling my right arm over my face to shield me. A lion bites down on it, his red glowing eyes widening when I scream in agony.

My lightning releases along my arm, electrocuting his maw and charring his face. He releases me, swiping his claws across my back when I try to veer around and escape. My skin tears open in red-hot agony and warm fluid soaks my shirt. I curl into a ball as the sting in my back is replaced by that familiar burn from my core.

I can't see anything in this position, but I feel a great deal: the weight of the beast on my back and his body falling away from me in charred chunks. I crawl forward and rise, my vision sharpened by the amount of magic coursing through me as fire engulfs my form. I should draw it back, save the energy this much flame is leeching. But I can't control it, my arm is appearing to take over.

Flames surround me, refusing to let go. Through the smoke I make out Shayna.

Her eyes ram shut as she uses her senses to take on the lion circling her. "He's behind you!" I scream, rushing forward.

"I know," she answers.

She whirls in a circle, driving her sword into the lion's chest when it leaps. Her feet press into his stomach as she falls onto her back, allowing his weight to impale the lion while using her legs to keep him from crushing her. The lion flails, clawing at the air.

"T, go!" Shayna yells. "Find Emme."

But Emme is already here. A lion jets over my head like a rocket, smashing into what remains of the house as more zombies pour out from the woods to hurtle themselves toward their freedom. Emme leads a cluster of small zombie children, the smallest one holding her hand. She's covered in blood, her nose is bleeding, and scratches litter her dirty face.

I stagger toward her, my body horribly weak and my soul aching to see her like this. Another lion appears, rushing her. But like I mentioned, Bren is protective and no way in hell will he let that beast hurt Emme.

Bren tackles him. Rolling along the beach with him as they fight. Emme urges the zombie children forward, her tears spilling like raindrops as they hurry toward the fire. Their hands reach out as if embracing a loved one, despite the agony the flame appears to cause them.

Emme leans forward, placing her hands on her knees to keep from pitching to the ground. "Taran, you have to get Savana," she calls to me, the fatigue in her voice as evident as the blood coating her face.

I compel my feet to move to where I feel Savana's dwindling pull. But this fire won't leave me, the energy it's taking from me making every move forward as arduous as treading through wet cement.

I round the giant inferno that used to be the house. The flames surrounding me withdraw, only to resume along my arm in an odd mix of charged lightning and fire.

"Behave," I beg my arm, recognizing how badly it's clashing with my magic then.

I catch site of Savana, standing on a makeshift raft with a sole zombie woman in a long brown dress beside her. The zombie digs a long pole into the water, using it to maneuver them across the lake and toward the opposite shore.

She sobs openly, crying in that mournful way.

With all the energy I have left I call forth my fire from my core. Instead of increasing my fire and withdrawing my lightning, the flames extinguish, leaving only the building energy of lightning. I jolt when a small wave of water touches my foot and reverts the charge back to me.

"Son of bitch," I mutter, glancing between me and the mere yards that separate me from Savana.

I give up trying to manipulate the magic from within my core and lift my arm, focusing on the skin and ignoring the bind containing its temper. "Burn," I tell it. "I need you to burn."

To my total shock, fire ribbons around it. I take a breath and point. But as I fire, another small wave of water splashes at my feet and my flame morphs back to lightning.

Electrified energy zaps every last cell in my body, rattling my teeth as a blue and white bolts of lightning stream in a rush toward Savana. It misses her and crashes into the water. She lifts her staff, vanishing in a funnel of gray smoke as I soar into the air.

~ * ~

Gentle yellow light flickers across my lids, coaxing me awake. I'm in the damn woods. Again. I'm not sure how long I've been out, but it couldn't have been too long seeing how the fire eating away at the house continues to rage.

Bren watches me in his human form as he tugs on his jeans. "Fuckin' A Taran. That was some heavy shit."

Emme shakes her head as she drops her hands away from my face. My head is cradled against her lap, but I'm not exactly comfortable seeing how there's a shard of bone sticking me in the ass.

"You shouldn't have risked your life that way," she tells me as I lift off her. "When I found you, your heart was beating in irregular spurts."

Shayna drives her sword into the dirt beside me. Her eyes, mercifully clear again. "Yeah, T," she agrees. "What you did was the equivalent of getting shocked by a defibrillator."

I stand, wishing I didn't have to. "It wasn't on purpose," I confess. "My lightning and fire were switching back and forth."

Bren frowns. "I thought you had it under control. You seemed to when you were fighting."

I shake my head, wishing it didn't feel so heavy. "No. Most of it was luck, at best."

Bren pulls the T-shirt out of the backpack Emme had left on the rowboat. It's then I notice the gash from his navel to his throat.

"Bren!" I say gasping. "What the hell happened to you?"

He shrugs like it's no big deal, but I catch the traces of his lingering anger. "Savana saw me as the strongest and thought I'd make a great sacrifice. Woke up in human form shackled to a table."

My eyes widen at the burn marks on his wrists. She must have bound him in cursed gold, the supernatural equivalent of kryptonite.

"To raise more zombies?" Shayna asks, her typically friendly tone clipped as she takes in Bren's blazing red gash.

"That's my guess," he says, glancing back at the burning house. "The bigger the sacrifice, the more bang for the buck when you're raising the dead."

"Is this common?" Emme asks, glancing around at the cluster of bones littering the beach.

"No," Bren thankfully admits. "I never heard of witch who could raise the dead like this. Usually, it's one or two zombies at best—sometimes an army for battle, but that's rare and something most witches can only manage for a handful of hours. But this . . ." He shakes his head. "If I had to wager a bet, I'd say her other magic was perceived as weak because her skill at necromancy overshadowed it, making it appear abysmal in comparison."

"Okay," Emme says softly. Like the rest of us she seems relieved, but more than a little troubled. She moves slowly toward Bren, placing her palms over his chest. "It's a bad cut. Let me help you heal," she offers gently.

He covers her hands, lifting them off him and putting some space between them. "I've got it," he says in a low growl that takes us all aback.

"Bren," she begins, sounding confused.

He whips around as if shocked by his own response. "Didn't you say you woke up at the bottom of a well to those zombie kids pelting you with rocks?" he asks tightly.

Her eyes rounded. "They didn't want to hurt me," she insists. "They were being forced, just like the rest."

"I know that. But they still busted up your face," he snaps. "The power you used to heal you and Taran alone—not to mention all the shit you had to do to get out of the damn well was more than you're used to. Save your strength, my wolf's got this."

I cross my arms, ready to argue and remind him that Emme's used more power than this in the past. But his hesitation to let her draw too near is odd and stops me. He's never been afraid to let any female touch him. Why is he acting like he needs to stay away from her?

"Bren," I finally say. "Just let her help you—"

"No," he snarls, meeting her stare. "She's already been through enough."

He stomps away, leaving us standing there. "The hell?" I say.

Shayna rubs my back. "His wolf's just cranky, T," she reasons. "Can you blame him after what Savana put him through? Come on, let's head back to the Jeep, peeps. We have to call our *weres* and give them the lowdown on Savana so they can break it to the witches that she's more hell cat than helpless kitten." Sympathy replaces the exhaustion along her small features. "You'll have to go to Genevieve," she adds.

"I know," I say, biting the words out. No matter how hard I tried, and regardless of everything we endured, it doesn't matter. I'm still obliged to bend to Vieve's will.

"Maybe Aric can talk to her, again," Emme says, her

focus skimming toward Bren as we make our way across the skull beach. "I mean, this wasn't exactly a fair test. No one could have predicted what Savana was capable of. Maybe there's another way you can prove yourself."

"I wish that were true, Emme," I say. "But bottom line, I had no control. And even if I did, I didn't complete the task as per our agreement. No way is Vieve going to let me out of this."

I tilt my head when I see that zombie Savana was beating with her staff sitting on a rock and staring at the flaming house. "What's she doing?" I ask.

"I don't know, dude," Shayna says. "She's been there for a while now. I think she's afraid to jump into the fire." She grimaces. "It frees them, yeah, but it hurts them, too. Did you hear them? They were in pain."

"I did," I admit. I hunker down beside the zombie. Her short spiky white blonde hair, tattered jeans, and black Alice in Chains concert T-shirt give me a glimpse of what she must have been like in life, but not much more than that. Her skin is as pale as my affected arm and dark circles ring her soft brown eyes. But her stare is gentle, despite how her skull remains indented from Savana's blows.

"Hi," I say.

"Ergh," she responds, surprising me by answering.

Bren returns to our side, crossing his arms as he examines her briefly. "She either overdosed on her own or Savana helped her," he says, keeping his attention away from us. "I can scent some of the leftover meth."

I take in the condition of her skin. It's dried and shriveled, and in some sections peeling away in patches to reveal the layers beneath. Yet she seems more whole than the others. "She hasn't been dead long," I reason.

"No, which made her the strongest and probably hardest to control," Bren adds. "I think that's why Savana was beating on her, she was trying break her."

Emme gasps. "But she seems so gentle," she says. "It wouldn't take more than an unkind word to break her."

"I don't think Savana was really into unkind words,

89

Em," Shayna points out. "She strikes me more as the torture first and ask questions later type."

Without thinking, I stroke the zombie's head. "Ergh," she says in a way that totally breaks my heart.

"I think you should go into the fire," I tell her gently. "It won't be long before it goes out." I straighten, hoping she does what I suggest. I don't have it in me to kill her outright and hope she doesn't make me.

She seems to understand, staring back at the smoldering flames yet making no effort to move.

"We need to get out of here," Bren says gruffly, marching toward the boat when Emme tries to approach him.

Shayna holds out her hands in true "oh, well" fashion when I gape. "He'll be fine once his wolf knows we're safe and he gets something to eat," she assures me.

"All right," I say. I glance back at the zombie. "Bye, Alice," I tell her.

That's not her name of course. I choose it because of the band name on her T-shirt. She's also very human in her own way and saying goodbye all on its own, after everything she's suffered, doesn't seem right.

I follow behind my sisters, fixated on the way the skeletal remains sink into the soil. Savana's magic is quickly fading. It won't be long before all traces of her darkness vanish.

I don't initially notice "Alice" trailing me. I hold up my hand when I realize how close she is. "No, sweetie. You need to go into the fire." I point back to the house. "The fire!" I say louder.

She blinks back at me like she doesn't understand and takes another step toward me. "You can't come with us," I insist.

You know those pictures of dogs at the shelter that people post online and on T.V. when they're raising awareness about animal cruelty? Alice reminds me of one of them. Hopelessness and fear encompass every inch of her pale face. But it's not her fault.

I turn away from her, unable to stomach the sadness

overwhelming her tall, emaciated frame.

Bren waits for me to climb into our rowboat before giving it a hard push and leaping inside.

"Ergh?" Alice says as Emme powers us through the water.

Even though I shouldn't, I glance over my shoulder. Alice is waving her arms, calling to us. "Ergh!"

I focus on the opposite shore. "Don't look at her," I tell the others. "With luck, she'll change her mind about leaping into the fire."

"Ergh!"

"Ah, I don't think she's changing her mind," Emme says.

Splashing has me veering back toward the small island. I don't know anything about Alice aside from the fact she must have liked punk music. But based on the way her limbs smack erratically against the water, girlfriend wasn't exactly an Olympic freestyle hopeful.

"Ergh!" she yells, swallowing water. She disappears below the surface. I'm not sure where she is or if she's okay until her hands grip the boat on my side and she pulls herself up.

She grins, appearing quite proud of herself. "Ergh."

Bren sighs and helps her on board.

"Bren!" I yell. "What are you doing?"

"Taran, she's not going to free herself. We've got two choices here: take her with us or set her on fire."

"I can't set her on fire," I tell him. "Look at her, she's . . ." I was going to say "cute" but considering her skin is flaking away in pieces, it doesn't seem like the best word.

"She's innocent," I say quietly.

Bren rubs his beard. "We can't leave her here," he says. "If Savana comes back, she'll reclaim her and use her to raise more dead."

Alice smiles at me, snatching the fly that lands on her nose and munching on it like a Skittle.

Emme gags, leaning over the side of the boat like she's ready to puke. I can't really blame her. It's moments like this I'm convinced the universe hates me. What I don't realize then is that the universe has more planned for me than a fly-chewing zombie.

Chapter Ten

Four days. That's how long it took us to drive back to Lake Tahoe. We would have flown, that was the original plan. But considering poor Alice was breaking away in pieces, taking her on a commercial airline didn't seem like the best plan.

Girlfriend wasn't looking too good until she spotted a dead possum in Nebraska. Then she perked right up. Bren pulled over so she could have what I interpreted as a hearty breakfast. Oh, but it didn't stop there. No, it did not.

Two thousand miles, a couple of raccoons, and part of a deer later, she was almost looking human. But still, not exactly well.

"Ergh," she says, peering out a window.

Shayna smiles happily back at her. "I think she likes the woods. Don't you, Alice?"

"Ergh-a."

Emme, who's been looking pretty green since she tried to wash Alice's hair and part of Alice's scalp peeled off, clears her throat. "Maybe we should call home. Let them know we're almost there."

Bren rolls to a stop at a light. "Good idea. We may need Celia's help to sneak Alice in if the other wolves are there."

I stop in the middle of rummaging through my purse

to find my phone. "Sneak her in? Why would we sneak her in?" I glance back at her. "I know she's not at her best, but since that dead crow, her scalp has healed up nicely."

Bren does a one-shoulder shrug. "Oh, on account of all the illegal shit going on here."

I can't see my sisters, but I know that like me, we're all gaping at Bren. "What do you mean, 'illegal shit?'" I ask.

"We're keeping a zombie. Well, technically a familiar—*your* familiar. I told you that it's one of the deadliest supernatural sins." He frowns like we're the stupid ones. "Why are you looking at me like that? It's the same damn thing I told you back in Kentucky."

The bottom of my stomach drops. "That's not what you said," I practically screech. "And she's *not* my familiar!"

"Taran, *you* saved her from Savana," he says, pointing. "I saw you. Alice saw you, too. Why do you think she followed you in the water? She attached herself to you as your familiar when you were nice to her."

"I wasn't going to be mean! An-and you never said anything about her being my familiar. You said we had to take her with us or else Savana would come back and use her to raise more zombies."

He thinks about it. "Same difference," he offers, stepping on the gas when the light turns green.

"No. It's not." I turn around. Alice smiles back at me with what remains of her teeth. "Jesus," I say, feeling my eye start to twitch. "How the hell are we going to keep her from the wolves—from Aric—from *Koda*? They live with us. You can't tell me they won't smell her. Son of a bitch even I can smell her."

"You shouldn't say Jesus and son of a bitch in the same context, Taran," Emme mentions quietly. Her face flushes when I glare at her. "It's sacrilegious," she presses.

"Taran, relax," Bren says. "We'll need to keep her at your place for a few hours, max. Just until my boy Danny figures out a way to lure her from you. It's no big deal. She can stay in our bathroom until we can find Savana, kill her, and break the spell keeping her here."

"Bren, Savana could be halfway to South America right now," I remind him.

He shakes his head. "Not with a zombie at her side. My guess is she's scouting out another out of the way locale, if she doesn't already have one, and getting back to business."

"To raise more Alices," Shayna says, stating the obvious.

"Yup," Bren says angling the car along a windy hill. "She'll hunt down a few sacrifices, combine her magic and the zombie's deadness or whatever you want to call it, and raise however many she needs to replace the ones she lost." He huffs. "For a necromancer of her caliber, it's not going to take her long. Especially if she can find strong enough beings to sacrifice."

"But why does she need all these zombies?" Emme asks quietly. "They don't eat human flesh, and they can't convert them."

"No," he admits. "Except she can force them to kill." He hooks his thumb behind him. "Alice may not look like much. But an angry zombie is dangerous and strong. All Savana has to do is feed them her hate and anger and she has an army of soldiers who aren't easily destroyed."

"What about Celia and the baby?" Emme asks, glancing at Alice. "We can't have Alice around if she could hurt her."

"She's not going to hurt Celia, Emme. She's Taran's familiar, remember?" Bren reminds her. "And Taran isn't going to order Alice to hurt anyone. Are you, T?"

"Of course not," I say. "But that doesn't change the fact that what we're doing is considered illegal. We're seriously screwed here."

"Relax," Bren says, turning onto the main highway that leads to Dollar Point. "It'll be fine. Just call the house, see who's there, and we'll form a plan. Seriously, it' no big deal." He gives it another thought. "Unless we get caught. Then yeah, we're seriously fucked.'

This time I swear in Spanish because I'm all out of swears in English. I tap my phone to dial the house. Celia answers on the first ring. "Hey. You guys okay? Are you almost home?"

"Um. Yeah. Can't wait to see you, and everyone. Who's home?" I ask.

Although I try to keep my voice casual, Celia picks up on the fact that not all is well in the weird world. "Aric, me, and Koda." She pauses. "Why?"

"We're stopping by the store. Could you check my bathroom to see if I need to pick up tampons?" Which is code for, "We're in deep shit, again, and I need you to get some place where Aric and Koda can't hear us."

"Sure," she says, through her teeth because she's already pissed. "Let me go check. I'll just be a minute, wolf," she tells Aric.

Some quick paces and two door slams later, Celia whispers into the phone. "What did you do?"

"Nothing," I respond.

"Taran, *what did you do*?" she repeats. "I thought you were okay and just needed time before you started training with Genevieve."

That much is true. We didn't tell her about Alice because, well, it's kind of like finding a mange-ridden puppy on the side of the road. It's best not to tell the family until you bring the critter home and you show them how badly it needs you and your love.

"*Taran*," she says, growling.

"Look, we picked up a friend. She's with us now," I say.

"'A friend?'" she asks. "What kind of friend?"

I sigh as I glance out of the window and toward the lake. We don't have a lot of time until we're home. "The kind of friend the wolves won't like."

"You picked up a vampire?" she asks. "Are you crazy? You know how they get if they don't have a master. And you know how the wolves get around them."

I glance back at Alice when she spits out what might be a molar out of the window.

She only has two left, Shayna mouths, holding out her

fingers for emphasis and reinforcing that *yes* that was a molar.

"Taran," Celia says sighing. "I don't want to spend the afternoon scrubbing blood and fur off the floor!"

"It's definitely not a vampire," I say.

"Then what is it?" she asks.

"Trust me when I say you're better off not knowing. Look," I say when she starts to press. "She's only going to be with us a few hours tops. But I don't want to upset the wolves." That much is true. "Can you get Aric out of the house, just for a little while? Shayna will take care of Koda since he won't want to leave until he sees her."

"Aric won't leave either," Celia insists. "He knows you're almost home and wants to make sure you're safe."

Shit.

"Tell him you want to go thong shopping," Bren offers.

"*Thong shopping?*" Celia asks, able to hear him loud and clear.

"Yeah. We'll come in, he'll see we're fine, and then you can distract him by asking him to take you thong shopping," Bren reasons. "There's this really hot lingerie place is South Tahoe called Spank Me. You should definitely check it out. They usually have good specials on chocolate body fondue. Tell Jeanette I sent you, she might give you a discount . . . then again, don't mention me. I think she's still pissed I—"

"Bren, he's not an idiot," Celia says, cutting off his tangent. "He's going to know something's up."

"I'm not saying Aric's a dumbass, Ceel. But you're his mate, he's a dude, and you're spilling hormones like a broken damn, making him that much hotter for you and easy to distract."

"I don't know about this," she says.

The sign for Dollar Point comes into view. "Ceel, we're home," I say quickly. "We'll be pulling into the driveway in another two minutes. Please, you have to help us out."

There's a brief moment with just silence. "*Fine*," she

says. "But don't get us in trouble."

I rub my face, knowing that's likely a promise I won't be able to keep. So instead of answering, I disconnect, hoping we can pull this off. "A few hours?" I ask.

"Three tops," Bren answers, his tone growing soft. "You know Dan is into all that nerdy shit. He'll figure out a way to loosen her attachment to you and we'll keep her at my place."

"Okay," I say. I turn around, keeping my voice gentle. "Alice, we're almost home. But I'm going to need you to stay in the car until we come back for you."

She stops smiling, glancing from me to my sisters and then back to me again. "It's all right," I assure her. "We just need a moment to get settled. Can you stay quiet and in the car until we return?"

Alice doesn't blink, ever. She also doesn't sleep. But if she could blink, I think she would now. As it is, all she does is stare at us like we're abandoning her. "I won't be long," I assure her. "Just a few minutes."

She makes this odd gurgling noise like she's close to crying. "Please, Alice," I beg, my voice growing desperate as Bren pulls into our development and rolls up our tinted windows. "Please."

She nods a little, but doesn't appear any less sad. If she could talk, I know she'd tell me she's had a rough life and very little kindness. I can tell by how attached she seems to us, and by the way even the small things we do for her appear to mean so much. If I had to guess, I'd say we're the only real friends she's ever had.

Bren hugs the curb away from our house, parking in front Mrs. Mancuso's thick bush to give us cover. "Show time," he mumbles.

Shayna and Emme hurry out. "Stay here," I remind Alice. "I'll be back shortly."

It's only when she seems to understand that I slip out with Bren.

The front door flies open. Koda releases the wards protecting the house and jogs down the steps. "Puppy!"

Shayna yells, skipping toward him and leaping into his arms in a straddle.

Koda clutches her to him, but then turns away grimacing and releasing a sneeze. "Do I smell bad?" Shayna asks crinkling her nose apologetically.

Koda doesn't like to lie, especially to Shayna. But it's clear he can catch traces of Alice even though we kept the windows down during the drive. That doesn't stop his chuckle or the sweet kiss he gives her. "Damn, baby. What happened?"

"Got stuck behind a garbage truck," Bren says.

That's true, but that was back in Wyoming. "I'm sorry," Shayna offers, tilting her head so her long ponytail swings to the side. "Want to help me clean up?" she asks with a grin.

Koda nuzzles Shayna's neck, making her squeal as he carries her into the house and past Aric and Celia waiting by the door. "Welcome home," Aric says.

Celia waits frozen by the door, trying to appear casual and doing a hideous job. Aric appears to notice. She notices him, noticing her, and hurries to Emme. "Hey, Emme," she says, hugging her tightly to mask her nervousness. "I've missed you."

The honesty behind her words are enough to placate Aric.

Well, at least for the moment.

She eases away from Emme, her nose wrinkling from taking in Emme's scent. Whatever aroma she picks up on spikes her concern. Her narrowed stare bounces between me and Bren as Aric strokes Emme's head affectionately.

"You okay?" he asks, honing in on Emme's mounting panic.

And because Emme is even less smooth than Celia she yells, as in *yells*, "I'm just tired from being in the car!"

Her response wouldn't be nearly as bad if she didn't run into the house like her tiny ass was on fire.

I pull Celia to me, clutching her hard when Aric fixates on me. "How are you?" I ask. I don't wait for her to respond, holding her at arm's length. "You look fabulous."

Oh, and good Lord, doesn't she look ready to slap me.

"Hey, Ceel," Bren says, whirling her around and leading her back into the house when her stare skips to the car. "Good to see you."

Bren keeps his arm around her. He hasn't been as affectionate with her since she and Aric were mated. Mostly because Aric's wolf goes all ape-shit when another male draws too close. And today is no exception.

Aric stiffens as Bren guides her back to the house. Bren isn't suicidal, but he is smart, causing the necessary distraction we need.

"Aric, stop it," Celia tells him when a deep growl rumbles in his chest.

"Oh, sorry, boss," Bren says, shoving her into his arms. "Didn't mean anything by that."

Aric watches Bren as he jogs into the house and I make my way onto the porch. I think there might be trouble until Celia clasps Aric's hands, soothing his wolf. "You know he's just my friend, and that you have nothing to worry about," she whispers.

"Sorry, love," he tells her, curling his body against hers. "But after what we've been through . . ."

"I know," she says. "Just don't worry about us, *please.*"

I hurry through the door and to where the small foyer opens into our large family room. I try to keep my steps casual as my heels click along the dark wood, but along the sweeping space, everything sounds that much louder and seemingly more distressed. I don't look behind me, knowing Celia and Aric are following, seconds from calling me out.

Bren flops on the couch, munching on a bag of chips he looted from our pantry. He shoots Celia a poignant stare as she and Aric make their way forward.

I brush off my black jeans in an effort to avoid making eye contact with Aric. Of course that does jack. And of course, the alpha badass picks up on it.

"Is there something you need to tell me," Aric asks,

pulling Celia onto his lap when he sits.

Damn these wolves and their supernatural senses.

I lift my chin and feign surprise. Aric clenches his jaw, but then his attention drifts toward Bren. "What are you keeping from me?" he asks.

"What's there to keep?" Bren counters. "We covered the legions of zombies we had to take on, Emme reliving that scene from *The Ring* with creepy dead kids, Taran getting smacked around by limbless hands, Shayna going blind, and me getting gutted. No offense, but I think I was pretty damn descriptive on the phone, boss."

Aric watches Bren as I shoot Celia another poignant look seeing how she ignored Bren's hint the first time around. She squirms against Aric's lap, again, and then again. If this is some kind of seduction thing, me and my girl need to have a serious talk.

Aric adjusts his hold around her waist when she does it yet again. "What's wrong, sweetness?" he asks, frowning at her erratic motions.

"My body's changing," she says, her voice taking that odd quiver it does when she's trying not to lie.

I gape at her, wondering how the hell she managed all those super-spy missions the vamps would send her on.

Aric's brow softens as he strokes her back. "Of course it is," he tells her. "Our baby is growing inside of you."

I'm not sure if he believes it, but he seems to need to, and because of it, I'm struck with a pang of guilt.

Celia, though, charges full speed ahead. Well, in her own awkward way. "Maybe I should buy some new panties to help me be more, um, comfortable."

Oh, and look at that, Aric's attention is no longer on us.

"Maybe you should invest in some thongs, Ceel," Bren says, making it a point to flip on the T.V. and turn up the volume, like he doesn't care either way, and that this isn't all part of his dastardly plan.

Celia's glare is enough to singe a hole through Bren's forehead, but Aric isn't noticing anything except her. His stare rakes down her body. "Yeah, sweetness," he murmurs. "Maybe you'll be more comfortable only wearing thongs."

Celia's cheeks flame red when Aric nuzzles her throat. As private and shy as she is, this isn't a conversation they'd normally have in our presence, or affection they'd so openly display. But Bren's suggestion, coupled with her response, is enough to make Aric's wolf go all beast and ignore the rest of us.

She clears her throat as Aric increases his motions. "Do you want to help me pick some out?" she squeaks.

"Yes," he breathes against her skin. "Let's go upstairs and look online."

"Ah," Celia begins, swallowing hard when Aric's tongue drags behind her ear. "Wouldn't you rather go out? So I can try them on?"

"Later," he says, standing and placing her on the floor in one smooth move. "Much later." His fingertips trail down her spine as he leads her up the stairs.

I don't miss how he palms her ass as they reach the landing. Just like I don't miss the seething look she fires my and Bren's way. She hates lying to Aric, but I think she's more pissed at how easily her mate fell for Bren's plan.

Bren fist bumps me when they disappear. "Give them a minute," he whispers when I attempt to stand and Emme pokes her head out from the kitchen.

I glance at the door, leaping to my feet when Alice crashes through it.

"Ergh!" she says, flailing her arms excitedly when she sees me.

"No, no, no, no," I say rushing forward.

The wolves and Celia appear at the top of the stairs, growling viciously. Celia lands in a deep crouch half a breath behind Aric and Koda. She lurches forward, her claws protruding.

Aric clasps her elbow, pulling her back and behind him. But instead of meeting me with all the protective rage Celia demonstrates, he and Koda stare at me like I nut-punched them.

"Who's this?" Aric asks.

Of course, now everyone is looking at me. "Um. Alice?" I offer.

Not the answer he was looking for. "When is *Alice* going back?" he counters.

I cross my arms. "She's not," I reply, keeping my voice casual. "She's with me."

Celia clasps her mouth, her eyes widening. But it's Koda who responds, his long wet hair sticking to his bare shoulders. "You brought a familiar into this house," he says, speaking slow enough to demonstrate the extent of his shock.

He managed to pull on a pair of tight black boxers, which is all I can be thankful for right about now. Shayna, hurries down the steps, gathering the front of her robe against her as I stand there in a pathetic attempt to hold my ground.

"A familiar?" Celia asks, dumbfounded by the news, and why the wolves aren't attacking.

Alice hobbles to the couch and plops down next to Bren to watch T.V..

And in three, two, one, Aric loses what remains of his cool. "Why is there a familiar in this house and in *your* presence?" he rumbles.

His head jerks Bren's way when I don't answer. Bren shrugs. "I tried to talk her out of it, but you know how she gets," he says, totally and literally throwing me to the wolves.

"You *asshole*," I snap.

"Taran," Aric bites out, cutting me off and storming forward. "Do you know the shit-storm you're hitting us with?—the trouble you're causing between me *and* the witches."

"They don't have to know," is my awesome comeback.

"You have to be fucking kidding me!" he snarls. "What you're doing is among our deadliest sins."

"I didn't know," I say watching Celia begin to pace. "I was just trying to be nice to her."

"Savana was beating her," Emme says. "We were only trying to help."

"Koda, don't," Shayna says when he marches forward. She cuts in front of him and presses her hands against his chest. "Don't hurt her. We're the only friends she has."

"She's not your friend," Koda tells her. "She's not even supposed to be part of this world. For Taran's sake, I have to destroy her."

My body lurches so hard, I barely keep my feet. I scramble toward Alice, my right arm erupting with blue and white flames.

I face the wolves with my hand out, pretending that the response of my magic is purposeful and that my arm isn't simply reacting to my anger and fear. It's safe to assume, I'm not fooling anyone.

Alice cowers behind Bren when she sees my fire.

"You're not touching her," I snap at Koda. I round on Aric. "Any of you. Look at her, she's scared. She's not a threat to anyone."

Aric's face darkens with rage. "I know that," he growls. "If she was, the wards protecting this house would have demolished her. That doesn't excuse the fact that she shouldn't be here."

I don't respond, which only pisses Aric off further. "Taran, she doesn't belong in life. She belongs in death—can't you understand? This slavery of the dead. I can't allow this."

"I'm not asking you to," I say. "And I'm not asking for help. What I'm telling you is that she's our friend, and as long as she's willing to live, I'm going to let her."

"Aric, please," Emme says. "Just let her be."

"She's a fresh, strong zombie," Bren says, taking a protective stance next to Alice when Koda releases an unearthly growl. "Exactly what Savana needed to raise the army she did. Like I told you, I've never seen anything like it. We couldn't chance Savana finding Alice again and reclaiming her. So we did the next best thing."

"No," Aric says, refusing to budge. "The best thing was to throw her into the fire." He ignores Celia's growing sympathy as she takes in Alice's trembling form. "She's an abomination of our natural law."

"The same thing could be said about your mate," Bren says, holding his ground.

And holy shit, doesn't Bren know how to push it. "Watch your mouth," Aric warns, taking a step forward.

"He's right, Aric," Celia says, luring his attention. "She's not supposed to exist. I get it, and believe me, I'm less than thrilled. But my sisters and I weren't meant to be either." She motions to Alice. "Look at her. She's innocent. She never asked for any of this."

"That doesn't mean I can allow her to stay," he insists.

"The dark ones feel the same way about us," she says, her focus skimming to Emme, Shayna, and me.

"That's different," he says.

She shakes her head, gathering the strands of her long wavy hair. "I don't agree," she says, walking slowly toward him and closing the space between them. She's not blind to her mate's position of power in the supernatural world. And to my knowledge, she's never asked him to do something that would jeopardize his status or require him to abuse his power. But she does then. "The time will come when her fate is decided, until then, leave her in peace and allow her to live what life she has."

The flames around my arm sputter and sizzle out in the silence that follows, the expulsion of energy causing it to fall limp at my side. I don't bother wiping the sweat from my brow, keeping my head up when Aric approaches.

"I won't order the kill," he tells me, meeting me with more anger than I've ever seen. "But I won't protect her either. She's neither family nor Pack."

"I understand," I say. My tone reflects strength and confidence I don't quite have. In truth, I'm terrified what could happen if the witches find out about Alice.

He doesn't flinch, not that I expect him to. "Then you must also understand that whether you knowingly attached her to you or not, she's *your* responsibility. I'll allow her presence, but I'll be damned if I permit her to jeopardize the treaty between my Pack and the coven."

Chapter Eleven

Genevieve couldn't wait to sink her perfectly manicured nails into me. When I entered my room, there spread neatly across the bed was my designated uniform: ankle length gray dress, white apron, white bonnet (don't get me started), and pointy black shoes (with freaking buckles!).

I think the shoes were my undoing. That, and the note:

Dear Lesser Taran,

Mmm and doesn't she like the sound of that.

It is my pleasure to welcome you to our program.

I'll bet it is, Glinda.

While I understand and respect the large role you played in abolishing the past evil that threatened our world, your position will equal that of your Lesser peers. No special considerations or accommodations will be made on your behalf. Nor will your alliances or family members influence or alter our time-honored way of teaching. You are to address your Superiors as such and treat them with the reverence they deserve. Insubordination will not be tolerated and will be dealt with in the same tradition we handle those who defy us.

In other words, behave or we'll kill you.

To insult or attack your Superiors is to insult me.

Okay, now she's just daring me to do something.

Take your role seriously, and my sisters and I will do everything in our power to help you master yours.

Sincerely,

Genevieve Lacoste
The Most Superior Head Witch, Lake Tahoe Region
I'm convinced she made that title up.

I walk out of my bedroom on my first day of Hogwarts, trying not to make a lot of noise so I can make a quick escape. Of course, it's not working.

It doesn't help that the small heels of these crap shoes *clip, clop* against the hardwood floors or that Alice is limping behind me. Danny put some kind of charm on an old necklace of mine. If someone else is wearing it, and that someone else stays in the house, Alice can't leave.

Well, in theory anyway.

"Ergh," she says, happily trailing me.

I shake out my hands, trying to shush her and wishing I could make her obey me. I told her to stay in her bed aka my bathtub. It may sound cruel, but it beats her shedding skin all over my carpet and having her watch me sleep like she had been doing.

"Ergh?" she questions, wondering why I appear so frantic.

"Taran?" Shayna calls as I reach the front door. "We made you breakfast for your first big day."

My shoulders slump and it's all I can do not to bang my head against the door.

"Taran?" she calls again, her light feet bouncing around the kitchen.

I glimpse at Alice. Considering she doesn't say much, her chastising expression speaks volumes and she can wield Catholic guilt like a seasoned nun.

"I don't want you to see me like this," I admit.

"Oh, come on," Shayna says, skipping into the family room. "How bad can it be?"

She stumbles to a stop when she sees how bad it really is. Celia and Emme shadow her, their grins slipping like melting snow along a tin roof.

"Oh, look at . . . *you*," Celia says.

"Kill me," I beg her. "You have the claws. You have the skill. Just make it quick."

Shayna's stare zooms to the floor. "What's up with the shoes, dude?" she asks, as if that's the only thing wrong with this ensemble.

My voice is about as tight as the bun in my hair. We're supposed to have all our hair up and away from our faces, but honestly, it's the only way I could shove on this the bonnet. "Lesser witches dress in honor of our fallen sisters burned at the stake."

"That's nice," Emme offers, because what else is she going to say.

"No, Emme. It's bullshit. I'm convinced the Puritans, or whatever the fuck, just meant to burn the shoes and the stupid wand-wavers were too dense to take the damn things off."

"I can see that," Shayna says, taking another good look at my footwear.

I used to be cute. I used to have style. I used to wear attire that drew attention for the right reasons, not because I resembled someone who belonged on a box of oats.

You'd never know any of this by the way my sisters are eyeing me. Oh, and look, here comes Aric and Koda because, why not.

They pause as they step out of the kitchen their eyes widening briefly.

Aric averts his gaze as if pained by the sight of me. "I'll be right back," he tells Celia. He kisses the top of her head, walking past me without looking at me and giving me ample space.

Koda follows behind him. Neither say much unless you count Koda's, "Jesus Christ," remark when he passes me.

I lower my lids briefly and take a few breaths when the door shuts behind me, hoping to release some of the pressure tensing my shoulders and to relax my balling fists. It does nothing for me or my sisters. They regard me like I remember our mother doing when she'd drop us off at school—back when we lived in an economically deprived city and in a war zone of a neighborhood—like she realized she had to let us go and was praying we wouldn't get our asses kicked during recess.

"I don't think I can do this," I admit.

Celia leans back to rest against the couch. "Which part, the schooling or joining the coven?"

I throw out a hand. "Oh, I don't know, maybe the part where I have to bow down to the witches and swallow whatever they force down my throat."

"No one's asking you to bow down, Taran," Celia tells me patiently. "There are rules to follow, tasks to perform, and a lot to learn. But all that is manageable and what you need to do until you gain control."

"Yeah, T," Shayna agrees. "What Celia said." The charm she's wearing to keep Alice put swings against her chest as she makes her way to me. She embraces me with her long thin arms. "It's just temporary, a means to an end. A few months might be all you need to gain control. Remember nursing school? How bad it was and how none of us thought we'd get through it?"

"Nursing school didn't involve cauldrons bubbling with enough juice to turn anyone in the vicinity into sea urchins. It also didn't involve spirit summoning or whatever that Séance Class is supposed to teach me. Did you read the syllabus? I have to slather myself with dirt from a freshly dug grave so I don't sprout hooves. *Hooves.* What kind of messed up shit is that?"

Shayna rubs my back. "I asked Koda about that. The good news is only two to three Lessers end up with hooves or tusks or even antlers a year out of like, *fifteen* students. Oh, and that dirt is supposed to be really good for your skin."

This is the ray of sunshine she offers.

Although it shouldn't be possible, my body relaxes against hers, relishing the feel of knowing someone cares.

"What if it doesn't work?" I ask.

"Koda says they can totally remove the tusks or antlers. The hooves are a little tougher, but he insists you'll only have to be chained to that rack for like three days, tops."

"I meant the schooling," I say, thinking about the nearest cliff to hurtle myself from. "What if I go through all this schooling and I still can't control my power?"

In the moments that follow, I realize that I'm not the only one who's given this possibility some thought. "You'll still have me," Emme tells me gently.

I lift my head from Shayna's shoulder, peering in the direction of our youngest sister.

"I can heal you," she reminds me.

"But what kind of life is that?" I ask, frowning. "Me counting on you to keep me alive? I wouldn't do that to you."

"You're not asking, I'm offering," she says, smiling softly. "It's no different than you being sick, and me providing the care you need."

"You would do the same for me," she adds when none of us respond.

That's not the point, of course we would be there for each other. It's an unspoken promise we made long ago. But what Emme is suggesting isn't solely based on my condition. She doesn't think she'll have anyone else to take care of, ever.

I watch her as she meekly strolls into the kitchen. Celia and Shayna pick up on what goes unsaid, tossing me worried glances. We're all concerned about Emme and whatever she's going through.

I'm ready to ask her about it, but my little life and death dilemma takes center stage and the focus reverts too quickly back to me.

"Come on, T," Shayna says, swinging her arm around me and leading me into the kitchen. "We can't send you off to Anti-Possession class without a hearty breakfast."

"That class isn't for another few weeks," I mutter, even though I have a virtual arsenal of garlic and holy water ready to go in my car. "The first session revolves around herbs and plants, along with spell reading and translation."

I slump into my chair as Celia lowers herself carefully beside me. "Is spell reading and translation dangerous?" she asks.

"According to the syllabus, no. Unless I accidently open some portal to hell, but that's not something I have to worry about until next semester."

"What about the plants?" she asks. "Or herbs? Tell us about that."

"For starters, it's commonly referred to as Plant Day, even though it takes place over several weeks." I brush a stray hair away that escapes my cap. "That's all about cultivating and harvesting plants with magical properties, belladonna, wolfs bane, things like that."

"That doesn't sound so bad," she says, sounding hopeful that my head won't be spinning and she won't have to clean up any pea soup I spew. Well, at least not this week.

"According to everything I read, it's a lot of chanting to empower the plants." I shake out my skirt. "And working in the hot sun in this little number. But yeah, it doesn't sound too bad."

"That's the spirit, T," Shayna says. She places a big stack of pancakes in front of me and plops down next to Emme.

"I'm sorry," I say. "I can't eat this during Plant Day."

Celia lowers her fork. "Why?"

"Because they're made from wheat that has been unfairly and unjustly taken from the earth," I repeat verbatim from the no-no list I was given.

"Eggs?" Emme offers, lifting the bowl filled with fluffy scramble goodness.

I shake my head. "Not unless you can guarantee it didn't fall on the sacred earth without it being thanked."

"You have to thank the egg?" Shayna asks, confused.

"No," I say, scanning the table.

"The chicken?" she presses.

"No, Shayna. You have to thank the soil for allowing the chicken to drop the egg on it." And yes, my tone matches my frustration and my "can you believe this crap" mood. "I also have to apologize on behalf of the chicken, for feeding on the grass, without asking for permission from the earth, to feed on it in the first place."

"Every time?" Celia asks.

"Nope, just during Plant Day, Plant Week, whatever you want to call it."

"Why?" Shayna asks.

I straighten. "Because apparently I'll be 'intimately' engaging with the earth and any negative actions or thoughts will be absorbed by the plant while I chant, thereby affecting the potency of the herbs and the magic I'm supposed to be harvesting within them."

"That makes sense," Emme offers, even though the expression riddling her angelic features reflects how messed up this whole thing is.

"So what can you eat?" Celia asks.

"Orange juice," I reason. "Since the oranges are picked and it's likely they haven't yet hit the sacred earth."

"And?" Celia presses.

"And more orange juice," I say, lifting the glass and take a swallow. "And probably all the water I can handle. Once the sun sets I can have a fish, but that's about it."

"Wow," Celia says. "So it's almost like a cleanse. Well, until evening."

"Pretty much," I say. I turn to where Alice is leaning against the counter watching us. She probably recognizes the food as something she used to eat. But it's clear it's not something she's craving. She turns her head like it disgusts her, causing her neck to make an odd cracking noise. The sound makes me cringe, but it's not until I realize that she's stuck that I know she's in trouble.

"Oh, no. I think she broke her neck," I say, rushing to stand.

"No, that can't be," Shayna says, although her shrill voice tells a different tale. "She probably just pinched a nerve."

We all startle, gasping when her head flops forward. Alice offers us a reassuring smile, which ordinarily would be sweet, but since the base of her skull is now resting between her breasts, and she's staring at us upside down, it only adds to the creep factor and makes Celia gag.

In Celia's defense, she's been queasy since Aric knocked her up.

Alice, being a trooper, hangs onto to her grin.

Even when a tooth drops to the floor with a *click*.

"Did, uh, anyone feed her this morning?" I ask, edging toward her. I stop directly in front of her, not really knowing what to do. My stomach flip-flops because yeah, her head is buried between her boobs.

"Koda used the charm to take her out back and along the trail sometime around dawn when he heard her wandering downstairs. But she kept trying to return to the house so he thought she was okay." Shayna places her hands on either side of Alice's head and tries to lift it. It seems to stay, but as soon as she steps back, it falls like a bowling ball, smacking hard against her chest and cracking her sternum.

We collectively jump at the sight of her concaved chest. Alice jumps with us, thinking it's some kind of game, resulting in her head bouncing and burying deeper into her chest cavity.

"Oh, *gawd*," I moan, pointing. "I think the muscles in her neck are starting to tear."

Shayna inches away when she hears the front door open. She keeps her smile despite the green color overtaking her skin.

"Koda, honey," she calls. "Could you take Alice out for breakfast? She could really use a bite of carcass."

A few days ago, this would seem like an odd thing to say. Today, not so much. That doesn't make the acid burning a hole through my gut any easier to bear.

I turn as I hear him and Aric step back inside the house. But they're not alone. Gemini stands there, his watchful stare taking in the scene. It pauses briefly over Alice, but it doesn't stay there, fixing on me in a way that grounds me in place.

I tuck my arm against me when it jerks, stepping far away from him.

"Ergh?" Alice question.

Aric rushes past me. I'm not sure why until I see Emme easing Celia to the floor. Between Alice's walking corpse aroma and delicate condition, Celia and *her* delicate condition don't stand a chance.

"I've got this," Koda says. He takes the charm Shayna

offers and pulls it over his head. But when he takes Alice's arm to lead her out, she breaks away.

From one sickening crunch to the next, Koda is left holding Alice's arm and not much else.

He lifts the severed limb, examining it closely. "Yeah, she could use a bite."

"Ergh?" Alice says, trying to crane her head as they pass me.

"It's okay," I tell her. "Just go with him, sweetie. I'll see you when I get home."

"Ergh!" she says, thick black sludge seeping from her eyes.

"Oh," Emme says. "She's crying."

"Ergh," Alice says.

It's like I'm going to work and leaving my new puppy behind. Okay, maybe not, but it's still hard to watch. I approach her, swiping the stuff from her eyes with a napkin. "Shayna and Emme will stay with you until I get back later tonight."

"Gurgla," she says.

"Yes, I promise," I assure her, even though I'm not positive that's what she said.

My assurance seems to satisfy her and she leaves without incident. Unless you count the toe on the floor that rolls after her. I want to go with them, to make sure she's okay. But with Gemini here, and the air thickening between us, I know I'm in for a lot more than a sad goodbye.

Everyone leaves us except for Aric, and Celia who doesn't look well.

Aric lifts her from the floor. "Let's get you upstairs so you can lie down."

She shakes her head, keeping him in place. Her stare travels in Gemini's direction. "Hi," she tells him. "I didn't expect to see you here."

"My apologies," he says, as if that explains everything.

He's in a pair of dark jeans that no-doubt hug his ass perfectly and draw attention to his long legs. But it's the navy

T-shirt that brings out his olive skin tone that holds my attention.

I bought it for him as a gift. I'm not sure if he remembers, or if he's playing some kind of game. Considering this wolf remembers everything, I lean toward the latter. I return to the table, drinking my orange juice as slowly I can, trying not to appear like I'm forcing it down.

"I'd better go," I say, reaching for my keys. "Later, Ceel."

"Gemini is here to accompany you," Aric says, lowering Celia to the floor, but keeping her tucked against him.

"No thanks. I'm good," I sing, taking off toward the foyer.

"You don't have a choice," Gemini snaps.

I turn on my heel, pegging him with a glare that causes my arm to smoke. I shake it off, ignoring the way the bind tightens against my skin, reminding me that it's there to keep me, and it, in place.

"If you're trying to convince me with your charm it's not working," I point out, smiling with all the friendliness of a Great White.

He crosses his arms. "As the liaison between the Coven and the Pack I play many roles."

"You made your role quite clear the other day when I found you with Vieve," I answer. Maybe I shouldn't be so harsh, but I always knew if I was out of the picture, Vieve would pounce on him like a cobra.

I just never counted on him falling for her. At least not this fast or this hard.

"I would tell you there's nothing between us, but it wouldn't make a difference would it?" he asks.

"Nope," I respond.

He tightens his jaw. "As I was saying, I hold many roles, and one of them necessitates ensuring your safe passage into the coven today."

"I can drive myself and deal with whatever comes," I insist.

"No, Taran," Aric interrupts. "The wards surrounding the compound will tear you apart. At the end of the day, you'll be granted full access so you can to travel alone. In the meantime, you must accompany Gemini in order to be allowed safely in. He and I are the only ones outside the coven empowered to enter Genevieve's domain."

"How convenient," I say.

"Come on, Taran," Aric says, dragging his hand irritably through his dark hair.

"She couldn't give me access the other day?" I ask. "No, I guess that would have been too easy."

"Emotions were heightened that day," Aric responds. "It wasn't the right time."

"I don't want to go with him," I say. "I don't want to have anything to do with him." That's not really true. I don't want all the bad between us. I want the good we used to share. But as my arm gives me another wicked shake, I'm reminded any sense of us is in the past and exactly where I should leave it.

Gemini swallows hard as if pained. But when he responds, my former lover leaves me and the Second in Command takes charge. "You have two choices: walk to my vehicle on your own accord, or have me throw you over my shoulder and carry you. Two choices," he repeats. "Pick."

I glance at Celia. If I was a total ass, I'd ask her if Aric can take me. But she's still nauseous, and it'll kill Aric to leave her, especially feeling the way that she is.

"Okay. Let's go," I tell him. "Bye, Ceel."

"Bye, Taran," she says, slowly, probably stunned stupid with how easily I give in.

I walk past Gemini, working the Pilgrim shoes like they're stilettos and I'm on the catwalk. My hand brushes against him briefly, the contact giving him the magical equivalent of sticking a safety pin into a light socket.

He shakes away the effect, growling as his dark hair stands on end. This here kids is what's often referred to as cause and effect. You piss me off, and this is the effect.

"Oops," I say, covering my mouth. "I hope this

doesn't happen the entire way up. It could make for a *very* long and uncomfortable ride up."

Okay. Maybe I am kind of an ass.

Chapter Twelve

"Heh."

"Heh, heh, heh."

"Heh, heh, ha!"

I step onto the porch, only to have Mrs. Mancuso, aka the devil's grandmother, laugh and point when she sees me in my get-up.

Not that she has any room to judge. Today she's wearing one of her more obnoxious house dresses, the one with large flowers and bees buzzing around it. Is it too much to hope one of those bees comes to life and stings her sagging ass? And yet despite how I was working my strut seconds before, the strut stops short. Mrs. Mancuso, for all I think she's some kind of demon spawn sent to make our lives miserable, is human. She has no ties or knowledge of the mystical community. But she possesses this rare ability to ruin your day in a single glance or a wave of a middle finger.

"Where did you get that *ridiculous* ensemble?" she sneers.

"Your mother," I respond, smiling.

And look, she's no longer laughing.

"Taran," Gemini warns. "Just ignore her."

I shake my head as she narrows her little beady eyes at me. "Too late," I say, recognizing she's getting into her warrior stance: which includes prepping her fingers to waggle a stiff one or fling one of her orthopedic shoes at my head. A thousand years old or not, the woman has crazy aim.

She rises from where she's tending to the flowers over Ginger's grave. Ginger was an old rescue dog Mrs. Mancuso had for roughly two months. In those two months the dog lived with her, she dug up our yard six times, used our front lawn for her daily bathroom privileges, bit Emme twice, Shayna three times, and picked a fight with Celia and the wolves every time she saw them.

Ginger was a bitch.

Yet oddly cuter and kinder than Mrs. Mancuso.

Ginger died, supposedly of old age. We're convinced she killed herself because death beat living with Mrs. Mancuso who'd force her into matching outfits.

In fact, I think the bee and flower print number is the same one Ginger died in.

Mrs. Mancuso lifts her gardening trowel, pointing it menacingly. "Women like you belong in dirty alleys, lifting your skirts for men of equal caliber."

Let me be the first to say, it's hard to look badass in these shoes. That doesn't stop me from stomping toward her or speaking like I'm dressed in riot gear. "And women like you belong knitting, silent, and far away from me. Jesus Christ woman, don't you have a set of dentures to scrub or a litter of kittens to drown?"

"May God and syphilis have mercy on your soul," she fires back.

"May your support hose choke you in your sleep," is my response.

"Taran, get in the car," Gemini says. He doesn't like Mrs. Mancuso, and hates how she treats me. But he has certain ingrained Japanese traditions which include respecting your elders. No matter how much of a pain in the ass said elders are.

"You *whore*," she spits out.

Point made.

"Better a whore than something the Angel of Death

wouldn't fu—"

"Taran!"

I glance up to see Emme dashing down the steps, her face as red as Mrs. Mancuso's roses. "I'm so terribly sorry, Mrs. Mancuso," she says. "You'll have to forgive Taran. She's starting a new course of study today and is under a great deal of pressure—"

"What's she studying? How to be less of a slut?" She narrows her eyes. "Are you and the rest of your floozy sisters enrolled as well?"

Gemini barely grabs me in time when I launch myself at her. "Have a nice day in anti-tramp school," she calls.

"Die," I tell her. "For the love of all just *die* and put us out of our misery!"

I mean to sound forceful, but my anger at Mrs. Mancuso fades when my body reacts to having Gemini so close. Instead of breaking free, my body conforms to his, relaxing against him despite how my protective instincts warn me to keep my distance.

The muscles of his torso stiffen against my back. I think he means to say something, I know him well enough to know as much. But his mouth stays silent, releasing only a warm breath against my cheek. It's reminiscent of our times in bed, moments before we'd drift to sleep.

God, I really miss him.

"You can't behave like this," he tells me quietly. "Especially around Genevieve."

He had to go and say her name. The image I had of him curling around me as he whispered goodnight, vanishes as quickly as it appeared.

"You're right, the last thing I want is to upset her. Whatever would you do to ease her distress?"

The sting in my tone is enough to cause him to release me, but not before I notice how he managed to hold me without touching my affected arm.

"Why does everything have to be a fight with you?" he asks, stepping away.

"Why is everything always my fault?" I counter,

placing a hand on my hip.

"You know how she is. Why do you let her upset you?"

"Are you talking about Mancuso or Vieve?" I ask. "Either way, I think I have a right to feel what I feel."

He leans back on his heels, his stare dragging down from the top of my bonnet to my buckled shoes. I shrink inward, as if I can somehow hide what I'm wearing. I do a double-take when I realize, he's no longer frowning.

"Why are you smiling?" I ask.

"You're threatened by Genevieve."

"I am not," I respond, lying through my teeth.

My former bae isn't a grinner, he's not one to flash a broad smile. His expressions, like his personality, tend to be reserved, subtle. It takes a lot for him to really let go.

So that knowing grin that crosses his face isn't something I'm expecting, or something I particularly appreciate.

"I see," he says.

"No, you don't."

He nods thoughtfully. "No, I think I do."

"You're pissing me off," I point out.

"That's nothing new," he adds, throwing in an unfairly sexy brood.

"Um, Taran," Emme interrupts. I look up in time to see Mancuso lift a particularly vicious middle finger. "Would you like me to help you with your school supplies?"

This time, it's my turn to smile, ignoring Mrs. Mancuso when she adds another finger. "I'll get it," I hold my hand out when Gemini tries to follow. "Would you be a gentleman and open the door?" He already appears suspicious, as he should be. "I only have a few things," I assure him.

"All right," he says, watching me closely.

The moment Emme pops open the trunk of my sedan, I lift the box of garlic and hurry to where Gemini is waiting at the end of a driveway. His nostrils flare, he already knows what's inside. But just in case I rip open the top, sending a cloud of dust in the air and making him sneeze.

I dump the box on the passenger side floor of Gemini's brandy new Mercedes SUV (can't leave without my school supplies ya' know). He whirls away, sneezing repeatedly, only to glare when I climb into the front seat.

I smile sweetly as I reach for the seatbelt. "Ready to go, lover boy? I don't want to be late for my first day. Oh, and I'll bet our Most Superior Broom Straddler can't wait to see her favorite liaison!"

Emme glances between us, clutching a smaller box filled with holy water as if it can somehow protect her from the anger riling Gemini's wolves. As it is, the head of his twin wolf punches through his back, tearing his shirt as he growls and snaps his jaws.

Gemini edges away, shielding the sight from Mrs. Mancuso.

"Where do you want this?" Emme stammers, making a face.

The wolf sneezes a few times before Gemini lulls him back inside him.

"Oh, just put it in the rear," I answer for him. "Wouldn't want to be a bother, would we, cutie?"

My comment earns me another glare. He takes the box from Emme, muttering a growl as he places it in the trunk.

"Bye, Taran. Good luck," Emme says, hurrying up the driveway and putting plenty of space between us.

Gemini throws open the driver's side door and hops inside, slamming it shut.

"I just love the smell of garlic, don't you?" I gush.

He snaps his seatbelt in place, cranking the engine and lowering all the windows. "Why must you make *everything* so difficult?" he asks, popping his SUV into drive.

"Whatever do you mean?"

"Harlot!" Mrs. Mancuso screams as we pull away.

I shove my head out the window. "Shut up and die!" I yell back, refusing to let her have the last word.

"You were saying?" I ask Gemini, kicking the box and sending an extra whiff of garlic in the air.

He groans. "You're not going to behave. Are you?"

"Now what makes you say that?" I ask, trying not to notice how what's left of his T-shirt dangles from his shoulders.

He stops at the end of our development, pausing when he catches me gaping. In my defense, no heterosexual woman alive could resist all that.

"It's hot in here. Don't you think?" he asks.

"It's okay . . ." I don't quite finish my thought. He tears off what remains of his shirt and tosses it onto my lap.

"Problem?" he asks, knowing damn well my nipples are now doing the Neh-Neh.

I laugh. "Not at all," I say. I hike up my skirt, revealing my hot pink panties (hey, no one said I couldn't wear a thong). "But you're right, it is a little hot." I fan the skirt, and a little more garlic.

This time, he doesn't sneeze, but he does look, past my thigh-high white socks and to where the hot pink silk peeks out. I managed a little naughty to a whole lot of dull, trying to hang onto the me that remains beneath all this heavy cotton.

As if it takes everything he has, he wrenches his stare from my thighs and back to the road. He punches the gas, his typically controlled driving now a thing of the past. I allow my skirt to fall back to my ankles. I'm disappointed he didn't look a little longer, and maybe I'm hurt that he didn't pull me in for a long deep kiss. It reinforces my belief that he belongs to someone else, who isn't me.

Who is more polite.

Who thinks before she speaks.

And who's simply *whole*.

I'm sure of it, until he veers onto a different road when we're almost to Squaw Valley. "Where are you going?" I ask.

"A different way," he responds. His stare shifts my way, but it's brief. "Don't worry, I'll get you where you need to be."

"I wasn't worried," I say. I'm not afraid of him. One

thing I've never doubted from the moment we met is that he would never hurt me.

Yet as he reaches the far corner of the valley, I realize I should be afraid. I know where he's going even before he pulls onto a small narrow path leading into the forest of thick pines. Most who pass by on their way to the ski slopes in winter or to mountain climb in the spring and summer might miss it, especially now that densely packed trees shadow the narrow opening. Some locals might mistake it for a service road, or even a back road leading to one of the larger and more eloquent estates that overlook the lake.

I know it as the way to a small field, where Gemini and I once spent a warm summer's night making love beneath the canopy of a thousand stars. It was one of my favorite memories with him. He'd built a fire, made me dinner, and laughed when the melted chocolate from my s'more dripped down my chin. I should have been embarrassed, to have a not so great vision of me before this vision of a man. But I'd laughed, too, falling back into the blanket he'd laid out when he met me with a kiss.

It was a perfect night, and the first time he talked seriously about marrying me.

My stare falls to my lap, and to where I'm tucking my sickly hand beneath my thigh. I never expected us to change, to become something so foreign and unwelcomed.

He rolls to a stop, cutting the engine. "Do you know where we are?" he asks, his deep voice quiet, reverting to that familiar timbre, the one that carries so much of his heart.

"Why are you doing this?" I ask in a way of an answer.

He knows what I mean. If he brought me here, there's a reason for it. But he doesn't answer right away, taking every inch of my being in, as if he no longer recognizes who he sees in front of him.

A portion of my soul chips away, another piece to add to the growing pile at my feet. "I don't know," he finally responds. "Maybe I wanted to see how you'd react."

I meet his eyes, his dark irises shimmering with all the

heartache I feel. "Why?" I ask. Jesus, can't he see how much it's killing me to be here?

His words are slow and sure. "Because there was a time when you were my everything and I was your world. And now, you're sitting mere inches from me and all I sense is you slipping further away."

I blink the sting stretching out across my eyes.

"Taran . . . tell me you love me."

Another crack in my soul. Another sliver that falls. "Don't do this, Tomo," I beg.

I use his real name, not his nickname, the one I'd use during our most intimate moments.

Maybe that's why this time, he's the one who turns away.

"I need to hear you tell me," he says. "Me, and my wolves, we need something from you that doesn't come from pain or anger, a reminder of what we had, of what we meant to each other." He shakes his head, frustrated. "Taran, give us *something*."

My right hand jerks up, smacking against the armrest hard enough to send a jolt of agony streaming to my shoulder. I clutch it against me, trying to hide it. But beneath the thick awning of branches shadowing the cabin, I can't hide its glow, even with the heavy white fabric of my long-sleeved shirt. The obnoxious light fades in and out slowly, a harsh reminder of everything it cost us.

I glance up at him, wondering if my features give away how sorry I am—for not being the same mate he claimed and for not being strong enough to save us from this torment. Anara, the werewolf Elder who chewed off my arm . . . I should have killed him. I should have set him ablaze or split him into pieces with my lightning. But I didn't. I charged him in a careless rush, letting my anger rule me instead of fighting smart.

It's *my* fault. *My* doing. I knew what I was up against. I want to tell him as much, except he's no longer looking at my arm or even me.

He withdraws, taking those words he shared back,

along with his heart.

I'm not sure if he thinks the response of my arm was intentional, or if he was simply reminded of everything that wedged us apart. Either way, the hurt that brews between us simmers to a boil.

He mutters a swear, the viciousness in his tone warning me how close he is to surrendering to the beasts that prowl inside of him. I still, wanting so badly to pull him back to me. But I can't, not when he feels so distant. It's as if the motion of my arm told him something he didn't want to hear, know, or remember.

Perspiration gathers along his crown and torso, the small clear beads widening until they drip along his olive skin, streaking his shoulders and chest, and cutting angry lines into his features. The muscles along his arms strain as he grips the steering wheel and takes very deep and laborious breaths, working to hold back his wolves and the turmoil of emotions plaguing him.

He's scaring me, not because I think he's seconds from attacking, but because of what it's doing to him.

"Are you okay?" I manage, my voice cracking.

"No," he growls. He starts the engine with a harsh flick of his controls and shifts the SUV in reverse, using the rear camera to guide him.

Silence overtakes the air, muffling even the sounds from the road. I don't bother trying to coax him into a conversation. For someone who accused me of being so far away, what seems like a lifetime of false memories fall like a barrier between us.

It's only when we're almost to the compound that he finally speaks. "The other witches, even the Lesser ones, will try to enforce their ranks within the coven," he tells me. "They're like wolves in that respect. Hold your ground, but don't challenge them to a fight, or give them a reason to interpret your actions as cause for combat."

He's trying protect me. It shouldn't surprise me, but considering these last few moments...

"I'm not going to let anyone walk over me," I assure

him.

The corners of his mouth curve a little. "I know you won't," he says, his serious demeanor returning as he tosses me an all-too-knowing glance. "But there's a difference between standing up for yourself and reacting in a way that lands you in a magical duel. You're not ready for that. Not in your condition."

I open my mouth to argue, but shut it quickly. He's right. And it sucks. I think a toddler witch with a plastic wand from a party store could crush me right now if she waved it the right way.

"All right," I say.

"All right?" he asks, hardly believing it.

"I'm not stupid, Gemini," I tell him quietly. "And even though I don't want to be here, I also don't want this thing to kill me." I almost motion to arm, but he knows what I mean and it's already hurt him enough.

"I know you're not stupid, love," he says, locking eyes with me.

The gesture is brief, but the effect lodges my breath deep in my lungs. He doesn't react, as if I didn't notice what he said and was speaking as if nothing had changed between us. But everything has. If there's a doubt, my hand gives another involuntary jerk.

My entire body jerks again when we pass through the first ward, that awful feeling of being shoved through plastic wrap returning.

"It'll get better once Genevieve gifts you with the ability to travel in and out of the grounds."

I nod, but don't comment. Genevieve's name alone casts its own wicked spell upon me, reducing me to this insecure teen with her own personal homecoming queen ready to trip her in the halls and point out her weaknesses.

As we pass the fields and rows of witches making their way with their buckets, I should be panicked about what's to come and whether I'll be able to handle it. But the only thing concerning me now is our eminent goodbye. This ride up, wasn't perfect, wasn't us. Not what we used to be.

But it's more than we've shared in a long while and I'm not ready to let it go.

And maybe he isn't either.

He rolls to a stop in front of Vieve's ancestral home. Before I can reach for my box, he takes my left hand and curls it around his fingertips.

Soft warm lips pass along my knuckles as dark irises weld into mine. "Good luck," he whispers. "I'll be close if you need me."

I stare at my hand as he releases me, wishing he could kiss the hand that most mattered...

Chapter Thirteen

I think, I'm really late, in fact I'm sure of it. But instead of rushing, I find myself moving slowly.

Gemini's contact was a reminder of all the care and kindness he always met me with. For a *were* who's very alpha and can rip the head off a charging demon's shoulders and kick it aside, it's his gentle side that always blew me away.

"How could you be so brutal during a hunt yet so tender with me?" I once asked.

"Because I love you," he'd answered simply.

"Do you want me to help you with that?" he offers, motioning to my box of garlic and drawing my attention.

His grimace makes me laugh. "Haven't you had your fill?" I tease.

"No. I haven't," he responds, pegging me with a lustful gaze that I swear could roast the three pounds of garlic in my hands.

I am the queen of awesome, inappropriate comebacks. If there was ever an opportunity for one, this is it. Quaker uniform and all, I return the heat sizzling my pointy girl parts and say—

"Lesser Taran. You're needed in the fields."

Yeah, that wasn't it.

Vieve's guard Christie, the blonde Bren banged like a

pair of horny cymbals, marches down the steps the bodice of her medieval brown dress threatening to choke what remains of her cleavage. She snags Gemini's attention, as do the four witches dressed in black trailing behind her.

Their stares are intense and very lethal. I'll give blondie this, when Gemini and I march closer, she stops, nodding respectfully at him. It's the long not-so respectful glance down his half-naked body that I take offense to. If I didn't think I'd end up in Witchcraft and Wizardry detention, I would have nailed her in the head with a bulb of garlic.

Hello. Ex-girlfriend standing right in front of you.

"What's this?" he asks her, both of us ignoring her "chop-chop" command to get to my station.

My place beside Gemini gives her the barest pause. "A hunt," she responds.

"For the Whisperer of the Dead?"

I don't have to guess he means Savanna. In the supernatural world, one of three things earns you a nickname: stupidity, incompetence, or evil. Savanna doesn't strike me as stupid or incompetent, which of course makes her evil that much scarier. Give me a dumb bitch any day to take on.

His stare passes along the witches, his scrutiny causing them to straighten, and the gemstones fixed to their talismans to flicker in alternating colors. It's a demonstration of their status and power. Cute. Gemini would tear them apart if they pulled any shit.

"Yes. We were given insight to her whereabouts. Sister Genevieve ordered her immediate capture."

"Genevieve didn't mention this last night," he says.

My head swivels slowly his way. *Last night . . .*

Christie's professional demeanor vanishes, reverting back to the personality she demonstrated when she'd told Bren to fuck off. She notices my reaction, and she likes it.

She smiles, apparently thrilled for being the one to inform me that her leader and my wolf were to together last night. "The location where she's hiding were only disclosed to us in the early morning hours, following your departure," she tells him, adding another kick to the stomach. "Our most

Honorable and Superior Head Witch plans to discuss the hunt, along with other important matters during your scheduled breakfast time."

Her words repeat in my head like a flock of woodpeckers punching their beaks into my skull. "In the early morning hours *after* you left". "During your breakfast time". How much time exactly does he spend here in Witchland?

Despite how I steel myself, it's not enough to mask my annoyance. Christie doesn't miss a beat, and I don't think Gemini does either. Not that he shows it. "They're new to their power and position," he says, motioning to the witches dressed in black. "Perhaps our Pack can aid you in the hunt."

"That won't be necessary," Christie tells, him, her smug smile widening. "The Whisperer of the Dead is our kind, and our responsibility. And, may I add, my sisters beside me were among the best in their graduating class. I'm certain our most distinguished Head Witch will assure you when you meet."

"All right," he says, although he doesn't seem happy.

She gives him another subtle nod, joining her besties as they hurry toward the parking lot, but not before tossing me a very predatory leer my way. It's something I could have done without, the digs over how chummy Gemini and Vieve are were enough. Speaking of witch.

"Good morning," the most distinguished head hag calls.

Vieve glides down the steps, her long silver gown sweeping behind her. I'm not sure if her feet actually touch the steps, or if her gown is an actual dress, or the nightgown she was wearing when Gemini left her last night. At the moment, I don't really care. Between the connection they share and how stunning she appears, sweating my ass in a field while donning pilgrim-wear is far more appealing than having a front and center view of how hard she's falling for him.

Or maybe how hard they're falling for each other.

She's smiling. I'm not.

"Welcome, Taran," she says.

You don't mean that.

"Thank you," I say, not really meaning it either. Especially when I catch how close she inches to my wolf.

Her attention skims over his broad chest because, hey, I'm not paying attention or anything.

"You set up a hunt without my knowledge or input," he says, not bothering to greet her or bend to her charm.

Weres have this thing about needing to know anything and everything pertaining to saving the world from evil. As the liaison between the coven and pack, she should have given him the heads up.

But then if she had, she couldn't have discussed the matter over a nice cozy breakfast, now could she?

Her smile fades as if she's upset she might have hurt his feelings. "I didn't want to disturb you during the early morning hours, Gemini. I've already burdened you enough with my troubles." Her smile returns, the warmth and affection behind it as obvious as my damn bonnet. "But now that you're here, I'm more than happy to share our intel and how we're proceeding."

"Good. Based on her experience with one of our own, she's not someone we can take lightly," he says. His attention travels to where the witch party are assembling by a vehicle. "The Whisperer tried to sacrifice Bren, a Warrior. If she'd succeeded, given what she can do, she could have raised more dead. But if she sacrifices a witch—"

"They won't be sacrificed," she says, cutting him off. Her voice loses its warmth, gathering a slight edge. "They're prepared for what may come."

He's not so sure. "It might not be too late for my Pack to be of use."

"No. And if the circumstances surrounding the Whisperer's capture require it, I will certainly connect with you."

Oh, honey, I have no doubt.

She motions to the front door of stained glass. "Shall we?"

His focus returns to me. "In a moment. I want to

ensure Taran makes it to the field."

"Taran will make it just fine without you," I assure him. I don't mean to sound so angry, but their exchange was like watching a play from the audience, both of them making it clear I'm not part of the show.

He lifts his brow, likely wondering what could have possibly pissed me off this time—

as if I shouldn't be bothered by how close they're standing, or the late hours that they're keeping, or that I look ready to churn butter while Genevieve floats on her cloud, or whatever the fuck, polishing her halo. It's all I can do not to hurl my box of garlic at them.

I stomp away, stumbling slightly when the skirt of my long dress catches on the buckle of my pilgrim shoes.

"You won't need your garlic today, Taran," she calls sweetly.

I toss the box on the sidewalk, storming toward the field. "Awesome," I yell. "Totally psyched for anti-possession class!"

"Don't trouble yourself," she tells Gemini. I haven't quite reached the end of the walkway, but I know her response is because he's lifting the box from the sidewalk. I don't know what's worse, how I continue to look bad, even though I don't want to, or these mixed signals he's sending me about the possibility of us.

Our supernatural world may be changing, and evil is constantly afoot. But we're no longer at war. He doesn't need to spend the time he seems to with Genevieve unless there's something more going on.

"It's no trouble," he replies.

"My dear Gemini," she says. "I'll have another Lesser house it in her room for storage."

After breakfast, but not before we have sex, she doesn't add. I know that's what she's thinking, her alluring tone is one that hungers for the taste of a sexy male. I know because that's how I feel when I'm with him, when we're not hurting or angry, or—

"Taran," he calls, reaching me and stepping in front of

me. "You're reading more into my relationship with Genevieve than what's there."

"Relationship?" I repeat.

"You know what I mean," he answers.

He searches my face, frowning and appearing insulted by my response. Seriously, is he that blind to what Vieve wants from him, or how much his choice of words *and hers* hurt me? "My dear Gemini," she called him. She knows he claimed me. But that doesn't stop her from calling him hers.

"I know what I saw back there," I tell him. "And it's not the innocent exchange you're making it out to be."

He releases a long dragged out breath, his attention dropping to the ground. "Every time I feel we take a step forward, you run us backwards as fast as you can."

"You're putting this on me?" I say. "Really? After that little display of affection between you?"

"All we did was discuss the hunt."

This time. I don't want to go there, but it's difficult not to.

I glance away, unable to stomach how horrible things are between us.

A few feet past the garden, a line of witches return from the field to fill their buckets at a spout. That's how late I am. They're already starting round two and I haven't even stepped foot on the field.

"I'll be here all day," he says, trying to lure my attention when I remain silent.

"With Genevieve," I say, not bothering to look at him.

He doesn't deny it, worsening the betrayal I feel. "When you're done," he says. "I'll take you home."

Maybe he's trying to give me a peace offering. But it feels more like pity.

I shift away from his hardening stance to where she stands waiting for him to return to her. "Don't bother," I say, wishing I could hide the pain gutting me open. "You've already done enough."

Chapter Fourteen

I start to walk away with what little dignity remains. "Don't forget your bucket, Taran," Vieve calls, because no one can kick someone in the balls like she can. "You'll need it to complete your tasks."

I double-back, lifting a large wooden bucket from the top of a carefully arranged stack and somehow toppling the rest over.

So much for dignity.

"Don't," I say, when Gemini tries to help me stack them. "Just go."

"No," he insists. "At least allow me this one thing."

I keep my stare averted. I wish I could yell or scream at him. Let him know everything I'm feeling and what he does to me every time I'm with him. But I don't have it in me to fight him. It's the last thing I want to do. And after this morning . . .

"Just let me help you, Taran," he says, sounding as weary as I feel.

"All right," I answer quietly.

We work quickly and in silence. But as I set the last bucket in place, I hurry away from him and the awful tension between us.

I reach the spout, forcing a smile and a small wave to

OF FLAME AND LIGHT

the witches who approach. "Hey. I'm Taran."

The ones filling their buckets pause, whispering quickly, eyeing me and my arm closely, and not bothering to wave in response. Okay, so far we're off to a banging start. The next few Lessers do the same as well as the ones who follow.

I edge to the rear where only a few witches remain in line so I don't cut in front and risk accidentally challenging them. But it's only until a short distance separates me from the spout that I hear what all the whispers are about.

"Give me fluid so you may drink. Drink so you may grow. Grow so I may strengthen."

Ah, yes, I skimmed through last night.

"Hey, there," a meek voice calls out. "You're Lesser Taran, right?"

The little witch I met before, the one with the red braid inches closer, smiling.

"Yes," I answer. "And you're . . . Pauline?"

The two Lessers in front of her laugh. "It's Paula, actually," she explains.

"I'm sorry," I say, not just because I screwed up her name, but because of the petty way the other two responded.

"It's okay," she replies, struggling to hang onto her smile as she looks at the two who laughed. "People forget it all the time."

The way she says it makes me think she's used to being ignored. But she doesn't have to worry about that with me. "Nice to meet you, Paula."

I try to take her hand when she extends it, but then her stare falls on my hand. "I suppose you've heard about this thing," I ask, pulling it back.

"We all have," she says quietly. "But I wasn't offering to shake your hand." She points to the bucket. "Give it to me. I'll help you. The elements can be persnickety and I don't want them giving you problems, especially on your first day."

I pass her my bucket. "Persnickety?" I question, wondering why someone so young would use such and old term, at the same time also wondering what the hell she means.

"You'll see," she responds.

Paula motions for me to follow when she backs away from the spout. The witch who laughed the hardest at her reaches for the lever, resuming her chant as she pumps. But the moment the water hits the bottom of the bucket, a watery arm flies up and grabs the Lesser by the throat. It drags her down, plunging her into what's somehow now an overflowing bucket of water.

"Son of a *bitch!*" I say, jumping back. My first reaction is to call my fire, but fire isn't what this young woman needs. Regardless, my arm gives an involuntary jerk, sending a twinge of pain shooting up the length. All eyes are suddenly on me, *not* the Lesser having her ass kicked by the bucket of water.

"I didn't do that," I say, watching as the Lesser flails and an overabundance of water soaks the ground around her. "I swear I didn't."

"Shhh," Paula says, shaking her hands out nervously. "Remember, they're persnickety."

The water releases the Lesser abruptly, dropping her in some seriously thick mud. She lands with a splat, her soaked clothes coated.

Paula wrings her hands nervously. "It probably thought she was insulting it or the chant," she explains.

"Hmm," the others agree, nodding.

The other Lesser who laughed, isn't laughing now. In fact, she seems terrified to pump the water in.

"You might as well get it over with," her friend tells her. She stands, albeit wobbly, swiping the mud from her face. "Come on, or we'll all be late."

Her friend walks carefully forward, reaching hesitantly toward the lever. She slaps at it nervously, releasing a drop. I don't think anything will happen, but like with her buddy, that small trace of water becomes so much more, swirling as it rises into another watery hand.

This Lesser gets off with a watery, if not insolent, slap across the face that sends her spinning into the mud pile.

I gape with my mouth dangling open. *This* is supposed to be my easy day!

"Do you want me to help you?" Paula offers. "I'll pump, you chant, and then we'll switch?"

No, I'd rather go home and munch off my toes. "I'm not sure I'm going to be very good at this," I admit.

"Oh, of course you will," she insists. "Just think positive thoughts, otherwise the elements and the plants will react in a not-so positive way."

"Um. All right. Thank you," I say, hoping the water doesn't think I was calling *it* a son of a bitch. Is it a wonder everyone seems skittish?

I place my bucket beneath the spout. "Ready?" she asks.

"Ready," I say, even as I prepare myself for a possible H_2O ass-whooping.

She brings the lever down. "Give me fluid so you may drink," I say.

My nervousness makes me forget the rest. "Drink so you may grow," Paula whispers.

"Drink so you may grow," I repeat.

She smiles, pumping hard so the water spills in slow steady streams. "Grow so I may strengthen," she says.

"Grow so I may strengthen."

I switch off, pumping while Paula chants, watching in amazement at how quickly the bucket fills. I wait until she's done and follow behind her, trying my best not to spill, and, I don't know, insult the water.

The water swirls in my bucket, but although I'm pitching from side to side through the uneven soil, it appears to stay in.

"It's the magic," Paula says. "The elements respond to our chants and give them life."

"Wow." I'm starting to understand why the witches feel so akin to the earth, not that I'm certain we'll share that connection.

I stumble over a stone sticking out from the field. How the hell does anyone get around in these shoe things?

As the earth evens out slightly more, I tug on my collar. I'm already sweating and high noon is still a few hours away.

"Here," she says, reaching into her bucket splashing me in the face.

I start to ask her if she's nuts when the coolness from the water spreads from my face to my shoulders, giving me a chill. "Better?" she asks.

"Yes. Thank you. How did you do that?"

"The chanting helps, but don't expect it to last." She makes a face. "And don't let the Snapdragons we're tending to see you take their water. They're a nasty bunch."

"The *plants* are a nasty bunch?" I ask.

"Oh, yes," she adds. "They have nothing on the water. Unless you dump it aside out of anger. You're not going to dump the water in anger, are you, Taran?"

"That wasn't the plan," I assure her. Not that I don't see why someone would do that given the conditions these Lessers work under.

"Lesser Dina did that," Paula says thoughtfully. "She was frustrated with the program and with our instructors. One day she had it and kicked over the bucket." She shudders. "Let's say it's not a mistake you want to make, and that your breasts look better positioned on your chest."

"Sure. Let's just say," I reply, slowly, wondering if they somehow ended up attached to her knees. Magic is some freaky shit. Believe it or not, I've seen worse.

I look ahead as we reach a small path leading through the woods. "You seem to know a lot. How long have you been studying?"

"Too long," she says, glancing down. "The magic I come from isn't very strong. Most of my family has never reached Superior witch status. They belong to Lesser covens composed of women who sell charms and herbs at fairs." She shrugs. "My mother thought I'd be different, that I'd have a better chance. So far, it's not working out. If I can't pass in these next few years, I'll never be a Superior witch either."

"If you have a few years, you have a shot," I say,

ducking beneath a low branch.

"I wish I could believe you," she says. "But if I did I would've graduated by now." She tries to smile. "But let's think happy thoughts, okay?" Her voice lowers. "Don't want to anger the seedlings or disturb the surrounding vegetation."

No. Heaven forbid we get attacked by irate pine cones.

We push through the small path, and when I say, "push", I mean it. Paula maybe more used to the shoes, but she's not exactly skipping along. We trek up another small incline and end up on the opposite side of Vieve's mansion where a small field stretches out, partially surrounded by a forest filled with tall sweeping trees. Below us is another larger field. It's rectangular in shape and runs behind the house.

Vieve's laughter drifts in the air as we step onto the smaller field. I turn in that direction, watching as she and Gemini venture out onto a stone terrace. He's a good distance away, but I can see he's wearing a shirt, likely one from the spare pieces of clothing all *weres* keep in their vehicles.

Or maybe it's a spare set he keeps in Vieve's room.

My mind wanders to when we first met and how things sped ahead once he started spending the night. He started with leaving some things behind, a change of clothes, a toothbrush, a razor, but within a couple of months, he'd moved in everything he owned.

I follow Paula blindly when Vieve laughs again. If he was upset. I guess he's over it now.

She sighs. "He's beautiful, isn't he?"

"What?" I ask. It's not that didn't hear her, but I'll admit seeing Gemini and Vieve is not an easy thing to watch. They take their places at a table. But even though they're already very close, the moment Gemini sits Vieve moves her chair closer.

"Sister Genevieve's lover," Paula explains, smiling.

Her lover . . .

"Oh, yes, he is," someone else purrs.

I glance up at the group of Lessers giggling as they

pass along the rows of seedlings.

"He's the best thing about Plant Day," a petite young woman says as she adjusts her bonnet. "Every time I need more water, I know that I'll at least get to see *him*."

Paula stops smiling when she catches sight of my face. "Ah. Do you know him?" she asks when more Lessers mutter in agreement.

I want to say that yes, that in fact, he's my lover not hers. But I can't say that anymore. I steal another glance in their direction in time to see Vieve place her hand over his. "He's best friends with Aric Connor," I answer. "My sister's husband."

Their laughter ceases and they exchange glances. I suppose Vieve was right, that maybe it is my weird magic that makes them wary. But now they're wary for different reasons. I'm not one to name drop, but I do want them to watch what they say in front of me.

"So you know him?" another Lesser asks, her dark curls sticking to her face as she sweat. "Gemini, the Second in Command?"

"I used to," I say. I switch the hold on my bucket when the weight begins to pull on my shoulder. "But I don't anymore."

I'm not sure what they infer from what I say, I only hope it's enough to keep them from saying something we'll all regret. I follow Paula toward a row of cultivated soil that's empty of Lessers. I stop in place when I take a good look at the seedlings. They're larger than any typical garden variety. Each leaf is about the size of my palm and there's some kind of hole at the center of their buds.

"They ward off curses," Paula whispers.

"But why are they so big?" I ask. "And what's up with the hole?"

"They're bigger because of the magic used to harvest them. Oh, and that's not a hole, it's a mouth."

"Of course it is," I mumble. The water freaks out on you if you insult it, why wouldn't the snapdragons have mouths?

"Here, I'll show you," Paula says.

She reaches into her bucket, cupping her fingers just enough to gather a small amount of water. Their little mouths open and close, drinking in the drops of water Paula sprinkles as she chants.

Oh, and look, they have teeth . . .

I back away. I'm all for being brave, but did I mention the little bastards have teeth?

A woman dressed in a light turquoise maiden gown steps forward, her long grey hair partially wrapped in a bun and a spider-shaped talisman holding a red stone at its center. "I am Superior Wilma. Are you Lesser Taran Wird?" she asks.

"Yes, I—"

"You're late," Wilma says. She whirls around and walks down a row filled with what resemble small human skulls clustered between shriveling leaves. "Ten demerits," she adds, keeping her back to me.

She doesn't let me apologize or offer an excuse. Not that it would help me and not that I'd dare follow. I'm so unnerved by these skulls and what they're doing here. Shit, how many demerits did these poor saps get to earn *this*.

"Don't look at them for too long," Paula whispers.

I follow her down the row of seedlings. "What are they?" I ask.

"Dead seed pods," she says, struggling it seems to keep her gaze away. "The group in charge of their care didn't chant and water as they should. They didn't take their tasks seriously and well . . ." She shrugs. "The seedlings died and took one of the Lessers with them."

"Is this a joke?" I ask.

"No," the large group collectively mumbles.

"Don't anger the snapdragons," Paula presses. "Come on, you need to start."

Good God. Plant Day sucks.

"Follow me, okay?" she says.

I shadow her, sprinkling the seedlings with drops of water until I learn the chant that empowers the plants with magic by heart.

"Skies above and sun most bright, hear my pleas."
"Cast the light and nourishment upon this soil."
"Feed it with your light."
"Moisten it with your waters."
"Embrace it with your life."
"Nurture the young."
"So it may age and feed us in return."
"Harvesting our magic, and giving me power."
"Power," we all repeat. "Give me power."

The whole thing wouldn't be so bad. But each time the Lessers return with more water, I hear more about Vieve and her "boyfriend", her "lover", and my personal favorite, "the wolf who rocks her world".

"Do you think he's the one?"
"Oh, he has to be, they're practically inseparable."

I stop over a particularly large snapdragon, only for it to latch onto my skirt and tug it insistently. I toss water on it, trying to tame it. It gulps it down like it's thirsty so I give it more, chanting like a maniac. But the little bastard spits it back out at me.

I wipe the water and what can only be plant puke off my face. This doesn't seem to faze Paula. She urges me ahead. "Keep going. They're testy for some reason."

The bud pulls up and down, stretching and shrinking its stem, appearing to laugh and mock me.

I continue to sprinkle water. At least, I try.

"Has Sister Genevieve's boyfriend claimed her?" someone asks, giggling as she stops to remove a pebble from her shoe.

"Oh, I'm sure he has," another says. "Lesser Maris says she heard them in her room one night."

"Claim? How is that done?" a Lesser about eighteen asks. The others laugh. "I'm serious," she says, blushing. "I know it's an intimate act, but I don't know much about it."

My head pounds in dull strikes, making it hard to focus. Don't go there . . .

"It's the most intimate of acts between *weres* and their

loves," another says. She strokes the sweat glistening from her dark skin. "During their lovemaking there's an exchange of sacred words where the *were* asks his mate to be his and takes her in return."

"What are the words?" the younger witch asks.

I don't need to ask. I know them well. And before I can somehow stop it, Gemini's voice echoes these same words in my head.

"Do you want me?" he asked.

"Yes," I whispered.

"May I take you?" he begged.

"Yes," I answered, speaking breathlessly.

"Then you're mine, forever," he promised.

But forever didn't last as long as we'd thought. I move on to the next seedling and sprinkle it with water. I mumble words that don't make sense, hoping the others don't notice my inability to concentrate, and doing my best to ignore what comes next.

The one sharing the low-down on the mating practices of *weres* removes her bonnet, using it to dab her face. "I think the words vary, but it's not something they share since it's private, an exchange of vows of sorts since once the claiming is done, they're considered married."

"So they're married?" someone else says. "Sister Genevieve *married* him?"

I grimace as the Lesser replaces her bonnet. "No one has said for sure. But according to *were* customs, if he claimed her they are." She laughs. "At the very least, they're having a good time."

"I bet they are," another says, making most of them giggle.

I'm trying not to let it get to me, really I am. But it's getting to me, and I'm not alone.

The snapdragons start sprouting more teeth. Long teeth. Jagged, long teeth.

I jump when one nips at my ankles. "What the hell?" I ask, smacking at the leaf when it stretches several feet to reach me.

"Taran, don't!" Paula calls.

The leaves from the seedling shoot up, snagging my calves and making me trip. I fall, spilling my water as someone screams.

I don't dare look in the direction of the scream, or the next one that follows. The water starts snaking along the rows, thickening and taking a serpentine form. At the far end of its very long body, a head lifts, glancing over its back to hiss.

Droplets of water drip from its fangs, and beneath my chin the tail lifts and rattles.

Chapter Fifteen

Fuck. Me.

Literal water snakes, lots of them, some in shapes of anacondas and others more like boa constrictors, slither from buckets at lightning speed. They fall into clear sloshing mounds at the buckled feet of the screeching Lessers.

I roll out of the way as the first one lunges. The witch who spoke of the claim isn't as fast. She tumbles backward when the snake slams into her chest and sends her sprawling on top of a row of snapping plants. And good Lord, doesn't that piss off the seedlings.

The seedlings attack the snakes, and us, biting anything that gets too close. I haul Paula, who is ready to mess her bloomers, and drag her along the rows.

The Lessers smack at the plants biting them, kick at the watery snakes attacking them, while I do the same, swearing like my verbiage of four-letter words can somehow reverse it.

"Taran, stop," Paula urges, tugging on my arm. "Your emotions are upsetting the plants, and the water, and...and nature."

I think she's exaggerating until our instructor, Superior Wilma, busts through the row of trees, the gem on her spider-like talisman emitting a bright light that paints the entire garden red. "What's the meaning of this?"

At least, I think that's what she meant to say. Evidently, red is not the color to shine upon the world when nature is angry. The white fir with overhanging branches snatches her up by the ankles, and *damn*, evidently some witches don't wear panties beneath dem dresses.

The fir branches toss her into the reaching branches of a cedar tree, and then to a sugar pine, and then to a different tree until she looks like Tarzan swinging on a vine, only not as graceful, or swoon-worthy, and definitely not by choice. Superior Wilma is screaming. Everyone is screaming, even the fucking seedlings.

The plants, and the snakes, and by now everything around us that doesn't like all the noise, reacts. Vines from the forest creep forward, snagging my legs and dragging me away. I'm hauled backwards as a cluster of water snakes gives chase, hissing as they open their maws.

Anger, fear, and pain tear through my veins, sparking that familiar tingle of electrical current from my zombie arm.

The bind strapped along my arm tightens, trying to squelch the building magic. It digs into my skin, adding to the pain as the vines cocoon my legs and waist.

My arm retaliates, jerking wildly as it builds the current. Maybe it should give me hope—make me think I actually stand a chance against what's coming. But I have no control. This arm is going to do what it wants, and right now, it wants to kick ass.

Like a building tsunami reaching its peak, my arm fights back. It involuntarily lifts, smashing against the earth and charging the air and ground with bolts of lightning. The waves of energy build, crackling against my skin. I can't contain it. Nor can I halt my screams when the first snake reaches me and clamps down on my arm.

Agony rips through me as a buzzing sound fills my ears, the crescendo swelling until a supersized current of lightning detonates from my arm and sends me soaring backwards.

When my sisters and I were very little, my parents

took us to see fireworks. They lit up the sky in pretty sparks of pink, yellow, and purple, followed by extra bright shots of white that seemed to fire across the universe. What happens, reminds me of those fireworks, except that this time around, there are no pretty pastels, only ass-beating blue and enough white to blind.

I land in a rather graceless mess of limbs, watching in helpless terror as the lightning bolt passes through the watery snakes, and rows of plants and bodies, zapping everything in its path.

I open my mouth to shout a warning, only for the field to explode like an overcharged light bulb. My legs shoot over my head. I roll several feet, stopping with the hem of my sizzling skirt over my head.

For a long moment, I don't move. My knees rest on either side of my ears and I'm pretty sure I blew my shoes to smithereens. But then the passing breeze skimming along my exposed butt cheeks gently prods me to act, reminding me that maybe, just maybe, this isn't my best look. Yet it's like every bone in my body is stiff, angry, and refusing to cooperate. I don't so much as lower myself as much as kick out my feet and pitch onto my back.

A whine has me pushing up my arms and shoving down the layers of cotton over my pink and rather fricasseed panties. I glance up as a midnight black wolf with a white left paw sniffs at my head. My bonnet, what's left of it, dangles from my neck.

The wolf sneezes when he gets an extra snout filled with what I'm guessing is burnt hair. I know who he is, which only adds to my mortification. He whines again, nudging me with his cold wet nose.

"I'm okay," I stammer, my words releasing in short, electrified bursts.

This half of Gemini has always been the sweetest and most gentle. But as I reach to pet his large head, his whines turned pained. His long tongue frantically passes along my zombie arm, much like wolves do in the wild when *they're* hurt and it's *their* injury they're tending to.

But it's mine . . .

"Don't," I say, stroking his head with my opposite arm. "I'm all right." His sad eyes meet mine, the torment behind his stare a physical force that cements me to the ground. He bows his head, his long thick tail sagging as he returns to where his human half waits.

Gemini, shirtless, stands by Genevieve in the mud-soaked mess the field has become. The seedlings crawl away from their holes, their roots pushing them toward Vieve like she alone (of course) can save them. But Gemini isn't watching the plants, the trees resuming their majestic stances, or the tangles of ivy and vines slinking back into the forest. He's not even watching Vieve as her hair and the skirt of her lovely dress flow ethereally around her. He's watching me as I lay in the mud, his dark expression heavy with concern.

His twin wolf gives me one last glance and one more whine before leaping into Gemini's back, his large form disappearing deep within his being. Yet the moment they connect, it's like all the sadness his wolf demonstrated paints across Gemini's handsome features.

The Lessers gasp in awe of the merge, and maybe with a little lust too, despite how everyone looks about as sexy as I do. They're oblivious to his sorrow, but I'm not. Maybe because I'm feeling it, too.

Gemini doesn't notice their reaction. He stalks toward me as I push from the mud on legs that refuse to fully straighten.

"How are you?" he asks when he reaches me.

"Great," I say.

"How are you really?" he asks, his tone straddling that line between beast and man.

I lift my chin as much as I can without losing my balance. "About as good as you are," I reply.

He mutters a swear, abruptly averting his gaze. I don't know what to interpret from his response, anger, hostility, frustration? Is it torment? That's what I'm feeling.

I can't bring myself to ask, just like I can't bring myself to wrap my arms around him. So I limp toward the rest of the group because that much I can manage without breaking down.

His wolf was upset and desperate to care for what he thought was a wound. But the man he's a part of . . . Jesus, I can't even begin to guess what he's feeling.

My fists clench at my sides. I don't want to think about how easily I once settled both the man and wolves within him by simply touching him and whispering gentle words that carried my love. But thoughts of the past easily invade what I feel in the present, making those steps I need to take so much harder.

I force my attention ahead, toward where a Superior witch with a machete chops at the vines fastened around our instructor's ankles. I'll say this, if anyone knows how to make a lasting first impression it's me.

I ignore the jolt I earn when I step into one of the puddles, staggering forward and pretending I didn't feel the zing shoot across my molars as I straighten.

Paula inches to my left. I motion to where our instructor remains dangling and panty-less. "Is Betty all right?" I ask.

"Wilma," she whispers, trying to tame the red afro her hair has become.

I grimace. "Sorry," I mutter at the same time my arm involuntarily jerks.

Without turning to look, I feel Vieve approach, and Gemini, too, because I don't have enough of an audience. After another two whacks of the machete, Superior Wilma lands as ungracefully as she swung at my feet.

"Here, let me help you," I offer, extending my hand.

She, I shit you not, crab crawls away from my hand like it's ready to bite, her eyes wild. I'm new at this gig, but I'm pretty sure my first day fiasco has earned me another demerit or two.

Yet she doesn't mention it. Vieve, conversely, has plenty to say.

"I suspect our plants didn't react well to your presence, Lesser Taran," she begins, her arm passing elegantly along the seedlings tugging on her skirt.

"What was your first clue?" I ask, forcing a smile as the seedlings, Lessers, and air continue to snap, crackle, and pop with static around me.

Gemini groans, pinching the bridge of his nose.

Vieve, bless her perfect looks and mannerisms, maintains her smile. "I had several clues, Taran, including: turning our beloved earth against your instructor, electrocuting your peers and plants with lightning, infuriating the elements, and pretty much soiling and destroying one of our most sacred and beloved tasks. I'm afraid you need more help than I could have ever predicted." Her smile dwindles in true "poor pathetic you" status as what I think is supposed to pass for empathy fills her stare. "But don't fret," she adds, placing her hand on Gemini's shoulder and giving it a rather suggestive squeeze. *"We're* here to help you, despite your limitations, struggles, and mounting imperfections."

"Mounting imperfections?" I repeat.

"Yes," she says, glancing toward Gemini as she drops her hand away. "I fear you possess more flaws than any of us could have predicted."

Worry and fear spread along Gemini's darkening features. Vieve gives his shoulder another squeeze, whispering something I don't quite hear.

"Thank you," he mouths as he turns to regard her.

They're having a moment, here and now, not caring who's present. I see it, and so does everyone else.

The Lessers closest to me gush, despite the mud coating their faces, their tattered pilgrim wear, and the frizz their hair has become.

Vieve grins up at him, as if only he matters.

It takes all I have not to punch her in her perfect teeth.

Chapter Sixteen

Someone is pounding on my bedroom door.

At least, that's what I think is happening. My face is buried in my pillow and my limbs are spread lifelessly around me, except for my zombie arm. It's buzzing because I suppose it's bored, pissed it's being restrained, or in need of attention.

I ignore the buzz and the pounding, immediately returning to sleep.

More pounding, hours later. Or least, it feels like hours.

"Taran?"

"Yeah?" I mumble.

"It's Celia."

"Who?"

"Celia," she insists.

"Who?"

"Your sister," she pauses. "The one with the fangs and claws."

"Oh." I roll over, certain it's to my death. That's what it feels like. I don't ever remember being so tired on so many levels. "Come in," I say. At least I think I do.

"She said come in," Celia says.

"Are you sure?" Shayna asks. "It sounded like she said, 'fuck off'."

"No, she said that at around ten," Emme responds, lightly.

I'm pretty cranky on minimal sleep. That doesn't stop me from feeling bad about what I said, even though I'm not entirely shocked I said it. My exhaustion, however, overtakes my guilt.

My lids fall closed again. I hear my sisters walk in, followed by some shuffling sounds. "No, honey. Not here," Emme says. "The bathroom, sweetie. You have to take it into the bathroom."

"Ergh?"

"Alice, no, dude. In the bathroom," Shayna urges. "You have to eat that in the bathtub. Yes, that's it. Good job."

The door to my bathroom shuts. "See. She's getting better," Shayna insists.

A sickening crunch has my eyes opening. I groan. "What is she eating?" I ask in time to see Celia growing pale.

"Woodchuck," Emme says, glancing at Celia when she covers her ears. "Bren was nice enough to bring it over after lunch."

"Lunch?" I ask, I try to shove myself into a sitting position, yet don't quite manage. I remember getting up to use the bathroom earlier, but not much more than that. My body slumps, surrendering to my fatigue. One by one, my sisters position themselves along my bed.

"What time is it?" I mutter.

"Almost two," Shayna answers. She hooks her thumb in the direction of the bathroom. "Ordinarily the wolves take Alice to eat in the woods, but she hasn't eaten in days and the poor thing has been falling apart. Just this morning she lost another foot in the kitchen and we found her kneecap in the laundry room."

"Why won't she eat?" I ask, doing my best to sit up.

"She refuses to eat without you here," Emme says. "She needs you. You're her person."

Poor Alice. My sisters have kept her company, but based on the ravished sounds of the next few chews, it hasn't been enough. She's famished, having clearly starved herself.

"What happened this week?" Celia asks. "You haven't been home until after midnight and leave before any of us are awake."

"It's been a rough first week," I add. Without meaning to, my focus falls to where her tight black tank-top hugs her tiny belly. There's been no change to her pregnancy, and no growth. In fact, she's still wearing her skinny jeans. I don't want to complain, despite what I went through. It seems petty compared to the stress she and Aric must be enduring.

"That's what we figured," she says. She didn't notice where my attention fell, ramming her eyes shut when we hear more munching.

All is quiet in the house. Too quiet. "Where are the wolves?" I ask. Aric and Celia have been practically inseparable. As pureblood and Leader to his kind, he has multiple duties and responsibilities. But since Celia's pregnancy, he organizes and manages the Pack from home, refusing to leave her. The rare times he's needed in person, Celia accompanies him to the Den. It's odd not to see him with her.

Celia's face gathers that edge it does when something wicked this way cometh. "The witches charged with finding Savana have been missing for the last few days. Aric and Koda put a search party together, but are organizing and strategizing from the Den due to the multiple teams involved and because of the large area their *weres* are covering." She pauses. "Bren's leading the hunt. They arrived in the Appalachian Mountains late Thursday morning."

"Why Bren?" I ask. As a former *lone*, his pack mates don't hold him in the same regard as they do the rest, not that Bren gives a shit what they think.

"He has the best nose in the Pack," Emme adds quietly. The way she dips her chin and averts her gaze tell me she's worried. I can't blame her, seeing how the last set of witches were supposed to be top notch on the supernatural ladder.

"Genevieve didn't want the Pack involved," Celia adds. "But Aric isn't giving her a choice since her witches have failed to phone in."

"I see," I reply. This isn't a good sign. If they're missing, and there's been no sign of them, chances are they'll need a good nose to find what's left of them. I huff. That is, once Savana finishes sacrificing them to her deity.

"So what happened this week, T?" Shayna asks. "Any luck with getting your arm to behave?"

"Not really," I admit, not wanting to say too much.

I fold my hands over my lap. Somehow I managed a shower before I crawled into bed and put on my favorite pajamas, a silky burgundy set I knew I'd sleep comfy in. It's Saturday, my first day off in what seems like too long.

"Taran . . ." Emme begins. "What happened to your hair?"

My hands pass over some of the dwindling chunks. A piece breaks off and I set it aside. If my hair wasn't as long as it is, I'd be left with random sections along my shoulders. I blink up at the light blue and white tiers that make up my ceiling, not wanting to discuss my experience, but knowing I have to. "I electrocuted myself."

"Um. How?" Celia asks.

"I pissed off the water I was supposed to be using to nourish the snapdragons." I shrug. "It spilled and turned into some kind of watery rattlesnake. There were anacondas, cobras, and boa constrictors, too, slithering out of everyone's buckets. But for some reason the rattlesnakes came after me."

"You pissed off *water*?" Celia asks.

I'll admit, that's a new one even for me. "Yup. The witches were attacked and they bit me—"

"The witches bit you?" Shayna asks, her ponytail whipping to the side when she gapes at Celia.

"No," I begin.

"She means the snakes, I think," Emme offers, her fair-freckled skin blushing on my behalf.

"That too, but also the snapdragons," I admit.

"The snapdragons bit you?" Celia asks, her husky voice reflecting their collective shock. "As in those pretty flowery plants?"

"Oh, yes," I say, nodding. "Because in the witch world, plants have perpetual PMS, and teeth, and will come after your ass if you don't water them correctly."

"Dude!" Shayna says, hardly believing it.

And she's clearly not alone. "I'm sorry. I think I misunderstood something," Celia says, holding out her hand. "You're telling me you were gnawed on by an army of angry flowers after the water from your buckets turned into snakes and attacked you and your cohorts?"

"Yeah, that about sums it up. The best part was when nature, *freaking nature*, turned against me," I add.

Emme, who had been covering her mouth in stupefied horror slowly lowers her hand, revealing her bright pink face. "What-what," she takes a breath. "What happens when nature turns against you?"

Her tone implies that she's afraid to ask, but I'm no longer afraid to tell. Funny thing about humiliation, after a few days, it's like you have to talk about it and lay it all out there. "Vines and ivy wrap themselves around you and drag you screaming back into the woods." I shake my head, remembering Wilma. "Unless you're an instructor, in which case, you're seen as more of a threat and more royally screwed. Tree branches latch onto your ankles and toss you around like they're playing badminton or some shit."

I sigh, rubbing my face. "The field was basically destroyed so in addition to attending the other classes, me and the Lessers in my group spent the entire week rebuilding it and tending to the PTSD inflicted plants that survived my supernatural meltdown. My only saving grace was that it happened to be the smallest field on the compound. Otherwise, I'd still be there and so would my peers." I look at them. "Still, you can imagine how many popularity points I earned with that debacle."

"But this can't be your fault," Celia says. "Can it?"

"It is because the funny thing about chanting and cultivating and all the magic swirling Vieve's compound. It responds to your emotions, all of them. If it's positive, the plants will grow and thrive. If it's negative, you get your ass kicked."

"Which caused your arm to freak out," Celia finishes for me.

"Yeah. Hence all the lightning, electrocution, and overall mass destruction," I mutter.

Shayna puckers her brow, watching me closely. "T . . . what made you so mad?"

"I wasn't exactly mad," I say.

"You weren't?" Emme asks carefully. "It sounds like you must have been furious."

I wasn't angry. I'm still not and that's the truth. Anger was there, but the overwhelming emotion was hurt. I don't admit as much, but my sisters understand when I explain. "Gemini spends a lot a time with Vieve. The witches call him her 'boyfriend' and 'lover' among other things."

Emme bites down on her bottom lip as Shayna reaches for my hand. Celia, true to her inner tigress meets me with the anger I deny myself. "When you say other things, what does that mean exactly?"

I let out a breath. Plant Day was awful, embarrassing, and physically painful with plenty of scratches and bruises to show for it. But it didn't compare to what I felt seeing how close Gemini and Vieve have become.

"Taran?" Celia says, blinking her tigress eyes away.

I tuck my knees against me, staring toward my large picture window despite that the blinds are drawn. "He's supposedly claimed her, and she's his new mate," I say, my voice growing distant.

"*What*?" she asks, her tone morphing into a growl.

"That's not possible," Shayna says, frowning. "You're his mate. Not Genevieve. You only get one, T."

"It's what they tell us," I say. "But you didn't hear what everyone was saying about them, and you didn't see them together. There's something between them."

"They work together," Emme says, her focus trailing to Celia. "Isn't that right? He's the liaison between the Pack and the coven. He's only there doing his job."

"This isn't just a working relationship. He means

more to her than that," I say, wishing it wasn't true.

"No," Celia says, her tone stern. "No way is this possible. Even if you severed your mate bond with him, it wouldn't change who you are to him."

Alice shuffles out from the bathroom, appearing distressed when she sees me. "Ergh?'

"I'm okay," I tell her, more because I need her to be. Christ, even after the woodchuck, she seems to be falling apart. Well, I suppose that makes two of us.

"Taran, I'm serious," Celia insists, refusing to let it go. "Look, I know what you're going through. I went through it with Aric when we were apart. All those females, throwing themselves at him, and our bond being broken like it was, I understand. You have to know that I do. But it didn't change his feelings for me. I remained his one true love and who he desired."

"What if you're wrong?" I ask, edging closer to her. "Aric is one wolf. With one beast. Gemini has two. Can that other half choose another mate? Because I'll be honest, that's what it looks like to me."

She tightens her mouth and doesn't initially answer. "That can't happen," she tells me. "He and his beasts only know you."

My eyes sting even though I'm fighting not to cry. "You don't know that," I say, the way my voice cracks causing an immediate silence. "Even his wolves return to where he stands beside Vieve."

Alice pats my back, appearing sad. "Ergh.'"

"It's all right, girl," I tell her.

"It's really not," Celia says, anger clipping her tone. She rises. "I'm calling Aric and straightening this out."

"Don't," I insist, snagging her wrist. "I'm serious, Ceel. I can't handle it if it's true. I can't handle much more."

My head falls into my hands as my sisters gather around and embrace me. They don't say anything, they're just there. But they always have been . . .

I don't cry, but it's like the tears I don't shed flow through my bloodstream, my body mourning the death of something I never should have allowed. I was never that person picking out her china or envisioning the perfect dress to wear on her big day. I never dreamed of that one guy. Then I met him, and everything changed.

Gemini's loss causes me so much grief I should cry, and fall apart. But damn it, I'm so tired of being weak and rejected based on what my body has become. So there aren't any tears. There's only my sisters holding me, assuring me that they aren't going anywhere. Except seeing how my experience with the witches has gone, and how my arm continues to react in spite of Vieve's bind, I can't be sure I'll be there for them. Or how much longer I'll survive.

So instead of pushing them away, and insisting I'll be fine, I give into their embrace, and their love.

I hear Alice shuffle away and back into the bathroom, followed by the sound of water turning on and what appears to be scrubbing. Lots and lots of scrubbing.

I lift my head. "Is Alice brushing her teeth?"

My sisters edge away and Emme exchanges glances with Shayna. "We'll get you a new toothbrush," she offers.

"Seriously?" I ask, not wanting to think too much of what Alice is scraping off her teeth, and thankful I brushed my teeth when I used the bathroom earlier.

"We had to teach her, T," Shayna says. "She can't afford to lose anymore." Something clinks against the sink, making her wince. "I'll fish it out before you go in there," she offers.

I rise, my stomach churning. Now is not the time to picture what's waiting for me in the bathroom or if it's going to try to crawl its way back in Alice's mouth.

"I think I should take her out," I tell them, sounding as nauseous as I feel.

"Hmm," Celia says, trying to agree, but growing pale again.

"You're going out?" Emme asks.

"I think it's best." I shove myself into the only pair of sweats I own. "Alice needs more ah, nourishment," I add. "Nourishment" sounds better than "decaying critters", but

Ceel's bleaching pallor makes me think my choice of words didn't help much. "I'll take her for a walk out back, maybe she can find something."

"Are you okay to go out by yourself?" Emme asks. "You haven't eaten all day."

"I need to clear my head," I admit. "I'll grab something when we get back." I zip up my hoodie and shove my feet into my sneakers by the door. "Hey, Alice. You hungry, girl? Want to go grab a bite outside?"

Like the sound of the dinner bell, she takes off, fast. I steal a glance at my sisters. "Alice?" I call, walking quickly. The door leading out to the deck slams open, turning my urgent pace into a run.

I bolt outside and to the edge of the railing, scanning the backyard before racing down the steps. Shayna grounds to a stop beside me as I reach the area where our lawn ends and the forest begins.

"Did you see her run in there?" she asks.

"No," I say, whipping around. "I don't know where she is."

Emme's screams from the front of the house have us tearing across the front lawn. Celia is sitting against the side of the house with her head between her knees.

"Ceel, what's wrong?" I ask.

She makes this funky motion with her hand toward Mrs. Mancuso's front lawn. Emme is bouncing in place and pointing to what remains of Mrs. Mancuso's flowerbed. Dirt and flowers are scattered all over the place. I don't know what's happening until I see Alice's feet sticking out from the hole.

"Oh, *gawd*," I say.

"What is she—"

Shayna covers her mouth, gasping. Emme yells, confirming our fears, "She's eating Ginger!"

Because my life doesn't suck enough, my zombie familiar is digging up my evil neighbor's dead dog for dinner.

"Son of a bitch. Alice, *Alice!*"

"I don't feel right," Celia says. Her face is soaked, but

instead of being pale, her cheeks are flushed.

"Get her inside," I tell Shayna, shoving her toward Celia.

She starts to motion to where the chowtime is taking place until she gets a good look at Celia. Carrying a bit of Koda's essence gives Shayna some strength. It's not a lot, but it's enough to lift Celia to her feet and bear most of her weight.

"Come on, Ceel," she says, the smell and everything is probably too much for all your hormones and preggy self."

I don't get a good whiff of that smell until I reach Emme. "Oh, man," I mumble, the smell of death smacking hard against my nose. Yet it's the crunching and slopping sounds that almost make me go horizontal. "Alice, leave it," I say. "Leave it!"

Like a dog who doesn't want to let go of her bone, Alice starts eating faster. "God damn it," I say, snagging her ankles.

"What are you doing?" Emme asks, who looks about as healthy as I feel.

I tug harder, glancing toward Mrs. Mancuso's house. "Trying to get her out of here before Mancuso sees her."

Emme points to the hole, gagging. "She's still eating."

I cringe. Good Lord, it's like Cookie Monster found a bag of chocolate chip goodness. Only it's not Cookie Monster, and for sure not cookies. I pull harder, managing to drag Alice out. "Emme, get Ginger."

She shakes out her hands. "I can't."

"Use your *force*," I say, jerking my head away when I realize Alice is gripping some sort of appendage.

"I'll still feel Ginger, even if I do!" she says, shaking her hands out harder.

I drop Alice on the ground, stepping over her and her meal. "Should we just let her finish?" I ask, keeping my full attention on Emme and not the horrific gobbling sounds taking place behind me.

She sways back and forth. "It looks like, like . . ." She bends forward, coughing and gripping her knees. I'm sure she's going to be sick. "It looks like she's had her fill," she says, somehow finishing and keeping her lunch where it belongs.

Like a happy and very satisfied puppy, Alice hobbles to my side. I don't look at her, because right now, I can't. "Emme, why don't you take Alice into the basement bathroom and help tidy her up?"

Emme's stare cuts to where Alice waits. "Taran, she's going to need a lot more than that."

"Okay," I say, trying to avoid visualizing what she must look like. "Then just see what you can do. I'll clean up here."

She nods, barely managing that much. "Go with Emme, Alice," I say, trying not too hard to look at her.

Thankfully, she doesn't argue. "Ergh," she happily agrees.

My shoulders slump and I groan when I see the chunks of leftover Ginger and the remains of Mrs. Mancuso's flowerbed. But Emme, being Emme, doesn't leave me hanging. Lumps of things that will forever haunt my dreams skim along the grass and back into the hole.

I run to get a rake and a shovel from the shed and go to town. Following the week I've had, I've pretty much accepted I don't have a green thumb. So instead of trying to replant all the flowers, I start shoving everything back into the hole, hoping Mancuso will think some stray dug up her stuff. I think I stand a chance, and that I might actually pull this off, until something hard smacks me across the face.

I land sprawled on my back, blinking back the dirt coating my eyes. Above me, Mrs. Mancuso is glaring, her giant broom gripped tight in her hands. I didn't even hear her approach. For someone as old as the dirt pile I'm lying on, she's unbelievably stealthy.

"You dirty tramp!" she spits out.

"I know what this looks like," I begin.

She doesn't exactly let me finish, smacking me across the face again with the broom. I roll away from her, but Mrs. Mancuso is no longer just my wicked neighbor from the

Planet Bitch. She's a hellion bent on making me bleed.

She repeatedly nails me in the head, each strike more vicious than the next. "Damn it, woman. It wasn't me!"

She doesn't care, hitting me harder as she chases me around the yard. Like some dumb blonde from a really bad horror movie, I trip more than once. But instead of some scary monster giving chase, Mancuso runs behind me, her freakish ability and desire to kill me, ignoring the years marching across her veiny legs.

"Knock it off. I didn't do it!" I insist.

I half run, half-stumble to the sliding glass doors leading out from the basement, hoping Emme left them open when she brought Alice inside.

I'm covering my head and breathing hard, trying to speak the magical word that releases the wards guarding the house."*Pace. Pace.* Shit. *Pace,* damn it!"

Either I don't say the word right in my haste, or the spell doesn't recognize my voice between my shrieks of pain.

I whip around when Mancuso gives me an extra hard whack, snagging the broom by the handle and pulling it hard.

She falls on her knees, crying.

"Oh, my God," I gasp. I didn't mean for her to fall. "Are you all right?" She doesn't answer, sobbing. I toss the broom aside and clasp her shoulder. "Mrs. Mancuso? Can you hear me? I need to know if you're all right."

"You hit an old woman," she wails.

Her face is buried in her hands, her chest and shoulders heaving with how hard she's crying.

For the first time since I've known her, Mrs. Mancuso doesn't resemble the Wicked Witch from Dollar Point. She's not angry, or bitter, or even slightly strong. She's broken, a frail old lady who's now hurt. I crouch beside her, thinking she made need an ambulance.

"I'm so sorry," I say. "I didn't mean to make you fall."

She lifts her head. There are no tears, no proof of pain. But there is a whole lot of bitch. She picks up a large rock near her feet and nails me across the shin with it.

Sharp pain shoots up my spine and into my skull, making me see double and knocking me on my ass. I wrench up, using the side of the house to balance and limp away as fast as I can.

I drag my leg as I hop up the deck stairs, falling forward when I reach the door leading into the kitchen. "*Pace,*" I yell, realizing Mrs. Mancuso is almost to the top of the steps. "For fuck's sake, *pace!*"

The wards hum, allowing me through. I yank the door open, slamming it shut and locking it. I turn, hoping she's not there.

Like a scene from a creepy and twisted horror flick, a stiff, wrinkled middle finger presses against the glass, sliding past me as the evil it belongs to heads toward the flight of stairs.

I sag against the counter. "This day can't get any worse."

I should know better than to say what I do. But the words slip out anyway as Shayna shoots down the steps. "Taran, something's wrong with Celia."

Chapter Seventeen

I ignore the lingering pain and run toward the rear staircase behind Shayna. "Call Aric," I yell.

"I did, he's on his way."

We move fast, reaching the next level. "Where's Emme?"

"She's with Ceel now." She turns around so quick, I almost crash into her, fear skimming her features. "Ceel won't let her near her."

"What?" I glance down the hall toward her and Aric's room. "But Emme can heal her, help her."

She shakes her head slowly. "I'm not sure if she can, T."

I push past her, running into the room without bothering to knock. Celia is sitting on her side of the bed, her legs dangling from the edge as she curls forward and into her belly. Emme is kneeling in front of her, her eyes glistening with tears.

"She won't let me touch her," she says.

I don't know how I get there, I'm just suddenly beside her. "What's wrong?"

Celia shakes her head slowly, her breaths are labored and it's like she can't speak. "Ceel," I say. "You have to tell us what's wrong so we can help you."

Again, she simply shakes her head.

"Jesus," I say, rising.

Alice is standing in the corner, watching her with curiosity and clearly not with the panic currently engulfing us. Shayna is in the bathroom running water. I think she's filling the tub and I rush in there to wash my hands and help her.

When I reach the sink, I realize she's filling a small basin. "She seems hot," she says, barely getting the words out. "Let's try and cool her off."

"Good idea," I say, drying my hands quickly and reaching for a stack of washcloths beneath the sink.

I touch her skin with the back of my hand when we run back into the bedroom. Celia is warm, and her face flushed a deep red. But the temperature seems off. It's not hot enough to gather perspiration along her brow, but that's what's happening.

Shayna's on her phone, speaking fast. "I need you guys to get here," she says. "Please, Koda. I need you here now."

"We're coming, baby," he says. "We're almost to you."

"Here. Lie down," I whisper, edging closer to ease Celia down.

"Don't move me," she says, her voice barely registering. "I'm all right."

"No, you're not," I say, fearing the worst.

My sisters and I are nurses by trade. Emme worked in Hospice, Shayna and Celia specialized in Labor and Delivery, and I worked in the Cardiac Catheterization Lab.

Celia retired from nursing when she decided to take a job kicking ass for the vamps. I took leave to get my arm and life together. We're seasoned nurses and good at our jobs. But right now, we're practically helpless.

I soak a washcloth and wring out the excess. "Ceel, you have to tell us what you're feeling." I run the washcloth along her forehead, patting her skin gently. "Are you in pain, does it hurt?"

She lifts her chin, her lids heavy what appears to be

exhaustion. "It's the baby," she whispers.

My hands fall away as tires screech to a stop in front of our house. I start to go numb as what sounds like an army storms into the house. The door is partly open, but the force Aric uses when he barrels through splinters the wood and breaks it from his hinges.

"Celia," he says, rushing to her. He moves fast, but when he gathers her to him, his motions are careful and gentle.

Her head falls against his shoulder, but she continues to cradle her belly.

"What happened?" he asks, his face and voice darkening with menace.

I back away, knowing I shouldn't be anywhere near Celia or Aric. And I'm not alone.

Koda links his arms around Shayna's waist, pulling her slowly and away from them. She starts to argue, but Koda cuts her off, whispering low in her ear. "Stay away from him, baby," he says. "With his mate hurting, his beast is unpredictable."

Emme is the only one able to draw near. Be it her gentle nature or her ability to heal, Aric allows her to close in. But I see, no, *feel*, Aric's beast charging to the surface. My vision clears as his power and Pack magic overtake the room.

My back presses against a very large front. I know who he is, even before his strong arms slink around my waist and he pulls me closer, guiding me in the direction of the door.

"Don't fight me," Gemini rasps when I tense against him, his breath teasing the sensitive skin along my neck. "Let me keep you safe from harm."

I want to break his hold, insist he leave and not touch me. But God, I'm so scared for my sister and her baby, I need him here. Even if it's only for this moment.

Emme reaches for Celia's hands. Celia moves them away from her, but keeps them against her belly.

"Sweetness, please," Aric begs. "Let Emme help you."

Celia shakes her head. "It doesn't hurt," she says. With what seems to be a great deal of effort, she pulls her stretchy black shirt up to her chest. She takes Aric's hands, covering them with hers and gliding them over her tiny baby bump.

Yellow light, so pale in color it's almost white, permeates from her skin, surrounding her belly like a halo.

As we watch in stunned silence, Celia's stomach begins to grow. It's slow, subtle, increasing her breaths, but it's there. Her baby is growing beneath her skin.

Emme edges away to stand near Shayna and Koda. Aric's eyes are wide, and his body so still, I can't be sure he's breathing—or if any of us are. But Celia is breathing hard enough for all of us.

I don't know much about pregnancy, just what I learned in nursing school, and what Celia and Shayna discussed. But Celia barely looked pregnant before. If I didn't know her like I did, I wouldn't suspect she was pregnant at all. Now, there's no doubt. I'm not sure how far along she is, but it's clear there's a baby thriving inside of her.

I'm in awe, we all are. Emme and Shayna are gaping, and fighting the start of happy tears. But then something happens that none of us could predicted, and I swear, I don't think I've ever seen anything more beautiful.

A tiny bump, like a fist, passes beneath the skin of Celia's belly, pushing across until it disappears under Aric's hand. Aric freezes, completely awestruck.

Celia smiles softly, despite how she seems seconds from collapsing. "You know who your daddy is. Don't you, little one?" she asks.

I'm certain my sisters and I will cry first. But it's Aric's eyes that brim with tears. "I can feel him," he says quietly. "He's moving."

Celia rests her head against him. Aric's other hand cups her cheek and he kisses her gently. "Are you all right?" he asks, a mix of fear and wonder, seeping into his voice.

"Yes. Just tired," she responds.

"Did it hurt?" he asks.

"No," she says, although I'm straining to hear her. "It feels like a good stretch following a very long run." She laughs a little. "A very, very long run."

We wait, none of us daring to move until she speaks again. "He's growing," she says. "He's going to be okay." She pauses like it's taking all she has to stay awake. "I need to sleep."

"Not eat?" Aric asks. "It looks like he took a lot out of you to grow."

I do a double take when I realize how much thinner Celia is. "Sleep first," she mumbles.

I don't think she quite finishes before she falls soundly asleep. Aric lowers her to the bed, positioning himself so he lies with her tucked against him.

Emme, Shaya, and Koda pile out. I trail them, but when they gather along the hall, I keep going, down the steps and into the kitchen. I wash my hands again, drying them quickly so I can rummage through the fridge and see what we have.

"What are you doing?" Gemini asks. He's leaning against the doorway that leads to the rear steps, and to our laundry room and garage.

It shouldn't be so hard to form sentences around him. But given what just happened and my week with the coven, it's harder than it should be. "Celia is going to be ready to eat the moment she wakes up. I'm seeing what I can make her."

"Don't," he says. "Let Aric do it."

I lift my brows. "Aric can't cook, remember? Unless you count those grilled cheese and bacon sandwiches he makes her." I shake my head, remembering how much muscle she seemed to lose in those moments it took her to grow her baby. "She's going to need more than that."

"He'll hunt for her," he says, motioning upstairs with a tilt of his head. "His primal side will compel him to provide for his mate and his wolf will demand blood."

"Nice," I say, giving him my back. It's always about blood and mayhem with this group.

I reach for a glass pitcher and fill it with ice water,

then start slicing cucumber and lime since I know Celia likes both in her water. But when Gemini comes up behind me, and his front presses against me like it did upstairs, I stop slicing, and moving, and functioning.

"I don't like you ignoring me," he says. "I want you with me, like you were upstairs."

I lower the knife in my hand, turning slowly to face him. "Upstairs, I was scared," I admit.

The knuckles of his hand run brush my left arm. "No, upstairs you needed me."

Warmth spreads from his touch and along my skin. "What about you?" I ask, my vulnerability peeking through. "Did you need me, too?"

"Yes," he responds, his tone reminding me of all the strength he carries as easily as he holds my heart.

"Oh."

I mean to say more, but I can't then. The intensity in his stare surges, so does his adoration. It melts me, pulling me closer. For a second I see the man I remember and love, the one who claimed me as his mate. But it's only for a second.

His dark stare falls to my zombie limb and it's like I can feel him struggling to stay in place.

Aric gives him a reason to turn away. He steps into the kitchen with Koda at his heels. He leans forward, gripping the edge of our granite counter so tight, I'm sure he's going to break the damn thing half. "I need to kill something," he says, looking up at me.

I take a few steps back. "Okay," I say, hoping it's not me.

"Will you stay with her?" he asks, his stare cutting between me and Gemini. "I can't leave her alone. Emme, Shayna, and Alice are upstairs, but . . ."

"I won't leave her, Aric," I tell him. "I promise."

He nods stiffly and slowly releases the counter. "Thank you."

I expect Gemini to give him the same assurance, but he doesn't say a thing, nor does Aric wait for it. Aric yanks off his shirt and so does Koda, stalking behind him and kicking out of his boots.

Wolves hunt in packs so I'm not surprised Koda is accompanying Aric, and I suppose, Aric needs a "wing man" given his current overly-protective and semi-psychotic state.

Yet I am surprised Gemini isn't joining them. These beasts are as close as I am to my sisters.

Aric opens the back door and steps out. I hear his denim jeans fall a few breaths before four paws thump across the deck and leap over the rail. Koda waits by the door, giving Aric a head start so he can make the first kill.

"Will you take care of it, all of it?" Koda asks Gemini.

"Yes. Aric is needed here. I'll speak on behalf of the Pack."

Koda tilts his head in thanks, but his glimpse my way gives away who Gemini will be speaking to.

"You're going to see Vieve, aren't you," I ask before my pride reminds me it's the last thing I should ask.

"I have to," he explains carefully. "Aric was going to, but he needs to be here and provide for Celia."

"Did something happen?" I ask. If Aric was meeting with the witches, instead of Gemini, something major went down.

"Bren and his team found the witches a few hours ago," he responds, barely blinking. "Out of respect for our roles in the supernatural world, Aric is obliged to share the news in person."

"Bren didn't find them alive. Did he?" I ask.

"No. He and his hunting party found the witches in pieces, their hearts missing." His already ominous stare darkens further. "Savana is getting stronger."

Chapter Eighteen

Anti-possession class.

Anti. Possession. Class.

I can do this.

Maybe.

Who am I kidding? This is bullshit.

Screams echo from down the hall, followed by a shriek that chills the ridges along my spine.

As one, the Lessers and I rise to our full height, a mix of shock, fear, and holy-shitness riddling our features . . . Except for the little brunette beside me who looks ready to puke.

In her defense, she doesn't puke. She does, however, take off in a mad dash, down the catacombs of halls that make up Vieve's basement.

"That's Tori," Paula whispers. "She was possessed last time."

"She was *possessed*?" I ask, trying not to shrill my words, but of course, not managing.

Paula nods. "And the time before that, and the time before that." She shakes her head. "The spirits of dead evil witches seem to like her."

"And demonic dogs," another points out.

"Oh! And that dead werehyena," a really tall Lesser

says. "Remember that creepy laugh?"

Paula shakes her head. "No, the creepy laugh belonged to the dead witch. The biting, *that* was the werehyena."

They start arguing among themselves. They stop arguing when the dungeon doors (because I'm sorry, that's what they resemble) are kicked open and a Lesser is dragged out by two Superiors struggling to keep her from clawing at her face.

"Get her to Sister Genevieve," our instructor Superior Nora calls from the door.

I hug the wall with my back, clutching the box of garlic in my arms as they drag the Lesser in our direction. Her completely white eyes fix on my stare as a forked tongue slithers out through her teeth.

"Popcorn. Motherfucker. Gum drops. Twizzlers. Ass wipe," she hisses in another-worldly voice that send the tiny hairs on my arm shrinking inward.

"Um," I say, knowing I'll never look at the movie theatre concession stand the same way again.

Like me, the other Lessers don't take to her presence well. They glance away as the poor possessed wanna-be witch is dragged away, lifting their boxes of garlic to shield their faces.

"Demon," Paula says. "Possibly from the third or fourth realm." She thinks about it. "Or maybe the fifth. I think I read the fifth was more chatty."

"Who cares where it's from?" Lesser Merri asks. "I'm ready to pee through seventeen layers of cotton here." She glances to where the witches disappeared. "I don't need this shit. I coulda been a lawyer."

"I'm sorry," Paula says. "I was just trying to help."

"We know what you were trying to do," the short Lesser near the door says, rolling her small green eyes.

Paula quiets, her stare falling to the ground. I've noticed a lot of Lessers don't like Paula, and consider her a know it all. They're not seeing what I'm seeing, that she's just as scared as the rest of us.

"Excuse me," I say, waving my hand and drawing the Tiny Green Eyes' attention. "I'm sorry. I don't think I caught your name."

"It's Cynthia," she answers, scowling. "*Cynthia Morton.*"

I put one hand on my hip and lean forward. "In that case, shut the fuck up, Cynthia Morton. We're all a little tense here."

She narrows her tiny and rather eerie green eyes, but keeps her mouth shut. I glare at her until she looks away first. It's a domination thing, something I learned from the wolves to demonstrate you won't be pushed around. Technically, I'm challenging her, and according to the rules, she has the right to challenge me to a magical duel. She doesn't though, and I think I might know why.

Something switched near the end of the Plant Day term. The plants began to crave my presence and thrive, tugging on my skirt for attention. Superior Wilma couldn't believe it, and tried to discredit me by moving me where some of the snapdragons were beginning to die. Somehow they didn't, coming back from the dead. It's not because my chants were any better or louder. But I noticed a change when I'd only feed them with my zombie arm and when I'd focus all my energy, positive *and* negative into the water cupped in my hand. They, I don't know, liked it. My guess is because like nature, the magic that created this appendage is as old as time.

The other thing that changed wasn't so good. The deaths of the witches hunting Savana had a profound effect across the coven. Some stepped up to hunt, furious over the loss of their sisters, but the underlying current is mourning and a quieter respect for life.

I turn to Paula and smile, even though I'd rather run back to my car when more screams erupt from room and something hard bangs against the door.

We exchange glances. "It looks like they're almost done," she says, when the screaming abruptly stops. "I think they banished them."

"Them?" the tall witch asks. "What do you mean

them?"

Paula makes a face. "We're technically a more advanced class. They'll call forth at least five entities to stalk and attempt to possess us."

I glance at my box. Some days, there's just not enough garlic in the world.

Mutterings fill the hall as people rummage through their supplies, shaking bottles of holy water to make sure they're filled to the brim and tugging on sacred necklaces. Unlike the Superior witches, and those who are more advanced in abilities, we haven't been given talismans, much less the stones that are supposed to amplify the magic within us. Maybe that's a good thing. At least where my magic is concerned.

I edge closer to Paula when she starts reciting the power words that help abolish malevolent spirits. "Does it help?" I ask.

She tosses her long red braid over her shoulder. "Does what help?"

"Going over facts in your head rather than taking in all the creepy shit we're in for?"

The fear everyone seems to be feeling reflects in her round features. "Not really," she says. "Power words or not, I'm terrified to walk in there. I didn't make it the last time around and asked to leave before the first demon took form."

"You can do that?" I ask. "I'm surprised more people don't."

"You can," she says. "But every time you refuse, you have to start the training from scratch." She makes a face. "Which is why me, along with a few others, are repeating our studies and taking so long to master our magic."

"I see," I reply. Hey, I'll be the first to admit I'm not excited about this crap. But my door number two is death by psycho limb.

Something else strikes the door. As we watch, the door slowly creeps open. Two Lessers walk out. The first one, with pinkish hair dangling in messy strands from her bonnet, leans heavily on her larger friend.

OF FLAME AND LIGHT

"It's okay, Linda," her friend says. "Maybe next year."

"What happened?" I ask.

The Lesser looks up. "A brain-eating demon broke through her wards at the last minute. It didn't possess her, or eat her brain, but she couldn't fight it off so she failed the assignment."

"So she has to do this again?" I ask, taking in her sickly and obviously traumatized condition.

The small Lesser bursts into tears. I want to hug her, tell her how messed up this is. Mostly, though, I want to get the hell out of here.

Paula takes me in. "How do you do it?" she asks.

"Do what?" I ask, because right now, all I want to do is follow the other Lessers out.

"Show no fear and all attitude. For one, you looked right at Lorraine, or whatever that thing possessing her was, like you weren't afraid. I mean, it stared right at you and barely flinched."

"Oh, I flinched," I confess.

"But you still looked at her." She stops as if unsure whether she should ask what she does. "Have you seen a lot of that?"

"Possessions? Thankfully, no," I add shuddering.

"I mean evil," she says slowly.

I smile, but I'll admit, it's not with a great deal of warmth. "Yeah, that I have."

"You may leave," Superior Nora's voice echoes from the room. "Congratulations to those who passed."

She doesn't quite finish her verbal pat on the back before the group inside runs out, as in tears down the hall like something with fangs is chasing them. Supposedly, there are some sort of sacred bath salts you're given following Anti-possession class. They're meant to cleanse you of what you saw, and what you experienced, and basically wash the remaining evil away.

My guess is, it's bath time, and these Lessers can't wait to lather up.

177

"Come on," I say, when no one moves. "It's show time."

I stomp into the room like I own it, because it beats cowering. I'm going to need all the courage I can muster because holy bats and broomsticks, this place doesn't simply house evil, it reeks of it. The aroma of brimstone spreads across the room, dusting the air and coating my tongue with its bitter taste.

I'll tell you this, witches *never* disappoint with this whole eye of newt vibe. The room is enchanted, making it resemble a dungeon King Henry would pop wood for, its magic stroking my arms like it owns me and I'm its damn cat.

Pavers in different shades of grey and black make up the floor and walls, marred by deep scratches and blood stains from either demons or the poor saps who didn't pass the class the first time around.

Very large, flat, brass rings, are fixed to the floor in random patterns, separated with only enough space to walk or stalk through. The rings are about an inch thick in width, scratched and dented from use, and charred as if burned to protect something within, or maybe keep something else out.

Up until this point, Anti-possession class was mostly a couple of weeks of self-study, mulling over words of power to help protect, and a great deal of mediation to strengthen focus. Superior Nora didn't actually teach. She more or less paced between the rows of desks, verbalizing how to put our strength behind each word, the importance of being focused, and what can happen if we fail. Did you know an evil being can draw from your worst memories and play them out like a damn puppet show, using your intestines in place of the strings?

Well, now you do.

I highlighted a few passages in our text here, took notes there, and practiced my words. But seeing what we did in the halls, and what I'm seeing now, a Power-point presentation, some crib notes, and maybe even a YouTube video could have helped.

"Take a place inside one of the circles," Superior Nora

calls, her voice ricocheting from all sides. I don't see her at first. Well, until she rises from the floor like an apparition.

Before she swooped into class, because turns out Nora can fly an actual broom, I thought she'd resemble, or at least dress to match the ambiance a class like this invokes: dark and mysterious with just the right amount of creepy and "help me, Jesus".

She wasn't what I expected, but it's actually a great thing. Long braids with silver beads sweep against her back, and instead of a crushed velvet gown, a white silk dress covers her shapely body and gives her dark skin a subtle glow. She's not the angel we need to save us, and she doesn't give out that ethereal feel Vieve does. But what does surround her is a strong feel of power and wrath I've never quite felt. When dealing with demons or whatever is planning to rise from the depths of hell, you want someone who can take them down.

I step into what I think is a random circle and place my box on the floor. As I straighten she smiles, appearing impressed. "Very well, Lesser Taran," she says. "You may go first."

I'm sure I misheard. "Um. What?"

I glance down when she does, it's then I notice the number one etched into the brass. I also notice that the rest of my class took circles closer to the door and further away from me. I'm ready to argue, but end up shutting my mouth for two reasons: I don't want to look stupid or scared, despite how I feel.

"To summon the dark is to risk your soul and those you most cherish," Superior Nora begins. She walks forward and in the small space between the circles, the train of her dress dragging along the dank floor yet somehow staying clean, pure. "But there are those who are willing to risk much more for power, gain, or fortune," she adds.

The Superior witches who dragged away poor possessed Tori return, taking point on either side of the door as it closes shut, their talismans flickering as they ready for what's to come.

The sound of the door closing against the frame and the bolts surrounding it clicking shut echo along the room and beyond. I blink toward the wall as it shakes in blurry waves, like it's under water. It's a reminder that everything isn't what it seems, and that the room extends beyond what we can see.

"To be possessed is to be weak of heart, magic, and strength. Do not permit this, young Lessers. Do not be weak in the face of darkness." She pauses. "When I call forth the dark ones, they shall be bound in chains and therefore bound in hell. They cannot fully leave or drag you back with them, but they can house themselves within your spirit and extend their time among us. Do *not* let them," she stresses, her tone sharpening and causing the clear stone around her neck to glisten. "The Power of Good may limit their time here, but in the time they have they can cause tremendous harm."

My hands lay at my sides, pooling with sweat the more Nora reminds me of what's coming. I have experience with the offspring of demons. I've seen them, fought them, and lay helplessly watching as they carried off my family. I hate them, but I also fear them in a way that can paralyze me.

"The strongest in hell may leave independently and sporadically," Nora continues, the reminder pushing the first drop of sweat to trickle down my moist fingers. "These are dark times we face. We cannot rely solely on the Power of Good. You must rely on the power within you." She meets my face. "Three minutes. That's how long each will stay."

The way Nora regards me and emphasizes her last words, she's trying to make sure I understand that since there will be more than one, that window of danger will extend past three minutes. I nod because I get it, and because I'll be the first.

"Are you ready?"

I nod again as the others call out, "Yes, Superior Nora."

"Then begin," she says.

The tearing sound of boxes opening and flasks of holy water hitting the ground seem too loud. I ignore them, hurrying to place the bulbs of garlic along the exterior of my brass ring. I know the majority of the Lessers will place their garlic on top of the ring. But having had first lines of defenses fail me in my past, I'm all about the backup plan.

I whisper a power word against each bulb I set, putting all of my will into it and envisioning an aura of white light surrounding it, just like we were taught.

"Protegeme" I say. *Protect me.*

I choose the Spanish version since it's the language from my mother's side and closer to me than the Latin were taught. Vieve does that, choosing words in Italian to honor her ancestors. Nora chooses Swahili. "If another language calls you to that power word, use it," she'd said. "Whatever helps strengthen you."

The sound of breaking glass followed by a wail makes me cringe. Someone broke their bottle of holy water. But I don't dare look up, working fast when something shifts in the thick dusty air, sending a heaviness in the atmosphere that pushes against my shoulders.

"Work faster," Nora calls.

Again the air grows dense, the weight on my shoulders becoming more burdensome.

"They're coming," she says.

I place my last bulb of garlic.

"They're here," she says, her voice murmuring against my ear.

Chapter Nineteen

I don't look up, concentrating on dripping the holy water onto the brass ring. "*Defiendeme,*" I say. Defend me.

Like a gasoline circle that's been lit, the brass ring ignites. Bright light shoots from the base, creating a wall of breath behind the demon that collides against it. I fall back, barely staying within the confines of my protection as a tongue as long as my leg slides against the wall of blue light.

I bite back a scream. But not everyone manages, the gamut of their fear threatening to bust my eardrums. Except I'm too busy gaping at the creature in front of me to seriously give a damn.

Demons come in all shapes and sizes. All are scary. All are evil. And all are butt ugly. This one is no exception.

A head, the length and width of my body make up its form and a mouth with jagged teeth split down its center. Eyes the size of softballs perch on top and claws dangle down from its enormous hands to scrape along the pavers. But it's the three sets of testicles, dangling like shriveled grapes off a vine beneath it, which adds an extra dose of nasty.

My body is shaking so hard I'm bouncing in place. The demon lifts his claws, slamming them against the protective wall, the points scraping against it like glass. The shield splits as the demon drags his hands down, opening gashes wide enough to allow the aroma of brimstone to seep in.

Protegeme," I stammer. "*Defiendeme.*"

The protective walls burst with light, sealing the breaks close.

Another demon appears, this one with the body of a lizard and the head of a boar. It ransacks the wall, splintering it, and damaging the base.

"*Protegeme,*" I yell. "*Defiendeme!*"

My power words seal the cracks, igniting the wall with more light. The two demons roar, infuriated as they pound against the wall and a third demon appears.

A slug-like body slithers across my barrier, soaking it with a tar like substance that seems to eat away at my protection. He presses his humanoid face against the melting wall. "*Taran,*" he hisses. "*Taran Wird.*"

I cover my ears, screaming my power words with all that I have. It should be working, but then another demon appears, charging my protection and breaking through.

Light and sound detonate around me. Like an axe coming down on my head, my skull explodes in pain.

Something wet slides along my jugular, burning through my skin and jarring me awake. Eyes like bottomless wells sear through me as a tongue wraps around my throat like a noose. People are shrieking around me, I think I hear Nora shouting words in Swahili, and bright gemstone lights from talismans spinning like strobes in a dizzy swirl. Yet all I know is my desperation to draw air.

My hands slap against leathery skin, my thoughts shouting my words of protection. *Protegeme. Defiendeme.*

My fingers clasp around something cold and metal.

Protegeme.

Heat builds within my arm.

Defiendeme.

Lightning strikes.

Protegeme.

Tears leak from my eyes.

Defiendeme.

And what breath remains abandons me.

My lungs sear in pain, but it doesn't compare to the burn that combusts from my core *and* arm, or the crash of lightning that booms, electrifying the atmosphere.

I don't remember leaving my circle. Nor do I feel my back scrape along the floor. But I remember the impact of my spine driving against the grey pavers that make up the far wall.

My focus fades, from far away where my classmates are gaping at me from the safety of their circles, to near my feet where the Superior witches wait.

Nora, kneels beside me, shaking me. "Taran, can you hear me?"

I try to nod, instead my head turns off-kilter. What remains of my brass circle is nothing more than warped pieces of broken metal. In five different spots, gray piles of goop smolder, reeking of sulfur and mixing with the scent of brimstone.

Nora glances behind her, to the other Superiors. "I've never seen anything like this," Superior Kanah says.

The other Superior shakes her head. "Excuse her, Nora," she says, turning away like it's too hard to look at me. "The others can try tomorrow."

"What happened?" I mumble. I barely get the words out and I'm not sure if Nora can hear me. Somehow she does.

"All five demons came after you," she said. "They were drawn to you like nothing I've ever seen. I tried to return them to hell, as did my sisters. But they swarmed you, something within you keeping them here and thwarting my will."

"I didn't keep them here," I say, my throat so dry it hurts to speak.

"No," Nora says, her attention falling to my arm. I don't realize it's glowing until the light fades in and out across her skin. "But I think your appendage did. These demons didn't want to possess you, Taran. They wanted you dead." She strokes my hair. "But your arm and your will wouldn't let you die."

I'm not sure what she's saying or if she understands it herself. But I'm done. "Am I excused?" I ask. I don't really want to ask, but if I don't follow protocol or if I fail to respect her, I won't pass. And if I don't pass, I'll be back here again.

No way in fuck do I want to do this again.

"You are," she says. "You passed."

She tries to help me to my feet, but I stumble away from her.

The image of the first demon's face flashes in front of me before I make it to the door. It's the remains of the evil, mocking me. I shouldn't let it get to me. I should know better, just like the Lessers in the class before us. But like them, I take off, running fast.

Unlike them, I'm not moving in a straight line, I'm bouncing off the wall like a pinball as Nora calls to me. "Taran, wait. You'll need to wash."

Another image appears, this one of a different demon, the one like a boar. I dig through my pockets, pulling out my keys as I reach the first level.

The late afternoon sun blinds me as I practically fall down the front porch steps when I make it outside. I welcome the light, thinking it will keep the darkness away. But they continue to come.

All of them

I'm trying to slide my key into the ignition of my sedan when a humanoid face slides along the windshield. I think I'm going crazy, especially when my darkest memories pop in and out of my mind like a strobe light.

Common sense begs me to stay, compelling me to return to the mansion because I need help. But fear urges me to leave and put distance between me and this place.

I stomp on the gas, not realizing I still have my emergency brake set until I'm almost out of the compound. I don't remember the drive home. Nor do I answer my phone ringing relentlessly through my Bluetooth.

Under other circumstances, I wouldn't drive, not like this. More than once, I almost run off the road, the images of those dark creatures and memories popping in front of me and making me lose control. As I pull into my neighborhood, what little focus remains abandons me. I ram up the small incline on our front lawn and leap from my car, not bothering to set it in park.

Koda speeds past me as the car rolls down the hill. My sisters call after me, but it's Aric's voice that rises above them.

"Celia, no," he growls. "You can't be near her. Not now."

I race forward, crashing against the wards when they won't let me through. Emme and Shayna clutch each arm as I fall back. I think Emme's crying, maybe Shayna is, too. But Shayna pushes through it, hoisting me up.

"The wards sense the evil that remains, T," she says. "Let us help you through, okay?"

I don't answer, letting her speak for me. "*Pace*," she says.

I'm trembling, the adrenaline shooting along my veins mixing with my residual fear. I pitch from side to side like I'm standing in the middle of an earthquake. I barely keep my feet as Shayna and Emme cut a hard left, past the front staircase and down the hall to my room.

Alice babbles as she trudges behind us, completely beside herself.

"It's not real what you're seeing," Shayna says. "It's memories and all that leftover darkness."

I know as much, that doesn't stop the mind-screw of images parading across my line of sight.

My mind latches out to images of our dead parents, lying unmoving and covered with blood before the demon with the long tongue shoves them aside, its tongue flapping, eager for another taste.

"God *damn* it!" I scream, kicking at the air.

"It's okay, honey," Emme says. "We know what to do."

They guide me into the bathroom where my extra-large tub is filling, the water almost at the top. But I still see those wicked faces getting closer and the nightmares of my past growing more vivid.

Emme and Shayna work fast, stripping me out of my clothes. I didn't tell them any specifics, and assume someone else gave them the heads up. I'm not sure who until Shayna says his name. "Gemini is coming. He's almost here with the salts you need to cleanse this stuff," she says. "Do you hear me, T? He's going to help you."

Pale yellow light surrounds me as soft hands cup my face. The pain along my back, knees, and head, secondary to what I'm seeing, lifts, along with that awful weight. The moment it's gone, they remove the last of my uniform, leaving me only in my panties and bra.

Gemini races into the room, his feet stopping where my stare has fallen to the floor, a small burlap sack in his grasp. I don't want to look at him, worried I'll see the face of a demon where his face should be.

Maybe he knows. He sweeps past me, tearing open the bag and dumping the contents into the water.

"I healed her injuries," Emme says, her voice carrying all the fear she feels. "But she's not well."

All five demons appear at once, their faces swirling in a circle on the floor and making me dizzy.

"They're here," I manage to tell them.

"No, they're not," Gemini says. His shirt falls over the faces of the demons, along with his jeans, shoes, and socks.

"Giver her to me," he says, tucking me against him with one arm.

Shayna and Emme leave as he reaches for the clasp in my bra. The door closes softly behind us as Gemini's black boxer briefs hit the floor.

My bra and panties quickly follow. I don't fight him, my face resting against his shoulder as a sob rips through my throat.

"Shhh," he murmurs. "Nothing will hurt you as long as I'm here."

He lifts me, lowering us both into the tub. I gasp when the warm water surrounds me, that awful filth seeping through my skin and drifting away.

The relief is immediate, as if I'm drawing my very first breath after almost drowning in a pool of liquid cement.

I fall limp against Gemini's chest. He hooks his arm across my waist, lowering me with my head against his shoulder so only my face skims above the surface. My body remains pressed to his as he reclines against the side of the tub.

"I'm going to bathe you," he whispers against my ear.

My heavy lids and thick lashes veil my vision. But I feel everything he does to me. He passes a sponge along my face until the last speck of darkness is nothing, but a memory.

Yet his touch remains.

He sweeps the sponge along my side and down to my hip, barely grazing my curves until he reaches my backside and something changes. He tucks my legs against me, squeezing the water from the sponge above my knees. The water drips in a slow cascade, trickling over my breasts as his ankles fasten over mine, keeping me close to him.

If he's trying to keep his motions innocent, he doesn't quiet succeed. Each stroke turns more sensual, teasing, erotic, building the heat inside me.

His hands drop to the swells of my heavy breasts, circling each, spiraling closer to the center until the edges of his fingertips graze my very taut nipples. I want to arch my neck and kiss him. But I don't dare move, needing him to prove I'm the one he desires.

Except my body doesn't fully obey. My spine arches and my hips grind against him, speaking my need while my voice gives nothing away.

The sponge he held floats by me as his hand skims between my breasts to cup my jaw, lifting it up and exposing my throat.

His lips dip down, passing sweet kisses along my wet skin. His other hand wanders lower, his fingers stretching open as they pass my belly. He pauses above my throbbing center, my desperation for his caress almost making me cry out.

He's holding back, likely unsure if he should proceed.

But I want him to, and prove it, placing my hand over his and gliding it down.

I don't realize it's my affected arm that's pressing him to me until my hand slides past his and he lifts his lips away from my throat.

"I should go," he tells me.

He stands, moving stoically away from me.

Water falls down his bare skin in streams as he steps onto the cobalt blue tile. "It's gone," he says, keeping his back to me. "Whatever remained has been purified by the water."

I'm supposed to answer and pretend he didn't touch me the way that he did. But I can't. Not when my body is still seething from his touch.

"You can stay in the tub if you'd like," he says, his voice strained. "What remains can't harm you and the water and salts will help you relax."

"Relax". That's a funny word considering what he just did to me.

He bends to retrieve his clothes. He may be talking to me, but it's like I'm not even here and his hands never touched me.

I use my legs to push to the side of the tub, placing my arms on the ledge to keep me in place. "Why are you doing this to me?" I ask.

His response is immediate. "I wanted to help," he explains, keeping his face forward. "Your instructor told us what happened and how you left without treatment."

"Us?" I ask, not that I need to ask who he was with.

Against the large wall mirror, I can catch sight of his profile and how the muscles along his jaw tense as if pulled. His focus stays fixed to the way out. Not that I would expect anything different form him.

"You know I was there," he says. "I've been there every day since you started your training."

"Don't pretend you're there for me," I bite back.

"Taran—"

"I don't want your help," I say, disturbed by how vacant my voice sounds. "Not when it leads to this."

He bows his head, frustration scrunching his features. "You don't understand. You *never* have."

"I think I do," I reply.

Today was literally hell. There was pain, demons, fear, and evil. But it doesn't quite compare to the torment he alone brings. No, this is an entirely different kind of agony.

"I don't want you here anymore," I say, realizing for the first time how much I mean it. "Nothing good ever comes when you're near me."

"*Don't tell me that,*" he growls, pinching the bridge of his nose. "You don't know what you're doing to me!"

My face falls against my arms. I may have felt numb before, but that feeling is gone. At once, everything I feel for him surges, causing my arm to twitch, its need to unleash fighting against Vieve's bind.

Vieve.

Genevieve.

Damn it.

I pull my arm closer, trying to shield it as I crouch there naked. "Just go," I say. "I need you to leave me."

I'm not sure if he will. But when he whirls around and sees my spastic arm banging against the side of the tub, he does.

My other hand passes over my zombie limb, stroking it, trying to soothe it. The trembling ceases, yet the glowing resumes, casting light across the wet bathroom floor.

As much as Geminis actions and words upset me, his leaving crushes me more.

"Nothing will hurt you as long as I'm here," he'd said.

He's wrong. Everything hurts because of him.

Chapter Twenty

I adjust the damn bonnet on my head and stare out at the marsh. It's bad enough to go trekking through a cornfield at six in the damn morning, without coffee mind you, because hey, that's not allowed either. But now my pilgrim shoes are sticking to the thick mud, and you know that's going to earn me demerits or whatever the fuck.

Three weeks. That's how long it's been since Gemini marched out of my bathroom. That doesn't mean I haven't seen him. He's here every day, but he's not here to see me.

He's tried to approach me, and say hello. But I don't bother with a 'hi' back, or even a glance his way. It infuriates and hurts him, the tension between us growing more pronounced every time I walk away.

He doesn't realize it hurts me, too. I want something, *anything* between us at this point. But it's just not possible.

Vieve is always close, never far from his side. It's hard to see. But even when I don't see them, I hear all about them.

I sit in class, listening to my cohorts ramble on about how hot, sexy, and smart Genevieve's "boyfriend" is. I want to tear my hair out and pretty much shove what I pull up her ass.

"It's not true," Celia insists. "Aric is adamant that

there's nothing but friendship between them."

But she can't sniff lies and I know Aric is doing all he can not to upset her.

Paula squishes to a stop beside me as I reach the edge. I step to the right slightly, doing my best not to place my feet in the gooey embankment. "Hi, Taran," she says.

"Hey, Paula," I reply, wishing I could offer a better smile than I do.

The others nod my way. We're not all exactly buds, but I'm slowly starting to get to know everyone. All it took was getting swarmed by five demons, and sending them back to hell in pieces when they tried to kill me, to earn me some respect. Had I known, I would have done it sooner.

Never mind, I'd rather set my eyebrows on fire.

In the distance a large bird squawks, shaking out its dark feathers when it lands atop of a nearby tree. The marsh is enchanted, as in not real. Most likely it's a small lake or even a creek that's been enlarged and majicked to resemble one.

What appears to be ancient weeping willows gather around the oblong-ish perimeter, the tips of their wispy branches skimming across the mist-colored surface. A few frogs sing from their spot on a large boulder while a crane lands on a drifting log. Whoever cast this spell meant to flex her magical muscles and intimidate all of us "Lesser" beings.

"You doing okay?" Paula whispers.

"I'm fine, cutie," I tell her, my voice catching when I take a good look at her.

Her fair skin is an odd shade of white. She's scared. My head whips from side to side, everyone's scared. I was mostly too sleep-deprived to notice on my walk in, and in a way I still am. That doesn't mean I'm not starting to wake up now.

Everyone around me is emitting that awful vibe you feel when you're at a funeral and the first mound of dirt get tossed over the casket.

"Did someone, like, die?" I ask.

Courtance—or whatever that Lesser's name is—keeps

her attention ahead. "Not yet," she answers, totally not joking.

Okay, following Anti-possession class, and with Séance class still weeks away, I determined nothing could get worse until finals. As I scan the faces around me, I wonder if perhaps I made an erroneous assumption.

"Didn't you read the syllabus last night?" the Lesser with the tiny lips asks.

No. I was too busy sleeping from all the damn weeding and chanting following another round of Plant Week.

"Of course," I lie, because we're not exactly besties. In fact, just yesterday she laughed at my chanting and rolled her eyes at my watering.

I start to press for more information when I see a long gray body skimming across the water's surface.

For the first time ever, I want it to be a dead body— something that may or may not have pissed off something powerful and may or may have not received what he or she deserved. But this isn't a human body. Not even close. Not with all the spikes along its back and a snout as long as my torso.

Who needs coffee? A crocodile coming at you—oh, and look, here come more of his friends—is all the virtual java a gal could ask for. I back away from the water's edge, and I'm not alone. The three witches in front of me practically tit-punch each other in their haste to scramble up the hill.

"Problem, ladies?" a sweet voice echoes, halting us in place.

That sweet voice is layered with lots of magic, the kind that snags your attention and makes you pay attention, despite what's around you. I shudder, trying to shake it off, and hating how it seems to tug at my clothes and lift my chin in its direction.

I try to fight the pull, scowling as my neck is wrenched to the right and my arm twitches in annoyance.

Agatha, the Superior witch with the grannie blue hair and silver staff, who is about as endearing as a pit full of snakes, appears through the parting mist.

She steps down from the boulder she's standing on

and into the marsh, hovering above the water like she's walking along the surface. It's yet another peek at her power, meant to further intimidate and make us believe she's more than she is. Is she a mystical powerhouse? Totally. Can she likely kill us all? Sadly, yes. But that doesn't make her any less of an asshole.

Lessers scatter when they see her roaming the halls, and have left running and sobbing from her classroom.

Rumor has it dozens of wanna-be witches have dropped out of the program under her tutelage and a small few have gone insane following her Runes class. There's even talk that she killed a Lesser she felt insulted her and that she's not afraid to do it again.

Fine. But if she does try to kill me, I guarantee I'm going to make her work for it and that my middle finger will be last thing she sees.

Unlike me, the others aren't scowling, their expressions oddly terrified yet mesmerized by the pull of her voice. I wonder if they could break away from the enchantment if they tried. Based on how enthralled they appear, I'm not so sure, or even if they care enough to try.

The breeze gathers around Agatha as she moves to the center of the marsh, lifting her short blue hair and fanning it in perfect motions along her narrow face. About seven crocs form a circle around her, closing in as she advances, their milky white stares glossed over with hunger.

The Lessers collectively gasp as a croc leaves the circle and slithers toward Agatha. But Agatha keeps both her attention and smirk on us, assuring us she's in complete control. "By now, you're all familiar with vampires," she says, her tone maintaining that haunting edge.

"Yes, Sister Agatha," everyone answers.

She tilts her head in my direction when she realizes I don't respond in turn. She must guess I'm not impressed, or afraid, so she tries to assure me she's someone to fear.

Like some kind of freaky dolphin, the crocodile lifts up from the water, curving its spine so its snout points upward. "Vampires are beautiful, immortal, and strong," she

OF FLAME AND LIGHT

says. "They're also *dangerous*." She strokes the head of her pet as if it's a gentle creature that would never sever her face off if given a chance.

"Ever anger a vampire?" she asks, her smile widening.

Yup.

"I have," she says, oblivious to my thoughts. "It's a sight to behold." She stops smiling. "But not to fear. They are less than us. We are the superior race."

It takes all I have not to roll my eyes because, sweetheart, they feel the same about you. As far as angering a vampire, it's more like when *haven't* I pissed one off?

Judy (I think that's her name) raises a hesitant hand. "But, Sister Agatha, I thought vampires aren't allowed to attack us unless provoked, or if their master is in danger," she says, fear making her stutter.

Agatha smiles. "Well perhaps I did some provoking," she answers, earning a few more gasps.

Okay. This time, I have to roll my eyes. Misha Aleksandr is among the most powerful master vampires in the world. He and his vamps are the only ones who reside in the area—and badass witch power or not—even the slutty ones who dress like naughty Catholic schoolgirls would rip Agatha's hands off and smack her across the face with them if "provoked". So this tells me two things: she's either talking about something stupid she did long ago—and to another vampire clan—or she's full of shit. I'm leaning toward the latter because there is such a thing as trying too hard and damn it all, this woman is really pushing it.

Agatha's fingertips slide underneath the croc's jaw as she releases it back into the water. "Who can tell me what bloodlust is?" she asks.

Tina raises her hand. Like the others, she seems terrified, but that doesn't stop her from trying to kiss up to Agatha or toss a nasty grin my way. "In a vampire or wolf, Superior Sister?" she asks.

I take a deep breath and briefly lower my lids, knowing it's a dig on Aric. Now, everyone's looking at me. They heard the rumors about his moon sickness—aka the

195

equivalent of bloodlust for a *were* that usually results in his quick death, but not before plenty of bloodshed. I make a mental note to punch her in the face come graduation, if by some miracle I manage to graduate and not die.

What happened to Aric was no joke, and one of the hardships he and Celia just barely survived. So when I answer, my anger reflects in my tone. "Moon sickness affects *weres*, and is caused by a curse cast by a *witch*," I snap. "Bloodlust in a vampire comes in two forms: acute, which results when a vamp has gone too long without feeding, easily remedied by providing a feed, or chronic. Chronic occurs when some psycho witch curses him or poisons his bloodstream. There's no cure for chronic bloodlust. Nothing to do, but put down the vamp." My face meets Tina's. "And supposedly there's no cure for moon sickness, but my brother-in-law Aric managed to fight it off."

I'd cut Tina off, and failed to address Agatha by her "Superior" title. But honestly, I could care less.

"My," Agatha says. "You seem to have a lot of experience with both."

"You can say that," I agree, returning her smile with equal kindness.

She laughs, unimpressed, not that I expect anything less. "It's forbidden to keep a bloodlust vamp alive. Yet I must teach you to kill one." She stretches out her arms, motioning to the crocodiles. "I suppose my babies will just have to do."

I groan, despite recognizing this is where she was headed.

"A vampire inflicted with chronic bloodlust knows only hunger," she says, adding an extra ping of drama to her voice. "No amount of feeding will satisfy him, reducing him to a mindless predator who will viciously murder everything in his path." Again, there's that wicked smile. "These creatures represent the lethal equivalent of one vampire in his early stages of bloodlust."

Again, more gasping as another five crocodiles join those circling Agatha. I'd like to say she's exaggerating, but she's not. I'll give her this, she paints an accurate picture.

She loses her smile. "Your task is simple: fight and survive. It is only by knowing your enemy's power and strength can you hope to defeat him."

There's no hesitation. From one blink to the next, Paula is ripped from the spot where she's standing beside me and flung into the water.

The force from Agatha's pull is so harsh, Paula's arm smacks against my cheek, hard enough to leave a mark. The slap is intentional, meant to put me in my place and shut me up. I get it. But considering Agatha demands respect, there's none shown to poor Paula.

And it really pisses me off.

Agatha selected Paula because she knows she's the weakest in strength and ability. She's also the one who appeared most frightened. Agatha means to stir fear and cause everyone to panic.

Not that she doesn't succeed.

The group jumps when Paula falls shrieking, some of them failing to muffle their screams. The crocodiles don't wait, diving in the direction Paula disappears. I rush to the edge, losing one of my shoes in the mud in my urgency to reach the water.

The mist in front of me forms into long spindly hands, slamming into my shoulders and holding me in place. I struggle to wrench free, my arm glowing in protest as I square my sights on Agatha. "Get her out of there," I snap. "She can't fight like this. She isn't ready."

Agatha talks over me. "As witches, you must always be prepared for battle."

Jade and red lights spread across the murky water as Agatha adds an extra boost to her spell. Paula's hand shoots up only to be quickly ripped downward. I swing my arms against the mist holding me back, sparks of blue and white energy erupting around me.

I don't know what magic Agatha is working, but my magic can't counter it, and my hands swipe through the mist as it keeps me in place. "Get her out of there!" I yell, calling my magic from deep within my core.

The misty hands solidify to gray, falling away like ash. I'm not sure what I did, and neither is Agatha. Her eyes widen with shock, but they don't stay on me. Her focus whips to the murky water and she sighs as if annoyed. She dips her staff into the water, swirling it once and flinging Paula back onto the shore.

Paula lands by my feet, gagging, choking, and sobbing. Her clothes are in tatters, every inch of her covered in muck . . . and blood. I tug down her sleeves, examining her arms.

Puncture marks and scratches litter her exposed skin in alternating patterns. She didn't manage to fight these things off, but she effectively used her magic to protect her. Against a vamp infected with bloodlust, she might have managed to stay alive. Her wounds aren't deep and none of the injuries lethal. To me that's a win.

I gather her to me when she falls into hysterics, trying to console her. "It's okay. It's over, Paula. You did well."

"Don't lie to her," Agatha tells me, her voice more like a snarl.

"I'm not," I fire back. "She protected herself against a mortal injury. A human would be dead—"

"She's not human," Agatha reminds me. "And she's had enough training to fight back." She scoffs as the crocodiles line up beside her like her own personal army, ready to maul every last one of us. "An infected vampire is nothing—not compared to the new evil that's rising. I feel it every time the moon peaks in the heavens. *It's* coming, and will spare no one!"

She zooms across the water, spreading the mist into streaming bands of white as she looms over Paula. "You're nothing but a liability," she tells her. "An embarrassment to your teachers and our kind."

I can't see Paula, I'm too busy glaring at Agatha and wishing her herpes. But I feel her spirit crumbling and weakening against my arms.

Agatha scans the crowd, addressing our peers. "Who

can tell me what Lesser Paula did wrong?"

I lift my hand. "She got up this morning?"

"No," Agatha growls.

"She signed up for this shit?" I guess again.

The Lessers take a collective step back as ribbons of jade and red light swirl from Agatha's staff. Paula shrinks against me, but I hold my ground.

"You have a very big mouth," Agatha tells me. "I think I need to teach you to shut it."

I know what's coming even before the mist snakes around my waist like rope. But the motion is too fast, and not nearly long enough for me to take a breath. The cold murky water envelops me at once as I'm plunged deep within the marsh.

Chapter Twenty-one

Here's the thing about witches, there's a reason the word rhymes with "bitches". It's not bad enough I'm dumped into a freaking ice-cold swamp at the ass-crack of dawn with circling crocodiles ready to eat me. No. Not with this crew. After all, this "training" isn't meant to simply teach you to cast a few spells, ride a broom bareback, or in my case, keep me from dying. It's a mind fuck meant to break your will so only those most worthy are bequeathed the title of Superior Witch.

I may not want the title. That doesn't mean the Superiors aren't determined to break me.

My arm glows in the surrounding darkness as the dim sunlight above me slips away. My mouth is closed and while I don't have a lot of oxygen, my lungs aren't threatening to burst. That doesn't mean there's no need to panic.

My feet are heavy as if encased in blocks of cement that plunge me down further. I jerk when something green whips past me, only to whirl when something smacks me in the back. But it's what I see a few feet away that has me close to screaming.

Gemini is bound to the base of the marsh with gold chains. His head is bowed and blood from his partially eaten flesh intermix with the swampy water.

It's a trap. I'm sure it is. But when he lifts his head, and his agonized stare locks on mine, my need to know compels me to go to him.

I can't swim, and more or less flap my arms and legs in his direction. Yet it's the current pushing against my back that forces my attention away.

I barely catch sight of the infected vampire, but I see enough to recognize how sick she is. Grotesque muscles bulging with infection overtake her form, swirling putrid green liquid beneath her skin to the point of bursting, while bat-like features distort what had once been a beautiful face.

Except it's not so beautiful anymore.

Her long matted hair whips behind her as she torpedoes forward, her fangs exposed and her dagger-like nails elongating as she nears.

I lift my right arm as she lurches at me, trying to block her fangs from my throat. I spare my jugular, but not much else. Long, sharp points dig into my flesh and scrape against the bone.

I scream, releasing the air in my lungs by half. I shake my arm wildly, struggling to wrench her off me. She clings to it, cradling it against her as she bites her way across and closer to my neck.

Her eyes sear into mine, the lustful hunger behind them surging. I kick and punch uselessly, realizing my physical strength isn't enough.

Burn, I think, pathetically calling my fire.

Burn.

Tiny blue sparks creep from my fingertips, disappearing as they rise toward the surface. The vamp barely notices, chomping into my arm and tugging at the skin, appearing confused when she can't rip the flesh from the bone.

My skin holds tight. That doesn't mean it doesn't hurt. I feel every last tug, shrieking as her fangs clamp down.

More air leaves my lungs, the bubbles floating away like the sparks.

Come on, *burn*. Damn it, *burn*.

I don't think it's my will, not by how fear overtakes me. It's my arm reacting to the invasion and the vamp's escalating hunger. It trembles, rattling the vampire and detonating her into chunky green bits in one mighty explosion.

The pieces of flesh draw more vamps like raw meat to piranhas, but also to me. This time, I don't wait to be bitten.

My arm shoots out, sending blue and white fire jetting from my arm. It strikes the closest vamp, taking his head off his shoulders and enticing his friends to tear him apart.

More ripping flesh, more green putrid fluid, more chunks. The frantic results of the chewing and mauling distorting the water and blinding me. I scramble forward, or up—or freaking sideways. I'm not sure where I'm headed, my desperation to find Gemini making me frantic.

Something snags my ankle, dragging me down. I barely manage more than a minor sizzle within my core and aim blindly. The hold loosens, but not enough to release me. I kick out, tensing and allowing the fear to sweep through me and for that sense of power to ignite one last time.

This time when I unleash my fire, it releases like the rapid discharge of bullets. Clumps of vamp float up to my face, letting me know I struck it dead on. I try swimming up and away from the feasting vampires, but the weight at my feet keeps me from reaching the surface.

I catch sight of Gemini and move frantically toward him. He's made no effort to break free, or move, his head bobbing lifelessly. Son of a bitch. I know it's not him. My wolf would fight, show signs of a struggle—*something*. But that doesn't mean I can leave him!

I steal a glance over my shoulder to where the vamps continue to consume each other, the mix of blood and flesh causing them to fight and turn against the small and weak. Two males pounce on a female, tearing the muscles of her writhing limbs from the bone and adding to the carnage. My legs kick faster, my urgency to reach Gemini making my pulse race.

I don't have a lot of time before the vamps remember

me, but maybe I have enough.

The water, so thick with body fluids and God knows what else, makes it feel like I'm treading through gelatin. It exhausts my arms and makes it harder to hang onto my remaining oxygen.

I practically throw my arms around Gem when I reach him, my mind wrestling with how to free him and whether this is the last step in this twisted quiz.

My thumbs graze over his goatee as I lift his face with trembling hands, searching for any signs of life. His chin jerks up at the same time he breaks free and fastens his hands across my throat.

He forces my gaze onto his as he squeezes, his eyes flashing the putrid green of a cursed wolf. Now, I know it's not really him, and that the real Gemini is safe. But as the air is forced from my lungs, I'm the one who's in trouble.

My hands grip his wrists, calling forth my magic as darkness dims my sight. He clamps down hard, but pain and fear are the jumpstart I need to trigger my power and ignite him in blue and white flames. I press my feet against his chest, trying to push free—not wanting to watch that face that haunts my dreams blister and his skin melt away. Yet despite his cooking flesh, he hangs tight, forcing me to watch everything my fire does to him.

I know this isn't the man I love, the one who broke my heart and made me cry. That doesn't make it easier to watch him fall apart. Not when I'm the cause.

My body lurches against his, the force of my magic sputtering as if dying along with him, only to reignite from my arm like a firestorm.

Water boils around me, the heat so tremendous I feel it turn against me and burn my skin. I thrash back and forth, furious that despite Vieve's bind, my arm betrays me again. But it's the rage I feel seeing Gemini implode that propels my magic and launches me backward.

The last breath of enchanted air leaves me in a merciless rush when my back strikes against the embankment. I roll to my side, clawing my way across the mud as I choke on scum and what might be leftover vamp parts.

I'm not sure which side of the marsh I'm on until arms hook beneath me and haul me up. Paula's there, and the tall blonde whose name I can't remember. I'm retching, trying to expel whatever I swallowed. They hold tight as I struggle to keep my feet.

Shit. It seems to take forever before I can take a decent breath. But even then it takes me another few moments to realize no one's looking at me.

All eyes are on the marsh as it boils the remains of the crocodiles bobbing along the surface.

The smell is awful, the experience worse, and watching Gemini get stewed like fish—horrific. But it's that glare that Agatha is pegging me that makes me come undone.

I storm forward. She opens up her mouth to say something except she never gets a chance. I punch her so hard in the face she drops her staff. Be it my lack of balance or the unbearable weakness in my legs, I fall forward and on top of her, my common sense kicking in enough to shove her away from her staff.

We're not fighting like kids on the playground, those who smack and bat their hands. We are literally beating the shit out of each other, kicking, clawing, punching—her long fingers digging into my hair and scratching my scalp as she yanks me forward and nails me in the nose.

Stinging pain shoots between my eyes, instantly making me see double. If I'm being honest, I can't fight. Celia is the brawler. But I've seen her in action enough times to learn how she wins. She doesn't stop, throwing the weight of her body into each strike, and she doesn't give up, making each strike harder, more vicious. So I don't curl in a ball and beg for mercy, or crawl away crying. My elbow comes down on her face, again and again between punches.

The Lessers are screaming, hands blindly sweeping in trying to pry us apart. Yet even as they're separating us, we continue to kick, my stubborn will ensuring the last strike is mine. I'm dragged back, spitting mad. The last image I see as I'm hauled up the hill is what remains of the marsh. The weeping willows collapse into the simmering water as Agatha's magic shatters apart.

~ * ~

Once more, I'm in the principal's office. The principal isn't happy. Neither are "Mom" and "Dad". Aric drags his hand across his face as Principal Vieve gives him the deets on my smack-down with Agatha.

Celia sits rigid, with her hands clasped over her lap. She's trying not to react and keep her expression neutral. But I recognize that familiar, "Jesus, Taran" look she always gets when I engage in less than stellar activity.

"An assault against a Superior is cause for dismissal," Vieve says. Her voice maintains that smooth and relaxed tone, but the stern inflection behind it is as obvious as the mud and muck coating my hair. Her attention flickers my way. "It also gives Agatha cause to challenge Taran to a duel."

"Let's go then," I begin, only for Aric to cut me off.

"That's not going to happen," he says. Yet he isn't talking to me. "A direct challenge against my mate's sister will be construed as an insult against me and an act against my Pack."

"I know," Vieve responds.

She's not regarding Aric in a challenging way, at least not so directly his wolf would respond with force. But it's clear she's not happy about having to deny Agatha the pleasure of hexing me to possible death.

"However, I can't ignore the insult on my end either," she responds, turning back to me. "Taran, you punched Agatha in the face, demeaning her in front of Lessers who she must continue to teach."

It's one of those moments when "she started it" wouldn't work and neither would flipping her off. So instead of yelling and cursing which I'm damn good at, I tell her off the best way I know how. "Agatha chose Paula first. You know Paula, right? The one who every Lesser here regards as pitiful? The one who works harder than anyone else, yet has spent years trying to conjure magic most young witches master before puberty?"

"Yes, I know her," she responds, her expression unreadable.

"Well, did you also know Agatha flung her into a marsh infested with crocodiles which she enchanted to resemble infected vampires? And that she then hypnotized her so she'd see her greatest fear?" I don't give her a chance to respond. "Want to know her biggest fear? It's her mother dying. The one person who's always believed in her and told her she could be so much more." I grip the sides of my chair. "Agatha didn't care. She made it so Paula would watch the person she loved most mauled to pieces."

My voice quiets as I remember how hard Paula cried when she told me. "Agatha didn't choose Paula because she thought Paula would do well, or to give others hope they could survive this twisted test. She picked on someone weaker to instill fear. You call that effective teaching? I don't. I call it bullying and harassment. Agatha might as well have stolen her lunch money while she was at it."

Vieve's full pink lips press together, her way of demonstrating her distaste. But it's Aric who speaks. "Is that true?" he asks, even though he can already scent it is.

"Like you, Aric, our kind doesn't discuss our training methods. Perhaps if Taran would have actually studied our rules she would realize as much." She leans back into her throne-like chair, analyzing me closely.

Aric shifts in his seat to look at me. "And what did you see?"

"What do you think?" I ask, turning away when my eyes burn.

I don't have to explain. He knows what I fear. It's the same fear he holds when it comes to Celia.

"Like *weres*, we train ours to battle the very worst, at our very worst," Vieve says as a way of an answer.

"I'm not passing judgment," he answers, keeping his voice low and as hard as his expression. "But you're dealing with Taran. She's not a witch or a werebeast."

"But she is someone who assaulted a teacher," Vieve responds with equal force. "How would that have gone over in your Pack? Would the perpetrator even be allowed his next breath much less stand before you?"

If she expects to stonewall Aric it doesn't work. "Taran is different from us," he reminds her.

"And I've made allowances given she's not one of us," Vieve counters. "That doesn't give her permission to behave as she wants."

She rounds on me. I guess this is the part where I'm supposed to hang my head in shame and express my remorse. Too bad I don't have any. Instead I meet her perfect face, willing myself not to leap across her pristine desk and pummel her. She must sense as much, her chin tilting ever so slightly which on Vieve is the equivalent of me screaming and flailing my arms.

As if to remind me who's head bitch, she tugs on my leash. The bind around my arm tightening hard enough to make me flinch. But this time I don't. "I didn't behave the way I wanted to," I tell her.

"Really?" she begins, her brow lifting so slightly, I barely catch it.

"No. If I had, you'd be sweeping up Agatha's remains with one of your brooms." I ignore Celia's groans, and Aric's too, standing despite the tug on my arm insisting I sit and remain far beneath her. "I get that you're in charge, and that the Superiors are to lead and teach us as it suits them. Just like I understand that all this bullshit stress is designed to take us to our breaking point so we train our bodies and mind to push past our fear and react. I get it, because I've done it a thousand times over since being dragged into this world."

Vieve's voice is so laced with anger her power sparkles the gemstone on her talisman. "Then you know how imperative it is that every last member of our coven learn what you've learned, the hard way to survive," she says rising, She lugs me forward with a magical pull of the bind. I fall across her desk, my forearms smacking hard against the slick wood.

"*Genevieve*," Aric warns.

Celia growls, that deep growl she does before her prey literally loses its head.

We ignore them, glaring at each other. "There's a difference between teaching to perform under stress and what Agatha did today," I bite out through my teeth, ignoring the tightening around my arm. "Agatha wasn't taking Paula to her breaking point, she attempted to *break her*—break all of them by starting with who she thought was the weakest link. Maybe she is. Maybe she isn't. But what Agatha did was wrong."

My neck muscles strain as the bind digs into my skin, causing my sickly blue veins to bulge against their white landscape. "You want me to learn. You want me to do the work. I have," I remind her. "But I won't ignore my nature. Today, that nature compelled me to protect Paula. Weak or not, right or wrong—I don't care. You can expel me. I'd rather burn to embers. But no way in *fuck* will I allow someone like Paula to be treated like she's nothing."

My head is spinning. It could be something Vieve is doing, some evil hex that will make me sprout six tits, or it could be because every time I inhale, I can still smell Gemini's body cooking and falling away from his skeleton.

Time passes as my focus wavers in and out. But just when I'm certain I'll hurl, the nausea recedes and Vieve's grip on my arm releases.

As gracefully as I can, I edge away, watching her straighten. Something changes in her expression. Not that she appears any less pissed.

"Your tactics are designed to protect your sisters, but also the innocent," Aric reminds her. "Just as we *weres* guard and defend the earth and its human populace."

"I already made my decision, Aric," Vieve says, making it clear that nothing he says will change her evil plans.

"You think you know so much," she tells me, her precious blue stare morphing to steel. "Because of your experience and the courage you pretend to wield." She ignores my scowl. "So be it." She walks around her desk. At first, I think she'll walk toward me. Instead she glides toward the high windows that look out to her sacred garden. "Did you read your High Tasks?" she asks, keeping her back to me.

In general, I rack my brain trying to remember all the witchy stuff I'm supposed to know for each class. But I don't have to now. The High Tasks are spoken of in whispers between chants, meals, and those rare moments the Superiors are out of earshot. They are the equivalent of your witch boards. Three tasks that must be completed in order to graduate and earn Superior status within the coven. It takes a shit-ton of magic, power, and even more focus to achieve them. According to Paula, most in our class will never make it and leave the compound in disgrace.

"Yes," I answer.

I don't go in to detail, especially since I can feel the weight of Celia's and Aric's scrutiny. They're not familiar with the High Tasks, and they're not supposed to be. It's one of those, "If I tell you, I'll die," kind of deals. Seriously. The hex attached to spilling the details will blow me to smithereens.

She looks at me then. Knowing where she's going, I expect her to smile. One of those wicked smiles bad guys get when they're squeezing you by the proverbial nuts. Vieve doesn't smile. Yet the way she regards me is almost worse. "Pick one. Perform it. And you'll be allowed to return." Her eyes flash with the bright yellow light of her talisman. "If you fail, you'll have your wish and be allowed to burn."

Chapter Twenty-two

One chance, or I'll meet my eventual fate.

I not only know how to make my bed, here I am lying in it, tangled in the sheets, and suffocating myself with the damn pillow.

But this time, I'm not alone.

Paula, Merri, and Fiona, sit across from me. I'm in their room because not only did Vieve require the impossible, she's making me spend the next few nights here until I get it done. I'm not allowed any contact with my family, or anyone outside the coven.

Paula skims through the leather bound texts that list the High Tasks while Merri and Fiona flip through old notes from Lessers who have actually passed. These girls have been nice. None of the other Lessers opened their doors with arms outstretched lovingly. After watching me in a fistfight with the most feared instructor, I suppose they fear expulsion by association if there's such a thing.

I wasn't surprised, expecting ridicule and nasty comments. Yet as word spread I'd have to perform a High Task *way* ahead of schedule, they began to regard me like one of those deep sea creatures no one knows the name of, but everyone is afraid to approach.

The laughs at my expense, and eye rolls I anticipated

never came. What I saw was fear and a whole lot of pity. Which, incidentally, did nothing to boost my quickly deflating confidence.

"What about the Vanishing?" Paula suggests, glancing up from her reading. Ordinarily, Lessers aren't allowed to see the text until close to their graduation period which, for the four of us, is a *long* way off. But Vieve made the exception, permitting me access and any help that came from my peers.

"The Vanishing sounds doable," she adds. "I mean, how bad can it be if it goes wrong?"

"Pretty damn bad," Merri says, scratching at her bald head. She started out with jet black hair down to her butt. That changed after we mixed our first snapdragon potion last week. Whisker of Boar or whatever she added went horribly wrong. She cursed herself so badly the only hair she'll grow for the next year is on her feet, and by the looks of it, girlfriend needs a cut.

"My sister told me that her roommate, Karen, had this second cousin on her mother's side who overdid the Vanishing," Merri continues. "Instead of disappearing, she turned inside out." She holds out her hand. "Seriously, her guts spilled out of her and all over the front foyer, and her own hand was doing its best to push out her beating heart. She didn't pass, in case you're wondering, and it took like a week and a half to put her back together."

I blink back at her. "Okay, so I'm thinking no to the Vanishing."

Fiona swallows hard. She's thin, and so tall she has to tuck her head to pass under doorways. I haven't spoken to her much, but she's trying to help me and that means a lot. "What about Soaring?" she suggests. "You get to fly. That sounds cool."

Merri shakes her head. "Nah. My sister told me that some Lesser in her Rune-reading class did Soaring. Crazy freak sprouted wings and fangs. She did fly," she adds, thoughtfully. "But it took them a few days to find her and when they did she was in a field munching on dead rats."

So far, Merri isn't living up to her name.

Paula lowers her hand from her mouth. "It doesn't appear your sister studied with a very promising class."

Merri huffs. "Tell me about it. She lost an ear and part of her left foot before she graduated, but at least she graduated. I think about sixty percent of her classmates are now reading fortunes at carnivals, poor bastards." She shrugs. "They were all lower-ranked like us."

Sadness falls around us like an itchy blanket. For all I think I'm a freak, I'm starting to realize that I'm not alone. "We're going to make it," I say, because we all need to believe it. "We just have to keep going."

They don't seem so convinced, but as they exchange glances they smile. The motion is subtle, but I catch it.

"Well, that leaves one High Task," Paula says, frowning as her eyes skim down the passage.

"It's Mirror? Isn't it?" Fiona asks, leaning forward.

Paula holds up a finger as she continues to read, alerting us she needs a moment. She flips the page, her eyes passing along each line.

"What's Mirror?" I whisper to Fiona.

"You turn into something or someone else," she explains, watching Paula with interest.

"Some*thing*?" I ask.

She nods. "It can be a beast, a dog, a crow, a rat—"

"Don't be a rat," Merri interrupts. "You know that chick who sprouted wings? One of the rats she was found chewing on was her roommate. *She* picked Mirror, God rest her soul."

"I'll be a cougar," I say quickly, thinking I'll be damned if I let someone eat me.

Paula purses her lips, placing the journal down. "I wouldn't pick beast, not with so many *weres* in the area." She points to a section in the text none of us can see, not that I think we're supposed to. "According to rules surrounding Mirror, you're supposed to fool someone close to you into believing you're that someone or something else. You'll lose your natural scent and inherit that of the being you choose, but *weres* can distinguish a true beast from a fake one. Their animal nature makes it easy for them."

"What about another human?" I ask, thinking about all the *weres* occupying my house alone.

"That could work," she says. "But this is one of those High Tasks people dread the most."

I'm almost afraid to ask, but I still do. "Why?"

"It's designed for the supernatural equivalent of espionage, becoming someone else to gather secrets and information. In a Lesser, the spell is unpredictable. If it sticks, you'll have at least twelve hours once you change to fool your target. But if it doesn't, your form will dissolve as quickly as it comes. But Taran, I have to warn you, according to this, it's painful. We'll have to tie you to bed once you swallow the potion."

I don't mention it won't be my first time tied to the bed, and while I'm not excited about feeling more pain, the thought doesn't deter me. "Okay. Let's do it."

"You're not worried?" Paula questions. "About the pain, I mean. According to this, it's like torture."

The girls gasp as my vision sharpens. I don't have to catch sight of my reflection to know my irises have turned almost white. "Let's just say, I'm used to pain," I tell them.

~ * ~

Three days. That's how long it takes the four of us to chant enough to strengthen the herbs and plants we need for Mirror. I have to give it up to Fiona, Merri, and Paula. Our chanting was limited to the dead of night because this was considered an extracurricular activity.

It was colder than Frosty's ass cheeks. Merri had an easier time because of her hairy feet, but the rest of us were chattering through our chants. By the time we plucked our herbs and plants (beneath the light of a full moon of course), we were averaging four hours of sleep a night and still expected to be at our best during class.

My sisters have been calling me, despite knowing I can't call them back. They want me to know they're thinking of me and praying for my success. I want to text back and tell them I love them, and I would if it wasn't against the rules

I miss them and was pretty choked up when I heard Alice's "Ergh" on my voicemail. I hope she's okay and getting enough road kill to eat. Shayna left me a message telling me Alice isn't doing very well and that they're finding random body parts all over the house. A hand here. A leg there. But it was the nose sniffing around Celia and Aric's bathroom while they were taking a bath that was especially disturbing.

Poor Alice. She doesn't belong in our world, no matter how much I wish she could. Savana did a real number on her, and on everyone else who's been sent to hunt her.

I push my sweat-soaked hair away from my brow and reach for the potholders to lift our Crock Pot. Our potion has been slow cooking since we added the Acacia. For the last two hours we've been circling the pot and (you guessed it) chanting with our hands clasped.

The temperature in the room spiked from our combined power. So we're now standing in our panties and bras. It's not something any of us are keen on, but for some reason "more flesh means more power" according to Paula. Right now, we're two tugs away from being naked and afraid.

Merri wipes her sweaty feet with a towel. "How's it look?"

I lower the pot on the desk and onto our sacred stone, aka a random piece of granite we pass between us to dice herbs. "Like boiling mud?" I admit, gagging.

"I think that's a good thing," Paula says. "Do you have the picture?" At my nod she adds. "Then dip it into the potion and do your chant. We'll wait by the bed."

I try not to look in their direction. I'm all for a good time in bed, but the red satin sheets beneath, plus the shackles anchored to each corner, make it resemble something out of a bad BDSM dream.

Dom Fiona takes position at the foot of the bed, seeing she's the strongest and may have to lay across my legs if they can't restrain me in time.

I wasn't afraid of the pain before, but I'm plenty terrified now that the time has come. I lift the picture I ripped out of a lingerie magazine. I picked this model because she seemed almost the direct opposite of me.

Mirror is named for your inability to recognize your reflection once the change successfully occurs. Where I'm petite and curvy, she's tall, rail thin and small breasted. And while my long dark wavy hair falls past my shoulders, her tight thin curls in alternating tones of auburn and gold, barely reach her jaw line. Her eyes are the color of warm honey, but it's her beautiful mocha skin I envy. There's no hint of the porcelain white skin of my arm or blue veins.

I stroke my arm as I continue to study the photo. It's something I do a lot now, especially since the test involving the crocodiles. It was the first time my magic and that of my arm seemed to work together to save me. It was far from perfect control. But I felt the cohesiveness between them, however brief.

"You ready, Taran?" Fiona asks.

I take another look at the model's inviting smile. "As ready as I'll ever be."

I drop the picture into the vat of thick liquid. "Mirror, Mirror," I say. "Show me what I need to see." The edges curl as if burning, but then the potion pools around it, drowning the image and changing the liquid from thick muck to crystal clear. I can see the bottom, but the picture is completely gone.

"Mirror, mirror," I repeat, adding more force to my words. "Gift me the power of change."

Light flashes outside, blue like my lighting.

"Keep going, Taran," Paula urges. "I think it's working."

"Mirror, Mirror," I repeat, feeling that familiar surge of power expand from my core and along my limbs. "Change me now to the creature I seek."

My hands dive into the water. The steam rising from the liquid suggests that it's hot enough to burn. Yet be it the power I conjure, or the magic rising from the potion, I feel nothing, taking large gulps from my cupped palms.

The taste should be awful, making me want to hurl. And after all the belladonna and nightshade we added, it should very well kill me. But all I taste is tepid water. I swallow about half of it down, allowing some of it to drip onto my face and body, like the instructions say. But when almost half is gone, I start splashing what remains against my body, drenching myself and chanting loudly.

"Mirror, mirror, grant my change."

"Mirror, mirror, shield my skin."

"Mirror, mirror, blind those from who I am."

"Mirror, mirror, make it be."

I put all my focus into every word. But when the picture from the magazine appears at the bottom, and all the building power abruptly cuts off like the flick of a switch, I think something went wrong.

Silence isn't always golden. And right now, it sucks rhino balls. I turn to where Paula, Fiona, and Merri are exchanging glances. I sigh. "It didn't work," I begin.

As if on cue, their eyes widen and their hands fly out like they're trying to stop a large rock from bowling them over them.

"What?" I ask. They rush to me as the first wave of pain hits me like the strike of a mullet across my arm.

I scream as my left arm snaps in half, dangling to the side. "No!" I yell as they lurch me forward. "*No!*"

My legs give out, crushing to shards of broken bone. I'm fighting them off with all I have. I don't want them to touch me, or move me, or—

My head falls forward when my neck snaps.

I don't remember blacking out. I blink my eyes open, grimacing when I catch a whiff of Merri's feet.

Paula is shaking my shoulder. "Taran, Taran, can you hear me?" I'm sprawled on the floor that much I know. "We weren't able to get you to the bed," she explains. "You were thrashing too hard."

She seems ill at ease, as if expecting me to be injured. But I feel great, bordering on fantastic. I bounce to my feet in one easy move, energized and feeling like I can take on the world. I pause as I glance down, shocked by how much shorter she is . . . and the dark skin covering my body. I lift my fingers to touch my face. I don't need the mirror Fiona brings to know I'm different, but I take it anyway.

"Holy shit," I mutter, gaping at the woman from the magazine staring back at me. My hand passes along my throat when I realize how much higher my voice is, despite that I did little more than mumble.

"You did it," Paula says, jumping in place. "And you've been out an hour. That means your form will keep for several hours more."

Merri hands me a short coral dress. "That doesn't mean you have time to waste," she urges. "If you're going to fool your sister, we need to find her, and find her fast." She smiles hopefully. "You've got this Taran. This is your chance to make it right."

Chapter Twenty-three

Merri stomps her hairy feet on the gas. She's wearing flip-flops which ordinarily in her condition I'd caution against. But apparently, she can't wear her regular shoes and no one will lend her a larger pair.

"No way is Cecilia going to know who you are," she says.

I smile. "Celia," I correct.

My smile stays put, thinking she might be right. I chose Celia because she knows me best. And for me to get that "A" in Mirror, I needed to fool that one person I'm not supposed to be able to.

I lift my iPhone to my extra full lips to send a voice to text message, something the Superiors permit to complete my task. *Hey, Shayna. How are you?*

Dude, she texts back. *I miss you. Koda, Emme, and I just finished dinner. Are you okay?*

Fine, I respond, trying to keep it short and sweet. *Where's Celia?*

Shooting pool at Moon Song.

Perfect. And here I thought I'd have to lure her out of the house.

Moon Song is a popular *were* hangout located at a lodge that overlooks Lake Tahoe. It's good for a few pitchers of Witch's Brew, the supernatural beer equivalent that can knock a weregorilla on his ass, along with pool and live music.

Ordinarily, this isn't a place where Aric would take Celia. She can't drink, and she doesn't know how to play pool. But she's likely going stir crazy at home, and seeing how she's carrying the mystical world's version of the Second Coming, this is one of the safest places she can be. With so many *weres* under Aric's charge, nothing would dare attack her there.

Thanks, I text back. *I'll call later.*

Wait. Is your extra credit project done? she writes back.

Almost, I respond.

Did you pass? she presses.

I flip the visor back up after another good look at my new face in the mirror. I still can't get over these startling eyes. *Not yet,* I reply. *But I should. I have to go, but should be home tomorrow.*

Cool, she responds, and I can almost picture her smiling.

I shove my phone back into the shiny purse Paula gave me. This model never ate anything more than lettuce and the occasional bite of a celery stick. I'm sure of it. My crew couldn't find a bra that fit me so I went without. It seemed like a good idea at the time, but as the cool air rushes in through the windows and my nipples salute the night, I'm starting to think it's a bad idea.

Thank God, I had an extra pair of witch-wear and a new thong in my supply closet. The panties I'd worn during my chanting kept falling to my thighs. As pretty as this woman is, I'll admit, I prefer my own ass.

"They're at Moon Song," I say.

"Good, that's even closer," Merri says, cutting left at the light.

Paula and Fiona mutter in agreement from the back. They're incognito. Well, at least they're trying to be. They all have baseball caps and sunglasses. No, that doesn't look odd considering it's nighttime. The exception is Merri who's wearing a Ronald McDonald clown wig which, let me tell you, clashes brutally with the hair on her feet.

Personally, I didn't think the disguises were necessary, seeing how they've been holed up at the compound, and especially since all other supernaturals would only be able to recognize them as witches. They don't know my task, and hopefully won't figure it out. But these girls are going out of their way for me, and I'm really touched by it.

"Thank you," I say. "For everything."

"We couldn't let you do this by yourself," Fiona says. "It would have been too difficult."

"Yeah, you could have," I tell them. "The others did."

Merri smiles. "Nah. We're in this together."

Maybe we are.

It doesn't take long to reach the lodge. I wave goodbye as they pull away, then walk carefully up the stone steps. Two men heading out for the night whistle as I pass them. They're human. I can feel as much, but their responses do nothing for me. The attention I seek, isn't from some random stranger. It's from a wolf I can no longer have.

I cross the large lobby and head to where the sign for Moon Song lights up in white and red over the entrance. I'm feeling good, confident . . . until I reach the entrance and see Gemini sitting at the end of the bar.

He leans against the bar, taking a long pull from his bottle of brew, the motion bulging the muscles of his arms against the black T-shirt he's wearing. His back is to Celia and Aric. She's laughing as she bends over the pool table with a long stick in her hand. Aric curls his body around her, placing his hands over hers and guiding her hands forward.

She nods at something he says and pulls back her arm, ready to strike the ball. But Aric whispers something in her ear, causing her to miss entirely and almost scratch the surface. Although, I'm a good distance away, and the room is dim, I know her well enough to know she's blushing.

"Can I help you?" a gravelly voice asks beside me.

I play with my hair. My magical instincts letting me

know the big guy with the Mohawk beside me is all *were*. *Weres* can sniff a lie as easily as I breathe so I don't even bother. "Could you tell me where the ladies room is?" I ask, my lighter tone overtly flirty without trying.

"I'd rather tell you where my room is," he responds, eyeing me like he can already taste my skin.

Sure you would, buddy.

"Past the bar," he says, when I don't respond.

Of course it is. I'm not ready to walk by Gemini. Celia, yeah, but only because I've spent an entire car ride psyching myself up for this moment. But as I trail my fingertips down my super long and unfairly elegant throat, I'm reminded I'm no longer me. I'm supermodel me, and that's a hell of a lot better than some cheap disguise.

I lift my chin and force myself toward the bar area, noticing for the first time how different my walk is. It's a strut seething with confidence, similar to the way I used to enter a room, but different as the swing of my hips is more pronounced.

Eyes drift away from their drinks and their dates as I pass, all eyes but Gemini's. I give him a passing glance to make sure, my motion subtle and only enough to see his response. Yet aside from lifting his beer to his lips, he doesn't move, keeping that same slouchy position along the bar.

I stiffen slightly when Celia steps away from the pool table as I reach her. I'm sure she'll recognize me until she reaches for Aric and laughs at something he says. I keep my gaze on the door to the ladies' room, floored with how well this spell is working.

I don't need to use the bathroom, but I do need a moment to collect myself and take another long look in the mirror. I smile, allowing every speck of me to become this woman before me. She's hot, and she knows it. Seems to me it's time to own this role.

When I step out, I throw the door open, and really get the feel of these long legs. In the short time I was away, more *weres* have arrived. Some are sweaty, the familiar scent of a hunt permeates the room. We don't know what evil is rising, or when it will appear. But chances are it will appear very close to Celia and to the baby she's carrying. We also don't know where Savana is, something that's put supernaturals across the country on edge. Aside from me and my family, everyone who's found her, hasn't lived to share the experience.

I return to the bar in time to catch Aric's hand pass along Celia's baby bump. She bends forward and attempts to take another shot. But this time, he doesn't curl around her, locking eyes with the largest *were* who takes a seat at a nearby table. This *were* probably led the hunt, but the slight shake of his head demonstrates his team didn't turn anything up.

Aric nods, his shoulders relaxing, but only slightly. For now, there's nothing that threatens his mate and their child, but that can change from one prowl to the next. I pretend to fumble with the contents of my purse as I observe the exchange, taking a second to shut off my phone.

I'm supposed to be human and therefore blind to what's happening. So when I look up I'm smiling, like there's nothing out there ready to kill my sister. My teasing grin earns me a wink and a motion forward from the *were* who led the hunt to join him.

I keep my smile and play with my hair, flirting just enough before I turn to where Gemini is sitting. "Hi," I say, hoping my voice stays steady.

He doesn't answer, pushing his empty bottle away with a tap of his fingertips.

"Is this seat taken?" I ask a little louder. I know he heard me, despite the growing clamor around the room. But I'm pretending to be human, so I have to pretend he can't hear me over the noise.

He looks my way. He's not frowning, but he isn't exactly friendly either. Dark circles ring those heartbreaking eyes, his once neat goatee is scraggly, and his large muscles are threatening to split his shirt down his spine. But he doesn't look sexy.

Nope.

Not even a little bit.

Who the hell am I kidding? The man is one giant erection wearing a cape. As it is, my nipples are poking through this thin fabric, demanding he pay them the attention they deserve.

Except he doesn't even look. Well, at the girls, anyway. The way he's eyeing me is more like someone who's bored and unimpressed. I should be insulted, especially in this super suit. Instead, I see it as a challenge.

"Am I bothering you?" I give a one shoulder shrug. "If I am, I can find someplace else to sit."

"You can do whatever you want," he says, motioning to the stool. "The choice is yours."

He turns his attention back to the bar. The bartender returns, his stare cutting my way as he speaks. "Ready for another one, Gemini?" he asks him.

The way this bartender is looking at me would have earned him one hell of growl from my wolf if we were still together. But he doesn't so much as blink, even when I lean into the bar and the bartender's eyes travel the swells of my small breasts. "Sure, Steve. And whatever the lady is having."

"Oh," I say, my confidence building. I trail my nails along his bulky arm. "So chivalry isn't dead, is it?"

He doesn't respond to my words or my touch. But I lick my lips and pretend that he did. "I'll have a glass of champagne." Ordinarily, I'm a martini girl. But I'm not ordinary today.

"Champagne?" The bartender chuckles. "What are you celebrating, sweet thing?"

He doesn't care that I'm overtly flirting with Gemini. But again, Gemini, doesn't react. I lower my lashes, eyeing my former lover with all the naughty things I wish he could still do to me. "New friends, perhaps?" I suggest.

I make it plenty clear to Steve that he doesn't stand a chance. His focus trails to Gemini. "That's one hell of friend you're making," he mutters.

"Your name is Gemini," I say, trying to keep up my non-lying.

He looks at me then. "Gemini is a nickname. My real name is Tomo."

"I like that name," I whisper, lust building in my tone. Tomo is the name I always used when we were in bed and he'd climb on top of me.

Steve returns with a bottle champagne and pours into a long stem glass, his attention bouncing between me and Gemini. I glance away from him, losing myself in Gem's stare. With these borrowed eyes, I'm no longer afraid to look at him or fear what he may see. They won't give away how much I miss him and how hurt I am that we didn't work out. Yet they will permit me to reveal my need and desire to wake up beside him.

I'm safe to show him how much I want him, and I don't hold back.

He watches me closely. "What's your name?" he asks.

I lift my glass. "What do you want it to be?"

"Is this a joke?" he asks.

"No." I take a sip. "The choice is yours." I repeat his words, yet my tone suggests I'm offering a lot more.

"Who's this?"

I'm so enthralled by Gemini, and everything I'm suggesting, I didn't notice Celia or Aric approach. But I see her now and catch the sharpness to her tone. She's not happy to find me here with Gemini.

"A friend," I answer, meeting her with a naughty grin.

Funny enough, Celia's not smiling back. Her narrowing focus skims from me to Gemini. "You have to be kidding me."

Aric places his hand on the small of her back. He doesn't seem any happier, but where Celia is bordering on attacking, Aric's features shadow with concern.

Gemini leans back and takes a swig of his beer. "Celia, we're just talking. Nothing has happened between us."

"Yet," I offer, adding another impish grin that absolutely earns me no Celia points.

She looks ready to snap my freaking neck. I want to hug her, throw my arms around her and thank her for being the best sister ever. But I'm having too much fun.

"She's trash, Gemini—"

"His name is Tomo," I interrupt, glancing his way. "That's what you want me to call you, isn't it, big guy?"

Celia knows I'm the only gal who gets to call him that, and when and where that name is used.

"And what's your name?" she asks, taking a step forward.

"We haven't gone that far," Gemini say.

"Yet," I say, again.

Aric wedges his way between us. "Gemini, don't do this," he tells him. "You're making a mistake."

Gem meets his face with equal force. "It wouldn't be the first time," he tells him.

Aric stiffens. So do I. Shit. I wasn't sure he was willing to sleep with me, but I'm starting to think he might. And son of a bitch, who else has he been sleeping with? Vieve, yeah, I figured he would have rocked her broomsticks.

"Don't do this to Taran," Celia snaps, the tips of her nails lengthening. "You told me you've remained faithful. I believed you. Don't tell me you're giving that up for this slut."

"Hey," I say, growing defensive, at the same time damn impressed Celia is willing to kick my ass in my defense.

"I never claimed to be faithful. I only told you I haven't spent the night with another female," Gemini says, straightening and stealing a look my way. "Maybe it's time things changed. If she's willing."

"You *asshole*," she tells him.

"Gem, don't do this," Aric says, his voice a low growl. "You're making a decision based on anger and need."

My sister is spitting mad, her breath releasing in furious spurts. "Aric, tell him he can't do this," she pleads.

"I can't," he replies.

She whips around so fast, her long wavy hair sweeps across her shoulders. "Please," she begs him.

He reaches for her, frowning in Gemini's direction. "I can't interfere in something like this. No matter how much

I'm against it."

His last words were more a plea of friendship. Gemini stiffens his jaw, refusing to budge from his stool or his decision. He wants this body. In a way it destroys me despite that it's still me beneath. But this is why alcohol and heartbreak don't mix, and why it's easy to glide my hand down his thigh.

"You don't know what you're doing," Celia bites out, watching where my hand stops. "You deserve more than this."

I down my champagne, and pull out the big guns. "Oh. I see," I say, giving his thigh a squeeze. "If this is about numbers, you're welcome to join us." I lick my lips and flicker my attention to Aric. "I'm all about a good time."

Celia's claws stop mere millimeters from my throat. Aric drags her away from me and out the door, hissing mad. The *weres* around us return to their drinks, likely disappointed in the lack of chaos and bloodshed. Hey, there's a reason why *were* bars are insured for extensive damage.

I return to my champagne when Gemini fills my glass. If he wants me, really wants me, and this whole thing wasn't for show, he needs to make the next move. For now I'm calm, cool, and all about class.

Too bad none of these attributes stay with me when Aric and Celia appear on the other side of the wall of windows. Damn, my girl is seriously pissed. I choke on my champagne as Aric sets her down. I can't hear what she's saying, but I see enough.

Her arms are flailing and she's yelling, pointing at him. Aric crosses his arms. He's mad too, but it's frustration that overtakes his features. His hands are tied like he said, and like he's probably reminding her, which does little to comfort my hormonal sister.

Her glare turns in my direction. I offer a small smile and an even smaller wave, hoping to settle her, even a little bit. Aric snags her when she lunges at the window, dragging her away. She says something like, I don't know, "fuck off", maybe? It's the last thing I catch before they disappear across the parking lot.

"Hmm. Your friend there is really mad," I say, fluffing my hair.

"She tends to be protective," Gemini responds, returning to his beer.

I have another glass of champagne and fill another. I don't typically drink a lot, but in the silence and time that passes between us, there's not much else to do. How long do we sit there, an hour? I'm not sure. But even though the tension that followed our breakup isn't present, there is tension all the same. It's the kind that speaks of bare skin, teasing hands, and hard pounds.

I'm more than halfway done with the bottle when the ol' liquid courage kicks. I'm not smiling, or flirting, but my tone and the way my female regions begin to throb assure I mean what I say. "Remember what you said about spending the night with me if I'm willing?" I ask.

He lowers his beer, his dark eyes meeting mine. "I do," he replies, his voice husky.

I lean in close, gliding my hand along his chest. "I'm willing," I whisper.

Chapter Twenty-four

Gemini and I had this thing we always did when we were in public, on our way to very private. His fingers would skim down my back to clutch my hip, letting everyone in the vicinity know I was his. He's not doing that now, even as the attendant hands him the key to room 216. That's our room for the night. Second floor, somewhere in the middle.

In the past, he would have requested something bigger, grander. "Only the best for my mate," he'd say.

But I'm not his mate tonight. I'm a woman who looks nothing like her, a stranger who agreed to occupy his bed.

That familiar twinge of rejection twists my heart as we cross the lobby. There's at least half a foot separating us, enough so he won't risk accidently touching me or meeting my hand.

If I didn't know him, I'd have nothing to do with a man who treats me this way—even though I'm the culprit behind this one-night stand. But I do know him, and love him more than fucking life. So if it means one more night with him, I'll allow it.

He prowls forward, causing the couple stepping out of the elevator to scramble away. "Are you mad about something, Tomo?" I ask as we step inside.

"Why would I be mad?" he asks. "I thought you

wanted this?"

I edge closer, wrapping my long thin arms around his neck. In this body and in these shoes, I'm only a few inches shorter than his six-foot, two-inch frame. "I do," I say, leaning in to kiss him.

He jerks his chin away before my lips can connect. "Something wrong?" I ask, more than a little taken aback.

"There's only one woman I kiss," he says in a way that halts me in place.

"I take it she's not me?" I manage.

"No," he says, turning back to face me.

My hands slip away from his neck. I step away, trying not to freak out. I remind myself this is a role, and it's not personal. But when it comes to Gemini, it's almost impossible.

"I want you to wear a condom," I say, trying to embrace the charade I created.

He leans back against the wall and crosses his arm. "I'm not wearing a condom," he responds without blinking.

All right then.

"I'm clean if that's what you're worried about," he adds.

Weres are immune to disease. I know as much, but I'm pretending I don't. That doesn't mean he couldn't knock me up if I wasn't on the pill.

He pushes off the wall when the doors clang open, positioning his body against them to keep them from closing when I fail to move. "Are you clean?" he asks.

"Yes," I answer.

"Are you on birth control?"

I nod.

"Then that's all we need to know." He tilts his head down the hall. "After you," he says. When I hesitate he adds. "Unless you don't want what I have to offer."

My Gemini, the one I know so well doesn't speak to me this way. He murmurs lust-filled words intermixed love and a whole lot of naughty. He'd never suggest that this is sex and nothing more.

I let out a breath, watching the way he regards me. If I go with him, he'll take me. If not, there are plenty of women downstairs he can choose from, and one head witch just a phone call away. Either way he doesn't care. My wolf is done being the good guy.

"Well?" he asks.

He's being a purposeful prick so he knows what I'm in for and what not to expect. We're not going to make love, share it, let alone bask in it. No, this is going to be angry sex based on the underlying growl beneath his words: hot, fast, hard. The kind that will leave me sore in all the right ways.

I weigh my options, at least I try to. But it doesn't take me long to decide. I walk forward, keeping my attention ahead as I sashay to room 216.

I glance over my shoulder when I realize he's the one appearing to hesitate.

"What's wrong?" I ask, stopping in front of the door to our room. "I thought you wanted to fuck me."

From one breath to the next he's there, his eyes flashing with need. My comment earned me back control. I like it, and the confidence it stirs. I edge toward him, palming his erection.

I gasp, as he drags me to him, our bodies colliding. "Do I scare you?" he asks, his dark stare latching onto mine.

The only thing that scares me is him walking away. As my heart pounds brutally against my chest, I know there's only one thing to say. "No. My body is yours to take."

My breath hitches as his lips crash against mine. The kiss is deep, lustful, bordering on crazed. I can barely keep up, my head swimming with desire. But as hard as he grips me to him, he yanks me away with equal force.

"I thought there's only one woman you kiss," I stammer.

"Tonight I'll make the exception," he responds, hauling me back.

He lifts me into a straddle, a slight breeze smacking against my back with how fast he moves. I remember spinning and the sound of a door slamming shut before his teeth find my neck and my back is shoved against a wall.

We're in the room, but I barely notice it. Gemini yanks my dress over my head, his chin dipping to pull my nipple into his hot mouth.

Jolts of electricity fire along my skin, standing the little hairs on end. I'm sure my lightning is building within me, until I remind myself that in this shell, I have no magic. It was taken from me as easily as Gemini peels off clothes.

He lowers me to the floor, freeing me of my panties, but leaving my high-heels in place. I unsnap his jeans, fumbling to pull them and his briefs down when his hand slips between my thighs.

I'm trying not to curse, to keep up the part I'm playing. But it's hard. Those fingers that once knew me so well swirl, exploring my soft throbbing skin, slicking it like the tongue passing along my throat.

"Tomo," I bite out, startling when he pushes his fingers inside.

My hands grasp his thick and growing length, twisting up and around in rough motions. A drop of warmth reaches the tip. Yet instead of allowing me to play, he kicks out of his clothes and carries me across the room.

He lowers me on top of the dresser, turning me to face the mirror. My knees are bent in front me. I'm not sure what he's planning, falling still as he yanks off his tight T-shirt. But then he shows me a lot more than I've ever seen of him, and me.

He pries my legs open. "What are you doing?" I ask.

"Giving me a better view," he murmurs, his teeth biting on my lobe and his fingers gliding to my center.

My eyes fly open. At first his movements are slow, steady, trying to find the right combination of speed and motion. But when he finds it—*damn*—my legs kick out, the points of my heels driving into the wall and leaving deep scratches.

The screaming and cursing I'm known for, release as I lose my mind. The building passion so hot and furious, it's almost too much.

But I want more.

My breasts bounce as my body moves with him, mimicking his movements and inciting his free hand to tease the tightening centers. My orgasm peaks, the force making me grunt with desire.

My head lolls back against his shoulder as my release recedes. But as I turn to kiss him, I'm denied.

"No," he rumbles. "I want you to watch what I do to you."

Again, he enters me with his fingers, exploring me deeper and faster. I should be embarrassed by my whimpers and the way my body rattles from the ecstasy shooting across my limbs. But I don't fight it, allowing myself to come undone and surrendering to what I've gone so long without.

I'm not quite finished when I shove away from the dresser, clumsily falling to my knees. Gem tries to wrench me up, to do whatever he plans next. But I don't let him, wrapping my lips around that part of his body I can't wait to taste.

He stumbles forward, cursing, as that familiar tickle reaches my throat. Back and forth, back and forth. I tighten my suction and going deeper yet. He wanted a nymph tonight, someone who's naughty and not very nice. That's what I give him. No way will he forget me now.

Anger and resentment stemming from all the nights I went without him, all those moments I saw him with Vieve when he should have been with me—all those times he rejected my body, my arm, because I was no longer whole, fuel each forceful pass. He likes it rough. He always has. Tonight is no exception.

His release is near. I can feel the pulses with each pass. I have him where I want him. Yet that's not where he wants me.

He yanks me to my feet, spinning me so I'm facing the mirror as he enters me. Given his size, he's always had to work to fill me. But this body I'm in has never had sex with a *were*, and he has to work that much harder because of it.

My palms slap against either side of the dresser as I

fall forward, groaning. I bite down on my bottom lip, watching each press of his hips join us closer. But once he's in, the care he used is gone.

Not that I miss it.

He hooks his arm behind my elbows, his opposite hand wrapping around my throat to turn me and allow his kiss. But those thrusts are beast-like, true to his nature, and so delicious, I jerk away from his lips.

I'm no longer trying to be quiet. I can't. Not with him pounding behind me as rigidly as he is. So I don't try, begging him for more.

I'm not sure how many times he finishes me. But as he pulls out, and steps back and onto the bed, I know he's not done. His skin is flushed red, his breaths are pronounced, and sweat trickles across his broad chest. He sprawls across the bed, tucking his hands behind his head. He appears relaxed. But as his lower half lengthens and grows thicker, I know sleep is the last thing on this wolf's mind.

"Your turn," he tells me.

Chapter Twenty-five

I don't know what time it is. The digital clock in the room was smashed to bits along with the lamp when Gemini took me against the nightstand sometime around three. I lift my head from where I fell asleep on his lap. I think I could have slept forever with him like this. But the pain in my right arm reminds me "forever" with Gemini died almost a year ago.

Shit.

Traces of the bind appear across my borrowed body's skin. It's not enough to notice from afar. But I'm close enough to see it won't be long before my real form returns.

My "real" form, the one that Gemini no longer begs for. Not like he begged for this body.

The building resentment that made the sex so primal and raw returns at once. But instead of fueling my need to bury my face in his lap, it fills me with sadness, and maybe a little anger too.

I carefully push away from him, stopping briefly once he stirs. When we were together, and he'd feel me wake, he'd clutch me against him, if I wasn't already buried deep in his embrace.

Today is different. He rolls away from me and onto his stomach, putting some distance between us. It shouldn't bother me as much as it does. This was a one-night stand. No promises were made. No proclamations of love exchanged.

Angry sex, wasn't that what people call it?

It's funny, but as I rise on the opposite end, the physical intimacy we shared is the last thing on my mind. My anger isn't far away, and neither is that familiar pang of hurt.

I dress quickly, once I find my discarded panties, careful not to make too much noise, yet unable to pry my eyes off him. He remains on his stomach, one leg bent, bulging the muscles on his back, thighs, and ass.

A sheet tangles around part of one thigh. I have a few pics of him like that, some with me in them, but most solely of him. He never seemed to mind, often lifting his head enough so I'd capture his heat-filled gaze.

"You're not so shy for the camera. Are you?" I'd teased.

"Why should I be?" he'd ask smiling with all the sin I felt as I snapped the first of many pics. "It's proof that I'm yours and that you belong to me."

In other words, I don't give a damn who knows we're having sex.

As I lift my purse, I'm tempted to dig out my phone. One last photo, one last shred of evidence that we were together. But I can't. Night changes everything, something about it making us take chances and lose our inhibitions. In the daylight, common freaking sense kicks in and so does a nasty amount of logic.

I remind myself that last night he was with someone else. It doesn't matter that it was me beneath those unfamiliar layers of skin. In his eyes, I was a stranger. Someone who will never really know him, but maybe that's what he needed.

I needed him anyway I could have him. And even though I still want him, he won't feel the same the moment I change back.

He adjusts himself in bed, further away from me, reminding me how little I matter to him, even now. I doubt he'd pull that with Vieve, and not just because of her ranking among the supernatural elite. No, she means more to him than that.

"There's only one woman I kiss," he'd said.

I fooled myself into thinking it was me. But considering it didn't take him long to change his mind, I'm wondering if those kisses come to anyone willing to gratify his beast.

As that familiar tinge of jealousy wraps around my throat and gives a tug, I whip around and head toward the door. Jealously leads to hurt, and I'm done feeling all this pain.

"Where are you going, Taran?"

I freeze in place with my hand on the knob. I don't turn around right away. But when I do it's like my jaw unhinges. Christ. If this were a Looney Tunes cartoon, I'd have rug burn on my chin.

He huffs, pushing up on his elbows. "Give a wolf credit for recognizing his mate, no matter what ridiculous form she takes."

"You . . . how could you?" It would be cool if I could form a single sentence right about now. "You didn't think it was so ridiculous last night," I finally snap.

"You're right," he says, keeping his tone and expression deadpan. "Come back to bed."

"Bed". The way he says it carries as much lust as the steady pound of his hips. As it is, my puny nipples are pointing to where he's waiting, just in case I missed his naked body sprawled across the bed.

"No," I manage.

He stalks forward, hardening with each step. "Come back *to bed*," he repeats, punching each syllable with all the passion circling us.

The space dissolves between us. He's not holding me, but the way his body is pressed against mine, it's like he's already clutching me and we're already making love. "Do you think I could forget the way you look at me when we make love?" he asks. His fingers trail down my arm to circle my palm. "Or how it feels to have you touch me?"

"When did you know?" I ask, wishing he didn't make it so hard for me to speak. "We didn't make love right away, and I barely touched you before we did."

"The moment you walked into the bar," he answers gruffly. "My wolves latched onto your presence and it was all I could do to keep them in place."

Somehow, I manage to pry my eyes off him. "You lied to me," I say, tripping over my words, because right now, considering what's poking my belly, I have nothing better.

"And what do you call what you did to me?"

"I didn't lie to you," I say, meeting his face.

"All right, would you prefer connive, scheme, conspire. I have other words if *lying* doesn't work for you," he tells me, his voice growing louder. "Whatever you call it was meant to deceive me."

"No. It was meant to deceive Celia." I square my shoulders. "You just happened to be in the way."

"How was I in the way?" He spins me so abruptly, I barely register my breasts sliding against the wall.

Slowly, he presses his hard front into my all too willing back. "Like this?" he murmurs.

My body shudders, and so does his. I should be pissed that he lied and fooled me and—and—

I moan when his lips find the back of my ear and he tugs down my panties. Without thinking, I spread my legs open, angling my chin to welcome his lips.

When he kisses me, it's not in that demanding way he did last night. His sweet lips pass over mine like they used to, full of a yearning that carves its way into my soul.

I love you. God, I love you.

He deepens our kiss, my body quivering as he bends his knees and prepares to enter me. But as he pushes his way in, and I shudder again, I feel his abrupt withdraw.

He swears, releasing his grip to my waist and smacking his hands against the wall.

"What's wrong?" I ask, the need for him to merge us, making me sound desperate.

We're both breathing fast, but as I look to where he's staring, I realize his feelings don't stem from the desire I feel. My arm alternates in shades of dark to light, attempting to push through the spell.

I turn to face him. It's easy, he's given me plenty of space.

"I see," I tell him, all the love I felt dissipating in the air between us.

He wrenches his gaze from my arm back to my face. "No, you don't," he fires back.

"Don't I?" I yank on my panties and motion to his dwindling erection. "You could have fooled me."

He grabs my left arm when I reach for the door. "That's not what this about."

"Spare me," I say, fury making my head pound. "I'm done with your lies and your fucking pity."

I pull away, tucking my arm as I stomp down the hall. By some mercy of God there's no one in the elevator when I reach it. I take a few calming breaths, almost crying as I cradle my arm.

I stroke it, trying soothe it, and me. I don't expect it to respond to my touch, yet as the elevator begins its descent, the skin resumes the dark tone of my borrowed half.

My heightened emotions—this time *love* of all things!—triggered my arm to react. It makes sense, hours have passed and the spell is weakening.

My hands fall away when I catch my reflection against the doors. I shouldn't be surprised at the amount of hickies taking residence along my exposed skin. But even in the blurry image I can tell I'm covered with them.

For the love of all, I might as well be holding a sign that says Walk of Shame in Progress.

I'm bra-less, barely dressed, and my hair screams that I've had a crazy amount of sex (and loved it!).

I step out of the elevator, trying not to groan when the woman walking toward me yanks her child away from me. Her husband on the other hand inches closer. That's awesome. So are the looks I receive from everyone returning from brunch because clearly, I'm not feeling trampy enough.

I shove my hand in my purse and pull out my phone, cursing when I realize my battery is dead even though I'd turned it off. I can't call Paula, Merri, or Fiona. I don't know their numbers by heart.

But I do know my sisters'.

The concierge's eyes widen when I approach. "Good morning," I say, forcing a smile. "May I borrow your phone please?"

His stare travels to my neck and a little further south. I shove my phone in his face to keep his attention away from me and on task. "My battery died." Without another word he passes me the phone and steps away.

Celia answers on the third ring, her sleepy voice clueing me in that I wasn't the only one up all night. "Hello?" she says.

"Hey, Ceel. It's me, Taran," I begin.

At first I think the line went dead, the silence on the other end so profound it's like a physical force being shoved against my ear. "Ceel, are you there?"

"This isn't Taran," she snaps, her voice lowering with anger. "You're that stupid tramp from last night."

It's times like this where I'm reminded how good my sister's memory is. "No. It's Taran. I'm in disguise."

"You're in disguise?" she repeats, her tone mocking. "Honey, you're messing with the wrong person."

I hold the phone away at her growl, speaking fast. "Ceel, last night, it was me getting a rise out of you and Aric."

"You're disgusting and a liar," she tells me.

"You don't have to be mean," I say, growing defensive. "Look, I'll prove it by telling you something only Taran would know—"

"If you've done anything to hurt my sister, I'll kill you. Do you hear me? I'll tear your skin off in ribbons and tie them into little bows."

Holy. Shit.

"Okay, I'm going to stop you right there, Ceel." I glance around to make sure no one is within hearing distance. "Right now, you're tired from being up all night having hot make-up sex with your mate, Aric. The fact that you're even speaking to me means he's probably at the Den, getting what he needs to get done, done, so he can return to you and finish making it up to you for not stopping Gemini from sleeping with me, even though it was me. I'm at the lodge. Come get me. You'll be back in bed, waiting for Aric before you know it. Oh, and you like bacon. Like, a lot."

There's a brief pause. "I'll be there in ten minutes," she says.

She disconnects. Okay. So far one thing went right today. A little old man who's been watching me shuffles forward. "How much?" he asks me.

I stare down at his little spotted head. "How much for what?"

He smiles bashfully. It's then I'm torn between smacking him upside the head and feeling sorry for him. Lucky for him, I err on the latter. He's old and probably lonely.

I reach for the pad and pen on the desk and scribble Mrs. Mancuso's number.

"She'll take care of you," I say with a wink.

I strut across the lobby, trying to hang on to what little dignity remains when more lascivious stares trail my way. Damn it, it's not like I forgot my panties.

Celia can't arrive fast enough. She rolls Aric's black Explorer to a stop in front of the lodge, but she doesn't disengage the lock. I almost break a nail when I try to open the door and the handle slaps back.

Okay, now I'm annoyed.

"Are you going to let me in or what?" I ask. She watches me briefly, hitting the button to unlock the door .I throw it open, slumping into the front driver's seat and tossing my purse on the floor. "You're not going to believe my fucking night," I tell her, slamming the door shut and clicking my seatbelt in place. "It was totally hot, wicked, and awesome. I swear if angels had flown out of my vagina, I wouldn't have been surprised." I pause when I realize she's gaping at me.

"Oh, my God," she says barely above a breath. "It really is you."

"Of course it's me, Ceel." I throw out my hands. "And here I was certain you'd figure me out."

Her stare travels from my out of control hair to my lap. "No way. I didn't have a clue." She shakes her head. "But why?"

"It's something I can't talk about, but something that will allow me back into coven hell."

"I see," she says, the nostrils of her small nose flaring. She grimaces, cringing slightly.

"What's wrong?" I ask.

She swallows hard. "I can smell you."

I sniff on my clothes, thinking I need deodorant or shower. "No," she says, swallowing again like she's trying not to be sick. "I can smell you *and* him."

Based on the way she's looking at me and how I feel the color drain from my face, I know what she means, but ask anyway. "You don't mean our natural scents, do you? The ones we always carry."

She covers her eyes and shakes her head. "God, Taran. It's one thing to scent this aroma on Aric, it's another thing when it's on my sister."

"Yeah, I totally get it," I agree.

My words cut off as Gemini plops into the back seat.

Guessing by Celia's reddening face when he shuts the door, she gets another whiff of us. I suppose doubling the sex fiends, doubles the aroma.

"Celia," he says.

"Ah, hey," she answers, rolling down the window and pulling away from the curb.

"Wait, where are you going?" She doesn't answer me. "You can't take him with us."

"I can't just leave him here," she says. "Aric needs him at the Den."

"The hell he does!" I insist. "I'm not riding in the same car with him."

"Taran, you need to get back to the coven, he needs to return to the Den. What do you want me to do, throw him out of the window?"

"It would be a start," I answer, smiling.

"You'll have to forgive my mate, Celia," Gemini says. "She's irritable when she hasn't had any sleep."

"I'm not your mate," I snap, wishing he didn't go there.

"You're wrong," he adds.

"And I had sleep!" I add because I have nothing better.

Gemini doesn't seem riled, keeping his tone easy. "You needed sleep considering what happened between us." He pauses. "Or should I say what didn't."

I veer on Celia who's shrinking in her seat. "Can you believe this shit?"

Her hands tighten on the steering wheel. "Please leave me out of this," she begs.

I whip around to face him. "Yes. Leave her out of this. Do you think my sister wants to hear how you bent me over on the bed?"

And over the sink.

And against the wall.

And in the shower.

Oh, and the closet too—but that was an accident seeing how we fell into it when we were up against the wall.

My girl parts sing *Halleluiah* at the memory, and the way he gripped my ass when he threw my legs over his shoulders and—

"Oh, God," Celia moans, rubbing her face when she stops at a light.

My body heats as I watch his skin flush. His short dark hair is slightly mussed and his stare carries that familiar glaze it did when he yanked my hair back and pounded into me. But he doesn't look hot.

Not at all.

Okay. Maybe he does.

Celia punches the gas, racing toward Squaw Valley as fast as she can go. By now, she has all the windows down and she's practically driving with her head sticking out.

"You want to talk about last night?" Gemini asks.

"No," Celia and I say at once.

He ignores us both. "While this isn't something I'd normally discuss with others present, I think I should take advantage of this situation, seeing how you've spent months ignoring me, blocked my number, refused my calls, and rejected any attempt at cordial communication."

"The only thing you took advantage of was me. Last night."

My comment makes him smile. A really sexy smile. God damn it.

"Did I approach you?" he asks. "Or was it the other way around?"

"I just needed a place to sit—near Celia because she was my target. I didn't even know you were going to be there!"

"There were other seats," he reminds me.

"You mean with those other *weres*? The ones who couldn't keep their eyes off me when I walked in? Or by the bouncer who asked me to his room the moment I arrived?"

He stops smiling then.

I nod thoughtfully. "Yeah, looks like you weren't the only one who noticed me last night. I wonder what would have happened if I did sit somewhere else."

"His heart would have landed beside you when I ripped it from his chest," he adds, the viciousness and truth behind his words immediately erasing my smile.

"Why?" I ask.

The intensity is his stare halts the world from spinning and time from moving. I no longer feel the road as Celia barrels up the mountain. I only see him. "Because you're still mine," he says. "Even though you choose not to be."

I turn around, facing the front, love and hate warring inside me and making my motions jerky. He had go and say something like that. Even though I'm not the one to blame.

He pulled away from me *and* my touch. So, he can say what he wants, but we both know it's not true.

I swipe the stupid tear that manages to escape, stopping when I catch Celia wipe away her own sadness. She knows what I'm feeling maybe a little too well. But the difference is Aric isn't going anywhere. Not anymore. And even though Gemini sits directly behind me, I don't think he's ever been so far away.

None of us speak the rest of the way, but I know we're all reacting. Well, at least me and Gemini are, seeing how Celia continues to maneuver the large vehicle with her face partially out. She scents the tension and guilt, and maybe some of the heartbreak, too.

But she also scents more than any of us would like.

She grimaces as the image of my thighs lowering on either side of Gemini's head pops into my mind and sends an extra dose of lust seeping into the air. Poor thing, I'll probably have to make it up to her with a bacon basket or perhaps some nice bath salts. Yeah, she'll like that.

"Thank you, Baby Jesus," she mutters when we finally reach the Den.

Tall wrought iron gates part on either side of the stone fortress that surrounds the property. The *were* on guard lifts his radio to his mouth, likely informing Aric of Celia's presence. Yet as we pass, his stare hones in on me. He doesn't know who I am, and in his opinion, I shouldn't be allowed in. But with his Leader's mate at the wheel, and the Second in Command in the rear, he knows better than to question.

Acres of lush green grass cover the mountainside and a thick stand of trees spread along the perimeter. Like Camp Coven, this place is fortified with magical defenses strong enough to prickle my skin. The combo of *were* and witch make it an on odd blend, at least from my perspective. But since both are natural and of the earth, they complement each other like a seasoned orchestra with a world renowned soprano. It's another thing about the witches I envy, they and the *weres* are a perfect union of magic. Gem and I are not. It seems odd to admit as much, since I never would have believed it before. But unlike with the witches, my magic and the Pack's clashed, resulting in an arm that wants me dead.

I should be mad at it, and maybe hate it too, as I've often done. But I find myself stroking it once more. More than anything, I wish we could be right together.

Just like I wish me and Gemini could be right together, too.

I catch sight of *weres* in their animal forms tearing through the wooded tree line: cougars, wolves, bears, and even a lynx, as Celia continues down the road. They're probably engaged in some activity to teach them to track and hunt, while the *weres* directly ahead of us wrestle and tumble along a large grassy field in human form.

Celia slows her speed as we reach the main road, where two and three story mountain villas, serving as residences, office space, and classrooms line either side. It wasn't too long ago this place was almost destroyed. But some things you can't keep down for long. And those things include *weres*.

Celia parks along the curb when we reach one of the larger villas. Aric jogs down the stacked stone steps when he sees her, his pace slowing and his grin dwindling when he sees me sitting in the front. I smile and wave. But it's not until he reaches Celia's side, and apparently gets an extra whiff of me and his bestie's hot night, that he realizes what's happening.

His head snaps back as if I brought my open palm down on his nose, making him stagger. His wide eyes shift from me to Gemini. "*Taran?*" he asks.

"Hey," I answer. "Wassup?"

I don't think our combined sex-worthy aroma quite reaches his nose a second time before he throws the door open and hauls Celia out, not that she's complaining since she can't seem to jump out of the car fast enough.

He clasps her hand, shaking his head as he leads her away from us. "That must have been a fun ride up," he mumbles.

I scramble out. "Wait. You said you'd drive me to Camp Coven!"

She steals a glance at Aric, my spine stiffening when the rear door slams shut and heavy steps stop behind me. "I think you guys need to talk," she says. "I'll give you a minute, and then drive you wherever you'd like."

"Thank you," Gemini says, coming to my side.

"Yeah. Thanks," I mutter.

She narrows her eyes. I narrow them back. "Don't get pissy with me," I tell her. "You're supposed to be on my side."

It's Aric who answers. "We are on your side," he says quietly. He nods briefly to Gemini, then slides his arm around Celia and guides her into the building.

I don't want to do this, but Celia took the keys with her and it's not like I can exactly walk off the mountain. But being so close to him, and not being able to touch him. You might say it sucks.

My arm buzzes and shakes, my riled emotions stirring its magic and reminding me that the spell I conjured doesn't have much time left.

"What happens now?" he asks.

I frown, unsure what he's asking. "What do you mean?"

He leans back on his heels, crossing his arms. "Between us, Taran."

"We go back to how we were," I say. I mean to sound tough. But tough is one thing I can't seem to be in this wolf's presence, not when he grips my heart as easily as he lifts me in his arms.

He rubs his hand along his jawline. "Do you mean before you left me, or before last night?"

I cover my face with my hands. "Don't do this to me."

"You're the one who's doing this to us," he says, each word laced with frustration and hurt.

I drop my hands away. "Don't you dare put this on me," I say. "Not after you spent the night making love to this perfect body, only to reject the first glimpse at the real me."

"This isn't what this is about," he says. "You are my mate—"

"Don't call me that!" I yell. "Mates are real. They're Celia and Aric, Shayna and Koda. They are forever. You couldn't even give me more than a couple of years—not after what happened. Jesus, Tomo, arm or not, whole or broken, I never would have walked away from you!"

He stares at me breathing hard. "I never walked away, you told me to leave. You told me not to come back. You rejected me in every possible way. As a *were*, despite our matehood, despite our claim, I can't be with someone who doesn't want me. Our laws of nature forbid it, no matter who I'm bound to and how strong that bond is."

I whirl around ready to bolt, only to turn back and face him. "Don't you blame me for this. Don't you spend a night craving this body only to shove aside the one beneath."

"I didn't shove you aside," he growls.

"You did when you rejected my arm." I lift it slightly. "It's a part of me. We're a package deal. You can't deny it, without denying me."

This time as I turn away, I mean to leave. To keep walking, toward the exit with the hopes I find Bren, Danny—anyone I know. But Gemini won't let me go.

Not this time.

He yanks me to him in one smooth move, pinning me against Aric's SUV and kissing me hard.

As much as I should wrench away, once more my body surrenders, molding with his and returning his affections with equal passion. My fingers glide through his hair as he slides his palm along my neck, between my breasts, and to my belly. I moan as something very hard, long, and quickly expanding presses against my hip.

I jolt when he nips the curve of my throat.

"Don't make me walk away," he rasps against my ear.

I jolt again as his hands grip my hips.

But as my right hand shakes and a burn grows painfully beneath my sternum, I know my reaction isn't a response to our desire, but rather the spell *and* my arm coming undone.

Oh, shit.

My volatile limb detonates like a bomb, sending Gemini soaring across the parking lot and me in the opposite direction. I crash land on the ground, my arm pounding the soil and sending waves of magic rippling across the Den.

The earth rumbles, shaking the buildings. "Taran!" Gemini yells. I think he's near and try to sit. But my spastic arm and the singeing pain coursing through my spine keeps me down.

Strong arms grip my shoulders. Until they're wrenched off, followed by a vicious grunt.

I don't know what's happening, the forceful movements of my arm bouncing me along so brutally, all I catch are glimpses.

"Celia, *no*. You can't help her!" Aric yells over the sound of the quake.

Growls erupt. "Everyone back!" Bren hollers. "Back away, now!"

"Don't *touch her*," Gemini snarls.

Flames, *my* flames, flare in and out. I scream, no, I *roar* from pain and the eruption of power. Like a rocket washed in fire, my magic launches into the heavens, lighting up the sky in giant flares of blue and white.

"*Call* Genevieve," Aric yells. "Gem, *call* her now!"

The distinct howl from my wolf fills my ears as I continue to thrash and lose control, the crackles from the escalating inferno my arm has become, feeding the chaos around me. My stomach churns a sea of lava, sloshing along the sides as my body convulses.

But I can't stop it, any of it, even though I think I'm capable.

God damn it, this is *my* body. I need to be the one in control!

I clench my hands, determined to settle and pull back the burn spilling across my chest. But it's no use. I'm helpless . . . until ethereal light as yellow as the summer sun appears like an angel.

It's soothing, beautiful, sweet.

Until the bitch angel hits me with the magical equivalent of a bucket of ice water.

I cough and sputter, freezing and abruptly snapping out of my shock. Celia and Aric stand to the side, near Bren and Gemini. Blue and white soot coat the wolves' shoulders, the exception being Gemini who resembles someone who has spent the last hour rolling around in a pool of flour.

A large crowd of students waits in the distance, cause if your leaders order you to keep away from the crazy chick experiencing the magical freak out, you stay away from the crazy chick experiencing the magical freak out.

My right arm buzzes, the bind tightening as if scolding it for the rude outburst. But I can't look at my arm then, or at Gemini, knowing our make-out session resulted in his ash-covered ass. I mean to glance away, but a small laugh, keeps me in place.

Vieve lowers a wooden bucket at her feet as she glides to a stop beside Gemini. All right, she did douse me with magical ice water. But she's not looking at me. She laughs again as her hand slides down his arm, leaving streaks from her fingertips along his caked skin.

"You're covered," she tells him in true "you, poor, poor, thing" fashion, rubbing in my mishap and adding to my embarrassment. "What *am* I going to do with you?"

She doesn't wait for him to respond, gliding toward me as only Vieve can. The wind was blowing away from the stacked stone steps when we arrived. Now it's blowing toward them, allowing her long hair to flow like an endless ocean of black liquid silk. I wonder if she somehow shifted the breeze in her favor, to give her that look. It wouldn't shock me, after all she has a spellbinding image to live up to.

Today, she's wearing a blood red maiden gown, the plunging neckline giving a generous view of her round, full breasts. And because that's not enough, the color somehow accentuates her fair and flawless skin with a saintly glow while painting her full red lips with a touch of sin that promises pleasure to any male who has the honor of basking in her glory.

Meanwhile, I'm lying in a pile of wet ash, wearing a dress that's currently suffocating my breasts and cutting off my oxygen supply, now that the real me is back. The skirt is torn, I've lost a shoe, and I'm pretty sure I swallowed enough soot to spackle my teeth.

"You're late for instruction," she says, calmly. Her smile is subtle yet smug, a reminder that she saved me, *and* everyone unfortunate to step in my destructive path, and by the way, you're welcome.

I push my dripping hair away from of my eyes. My face and body are soaked. My cheeks are likely wearing most of my mascara, and my eye makeup has likely taken residence along my forehead. I look like hell and she knows it. But there is something she doesn't know.

I grin with my ash-coated teeth. "My apologies, most Superior Sister. I was tired after spending all night fucking your boyfriend."

Chapter Twenty-six

My comment erased Vieve's grin.

And earned me a punishment disguised as a "very valuable lesson."

Her words, not mine.

I barely had time to shower and thank Paula, Fiona, and Merri, before I shoved on my spare Lesser uniform and was brought before Genevieve.

The breeze picks up again, lifting the strands of her dark hair elegantly away from her face while a stray piece of my hair smacks me in the eye.

Yeah, the bitch is doing this on purpose.

We're standing in the large field closest to the rear of the house, along the rows of Adder's Tongue we cultivated last week. The small green leaves are only starting to poke through. They're not attacking or appearing aggressive, unlike the snapdragons. Maybe because they're supposed to stop slander and promote healing. It should be a good thing. But since it's just me and Vieve, I have the feeling it's going to lead to bad. Very, very, bad.

"You passed your High Task," she says, nodding to a Lesser who places a bucket filled with water at my feet.

"I did," I respond, watching as the Lesser takes off in a run.

"You fooled your sister, and Aric," she adds. "Well done."

Wait for it.

"But you didn't fool Gemini. Did you?"

I laugh without humor. "No. But funny enough, that big hunk of wolf still couldn't keep his hands off me."

Take that.

She smiles with about as much warmth as I do. "Yet despite your efforts, and accomplishing such a complex task, a Mirror, you still lack control." She folds her hands in front of her. "Your outburst at the Den demonstrates how far you are from mastering and unifying your magic, regardless of my sisters' efforts, and our teachings."

She's taking her jabs. I can't deny they don't hurt, or that there's not a great deal of truth to them. No matter the bind, how hard I've worked, and what I've managed so far, my arm ultimately did what it wanted.

"I think we need to start from the beginning."

"The beginning, beginning?" I ask.

She sighs, in that patient yet not patient way of hers that's one step shy of calling me an imbecile.

"Your focus is what will ultimately secure your hold and help meld your powers. So often to move forward, it's essential you take several steps back."

"You're going to make me chant, aren't you?"

The upward curve of her lips assures me that yes, there will be chanting, and plenty of it. Oh, and PS, I hope it kills you.

"You will chant, for the next few hours until the plants compel you to stop. At that time, you will practice conjuring your fire."

"When the plants compel me?" I repeat, scanning all the little leaves surrounding me. Based on experience, I'm half expecting these little suckers to sprout clubs on their tips and mash my toes to dust. "What does that mean?"

And there's that patronizing smile again. "The air will shift, alerting you your task is complete and that the plants have had their fill of your energy and magic." She motions to the empty stand we've used to perch scarecrows. Mr. Scarecrow is gone. What remains is a long silk ribbon anchored at each end of the pole by two nails.

"Your goal is to light the tip at the end and gently singe the ribbon all the way to the top," she explains. "If you set the pole ablaze, you fail. If the ribbon tears, you fail. It's all about precision, patience, and command. All which you seem to lack."

I wonder briefly if this is how she insults everyone. Nah, I think I'm just special. "What happens if I fail?"

"Then you will repeat the task every evening following instruction until you do," she explains simply, seeing how it's not her ass on the line.

"All right," I say, frowning when the tips of my breasts sharpen to points. What the hell? My eyes widen when I glance toward the rear terrace and see Gemini march down the steps.

Vieve's looking in the same direction, smiling. "Best of luck, Taran. I have every faith this is exactly what you need."

She's speaking to me, but looking at him. Not that I blame her. He's freshly showered, and shaved. His goatee trimmed perfectly, his body an awesome blend of grace and strength. God, he's beautiful. Be it our night together, or whatever bond that remains, my body reacts to his.

Heat builds along my breasts, but mostly my heart.

I should feel that familiar sense of surging lust. Instead, my arms feel barren with the need to hold him.

I'm not sure if he's responding the same way. Not with Vieve gliding toward him in all her awesomeness.

She stops, directly in front of him, drawing his attention."Gemini," she says. "Good to see you at your best."

In other words, let's get naked.

I sigh, jumping when the little leaves pull at my pilgrim skirt, demanding attention. "Give me a minute," I whisper.

"Thank you for coming when I summoned you," he says.

"I would have arrived sooner and apologize for the delay," she adds sweetly. She laughs. "I'm afraid I wouldn't have been able to prevent your condition and the fate of that poor unfortunate goose."

That's the other thing. I accidently shot down a Canadian goose when my fire jetted into the sky. Thanks for the reminder, Vieve. You see, I didn't feel bad enough for roasting an innocent creature.

"You don't have to apologize," he says. "I'm grateful for your help soothing Taran, and so is the Pack."

The plants closest to me and further down stretch out their leaves several feet, tugging harder on my skirt. "I said, give me a minute," I mutter.

"May I have a word with her?" he asks, lifting his focus away from her, and onto me. "With everything that happened, I didn't have a chance to speak with her after."

I start to walk toward him, trying really hard not to full-out dash into his arms, only to be hauled back by Vieve's stupid little plants.

"My apologies," she says. Her back is to me, but as she lifts her hand, I just know she's trailing it over her perky girls. "But Taran has been assigned a very important task. One that will help control her magic's volatile nature."

"It won't take long," he says, frowning as he watches me kick at the plants and swear at them.

"I'm certain it won't. But just as it's imperative your teachings not be interrupted, my Lesser witches can't be disturbed either." Her hands fall away as if it's killing her to keep him from me. "I hope you understand."

The plants tug harder, pulling me back and twisting me to face the pole. It's all I can do not to land on my ass. "All right," he says.

"God damn it," I respond, slapping at the leaves when they elongate and tangle around my ankles.

"Taran," he calls. "I'll wait for you until you're done."

I crane my neck, watching as Vieve escorts him back to the terrace.

A leaf from a smaller plant shoots up like a Chinese

yo-yo, covering my mouth when I try to answer.

An image of Vieve's transparent face appears in my line of vision. "Focus on your task, Taran. For one who's so easily distracted, this will be the greatest lesson I can teach you, and the best gift I may provide."

And then she's gone.

Here's the thing about Vieve, she has this ability, gift if you will, to turn a punch to the boobs around and make it look like not only did you deserve said punch, but that you should be thanking her for jabbing your girls out of place.

Urgent pulls from the leaves and an insolent slap at my ankles yank me back to the moment. After a few choice swears, I lift the bucket at my feet and cup the water in the palm of my affected hand, muttering the sacred chant as I moisten the leaves.

"Skies above and sun most bright hear my pleas . . ."

I can't believe she wouldn't let me talk to him.

"Cast the light and nourishment upon this soil . . ."

I mean, she knows we were together.

"Feed it with your light . . ."

Is that her goal to drive us apart?

"Moisten it with your waters . . ."

Of course it is.

"Embrace it with your life."

She wants him now, and always has.

"Nurture the young."

But he wanted me.

"So it may age and feed us in return."

Last night and this morning, he kissed me. Against Aric's ride, not caring who'd see us.

"Harvesting our magic, and giving me power."

Is it possible he still loves me? I smile. *Yeah. I think maybe it is.*

"Power," I repeat. "Give me power."

My voice trails when I hear Vieve's laughter drift from the terrace. There she is, sitting with Gemini. A small table dressed with beautiful white linens and elegant crystal is the only thing that separates them. But even though they're mere feet apart, it seems too far for her tastes. She leans in close, speaking so low. He nods, listening intently as she moves her chair closer and loses the small space that remains between them.

A Lesser witch appears with a tray of food, smiling bashfully as if she's interrupted an intimate moment, her attention bouncing between them in awe. He doesn't notice her, but why would he? His full attention is on Vieve and very far away from me.

What. The. Hell?

I whirl around when he glances up at me. Sometimes I'm such a fool, I could kick my own ass. Here I was, ready to run to him the moment I saw him, only to watch him leave with someone else.

Again Vieve laughs, appearing to have the time of her life. Why is he there with her? Did last night not mean anything? Maybe not.

I stop moving.

Maybe the two years I gave him didn't mean anything either. I curse again, the blood in my veins coursing with sadness and hurt. But out of everything I could feel, betrayal and anger burn through me.

I storm down the rows of plants, repeating the chant, grinding out each word like rotting wood through a really pissed off wood chipper.

"Skies above and sun most bright hear my pleas . . ."

I can't believe him.

"Cast the light and nourishment upon this soil . . ."

I can't believe her.

"Feed it with your light . . ."

I love him.

"Moisten it with your waters . . ."

I love him.

"Embrace it with your life."

I love him.

"Nurture the young."

But he doesn't love me . . .

The realization jars my thoughts, making it hard to

speak the last few words.

"So it may age and feed us in return."

"Harvesting our magic, and giving me power."

"Power," I bite out. "Give me *power*."

Lightning crashes, paining my ears and blinding me, the raw force of it making me dizzy. As my vision clears, all I see is blue sky. I'm not sure what happened, but as I scan the field every last leaf of Adders Tongue is pointing up to the heavens, trembling as if electrified.

I have to admit, their behavior is odd. But then again Vieve did say I would know when to stop. I take it, along with the shift in air, as signs that the plants had their fill. I won't complain. It's hotter than a barbecue in Hades and the last thing I want is to chant until the sun goes down.

The air around me is strangely quiet and the dizziness I feel surges. I fight my way back to the pole, anxious to finish this task and go home. I can feel Gemini and catch traces of his voice, but I can't look at him while he's with her.

This whole experience has been worse than I ever imagined, opening old wounds I fought to keep closed. But I can't let it break me. I can't let Vieve win.

I reach the pole, my brow soaked with sweat from the relentless heat. I wipe it with the back of my hand, but I barely feel the motion. It's like I'm in a haze, the blistering sun beating down on me.

I try to clear my head and shake the strange dizziness. I'm lightheaded, bordering on nauseous, but I'm not done and can't stop now.

"All right, baby," I say. "Let's light this shit up."

I narrow my stare on the base of the ribbon, reasoning it's probably easier to start at the bottom and work my way up. "Come on, burn," I say, when nothing seems to happen.

The tip curls. I think something is happening, but then I realize it's just a passing breeze. I roll my eyes. Vieve is probably trying to fluff her hair again.

I take a breath, focusing hard.

"Burn," I whisper.

Again, the breeze picks up.

Damn it, Vieve, cut it out. "Burn," I repeat, adding more force to my words.

All I see is that tip, its fraying ends beginning to quiver. I clench my fists.

"Burn."

I tighten my jaw. "I said, *burn*."

My insides sizzle. The air charges and the world fades away. That fire, the one I once tamed like a wild colt flares, building and filling my core. I smile from the rush, my smile fading when the power escalates, charging out to my limbs like a wildfire. I startle as it releases, certain it's going to be too much. But then I see the ribbon's fraying edges ignite in a minute spray of white and blue.

Yes!

Nothing else matters, nothing but this small task. My fingertips quiver as I relax my hand, trying not to overdo the flame. My fire crawls up, as slow as a snail across the garden. But I don't rush it. I have something to do and need to do it right.

I'm not a lost cause or someone to pity. I'm Taran Wird, damn it, the loudmouth sister who always seems to screw up.

But not today. Oh, no, not today.

Sweat trickles down my back and between my breasts. My skin is soaked with the amount of focus I'm using to drive that miniscule bit of fire up.

I'm halfway there. The ribbon is fragile, but still intact.

"Come on, baby, don't fail me now," I say when the flame begins to sputter.

More.

Give me *more*.

The flame catches before it fully fades. It's so abrupt, I'm afraid it's going to be too much and snap the ribbon. I ease it back down, willing it to listen.

"Taran?" Shayna's voice calls from far away.

I almost lose control, but quickly regain it, sending the flame to smolder.

"Taran." This time it's Emme.

But I'm almost there, I can't stop now.

"Taran!" Celia is yelling, I think. Her voice sounds muffled, but I can't be sure.

I'm really dizzy now, so entranced by this ribbon and what I need to prove, their voices drift to the back of my mind.

I think they're still there, except I'm not sure. The outpouring of magic seeps through my pores, my concentration locked on the last inch of ribbon I need to burn.

The flame reaches the top, catching on the nail. But the ribbon is still intact.

I did it. *Yes.* I did it!

Take that Vieve!

The trance I'm in begins to clear in scattered pieces. At first all I see is fog. Lots of it. But it's hot. Why the hell is the fog hot?

Celia leaps in front of me, making me jump. She's wearing some kind of oxygen mask and waving her hands wildly. Something bumps my leg. I jump again when I find Alice sitting at my feat, munching on a dead squirrel.

The last bit of brain sludge loosens abruptly. A cacophony of screams, yelling, and roaring accompanies the hellish inferno surrounding me. This isn't fog. It's *smoke.*

Blue and white smoke.

I spin from side to side. Every last field in the compound is on fire. *Weres* and witches fall all over themselves, trying to control the blaze, the witches with their magic and *weres* with fire hoses and buckets of water.

Flames, *my flames,* eat away the remains of Vieve's house. The table—at least that's what I think it is—the one she and Gemini were sitting at moments ago—lies in smoldering pieces, the fine china and crystal in shards.

"Son of a *bitch!*"

Celia grabs my shoulders and turns me around to face her. "Are you all right?" she asks, barely audible through her mask.

My eyes are the size of Vieve's former dinner plates. I

shake my head.

"Dude!" Shayna says, her and Emme rushing forward.

Ash and soot coat their clothes and faces. I can't speak, I can't even . . .

Celia seems to understand, yelling to be heard through the mask. "You've been in a trance for *two hours*. No one could snap you out of it." She points to the table. "You started by blasting the terrace with lightning and then set everything on fire."

I motion to the pole. "I was only trying to burn the little ribbon," I say like a dumbass.

"Taran," she says. "You burned *everything* down."

"Was anyone hurt?" I manage, my voice shaking.

"Um. No," Shayna says coughing. "But T, the entire compound is destroyed. That's like bad, even for you."

I glance around, barely believing it. There's fucking up, and then there's this.

"How the hell did I do this?" I ask, waving my arms. "I mean, *shit*."

Emme trudges forward, gripping my hand, her face as white as chalk. "Taran, whatever you were feeling when you were chanting fed every last plant, tree, and shrub in the compound in a bad way."

"A very, very, bad way, T," Shayna says, smearing her face with more soot when she pushes away her bangs. "Whatever you gave them, they gave back to you, only like, a gazillion times more."

"I was only trying to burn the little ribbon," I repeat, my voice a pathetic squeak.

The crunching at my feet lures me back to Alice. "Why is she here?" I ask, panicked over the shitstorm of trouble I'm already in. But with Alice here. God damn it.

"She wouldn't stay behind and followed us here," Emme says. "At first we thought she sensed your fire and was trying to die. But she only wanted to be with you."

Bren in his large wolf form races toward me, *changing* into his human half as he comes to a stop in front of me. "You're awake?"

I nod, but just barely.

"Damn, baby," he tells me. "You don't do things halfway, do you?"

I ignore him, pulling on Alice's arm and trying to lift her to her feet. "We have to get her out of here before the witches see her," I say. "I can't let anything happen to her."

My sisters exchange glances, their expressions riddled with sadness. "Taran," Celia says. "They've already seen it. All of it."

My stare drifts behind me when their eyes widen. Vieve stomps forward, her blood red gown in tatters and what remains of her hair singed to a giant frizzy knot. A cluster of *weres* rush her, only to yelp and soar outward when her talisman explodes with bright yellow light.

"You—*you!*" she screams at me, pointing. "Only *you* could take sacred plants meant for healing and twist them into some fucked up version to tear me down!"

Right now, as I stand here with my mouth dangling open and Alice finishing off her road kill dinner faithfully at my side, I'm not sure if I'm more stunned Vieve is screaming, that I've destroyed everything she holds dear, or that she said "fucked".

Regardless, I know I'm screwed. Oh, and she doesn't stop there.

"You demolished my ancestral home, reduced my sacred fields to ash, and set my garden ablaze. You are a walking disaster, a freak of nature. I'm done with you, you crazy bitch."

"Now, Genevieve," Bren says, holding out his hands. "No need for name-calling girlfriend."

"Shut up, mongrel," she snaps, causing the *weres* circling her to snarl. "You're not fucking getting away with this," she says whirling on me. "No way in hell are you walking out of this untouched."

The wolves draw closer, holding their ground, but not yet attacking. Aric and Gemini appear in a rush, positioning themselves in front of me.

By the way the muscles along their broad backs

stretch against their singed shirts, both appear livid. But this isn't their fight, it's mine.

I try to step around them, but Gemini hauls me back. "Don't move," he warns.

"Genevieve," Aric says, keeping his gaze fixed on the bright yellow tendrils swirling from her talisman. "As Alpha and Leader, you have my word I'll make amends—"

"Amends?" she says, squaring her fury on him. "How will you amend all *this*!" she screams, waving her hands.

Yeah, you can say Vieve has totally lost her shit.

I don't know all the supernatural rules, but I know enough to guess she has a right to challenge me and maybe even kill me without repercussions. My knuckles crack under the force of my dwindling power. Plant mojo or not, I'm not at my best. My energy has been sapped and my legs are feeling wobbly.

But if she wants to fight, we'll fight. I'm not rolling over for anyone, and no way will I let anyone suffer for my mistake.

Gemini storms forward as her power lights up her form. "You swore to me you'd protect her," he snarls. "You gave me your word as a friend that no harm would come to her."

"But she couldn't show me the same respect back, could she?" Vieve says, the fury she's feeling like drops of poison along each syllable."She's taken everything I have— everything that's *mine*!"

If he could, I suppose he'd tell her it was an accident, that I'd never intentionally do anything like this to anyone. But he doesn't bother to explain or offer sympathy. Oh, no, whatever she wants to do to me, he can feel, and it stabs his words like a dagger from a killer's blade. "You will *not* harm my mate," he grinds out. "You will allow her to walk away."

"No, she's not walking away unscathed."

Koda appears in his humongous red wolf form, growling deeply as he steps in front of Shayna and peeling back his fangs when she attempts to flank me. At the same time Bren wrenches Emme behind him. Celia . . . I lose her in

OF FLAME AND LIGHT

a rush of fur and fangs as a pack of humongous beasts surround her.

"Aric," she calls.

"Stay with them, love," he tells her, his concentration fully on Vieve.

My girls mean to protect me. They know this isn't going to end well for *were* or witch alike. Not with the way the coven appears behind Vieve, and not by the cacophony of growls behind me.

A line's been drawn because of me. It's no longer this harmonious union between those who worship the earth and those who guard it. Through my careless actions, I triggered the start of another supernatural war.

But I can't allow it.

I shove my way forward. "This is my fault, my doing," I say. "I take full responsibility."

Vieve, shifts her attention away from where it's locked on Gemini. "I *know* it's your fault. You've left me with nothing but a legacy in ruins."

"I'm sorry," I say, meaning it with all I have. "I'll make it up to you anyway I can. But this thing between you and the *weres*, it can't happen. Do you hear me, Genevieve? Don't start something that will hurt you and your kind for decades to come because of something I did."

She's listening, I can tell by the way the magic in her talisman seems to withdraw slightly. That doesn't mean she's any less pissed. "You want to make amends?" she asks.

"I do," I say, begging her to believe me.

"Start with killing your familiar," she tells me flatly.

My eyes widen briefly, but voice is sure. "No."

"You can't do one thing I ask, *one thing*," she bites out. "Your insubordination and your mockery of our laws disgust me."

Alice whimpers behind me in that way she does when she's scared or hurting. For all I think I fucked up, I'll be damned if I hurt her.

Gemini hooks my elbows lurching me back when I storm forward. I don't even see Aric move, he's just suddenly

263

there, hauling Vieve away from me. I fight Gemini's hold, struggling to break free. "Alice is not my enemy or my familiar. She's my friend. Don't you get it, she's a lonely being who wouldn't hurt anyone." My voice gathers an edge. "And I'm not mocking anything—"

"Then strike her down," she snaps, cutting me off. "Give me something, Taran. Something that proves you're as honorable as your mate has always claimed!"

Her comment grips my throat. It's not simply her acknowledging me and Gemini as one. It's her *believing* who I am to him.

I shove aside the emotions, speaking clearly so she won't miss a word. "You can do whatever you want to me. You can punish me—you can even try to kill me. But you're *not* hurting Alice or going to war with the Pack."

I mean to reach her, connect with her, or at the very least keep her attention on me. But she's angry, and an angry witch is a dangerous witch, her rage blazing her power and lighting her talisman like a torch.

Like rows of deadly dominoes, every witch in her coven follows suit. The air charges with magic as the *weres* gathered *change,* becoming fierce beasts bent on tasting blood.

"Don't do this," I yell. "Your battle is with me, not with them!"

My hollers are overshadowed by the scream of someone running forward. Paula appears, tears zipping down her face as she carries a cardboard box dripping with blood. "Genevieve," she sobs, not bothering to call her by title.

The heated air around us dissipates and time slows. Paula falls at Vieve's feet, offering the box with trembling hands. "A murder of crows delivered them," she stammers, choking the words out.

Them?

Vieve bends forward, carefully pushing away the sides of the box. Her breath releases in pained bursts as she lifts the severed heads of her most trusted and strongest witches by their matted and blood soaked hair.

The blonde opens her eyes, her dead stare lifting to the sky. Dark liquid spills along her chin as her mouth opens and closes like a marionette.

"We're coming for you, Genevieve," her deep and haunting voice says. "*All* of you."

Chapter Twenty-seven

Since the dawn of time, there's always been a huge divide among classes: Rich and poor. Dark and light. Brave and weak. It's an "us" versus "them" mentality that doesn't seem to end. I don't think I've ever felt it as strongly as I have since first stepping foot on Vieve's compound all those weeks ago.

The Lessers are named as such for a reason. Their magic is limited and so is their ability to strengthen and master what little they possess. The Superiors . . . what can I say? The name speaks of who they are among their kind and what they can do.

But as the Superiors and Lessers form a circle and clasp hands over where Vieve's grand garden once stood, for the moment that divide is erased.

I've seen witches make it rain to wash away the remnants of darkness. It takes thirteen to call upon the power of nature like that, yet to cleanse an inferno like the one I created takes a great deal more. So much more they couldn't manage until Savana gave them what they needed.

Death has a way of uniting. Horror can have the same affect. Fear does something altogether different. Add anger to the mix and fuel it with the need for vengeance, and a coven has all it needs to call upon the elements.

The clouds gather from the distance, forming a dark

gray canvas over the circle the coven creates. Everyone is looking down at their sacred earth except for Vieve who stares up to the darkening heavens. I'm standing too far away to see her eyes, but not so far that I can't see the features of her porcelain and flawless face. The fury she felt toward me and at finding her sisters mutilated, culminates close to the surface and brews deep inside her. She uses it to feed her magic, draw from her sisters' strength, and cast the perfect spell.

There's no thunder or flashes of lightning splitting the sky. There's only ink black clouds that weep the unshed tears of the stronger witches and mourn with those unable to stifle their pain. Even from where we wait by Aric's SUV, I can hear a large number sobbing.

Vieve has returned to the Genevieve I'm most familiar with. The one with quiet composed power, who's beauty is only rivaled by her wrath. Rain, in large sad drops, sprinkle against my face as Aric leads Celia into his Explorer. By the time he shuts her safely inside, my hair and clothes are completely soaked. But I can't bring myself to leave.

I wasn't allowed or invited into the circle. Not that I expected to be after what I did. And while I respect their decision, I confess, I'm really upset.

I wasn't close to any of the witches Savana has killed. Nor do I believe any of them particularly liked me. But I valued certain things about them: That they had a right to live, and they didn't deserve what was done to them.

Aric positions himself beside Koda who carefully holds Shayna against him. From the back of Aric's ride, Alice presses her face against the window, watching me through the glass. Emme waits quietly beside Bren. I think she's crying, despite her lack of connection to the coven. But Emme always feels for others, even when they don't feel enough for themselves.

The *weres* from the Pack gather near their cars, some still in beast form, while others form an arc, quietly observing the witches.

Smoke rises as the rain begins to fall in sheets,

washing away the remains of my fire. Everything is so messed up. I only wish I could make it right. God, I just want to make it right.

I'm so caught up in everything I did, and all that's coming, I don't hear Gemini approach me. But I feel his presence even before he speaks.

"Come with me," he says. I look up at him, unsure what he's asking. "Please."

I follow him away from what remains of the house and down the road that leads out of the compound. It's a long walk, but in the rain, it feels even longer.

He stops beneath a canopy of trees that were somehow spared from Firestorm Taran. I'm soaked to the bone, but I'm too numb to feel the cold and too sickened to care.

Water trails along his temples as he turns to face me, his wet shirt clinging to his chest. He probably has a lot on his mind, but I don't wait for him to speak.

"This was a really bad day."

"It was," he admits, hanging his head.

"I'm sorry," I tell him. I lift my hand to motion around me, but I barely manage to raise it above my hip.

"I know you are, Taran."

I purse my lips. "So what happens now?"

"Now we mourn as one," he says. "As beasts we're not exempt from pain nor can the witches use their magic to completely shield themselves from it. But our grieving will be brief. There's no time to waste." He glances back to where his Pack waits. "Aric and Genevieve have called a truce. We'll be working together to bring Savana down."

"A truce," I repeat. I meet his face, unable to lessen the bite to my tone. "From a potential war that I started." I only say it because I know that he won't.

He doesn't exactly deny it. "We couldn't abandon you. Not when you're the sister of the Pack Leader's mate, and especially not being who you are to me."

His last words become my undoing. I try and push the misery aside. But I'm so touched he stood by me, my words release in an unsteady breath. "And who am I to you?" I ask.

His features harden to steel. "You know who you are," he answers.

Sometimes I think I do, like when he kissed me earlier, and when he rose to my defense. But when he turns from my arm—when I appear to disgust him, all that I believe dissolves into doubt.

Maybe he senses as much, averting his gaze briefly. "I know you think I'm here for Genevieve, and at first I was, for *Pack* business. But the moment your arm turned against you, and I knew what you were facing, I couldn't leave." He shakes his head. "I couldn't leave *you*, Taran. No matter how much you wanted me to."

A lump builds in my throat, but when his finger trails beneath my chin and draws my focus, the lump expands and I can taste the start of my tears. "Genevieve is a friend. And because she's a friend, she allowed me to stay, even after the business between my Pack and her coven was done."

"She wanted more than friendship from you," I remind him, unable to hold back.

Gemini's stare travels across my face, searching for something beyond what I say. "She may have wanted more," he admits. "But my wolves and I belong to you. We have since the moment we saw you, and you captured our souls with a mere glimpse from your eyes."

My visions blurs. It's hard to hear what he has to say, but maybe it's hard for him to say it, too. He speaks of love, but love can really fucking hurt.

For a long moment, we simply take each other in, but when the silence becomes too much, he finally speaks.

Yet I hate what he has to tell me.

"The coven and Pack have always believed that many will join the evil that's rising. If Savana is one of these many, than the evil is emerging faster than we anticipated, placing Celia and her child at great risk."

The evil that's rising is something I constantly think about and something we all concurred will eventually arrive. But to learn that it could be happening now, and that my pregnant sister is in immediate danger . . . Jesus Christ, she doesn't deserve this. Not after all she's been through, and not now that her baby is thriving.

"So the threat voiced through the severed head could have been directed at Celia, in addition to the coven and Pack?" As if on cue, the rain increases in severity, forming deep puddles.

"We have to assume as much, especially with the amount of power Savana's amassed." He crosses his arms. "Makawee is close to finishing the wards around the house where Celia is supposed to spend her last few weeks of her pregnancy, and give birth. But after everything that's happened, Aric wants her there as soon as possible." He waits, then adds. "And I want you there with her."

"Why?" My question comes out before I can be more specific.

He frowns. "Because you'll be safe there, and because she'll want you with her."

I lift my arm. "But she might not be safe around me," I remind him.

"Aric will be with her to protect her," he says in a way of an answer.

I straighten as the rain begins to decrease in severity. The witches are almost finished, which means our talk is almost done. "And where will you be?"

"I will be leading the Pack."

I shake my head. "No."

"As Second in Command, it's my duty."

"No, it's Martin's and Makawee's duty as Elders," I counter. No way in hell do I want him to be a part of this, despite knowing his obligations as a Guardian of the Earth.

"With everything that's coming, Martin is needed elsewhere. And with Celia's safety being our primary concern, Makawee needs to be at her side."

The way he speaks doesn't leave room to argue, neither do the eruption of howls from the direction of the fields.

It's a mournful song that honors the dead and grieves their loss. "It's a show of respect for the coven," he explains, despite that I've heard them howl this way too many times to count.

I expect him to howl with them in that thunderous and distinct voice his wolves give him. Instead he waits quietly beside me.

This is our goodbye. I know it is, yet I can't bring myself to tell him.

Aric's Explorer rolls to a stop beside us moments later. If I'm expecting a hug or a kiss it doesn't come. Gemini turns away, walking toward the rear of the vehicle to speak to Aric when he jumps out. He doesn't glance back, even when it's clear our conversation is over.

Alice shifts in her seat to allow me in when I open the door. Celia turns around from the front, her beautiful face plagued with worry and sadness. "Are you all right?"

I don't respond. I can't. It's not that I'm numb. It's more like I'm feeling everything at once. My senses are on overload, overpowering me.

Alice's hand finds my zombie limb when it involuntarily jerks, the bony prominences of her knuckles crunching when they squeeze. "Ergh?" she asks.

She's letting me know she understands the danger that's coming, and that she's scared. I don't know why I choose to answer her and not Celia. Maybe because regardless of all Celia's fear, Alice isn't as strong. She's fragile, and growing worse. "It's really bad," I admit.

Aric throws open his driver's side door seconds later, glancing briefly my way. He doesn't say anything, but his disappointment is palpable. I don't have to wonder why he feels the way he does. I already know because I'm feeling it, too. He thinks I should have said more to Gemini.

Celia strokes his arm, halting him in place before he can place the SUV in gear. "What is it love?" he asks when she hesitates.

"I need to call Misha, and tell him what's happening," she explains. His brows tighten at the mention of our favorite master vampire's name, not that it stops Celia from continuing. "He and the vampires stand to lose as much as everyone else. They'll help. I know they will."

"Only if it means their hides," he responds.

"They'll help for other reasons," she reminds him quietly.

Yes, they will. Because just like with Aric, Celia is Misha's one weakness. I never quite understood their friendship, and I doubted its genuineness more times than I can count. Until the day Celia almost died and Misha proved how much he loves her.

"Aric," she says when he growls. "He has to know."

He shifts the SUV into gear. "Fine. I'll call him."

"I think it will be better coming from me." She sighs when he adds a snarl.

"No. You're staying out of this," he says.

"I'm already in it," she responds.

Her voice remains calm, yet there's more to her thoughts that go unsaid. Aric acknowledges as much when his focus wavers from her face to her belly, even though it seems he tries to fight it. "All right," he says.

I'm not surprised that Aric gives in. He may hate Misha, but he loves Celia and their baby more.

I think it's all that love behind his decision that triggers the kick to the ass I need to act. That, and the way his Explorer jerks when he stomps on the gas.

"Aric, wait," I say, unsnapping my seatbelt. "I need to get out."

He eases to a stop, turning to face me. I don't wait for him to ask what's wrong. I throw open the door and race toward the sacred garden.

I'm not sure where Gemini is, I only know I need to find him.

My bonnet flies off my head as I sprint alongside the caravan of cars stuffed with *weres*. The rain isn't as heavy as it was, but the light showers that fall sting my skin as I run. By the time I'm almost to the end of the car line, I'm covered with mud from the waist down.

"Tomo," I call. "Tomo!" I use his given name knowing if he's close, he'll hear me and be more willing to respond. At least, that's what I hope. After all the times we've pushed each other away, I don't know what to think anymore.

I reach the last vehicle, an SUV with large tinted wheels. As it pulls away, I catch sight of what remains of the garden. My right side clenches in agony, I dismiss it as pain from the run and take in the battered and blackened soil. The witches are gone. There's no one here, but their magic and mourning falls within each drop of rain that pelts my skin.

I whip around as if pulled, my legs almost buckling when I see Gemini standing a few feet away, the downpour of rain that suddenly begins, drenching his hair and weighing it down. I stumble toward him and stop, and then stumble toward him again. It's not that I don't want to be with him, it's more like I no longer want to know life without him.

And yet because of too many mistakes on my part, and everything he'll risk during the hunt, there's a chance I'll lose him, and be denied the life I want with him.

My affected arm quivers. If he notices, he doesn't react, even when I cradle it against me and it begins to glow. "What are you doing?" he asks, his voice heavy and his focus intense.

It takes me a moment to force the words out. Not that they come out in the way I intend. "I want to say goodbye to you—not like how you're thinking," I add quickly when he bows his head.

"Then how should I think?" he asks.

"I want you to come to my place," I manage. "Tomorrow. At sunset."

His dark eyes scan my features as if searching for a clue to what his crazy ex-girlfriend, who blew up an ancestral mansion and seven fields, and caused a major riff between *were* and witch could be up to *this time*.

"Please say you'll come," I say. "I want to . . . I want to make things right."

Chapter Twenty-eight

Son of bitch.

I jump when the tiny votive candle explodes. I should have known better than to try to light it with my hand. I just had a little bit of time and, I don't know, I suppose I wanted to feel normal.

Normal means good in my world. Normal can even border on boring. But boring isn't so bad, in fact, boring can be fan-freaking-tastic. It doesn't involve murder, mayhem, and overall fucked up-ness.

I rub my side, where that awful ache that's been growing gives me another twinge of pain, and take in the mess. Small pieces of glass lay near my stiletto-clad feet. I frown a little, noting that some of the pieces appear melted.

Shayna pokes her head out from the sliding glass doors leading into the kitchen. "How's it going, T?" she asks.

"Fine," I say, ignoring the buzzing sound from my arm. But as I reach for the broom and pan I used to sweep the deck, the ache on my side builds, giving me pause. Shayna doesn't seem to notice. She bounces toward me and takes both from my hands.

"Here," she says, grinning and adding a wink. "You look too sexy to be sweeping anything up."

"Thanks," I say, dropping my hand away from my

side and hoping she's right.

As the ache recedes, I run my fingers through my wavy tresses. Shayna had to add layers to my hair after I fried it during my first Plant Day fiasco. They're finally starting to grow out and blend with the longer strands that survived the incident. Except they're still shorter than I'm used to, adding an extra bit of "big" to my already "big hair". I spent an hour styling it, hoping I managed elegance instead of just plain "Jersey".

The skirt of my shapely red dress skims above my knees as I walk across the deck to fiddle with the sheer fabric that make up the edges of the canopy. It took me and my sisters most of the morning to set up this makeshift tent, and I worried too many times that it would rain and ruin the setting I was attempting to create. But by noon the clouds had cleared, bringing the warmth of the late June sun and easing at least that one worry aside.

Not that I've stopped worrying. In addition to stressing over Gemini's arrival, and what will happen while he's here, something feels off.

I move toward the center of the deck. We barbecue out here almost year-round, its large size allowing us to move around and enjoy the spring when the first signs of warmth trickle in, the heat the summer brings, the colorful fall foliage, and the blanket of white that follows each winter storm. It's a great place to entertain and share a few laughs, but tonight I want it to be more intimate, a small little world to escape to where we're safe, even for a brief pocket of time.

Like the tablecloth, the sheer fabric and plates are white, as are the candles placed along the railing and in the centerpiece filled with wild flowers. It's going to be perfect.

Maybe.

God, I hope so.

At the very least, we'll have a good meal.

Thanks to Koda's earlier trek through the forest, I'm roasting a large chunk of venison stuffed with quinoa, pine nuts, mint leaves, and sundried tomatoes. It's Gemini's favorite and the last great meal I made him before our relationship turned into what it became.

I don't realize how I appear until Shayna dumps the broken glass into the waste can behind me and pulls me into her thin arms. "Don't be sad, T," she says. "Boyfriend's going to love this."

I want to tell her that I'm not sad, at least about how the deck looks. But I'm too sad about everything else to try to deny what she sees.

"You look beautiful," she says, releasing me to fluff my hair. "The dress, the shoes, everything is perfect."

"Thank you," I say, walking away from her slowly.

My fingers trail over the pretty gold and delicate holly embellishments on the front of my dress. Under other circumstances, I wouldn't wear a dress like this on such a warm night and so far away from the Christmas holidays. But it's sexy, the off the shoulder design exposing my deep olive skin while the long sleeves cover my arms.

I place my right hand on the tablecloth as I adjust the silverware, pressing my lips tight when I see how it blends in with the linens.

It's white . . . pure white like the tablecloth and napkins, and maybe not as sickly in appearance as I used to believe. I entertain the thought of adding gloves, but decide against it. For tonight, and for always, it is what it is, and just needs to be.

Koda steps onto the deck, his ultra-angry persona melting away when he sees Shayna and she skips into his arms. Me and Koda will never be close. We're too much alike in temper and stubbornness. But he loves my sister, and for that reason alone it's easy to love him back.

Shayna kisses his chin. "Doesn't this look great?" she adds, motioning around.

He gives me a stiff nod. "Yeah," he rumbles.

"Stop it," I tell him, mimicking his edgy tone. "You're going to make me blush."

He smirks, lifting the broom and garbage can with one hand, while his other presses against Shayna's back. He guides her into the house, pausing to glance over his shoulder.

"Hey, Taran," he says.

"Yeah?"

He waits as if he doesn't want to say what he does, but then meets me with a small smile. "Gem's going to like what you did."

"Thank you," I say, hoping he's right.

He frowns. "You just shouldn't have waited so fucking long to do it."

I grin and waggle a finger at him. "So glad we had this talk, big guy."

His deep chuckle doesn't quite compete with Shayna's giggle, but it's there. And maybe it's what I need to hear.

I walk to where I left my phone beside my sound system, debating whether to call Gemini. But as desperate as I am to see him, I don't want to look the part. Instead I turn on the sound system. The satellite station it's on is called Between the Sheets. Based on the heavy base love ballad that's currently playing, it should be called, "Songs to Get You Laid and Then Some".

I lower the volume so it's not blasting. The sun has begun to set in the horizon, casting orange and peach light along the pines covering the mountainside. I walk to the edge of the deck to take in the pretty colors, stopping short when that ache begins to build again.

Emme eases out through the sliding glass doors, trailed closely by Alice. She's wearing the necklace to keep Alice with her. That doesn't stop Alice from stomping toward me when she sees me.

"Ergh," she says excitedly.

I smile and force my hand away from my side. Maybe Emme's right. Maybe I am Alice's "person".

"Hey, Alice," I say, doing my best not to focus on how much more gaunt she appears.

"Sorry," Emme offers meekly. "I know it's almost time for Gemini to arrive, but I think Alice needs to eat, and I don't want to disturb you during dinner."

"It's all right."

My words cut off when I see the way Alice is staring

at the flames flickering from the long stemmed candles. It's similar to the way she looked at the fire I set when we first found her.

I'm not sure what to think. At the compound, she could have easily acted and found her peace. God knows there was plenty of shit blazing to choose from. But instead she sat at my feet, eating her squirrel.

I wish I knew what she was thinking, but mostly, I wish I knew how to help her. Her time on earth is limited, especially in her condition. But as my arm gives an involuntary shudder, and the ache builds deep in my gut, I'm reminded that my days are numbered, too.

When Vieve first bound me, for lack of better terms, I didn't feel that pain that threatened to burn me from the inside out. That changed at the Den when Gemini kissed me, and that familiar ache returned. When it diminished following Vieve's oh-so glorious intervention, I tried to pretend that at least for a time, it was over. But then when I chased after Gemini, I felt it again, and this morning it woke me from sleep. Now that it's worsening, I'm not so certain I'm all right.

"Come on Alice," Emme urges sweetly. "We need to get you something to eat, honey."

I almost let them go without a word, but that pain is still there, and feels like it's escalating. "Em, wait," I say, when Alice begins to follow.

She tilts her small angelic face. "Did you need something, Taran?" she asks when I don't explain right away.

"Um. Yeah," I say, trying not to panic. "Could you heal me before you go?"

She starts to ask something, but the dread blanching her face makes it clear she knows what's happening. She rushes over, reaching for my hands. "Are you hurting?" she asks.

"A little," I say, hoping I'm right. No matter what, I'll know soon enough when she finds the source of my pain.

Her pale yellow light surrounds me, fading slightly when she seems to hone in on the right spot. As it brightens, what once was hurt like an infected cut, cools.

I sigh, grateful for the relief and thankful it's over.

It's what I think, until Emme's eyes pool with tears. "You're burning," she says.

The world seems to fade away, a heavy silence building like a fortress between us. "No, I'm fine," I tell her.

"You're not," she stammers. "Taran, your organs—your insides, they aren't well, even now. I . . . I don't think you have much longer."

I don't move, unable to breathe.

Emme carries that light of hope with her, always. Even during the worst of times she's had it. For her to tell me this much means everything is worse than I could have imagined.

I want to insist that she's wrong, that I feel great, because I do now. Except deep down, I recognize she's right. Something clicks in my brain, connecting the dots to the intermittent pain I've been having. This . . . this is really happening.

I don't argue or try to make excuses. I don't think I even try to speak. The words simply spill out, along with all my hope. "I know," I reply.

Tears fall down her face in streams as Alice hobbles over. "No, you don't," Emme says. "We have to get you to Genevieve—or Makawee." She starts pulling on my hands. "We have to get you there now."

"No," I tell her, my voice strangely calm. "I'm not leaving."

"You don't understand, Taran. What I felt, it's like a time bomb narrowing to the final seconds. All I did was pause the countdown."

"Taran, Gem's here," Shayna calls. She doesn't notice me or Emme, giggling as Koda pulls her from the doors before she can finish opening them.

I glance from side to side, debating what to do. But as I hear the front door open and the murmurs drifting closer, there's only one thing left I know I should do.

"Go," I say, urging Emme toward the steps.

"I *can't*," she says.

"Emme, please—"

"You need help," she insists. "You're out of time."

I cup her sweet face, wishing I could tell I'll be fine and mean it—that she, and Shayna, and Celia, are going to be all right without me—that they *have to be*. Because whether I'm here or not, they need to be strong and protect Celia's baby.

"You're out of time," she repeats, her voice begging me to reconsider.

I swallow back all the words I want to say, searching for the ones that will make her do as I ask. "Then let me spend it with Gemini," I whisper. "Please. If these are my last moments, let them be with him."

She chokes back a sob, crying as she races down the steps. Alice seems confused, but equally distressed, moaning loudly as she limps cautiously after her.

I start to wipe my eyes, pausing when I don't feel the tears that should be there. Maybe I'm in shock.

Or maybe I don't want to be remembered as weak.

The door slides open and Gemini steps out. He's in jeans and a dark blue T-shirt. For a moment, it's like he can't rip his eyes from me. But then he quickly scans the area before returning his stare on mine.

"Hi," he says quietly.

"Hey," I say, trying to give myself a moment to get myself together.

"I wasn't expecting this," he says when I remain quiet. "If I was, I would have dressed the part."

I don't remember moving. I'm just suddenly there, lifting up on my toes to kiss his lips. If he didn't bend forward, I would never have managed even in these tall shoes. But he does, allowing me to welcome him like I should have long before this.

His care and warmth shakes me out of my shock, and those tears that should have fallen in Emme's presence, burn their way across my eyes. "It's okay," I say, my voice quivering. "I mean. how could you have known, right?"

I start to pull away, but he reaches for my good hand, holding me in place. "What's wrong?" he asks.

Even if I did want to lie to him, I can't. So I tell him as much as I'm able. "I just think I waited too long for this."

He cocks his head, as if he doesn't believe me, but allows me to lead him to the table. "Have a seat, okay? Dinner will be ready soon. I made venison the way that you like it."

"I know. I could smell it when I pulled into the drive way."

He releases my hand and lowers himself into his seat. I know he's watching me as I reach the small table where I set up the wine. He likes red with venison. I know this, but I can't think straight. Not now.

I'm dying, and there's nothing I can do about it.

I lift the bottle of white I have chilling, speaking fast because if I stop, I'm sure I'll fall apart. "I picked up a harvest Riesling for dessert." I shove the bottle back into the ice bucket, reaching for the red wine beside it. "But I have a red blend if you prefer."

Gemini appears behind me, sliding his hands along my waist. He dips his head, pressing a long sweet kiss against my shoulder. "We did wait," he murmurs. "Too long."

More tears fall, stilling him in place. "Taran . . . what is it?"

"I think Celia and Aric are leaving in the morning."

He straightens, likely suspecting there's more to what I'm saying. "She's sleeping now," I add. "She's been more tired since the baby's growth spurt. Aric's with her now, but I can get him if you need to speak to him."

"We have a plan in place," he explains slowly. "But I'm not here to see him."

I nod, but the motion is jerky. I don't want to scare or worry him, but I don't know how much time I have left, and it's starting to show in my behavior.

"When are you leaving?" I ask. "For the hunt? When do you go?"

I'm speaking too quickly, giving away my fear. But he misinterprets that fear. "This evening, but not until later. I'm meeting Genevieve around midnight on the Nevada side of Tahoe . . ."

More tears. More regrets. "Taran," he begins.

"Please don't say her name. Not now, okay?" My head falls forward, unable to carry the weight of all the thoughts spinning through my head.

He pulls closer, like he used to, his hold loving and shielding, as if only his body could protect me from the world.

We stand there in this position for what seems like too long, but not long enough. The music switches to another ballad, one that's more recent. But when *She's Got a Way*, that really old song by Billy Joel follows, Gemini pulls away.

I think he means to put some distance between us, instead he regards me with so much sadness, the tears finding their way from my eyes fall faster.

"Will you dance with me?" he asks.

I don't quite answer, wondering how he'll manage without touching my right hand.

But then he does.

It's my affected hand he reaches for, leading me to him as he curls his free arm around my waist. "This song has always reminded me of you," he tells me quietly. "You have a way with words and everything else."

I laugh though the tears continue to fall, swaying slowly to the beat of the music.

As I relax against him, I'm reminded how I always wanted to be everything for Gemini.

Except now I'm too late.

"I'll come back," he tells me. "I *swear*, I'll come back to you."

"I don't know if I'll be here," I say. I don't want to tell him the truth, except I feel like I have to. "Tomo . . . I'm not the same anymore."

He stops in place, halting our movements. "No. You're not," he admits.

He lifts my right hand, curling my fingers around his as he peels the sleeve down with his opposite hand. His movements are slow, seductive, tugging on the fabric as if stripping me bare.

His eyes are on mine, his breath a mere whisper, exposing my arm until its bright color clashes against the tones my body. Old and new meet in what once was a startling divide. But it isn't anymore. It's just . . . me.

Those dark eyes that peer down to my soul take me in as if seeing me for the first time. I start to pull away, but he won't let me. His hold and his words, keeping me in place. "I've never stopped needing you," he rasps, fixing on the glow of my arm as it fades in and out. "And I'll be damned if I ever stop wanting you."

He kisses my knuckles, clasping my arm against his chest, the care he uses as gentle as a man caring for a wounded bird.

It's too much to see, and even more to bear. "I thought you hated it," I say before I can stop myself, my chest heaving as I sob. "And I thought you hated me because of it."

My cries garble my speech, but he understands them enough. His frown is deep, angry. "Is that what you think?" he asks, drawing me closer and grasping me tight. "Taran, this has *never* been about you. It's been about *me*. How I failed you as your mate, and how you've suffered because of my weakness."

His voice so rough with emotion, threatens to bring me to my knees. But it's his confession that glides tears down my cheeks and soaks my chest. "I saw what he did to you. I watched as he tore your limb apart." His stare drops to my hand. "I heard your screams. I felt your pain. And there wasn't anything I could fucking do about it."

My heart seems to stop, and I'm unsure I can breathe. "You watched . . . everything?"

His nod barely registers. "I was paralyzed, not unconscious. Neither me, nor my wolves could reach you." He averts his gaze briefly, his face scrunching with all the agony he feels. "I have the power of three: two wolves, one man, and it wasn't enough. Taran, *I* wasn't enough."

My chest caves in and out with how hard I'm crying. I never knew. He never told me. But I can guess why. Nothing is supposed to happen to your mate. Ever. And here it did, and he watched it all.

"Every time I see it," he says. "And every time it hurts you, I'm reminded of my failures and how much it cost you."

"You didn't fail me," I insist. "You're not the one who did this."

"No. But I should have stopped it." He leans in, pressing his forehead against mine as I weep. "Nothing must harm you with me at your side. Because it did, it destroyed me. You tell me you're not the same. Neither am I. That doesn't mean you're still not everything I desire." His lips brush gently over mine. "I love you," he whispers against my mouth. "You're *my* perfection."

A kiss can warm, incite, and speak words left unsaid. This one does more. It melds us, joining our souls, welding our hearts, and sealing what was once so broken.

Yet as I slink my arms around his neck I don't find that peace I so longed for. The burn from my core ignites, searing my organs and making me scream.

My spine bows back in anguish as hollowed out voices call my name from deep inside my skull.

Taran!

Taran!

They're shrieking, desperate to have me.

The pain escalates. I try to wrench free from Gemini. But he won't let go.

"Taran—*Taran*!" he yells.

The pain accelerates. My time has come.

"Go!" I groan, struggling to suppress the rising flames inside me. "It's my fire—you have to let go!"

My body trembles like a spaceship seconds from taking off. Gemini holds tight, howling for the wolves. The force of the building power sends us spinning across deck, slamming us through the railing.

Gemini turns us in mid-air, taking the brunt of the impact as we crash on the ground.

The pain increases.

So do the screams in my head.

"Taran!"
"Taran!"
"Taran!"
There's yelling, hard feet pounding from every direction. I hear my sisters' voices and the wolves.
But I also hear Paula, Merri, and Fiona.
The voices fade in and out, along with my vision.
Something detonates and I'm sent soaring across the yard in an explosion of power.

Chapter Twenty-nine

Light pushes against my closed lids. I expect the summer sun, along with its warmth. But as I pry open my too heavy to be normal eyelids, I don't see sun. I see feet. Very hairy feet.

The feet move quickly aside as Emme's healing light recedes and Merri rams her face into mine. "She's coming to," she says. "Thank Christ, I thought she was dead."

I push up on my arms wondering where I am, and why I'm so cold.

Emme slips her hands from my face and falls back to sit on her knees. I shove down the sleeve of my dress, trying to hang onto my body heat. As my vision adjusts to the dimness, I realize I'm in a cave.

Okay, not really a cave, more like a very dark, very bland stone enclosure. Runes in varying patterns are carved into the stone floor while the smooth gray slate that makes up the walls and ceiling await unmarred.

Aside from the carvings and the torches fixed on the wall every few feet, there's not much else here.

I place my hand on my side, searching for that ache. The pain is gone, but I'm stiff and need help standing.

Shayna and Emme pull me up by my arms as Alice shuffles over. She seems scared, not that I blame her. In fact, I'm just about there. But it's the Lessers from my class, and how they appear at a loss as they wait for me to speak, that momentarily suppresses my fear and adds to my confusion.

"What happened?" I ask.

Emme and Shayna exchange glances, but no one answers right away. "What happened?" I ask again, this time louder.

Shayna shrugs at Emme, likely guessing there's no sense in sparing me. "You know how trouble always seems to find us, T?" she asks. "How we always seem to fall into a pit of bad, nasty, evil—Oh, and body parts, too?"

"Yeah?" I answer her slowly.

She stretches out her hands. "Well, here we are again, dude."

"Ergh," Alice agrees.

My swears cut off as I realize I'm still in the red dress I had on for dinner. All at once, I'm jarred awake. "Where's Gemini?" I ask, glancing around.

"He's back at the house, I think," Emme offers, speaking quietly. She steals a glimpse toward the witches. She doesn't trust them, and rightfully so, but finishes explaining since honest to God, there's not really a choice. "Your arm went crazy and I think started burning you. He wouldn't let go until your arm forced him off you, and both of you went flying in opposite directions."

"You landed at the edge of the property line," Shayna adds. "He hit the side of the house and left a really bad dent." She gives it some thought. "I think we may need to redo the side of the house." She holds out her hands when my jaw drops open. "But I think he's okay. The others ran to him. Me, Em, and Alice ran to you and were dragged here with you."

"That was our fault," Paula explains. I hadn't noticed her hiding in the shadows until she steps forward. "Merri, Fiona, and I accidently summoned you here. When we helped you cast Mirror, it bonded our magic, not that it's permanent," she adds in a way of an apology. "And we only meant to *call* you and tell you we were in trouble. But somehow, it brought you and your family here."

"And where is here?" I ask.

"A fortress beneath the north side of the compound," Merri explains. "Genevieve created it in case we were ever attacked, or if the apocalypse or whatever came and we were gonna die. We've been using it as our new home since, you know, you blew our last one to shit."

I cover my eyes until an unearthly growl and the sound of claws scraping against stone gives me a reason to quickly drop my hands away.

"What's that?" I ask, only to be silenced.

"They'll hear you," Paula says, batting her hands.

"Who?" I mouth.

"The monsters," she says, like that's supposed to explain anything.

"You're going to have to give me more than that," I press, hoping I'm being loud enough that she can hear me, but not so loud that whatever is stalking the exterior notices.

Emme gently touches my arm. "They're not sure," she whispers. "They've been trapped here since we left. Some of the younger witches went missing when everyone was trying to settle in. The Superiors went to investigate and they never came back." She pauses. "Including Genevieve."

"You *have* to be kidding me," I say. I'm not crazy about Vieve, but I've only wished her scabies, not death. And if the strongest among them is gone, that means someone stronger is here.

A deep sniff follows a heavy growl that reverberates down the hall and sends some of the witches scurrying back. "They can smell us," Paula whispers.

Yeah. They can. But death by mutilation is not the way I want to go. I clench my fists, cracking my knuckles. My arm starts to buzz, but instead of turning against me, and causing me pain like the rest of me, it feels ready to act. I stroke it, feeling slightly reassured. But then it's like the motion increases the buzzing, but also its strength.

Holy shit. It's listening.

I step forward since now is not the time to analyze what's happening, and it's especially not the time to die. "Take up the rear," I mouth to Emme.

She nods, urging Alice behind her.

Shayna is ahead of us, but I don't need to tell her what to do, especially when the growls turn more challenging. She lifts a torch from the wall and blows it out. Using her gift to manipulate the metal, she stretches out the tip, separating it from the rest of the handle and converting it into a dagger while she transforms the remainder into a long and deadly sword.

I follow behind her, but hate how dark it is. The torches along the walls barely cast enough light to see. We pass an open doorway where two sets of bunk beds are pressed against the wall. Another similar room follows, but as we near the corner, what appears to be a dining area opens up on the opposite side, a long wooden table set at the middle of the cramped room.

Scrape. Scrape. Scraaaaaaape.

Shit.

Whatever this thing is has big claws. Shayna tucks her dagger in the waistband of her skinny jeans then adjusts her grip on the hilt of her sword. We inch toward the scratches, doing our best to move quietly.

Emme trails me, she's in sneakers. Shayna is in a pair of old flip-flops while I maneuver in platform stilettos. Alice is in bare feet.

Guess who makes the most noise?

"Ergh?"

"Alice, quiet," I whisper.

The scratching sound increases, growing frantic as does the sound of sniffling along the ground.

"Ergh?" she calls out, this time louder.

The wall shakes and dust falls from the ceiling. What resembles a paw stripped of its fur pushes beneath a crevice, scratching three lines into a rune that's supposed to ward off evil.

"Ergh!" Alice yells.

I fall back as the wall shatters and three large forms bust through. The one in the lead growls, the tone distorted as it charges.

My arm shoots out as a long row of sharp fangs clamp down.

I don't feel pain.

All I feel is fire.

It spreads along my limb in ripples of blue and white, illuminating the creature.

Patches of fur and muscle peel away in strips from his long snout while sunken eyes widen in torture. My flames consume him, spreading out across his sagging brown pelt like pieces of carpet lit on fire.

I push onto my feet as he releases me, shaking out my arm as he writhes and bounds away. But instead of racing back outside, he ricochets toward Shayna and the creature she's fighting.

"Shayna!" I scream.

With ballerina grace she pivots, bringing down the sword and decapitating her opponent. As she leaps out of the way, the creature I engulfed in flames crashes into the one she fought, igniting him as if doused in gasoline.

"Taran, Shayna, *move!*"

Shayna and I press our backs against the wall as Emme shoves a third creature past us, this one appearing more feline, unlike the wolves that attacked me and Shayna. Perspiration builds across her brow as she marches forward with her hands out, the magnitude of her power skimming across my skin and making my arm twitch.

The creature refuses to submit, its aggressive nature causing it to flail and viciously swing its limbs. Claws rake the air inches from my face as it jerks and struggles to break free. But Emme hangs on, slamming it into the opposite wall before launching it into the others.

My flames eat through them like piñatas, their agonized howls threatening to rupture my eardrums.

As they burn to ash Alice hobbles to my side, moaning softly while the rest of us work to settle our breathing. Tears glisten Emme's and Shayna's eyes. Emme's because of the raging heat, but Shayna because of something entirely different. "That was a werewolf," she says.

"I know," I respond, struggling to relax my hands.

"Yours was, too," she adds.

I nod because this is too messed up to be real. Paula edges forward, followed by Merri, and Fiona, and a few Lessers who didn't run and hide. "What are they?" she asks.

"Zombies," I explain, biting out the words. "Savana is raising dead werebeasts."

~ * ~

Shayna stands guard by the caved-in wall, one foot on the rubble, her sword out. I don't like her there, but her senses are more heightened than ours and she'll latch onto trouble sooner than we will. "We can't stay here," she says, keeping her gaze fixed out toward the darkness. "Whatever else is out there could have heard the fight. But even if they didn't, they'll track us, just like the others."

"I know," I say. I kick at the runes etched into the floor as I work through what's happened. "Did Genevieve strengthen these markings?" I ask. After studying them a few weeks ago, I recognize their meaning, and know they've been bespelled to protect. Yet seeing how three very deceased werebeasts not only found the location, but broke in here, clearly they're not working and it's so not a good sign.

Paula realizes as much, wringing her hands. "Yes. One of her duties requires her to strengthen them every quarter moon. The most powerful in her coven, and her most trusted guards, accompany her to help her reinforce the spell."

Emme looks at me. "What does that mean?"

"It means we're screwed," I tell her, walking forward.

Her shoulders slump. "It's worse than we thought. Isn't it?"

"Oh, yeah. For starters, her guards are dead. Their heads were the ones in that box," I remind her. I tap my foot against one of the runes. "And if these aren't working, the Superior witches are dead, too."

One of the Lessers begin to cry, then another few more after that. "I don't think Genevieve's dead," Paula begins.

"Wake up," Cynthia snaps, her face swollen from crying. "These runes did nothing and the others didn't come back. Of course Genevieve's dead, along with everyone else."

I ignore her, focusing on Paula. "What makes you think she's alive?"

Paula glances at Cynthia as if afraid to answer. I step forward, blocking her view. "Don't worry about her," I say. "Tell me what you know."

"The Whisperer of the Dead—Savana, I mean, can't raise werebeasts without sacrificing a ton of magic." Her voice drops. "And she's not going to sacrifice her own."

I glance briefly at Emme before addressing Paula. "So she's leaching from Genevieve, and possibly the others?" She nods. "You're sure?"

"A werebeast's spirit is too strong to raise otherwise. It's the reason it takes years for their bodies to decompose, and why they appeared as whole as they were, despite their dismembering parts."

Emme's eyes open wide. "That's why all those witches never came back. She must have used them to raise at least a couple of beasts."

"Which then helped her kill more witches, so she could raise more *weres*," I finish for her. It's like a twisted circle. But an effective one.

"T?" Shayna calls, her voice shaking. She keeps her attention outside, not waiting for me to ask what's wrong, even though something obviously is. "All the *weres* who died during the war were brought back and buried in Squaw Valley, at the base of the Den where generations of *weres* have been laid to rest."

The others gasp around me and I feel the blood drain from my face. Everything suddenly makes sense, not that I'm thrilled by the news. "This is why Savana came here to begin with. She wasn't trying to join the coven, she was getting a feel for the witches and staking out the area." I start to pace. "We're not just looking at a few werebeast*s*, we're looking at a potential army if Savana's draining enough of Vieve's juice."

I stop in my tracks. "I take it none of you have cell phones?"

The Lessers shake their heads. "Naw," Merri responds. "You melted them to nothing when you burned down our house."

"Thanks for the reminder," I say, lifting a hand. "Shayna, any chance Koda knows where you are?"

She closes her eyes briefly and breathes slowly. "What's she doing?" Paula asks.

"They're mated," I explain. "He can sense her distress and longing. If he's close enough, he can hone in on her presence."

"So there's a chance they'll know you're here?" Merri asks, jumping in place hard enough to bounce the hair on her feet.

"I can't be sure," I admit. "The *weres* don't know of this place, do they?"

The Lessers collectively shake their heads. "Only the head witch and her most trusted circle was made aware," Fiona explains. She's been noticeably quiet, but like the rest, she seems scared out of her mind. "The rest of us were told only after we arrived."

I curse under my breath. "In that case, we have a real problem. Gemini was supposed to meet Vieve at midnight, on the Nevada side of Tahoe to begin the hunt."

"That's a good hour from here," Paula says. "And it's only about eleven now."

Not to mention the north side of the compound where we are is nowhere close to the remains of the mansion, and the furthest away from the road. The *weres* wouldn't have a reason to come, and even if they did the amount of rain the witches cast would make tracking us harder.

"Shayna," I ask. "Do you feel anything?"

She opens her eyes. "Nothing, T. Koda isn't any place near me." She pauses. "Are you getting anything from Gemini?"

Cynthia frowns. "Why would she?" she asks.

CECY ROBSON

"Because he's my mate," I respond.

Oh, and don't I have everyone's attention then?

"You're a liar," Cynthia says. "He belongs to our most Superior Genevieve."

Emme whimpers as I stomp forward and ram my face in Cynthia's. Knowing you're going to die by your own fire, if some scary zombie werebeasts don't kill you first, while you wait in some dingy crypt-like hole in the ground, as the most evil and powerful necromancer witch ever known stalks you in the dead of night has a way of shoving petty insecurities aside. "He belongs to me," I fire back. "And if you say one more negative thing against me, or anyone here, I'm going to set your ass on fire and use what remains as bait. Got me?"

Her scowl dwindles and she nods.

I turn back to Shayna. "I don't feel Gemini, but we can't wait for them to show. We're not too far from the Den. Is there any way you can howl and *call* for help?"

Shayna can't go all furry, and her howls are pathetic at best. But any *were* belonging to the Pack will recognize her voice and alert the others. It may be all that we need, not that it gives us a lot of time.

"I can, but we're far, T." She adjusts her hold on her sword. "And anything out there will hear me, too."

"I know. But we need to move and need more help." My thoughts ground to a halt when I see something in Paula's expression change. "What is it?"

"I can make her howl louder," she says. "There's an amplifying spell that's supposed to work to enforce charms, but it can also work on voices. It should also intensify your emotions and help you reach your mate so he can find you."

"Okay," I say. "Do it. We have to move fast." I move to take over watch duty as Shayna hops down and a group of thirteen witches surround her.

I don't bother participating in the spell despite how I'm somewhat familiar with it. My arm is behaving, but the witch who bound it is either dead or being leached of her power. I can't count on its good behavior to last, and I don't want to screw up our last chance to call for help.

I carefully step through the mound of rubble. These shoes are the absolute worst footwear I could have been transported into the woods with. Stones and bark litter the terrain and the ground isn't exactly flat. I can't go barefoot, but I can't exactly charge into battle in these things.

"Anybody have an extra pair of shoes?" I ask, not that I think any sort of pilgrim-wear is much better.

"Oh!" a little witch calls out. "I found a pair beneath my bed." She hurries away from the crowd gathered around Shayna as they cast their spell.

Whispers fill the corridor as the witches begin their chant. They're almost finished when the little witch returns with a pair of pink bunny slippers.

It shouldn't surprise me, after all this pretty much sums up the kind of luck I have. "Ah, thanks," I mumble, switching out my shoes.

The good news is they're heavily cushioned to somewhat protect my feet. They also wrap around them entirely and will, hopefully, stay on when I'm running for my life. I almost laugh, thinking about what Gemini would say, but my smile fades the more I think of him.

I step through the opening, and a little further out when I fail to sense any nearby danger. The full moon peers at me from the heavens. Despite its brightness, it takes some time for my eyes to adjust.

This part of the compound survived my fire, though the lingering smell of charred wood remains. It will help camouflage our scents, but the thick stands of trees will make it harder to see and trek through. It will also make it harder to see what's coming.

I'm not sure how long I have and I'm not positive any of us will make it out of here alive. So I take a moment to speak to my mate even though I can't be positive he's listening.

"I don't know if you can hear my words or thoughts," I whisper. "But if you can, I'm at the north side of Genevieve's compound. Savana is raising dead werebeasts using Genevieve's power. I'm with Shayna, Emme, Alice, and the Lessers. We're moving out toward the main road. We might not make it, and I need you to know something in case we don't." I take a breath, trying to keep my composure, but barely managing to do so. "You told me you love me. I believe you . . . because I'll never stop loving you."

I don't realize I'm crying until Emme steps to my side and squeezes my hand. "Are you okay?" she asks.

I shake my head. "No, but I need to be."

I glance behind me to where the Lessers are gathering behind Shayna and Alice. "Are we ready?" I ask.

Shayna nods, lifting her sword. "Yeah, T. It's time."

Chapter Thirty

"Okay," I say. "We have to get to the river that runs along the main road. It's the only chance we have to lose our scent. My sisters and I have more battle experience. We'll lead. But there's a lot of us and so we'll need to separate out into three groups. Get behind us and form a line. Paula, Fiona, and Merri will lead each—"

"Why them?" Cynthia interrupts.

Good God, I may have to literally throw her to the wolves.

"Because right now, they have some of my residual power, making them stronger," I remind her.

"But I'm not sure how long it will last," Paula points out.

She's as averse to leading as the rest of the Lessers. "No, but for now you have it, and it could last long enough to help you fight and get everyone out of here."

"But, Taran," she says.

I cut her off, gripping her shoulders. "We don't have time to argue, and this is not the time to be weak," I tell her. "I believe in you. If you want to live, you have to believe in yourself."

My hands slip from her shoulders as I face the remaining Lessers. "Tonight you're no longer those so far beneath the rest. You are the coven. Use your magic to hex and curse those who seek to harm you, but most of all to protect each other. Don't be pussies, it's time to become the witches you were born to be."

The coven nods in affirmation, their expressions scared yet determined. My speech roused them, and perhaps under other circumstances I would be met with applause. But now is not the time, nor do I wait for it.

I stomp forward in my bunny slippers which—I shit you not—open and close their mouths as I walk.

Shayna and Emme hurry to flank me as Alice trudges beside me. Alice seems to be having trouble walking and I worry she won't be able to keep up. "Keep her close to you," I whisper to Emme.

Everyone does their best to keep silent, but with a group this large wearing the shoes we are, it's almost impossible. My bunny slippers alone are picking up debris and the coven sounds like they're stomping out fire every time they take a step.

I don't think we make it a half a mile before Shayna grounds to a halt. My vision clears as dark magic charges the air around us, circling us like a swarm of vultures.

"Something's here," Shayna whispers.

Panic spreads behind me and Alice begins to moan like she's in pain. I jerk to the left, then right, that awful energy that's closing in sparking my magic from my core and setting my arm aflame.

"Shayna, howl," I tell her.

She squats slightly, lifting her blade in front of us. "You sure?" she asks.

"They already know we're here," I respond.

In the past, Shayna's howls have bordered on squeals. Not this time. She lifts her head toward the moon and cuts loose, her *call* so deep and resounding it rumbles the ground as the first of the zombie beasts attack.

The lead one gunning for Shayna never reaches the tip of her sword. My arm shoots out a spiral of blue and white flame, blistering the leathery hide of a *werebear* and bursting open its decomposing flesh.

Chaos erupts as the coven spreads out, their magic clashing against the dark energy surrounding us as they cast their first hex. Yet it's the howl from the distant mountains that has me whipping in that direction.

Shayna leaps in front of Emme, striking a boar across the legs and forcing it to the ground. She cuts off the head while I send a fireball into the cougar behind it. "It's Koda!" she yells, veering toward me. "They're coming!"

"Get to the river!" I scream, sending a lightning bolt into the next wolf that attacks.

The strike barely affects it. He stumbles and shakes it off, gunning for me. If not for Alice, throwing herself on top of it and ripping off his head, it would have killed me.

"Ergh!" she yells, lifting the decapitated head over hers in triumph.

I'll admit, this gives me pause. But like Bren said, an angry zombie is dangerous and strong. And Alice is plenty pissed. I shake out my arm, trying to gather more fire, but the flame flickers out, despite the amount of power coursing through it.

The decapitated boar head snaps at my feet. Emme sends it soaring, but as it lands it spurts into flowers. "Take that, bitch!" Merri hollers.

The Lessers are fighting back, calling to the trees and earth around them. Paula is in the lead, her fear as evident as her determination. She clasps the hands of the Lessers on either side of her. "*Imptetus!*" she yells.

"Attack", she means. And damn it, nature does!

Vines snake from the brush, tangling a cluster of werebeasts. Rows of ivy muzzle their snouts and fasten around their legs, pulling them down as the earth swallows them whole.

I clench and unclench my hand. "Come on," I beg, trying to will it to work as a cougar bounds toward me.

Large branches smack her away from me. I think it's Emme using her *force* until I see Fiona, moving her arms in the air as she manipulates the tree branches to defend us.

The Lessers are kicking ass, but when I see the blood-soaked remains of a uniform, I'm reminded that we're simply not enough.

Flames involuntarily envelop my arm, but quickly sputter out. I'm shaking it, trying to rouse it when Alice takes off, away from the river and deeper into the forest.

"Alice!" I yell, charging after her. "Alice!"

A wereraccoon, about the size of a dresser tackles me as I reach a dense stand of trees. I ram my fist into its mouth, coughing as my magic lights it up and what remains of its body begins to smoke.

I roll it off me as it breaks apart, pushing into a sprint when Alice moans in agony. But even in her condition she's faster than me, and she already sounds far away.

More howls erupt, I almost stumble when I recognize them as Gemini's wolves. He's close, so are the wolves who answer his *call*. But instead of running back toward the river where I need to be, or in his direction where I know I stand a better chance of surviving, I race toward Alice, recognizing she's in pain.

A wave of nauseating magic surrounds me as the space between the pines narrows, slowing my steps. Again fire ribbons around my arm, squelching the sickness I'm feeling until it vanishes. I'm not sure what's happening, but when the nausea and flames recede completely, I pet my arm in gratitude.

"Thanks," I say.

I push forward, this time much slower. I'm not sure where I'm headed or where on the compound I am.

"Alice?" I call when I can no longer hear her. "Alice?"

Whimpering trickles from a small distance away as the trees begin to thin out. I step between a smaller collection of pines and onto a rockier terrain, using the moonlight to help guide me. It's there I find Alice, standing near the edge of a cliff and crying large black tears.

"What's wrong?" I ask. I gasp as I take in the vast clearing below us, gripping her wrist and yanking her down.

At the center of the demolished field, three long stakes poke through the ground from the points of a triangle, lifting a lifeless and impaled body from each, several feet into the air. Rows of more bodies outline the shape. We're far. But even from this distance, I know they're mortally wounded, if not already dead.

Another similar triangle has been created at the far end of the field, and yet another near the left side. We found the missing Lesser witches, but it's the Superiors Savana chose to leech of their power.

In the middle of the center-most triangle, Genevieve's spine bows in an arc. I know it's her by the way her long dark hair sways beneath her. Like the other Superiors, she's been impaled. But unlike the rest, I think she's still alive.

Triangles in the spirit world are often a symbol of evil. In this case, they're also sacrificial. Savana has cast enough mojo to lock Vieve inside and drain her of her magic. But to raise the werebeasts she needed more than strong witches. She needed a zombie.

On a smaller stake beside Vieve awaits the other half of Savana's spell. Unlike Vieve, this zombie wasn't forced through a stake. She's tied to it with rope, moaning loudly and giving me a small glimpse of her pain.

I can't see the zombie's face, but I recognize her by the long brown dress she's wearing. She's the one Savana took with her when she escaped. I look back at Alice as she breaks down, sobbing.

"You know her, don't you?" I ask.

Thick black tears drip down her deeply gaunt features. I swallow back my sadness, but it's still hard to speak. "She's the reason you stayed, isn't she?"

More tears fall, staining her sunken cheeks. She tugs on my sleeve and points. I nod. "I'll help them," I promise, even though, I'm not sure how.

"Taran!" Emme calls. "Taran!"

I scramble to stand and hurry back toward the trees. Alice doesn't follow, not that I expect her to, and not when she's hurting as much as she is. I don't see my sisters right away, but Shayna sees me.

"T!" she yells, rushing toward me with Emme at her heels.

She throws her arms around me before I can explain. "We have to get out of here," she says. "Koda howled again, but this time it was different. It's a battle cry, the *weres* are positioning themselves to attack."

"I can't leave," I say. "The *weres* can't destroy these things without fire and I'm the only one with the flame to do it."

My sisters exchange glances. Before anyone can respond, a pack of werebeasts howl in the direction I left Alice.

The Pack has arrived and they're ready to fight.

Emme places her hand on my shoulder as my arm begins to glow. "Can you do it?" she asks. "Can you summon that much magic?"

My focus falls to where the glow emanates in and out beneath my skin.

"I have to," I say, my voice shaking with my growing fear. "I found Genevieve."

"Dude. She's *alive*?" Shayna asks.

"Only barely," I say. "This way. Just stay down, okay?"

My sisters and I have seen our share of bad, but I have to say, the condition the witches and Alice's friend are in is hard to take. Both gasp as we fall onto our stomachs and take in the scene.

"If I can reach her, I think I can heal her," Emme says.

"I think we're too late for that, Em," Shayna says.

From the end of the field furthest away, we see them, rows and rows of mangled and dead werebeasts lining up. Savana is perched on the back of the elk in the lead, the staff with a skull at its center twirling gray smoke as she holds it against her hip.

Her confidence makes her sit ramrod straight despite her ride isn't ideal. I can't stand her arrogance, but I'm not too stupid to recognize she's secured the upper hand. *Weres* are outrageously bigger than the beasts they resemble, but Savana's steed is more massive than most I've encountered. It's also creepier than shit.

More skeletal than flesh, its ribs expose what seems to be a beating heart beneath. To add to its lethality, a rack almost as tall as its length protrudes from his head, the points appearing as sharp as Shayna's sword. And whether by coincidence or strategy, most of her zombie army are made up of the deadliest forms of werebeasts: bears, cougars, wolves, even hawks. But I suppose evil is as evil does and it's not like she's going to raise an army of wereducks.

Emme's breath hitches. "There's Koda," she says. She turns to me. "And Gemini."

She didn't have to tell me. I saw his twin wolves step forward at the opposite end where the Pack is lining up. Their howls rumble as they prepare to attack. But if Savana's triangles of death and dismay are away from her and her immediate reach, they must be cursed to hell and back, giving her enough assurance to leave them.

The Pack is outnumbered by their dead brethren. And their dead brethren won't easily die. Savana is using Vieve's power and a zombie to raise the dead. But I have power, too, and a zombie of my own. Well, at least a zombie limb.

I fall into a kneeling position and tug down the sleeve of my right arm. "Shayna, give me your knife," I say.

"Why?" she asks, her eyes widening.

"The Pack needs a hand," I insist.

Alice lowers herself beside me, snaps off her hand at the wrist, and drops it into my outstretched palm. Something, with at least ten legs, skitters from the hollowed out bone. It races across my skin and leaps off my fingers. I swallow hard, and as politely as I can, returning her body part. "That's not what I meant, sweetie."

"Ergh?"

I close my eyes, calling forth the magic I once held like friend. The familiar flicker of warmth and pain stirs my core as the flames gather more strength. The sting isn't as bad, but it's growing, and I know it's going to get worse.

"Taran . . . what are you thinking," Shayna asks.

"That we're out of time, and I need to act."

As if to prove my point, the Pack charges, gathering speed as they tear down the field. Savana screams, not in terror, but in impeding victory.

"They need my fire," I stress, speaking fast. "The Pack won't make it without it."

Shayna's head whips toward the fight as live and dead werebeasts collide. Savana casts her first death curse, narrowly missing Bren, but killing the wolf beside him.

"Oh, my God," Emme says, covering her mouth.

"T, don't," Shayna pleads.

"I have to release what's inside of me," I tell her. "It's the only way with all these zombies. Remember what Bren said, unless they burn to ash, they reassemble. Our wolves don't have that option, Shayna."

Emme may hear me and understand, but her tone reveals her panic. "If you cut that bind, your magic will explode like a grenade. You could blow yourself to pieces—"

"And take everyone with you," Shayna points out. "T, according to what Genevieve said, that's a storm that's been brewing inside you, waiting to blast all at once."

My eyes scan the growing anarchy, as more zombie werebeasts rush out from the forest. These creatures are everywhere and there's likely more to come.

"Maybe you're right," I say. "But you can't stop a storm."

I snatch the knife from her hip. "*Taran*," she pleads.

"I have to do this," I snap when she tries to take it back. "For the Pack and for the coven."

"But what if you die?" she counters.

"I'm already dying, Shayna." I don't mean to be so blunt, but it's the truth and I can't stop now. "Ask Emme if you don't believe me. I only have a few hours at best."

Emme stands, pushing her blonde hair away from her face as she chokes on her cries.

"But . . ." Shayna looks at Emme. "Can't you help her?"

"No," I answer for her. "But if I'm going to go, I'm taking these fuckers with me."

I stand and shove the blade beneath the strand closest to my elbow. But before I twist the sharp end up to make the cut, I meet their eyes. "I love you," I tell them over the howls of more wolves. "Watch out for Celia and her baby. Give him a kiss from me when he's born. And tell Gemini . . ." Damn it, I can barely speak. "Tell him I love him, too."

I wrench the blade up, slicing through the bind. I pause as the crook of my elbow starts smoking. "Um. You may want to step back," I warn, looking up at them.

They take off, dragging a moaning Alice behind them.

I'm not really sure what's happening, and despite all the bravado behind my heartrending speech, I don't love what I see.

Like a snake uncoiling, the bind unravels to my wrist and falls away while the smoke at my elbow ignites like a fuse, shooting out toward my fingers.

I know what's coming. That doesn't stop me from swearing when my arm blows me to kingdom come and I'm launched over the cliff.

The air smacks at my skin as I spiral downward. I call forth my fire, surrounding myself with it in a blink before I crash into the ground. Blue and white blazes spurt from the crater I create, but it's my fire, my will, and this time, I'm in control.

I climb out as the temperature builds around me, grabbing the protruding stones and roots along the sides to help me ascend. The hole I'm in is huge, and it takes time to reach the top. But instead of growing weaker, the flames encasing me feed my will and energize my spirit, compounding my strength *and* my fury.

"Power," I rasp as I reach the top. "Give me power!"

Like a rush of adrenaline, a torridity of heat expands along my veins, compelling my feet faster until I'm full-out running toward the fight.

A long deceased bison sees me and charges. I spread my hands, preparing to strike. Yet before I can launch my power the beast catches fire, as does the zombie hawk swooping down.

I'm covered in flames. Every part of me florid and crackling with blue and white, including the footprints I leave behind.

This is more than I've ever had or called. But instead of feeding my confidence, it prompts my fear. I can't control what's happening. I'm afraid, I'm about to erupt.

My body rattles as the firestorm within me builds into an inferno. I rush forward, hurrying toward where Vieve is impaled. A wolf from the Pack whimpers as I rush past, igniting the creature he's fighting, but also inadvertently burning him.

His packmates notice, bounding out of my way, but also herding their prey toward my increasing blaze. My flames rise and expand as the smell of singeing and festering flesh fills the air. The heat lighting up the zombies, but also somehow feeding my magic and making it hard to control.

I race forward, knowing I'm running out of time. The Pack must sense it, compelling them to act.

A mountain lion thunders toward the sacrificial triangle. Before it reaches it, a second hawk dives, digging its talons into the lion and carrying it away. Another *were* tries, this one a grizzly. She slams against an invisible wall and disintegrates. No smell, no particles, no evidence of who she was. It's no wonder Savana felt safe leaving Vieve, despite her being the primary source maintaining the zombies.

I don't know if what I have is enough to break through the wall of protection, I only know I have to try before it turns against me. I reach the triangle and hold out my hands.

The flames catch the invisible wall. I'm not sure if it's breaking through and try to move closer, but whatever is shielding the triangle shoves me back, making me almost fall. I try again, pushing forward until what feel like a truck bowls me over.

The earth beneath me smolders as I push up on my elbows, but again something rams me, flinging me hard and sending me rolling across the field. I come to a stop far away from the triangle, leaving a path of flames.

I look up to see Savana riding the wicked steed she used to mow me over. Christ, if my fire hadn't shielded me, I'd already be dead. As it is, I feel like I've been thrown down a flight of stairs.

"You bitch!" she screams. She raises her staff above her head, her magic building with gray light.

I don't wait for her to act, rushing to my feet and thrusting my power forward. My magic collides against the elk's chest, slapping away the rotting pieces of skin that remain, but not much else.

Savana laughs. That's right, *laughs*.

Tendrils of gray smoke surrounding her like armor. I shove all I have into her beast. Yet my magic has no effect. None.

But sometimes all you need is muscle in the form of two very vicious twin wolves.

Both halves of Gemini collide against the elk, tearing into the bleating creature. Savana topples from its back, screeching as her ride collapses on top of her and pins her to the ground.

I run forward, diving for her staff where it pokes out beneath the elk.

The moment my hand connects with the staff, magic as revolting and vicious as Savana jolts me like a bolt of electricity. I shake off my hands and reach for it again, swearing when another jolt slams into me.

Savana holds tight, spewing power into the staff as she writhes beneath the creature Gemini is mauling.

Again I try, again I'm zapped with something nasty. Fortunately, there's an old saying among werewolves, "If the hand of your enemy brings you pain and torment, bite it off."

That shit should be embroidered on a pillow, and is exactly what Gemini does. I snatch the staff when the wolf with the left white paw snaps Savana's hand off at the wrist.

"Good boy," I say, shaking the hand loose from the staff and sprinting back to the triangle.

I lift the staff above my head, forcing my will into it

as I speak the words of power.

"*Protegeme.*"

Protect me.

"*Defiendeme.*"

Defend me.

And most importantly, "*Véngame!*"

Avenge me.

I slam the staff against the invisible force covering the triangle, my power and Savana's colliding at once. Like a storm built from a thousand hell fires, a tornado of blue and white projects into the heavens, spiraling out and torching the sky.

Swirling clouds of black, blue, and white form, canvasing the night and blocking out the moon. Lightning bolts crash along the field, one after the other, splitting the clouds and making it rain clumps of freaking fire.

I am amazing. Awesome. A sight to behold.

Or I would be if it weren't for the smoldering bunny slippers on my feet and my right tit sticking out of my dress.

I toss the staff aside as that awful sense of death and evil builds, shoving my breast back into what's left of my tattered dress and racing to where Vieve lies suspended.

Blood pools from her mouth and her eyes are partially closed. I stroke back her hair as the fire surrounding me recedes, wondering if I'm too late, and if I'm not, how the hell I'm going to get her and the others down.

I startle when she turns her head slightly and smiles. "You accepted your arm and mastered your magic," she says, choking on the blood, spilling from her mouth.

"How the *fuck* are you still alive?" is my response.

She struggles to speak, but even though I'd rather she not try in her condition, it's like she has to. "Because we're both survivors and more alike than you think," she slurs.

"Maybe we are," I agree. "But why don't we keep that little tidbit to ourselves there, Vieve."

Her chest rises and falls sporadically, I think she's seizing and possibly dying, I rush to support her head when I realize she's chuckling. "You want to know something?" she asks, so softly, I barely catch it.

"What is it?" I ask, hoping it's not a warning of something else to come.

What remains of her subtle smile fades. "I never stood a chance with Gemini." She spits out the blood filling her mouth. "No female does with you around."

I ease her head down and step away, trying not to permit her words to affect me like they do, but not managing anything close to it. Maybe, though, I don't have to.

I whip around as an unearthly scream rattles the earth. Savana raises her staff and mutters the death curse. "*Muerte.*"

Her magic blasts toward me, fast and furious.

But not faster than mine.

The crackling energy from my lightning encapsulates my form, guarding me and rebounding the curse. It strikes her chest almost at the same moment Shayna's dagger flies over my shoulder.

The tip of the dagger drives through Savana's eye and into her skull.

Yet it's her own damn curse that makes her what she becomes.

Her chest caves as her body shrivels inward, decaying into gray wrinkled flesh. She peers down with her one eye as chunks from her face fall in pieces at her feet. I think she's turning into a zombie, and I think I need to set her ablaze. But then Gemini's wolves appear, saving me the trouble.

Their fangs latch onto her shoulders, digging in their points and tearing her in half. They bound away from me, flinging what remains of the big, bad witch into the mounds of fire burning the field. Around me the Pack is doing the same with their prey. But with Savanah dead, the deceased werebeasts are no longer bound to her. As I watch, all the zombies start flinging themselves into the fire, freeing what remains of their souls.

Except for two.

Alice wails as she clutches the zombie tied beside Vieve. I don't have to look at the zombie long to recognize there's a resemblance between them. They're family, I see it now.

Shayna rushes forward, cutting her loose. I look back at Vieve as Emme reaches her. "Go," Vieve says. "I can free myself."

She laughs a little when I look at her like she's nuts because hello, she is. "You're *impaled*," I remind her. "As in there's this giant stake sticking out of your stomach."

"Not for long," she answers weakly.

Vieve doesn't have her talisman, but I don't think she needs it. A flock of owls sweep through the skies as the clouds begin to recede. Their speed outrageously fast as they dive. I back away, bumping into Emme as the owls grip Vieve's limbs and carefully pull her up.

I expect her to scream and flail. I would. But she does neither, going flaccid as owls gently pull her up to the top, streaking her blood along the length of the stake.

She should be dead, I think to myself. But hell, so should I.

Emme cradles Vieve against her when the owls set her down, not waiting for them to leave before surrounding her with her healing *touch*.

The owls flutter away, their long wingspans stretching out as they move to the other Superiors not currently being freed by the Pack. I think Vieve is going to be okay, the knowledge easing the tension clenching my shoulders. But while I didn't harm her, I don't feel right hovering over her. She's hurt and needs her space.

I start to walk away, only to be intercepted by Paula. "We found the rest of the coven," she says, motioning to where the Lessers help carry the injured forward. "They were being leeched near the entrance to curse anyone who entered. The Pack figured it out and went a different way." She sighs. "They weren't able to free them, but we did. We helped them."

"No," I tell her smiling. "You saved them."

"Maybe," Merri adds stomping out her hairy and singed feet. "But you like, made it rain fire!"

"Yeah," I say. "Just don't expect that to happen

again."

I make my way toward Alice, rubbing my arm as I come to terms with finally accepting it. I mull over when exactly it happened, my thoughts automatically returning to when Gemini brushed his lips over the knuckles and finally appeared to accept it himself. But then I concur it wasn't one single moment, but rather a culmination of many, and that perhaps the love he demonstrated was the final piece I was missing.

I smile softly as the fingertips of my left hand trail over the bright white skin. "Thank you," I tell it, my eyes welling with how much I mean what I say.

I look up to where Gemini's wolves, along with Bren, Koda, and their packmates are rounding up the leftover zombie parts that remain. It must have been hard, battling and now destroying their fallen friends and family members. But evil like Savana doesn't care: one more reason she needed to die.

Alice is so enthralled with her sister when I reach them, I'm not sure if she'll notice me. Yet she does, throwing herself on top of me when she sees me. I start crying the minute she connects, knowing this is goodbye.

"Thank you for being my friend," I tell her as Emme quietly steps toward us.

"*Ergh,*" she wails.

She doesn't want to leave and grips me tighter. "It's okay," I say, rubbing her back. "Go and find your peace. You deserve it, sweetie."

She releases me slowly, nodding stiffly and reaching for Emme.

"Wait, she's going?" Shayna asks when Alice clutches her. As much as she wanted Alice to find eternal rest, like me, she's having a hard time watching her go.

I hug her and Emme as Alice clasps the other zombie's hand. Together they hobble to the nearby cluster of flames. "She was waiting for her sister," I explain, which of course only makes us cry harder.

If Alice and her sister feel pain, they don't show it.

They simply walk into the fire unafraid. But that's what sisters do. We're there for each other through good, bad, and even death.

"Taran?" Vieve calls.

She's standing with the help of the Lessers on either side of her. She's beat up, having just survived torture and a stake through her gut. Yet somehow, Vieve makes weak and tormented look good.

"Yeah?"

"Would you like to help us squelch the fire and make it rain?" she asks.

The corners of her mouth lift in that soft and regal way. She's trying to be nice, and I appreciate it. But she has her sisters and I have mine. "Do you need me to?"

She laughs, shaking her head slowly. "Not at all. But just as you helped us, I swear on my honor we'll be here to help you."

Her vow makes me smile, so does the sincerity behind it. Vieve and I will never be buds. But her kindness comes from the heart, and doesn't this world need more of that.

"I appreciate the offer," I say. "But I think I'm better at blowing shit up."

She chuckles softly, appearing weak yet determined. Before she can turn away I ask. "Hey, Vieve. What did I sacrifice?" I lift my arm and point at it. "You said I had to sacrifice something, accept my arm, and learn to focus. I get everything else, but what did I give in return?"

"You sacrificed yourself to save both the Pack and your coven," she explains.

"How?" I ask, not understanding.

She tilts her head as if I'm missing the point. "In cutting the bind, you unleashed a power that could have killed you. Not for your stubbornness or gain, but to help us all." She considers her words as remnants of her magic trace across my limb. "There may be times you'll struggle, as I find your arm to be almost as strong-willed as its owner. But if you continue to work with it, instead of against it, eventually, it will become a treasured part of you."

"Thank you," I tell her quietly, not only because of what she tells me, but also because of how hard it was to say what she did, giving her weakened state.

She and the coven shuffle away from me as Koda and Bren race forward. Koda *changes* from his giant wolf form, back to the male who can't wait to hold his mate. I'm not surprised, but I practically keel over when Bren *changes* and pulls Emme against his naked form.

"I was scared I lost you," he murmurs quietly.

What the *fuck*?

I back away fast, wondering what the hell I missed, and unsure whether or not I'm imagining things. Along the field, a caravan of SUVs barrel forward, stopping in a line a few yards away from the smoldering flames. I recognize Aric's vehicle at the center. He steps out, reaching for Celia's hand and keeping her back.

They didn't leave for the stronghold. And maybe now, they won't have to.

I trudge toward them, not realizing how tired I am until I catch glimpses of the sun rising in the east. I don't think the witches utter more than the first few words of their chant before sprinkles of rain begin wetting my face.

Tired maybe how I feel, but loneliness isn't too far away.

Alice, sweet Alice, is gone. And me and Gemini, what can I say? We've worked through some things, but I can't be sure we're okay.

I'm almost to the last mound of burning flames when twin wolves race past me on either side. They ground to a halt a few feet away, joining to become one. Gemini's back curls slowly upward as he stands, transforming into the man I've barely lived without.

He storms forward, his dark eyes glistening in the remaining flames as he dissolves the space between us.

"I have to finish searching the grounds for any evidence of zombie werebeasts that remain," he says in a way of a greeting.

"Okay," I respond, confused as to why he seems so

angry.

He starts to turn, but I can't let him leave me like this. "Are you mad at me?" I ask.

He freezes in place. "Yes," he says, peering over his back. "I shouldn't be, but I am."

I ram my hands on my hips. "Why? Yeah, I set the compound on fire, *again*. But damn it, it all worked out in the end."

He stomps forward. "You thought I hated you," he growls. "You are my mate, yet you thought I hated you."

The full impact of what he's feeling causes a burn in my heart that has nothing to do with my fire. "What else could I believe when you turned away from me like you did?" I ask, the sadness I feel leaking into my voice. "All those times you rejected me and pulled away. What did you expect me to think?"

His chest rises and falls with the extent of his rising fury. But it's not fury. It's something else. "I've used these hands for revenge and to protect the innocent from harm," he tells me holding out his arms. "I've used them to kill monsters, and to carry the fallen and those too injured to fight." His hands slowly grasp mine as a single tear cuts a line down his face. "But the best thing they've ever done is hold you."

"I . . ."

He kisses me as I clutch him against me. It's a deep, long kiss, heavy with love, but as gentle as the breeze passing along our skin. I don't want to let him go. No, I never want *him* to let me go. Except our lives being what they are, he has to. At least for now.

"We have things to talk through," he murmurs as his lips leave mine to trail along my jaw. "But I'm done being without you."

"Okay," I agree.

He pauses. I suppose he expected me to argue. Can't blame him, I'm what some may refer to as slightly challenging. But like him, I don't want to know another day without him.

He presses a kiss to my forehead. "I'll be at the house as soon as I'm finished. Will you wait for me there?"

"Yes," I promise.

"All right," he says, releasing me slowly. "I won't be longer than necessary."

I watch him walk away, splitting into two wolves as he leaps, the heavy paws of his beasts pounding against the earth as they speed forward.

Everything Gemini told me hits like a tidal wave of emotion that keeps me still and only barely breathing. And yet as a familiar brush of power presses against my back, I wipe my eyes and straighten.

The being approaching isn't one I can be vulnerable around. Nor can I ever demonstrate weakness around him.

Through the lingering smoke and flames, and as the rain continues to fall, he stalks forward, his long blond hair fanning out as he prowls in my direction.

The way his black silk shirt and finely tailored black pants hug his tall frame make him appear more model than man. But Misha Aleksandr is no mere mortal and neither are the vampires flanking his sides.

He stops directly in front of me, his gray eyes briefly scanning the smoldering landscape and lingering remains of battle.

Along with the holes on the front of my dress.

"Impressive," he says.

I smirk. "The destruction or my rack?"

And there's that sinful smile he's known for. "Perhaps both."

"You're late," I point out, motioning behind me. "We could have used you and your peeps when the zombie werebeast army tried to eat us. Oh, and when the psycho witch who raised them *and* imprisoned most of the coven launched her first curse."

"No," he disagrees. "It seems I arrived just in time." He stops smiling then. "I have a proposition for you, Taran. One I have no doubt you're the right sister for . . ."

Reader's Guide to the Magical World of the Weird Girls Series

acute bloodlust A condition that occurs when a vampire goes too long without consuming blood. Increases the vampire's thirst to lethal levels. It is remedied by feeding the vampire.

Call The ability of one supernatural creature to reach out to another, through either thoughts or sounds. A vampire can pass his or her *call* by transferring a bit of magic into the receiving being's skin.

Change To transform from one being to another, typically from human to beast, and back again.

chronic bloodlust A condition caused by a curse placed on a vampire. It makes the vampire's thirst for blood insatiable and drives the vampire to insanity. The vampire grows in size from gluttony and assumes deformed features. There is no cure.

claim The method by which a werebeast consummates the union with his or her mate.

clan A group of werebeasts led by an Alpha. The types of clans differ depending on species. Werewolf clans are called "packs." Werelions belong to "prides."

Creatura The offspring of a demon lord and a werebeast.

dantem animam A soul giver. A rare being capable of returning a master vampire's soul. A master with a soul is more powerful than any other vampire in existence, as he or she is balancing life and death at once.

dark ones Creatures considered to be pure evil, such as shape-shifters or demons.

demon A creature residing in hell. Only the strongest demons may leave to stalk on earth, but their time is limited; the power of good compels them to return.

demon child The spawn of a demon lord and a mortal female. Demon children are of limited intelligence and rely predominantly on their predatory instincts.

demon lords (*demonkin*) The offspring of a witch mother and a demon. Powerful, cunning, and deadly. Unlike demons, whose time on earth is limited, demon lords may remain on earth indefinitely.

den A school where young werebeasts train and learn to fight in order to help protect the earth from mystical evil.

Elder One of the governors of a werebeast clan. Each clan is led by three Elders: an Alpha, a Beta, and an Omega. The Alpha is the supreme leader. The Beta is the second in command. The Omega settles disputes between them and has the ability to calm by releasing bits of his or her harmonized soul, or through a sense of humor muddled with magic. He possesses rare gifts and is often volatile, selfish, and of questionable loyalty.

force Emme Wird's ability to move objects with her mind.

gold The metallic element; it was cursed long ago and has damaging effects on werebeasts, vampires, and the dark ones. Supernatural creatures cannot hold gold without feeling the poisonous effects of the curse. A bullet dipped in gold will explode a supernatural creature's heart like a bomb. Gold against open skin has a searing effect.

grandmaster The master of a master vampire. Grandmasters are among the earth's most powerful creatures. Grandmasters can recognize whether the human he or she *turned* is a master upon creation. Grandmasters usually kill any master vampires they create to consume their power. Some choose to let the masters live until they become a threat, or until they've gained greater strength and therefore more consumable power.

keep Beings a master vampire controls and is responsible for, such as those he or she has *turned* vampire, or a human he or she regularly feeds from. One master can acquire another's keep by destroying the master the keep belongs to.

Leader A pureblood werebeast in charge of delegating and planning attacks against the evils that threaten the earth.

Lesser witch Title given to a witch of weak power and who has not yet mastered control of her magic. Unlike their Superior counterparts, they aren't given talismans or staffs to amplify their magic because their control over their power is limited.

Lone A werebeast who doesn't belong to a clan, and therefore is not obligated to protect the earth from supernatural evil. Considered of lower class by those with clans.

master vampire A vampire with the ability to *turn* a human vampire. Upon their creation, masters are usually killed by their grandmaster for power. Masters are immune to fire and to sunlight born of magic, and typically carry tremendous power. Only a master or another lethal preternatural can kill a master vampire. If one master kills another, the surviving vampire acquires his or her power, wealth, and keep.

mate The being a werebeast will love and share a soul with for eternity.

Misericordia A plea for mercy in a duel.

moon sickness The werebeast equivalent of bloodlust. Brought on by a curse from a powerful enchantress. Causes excruciating pain. Attacks a werebeast's central nervous system, making the werebeast stronger and violent, and driving the werebeast to kill. No known cure exists.

mortem provocatio A fight to the death.

North American *Were* Council The governing body of *weres* in North America, led by a president and several council members.

potestatem bonum "The power of good." That which encloses the earth and keeps demons from remaining among the living.

Purebloods (aka *pures*) Werebeasts from generations of *were*-only family members. Considered royalty among werebeasts, they carry the responsibilities of their species. The mating between two purebloods is the only way to guarantee the conception of a *were* child.

rogue witch a witch without a coven. Must be accounted for as rogue witches tend to go one of two ways without a coven: dark or insane.

shape-shifter Evil, immortal creatures who can take any form. They are born witches, then spend years seeking innocents to sacrifice to a dark deity. When the deity deems the offerings sufficient, the witch casts a baneful spell to surrender his or her magic and humanity in exchange for immortality and the power of hell at their fingertips. Shape-shifters can command any form and are the deadliest and strongest of all mystical creatures.

Shift Celia's ability to break down her body into minute particles. Her gift allows her to travel beneath and across soil, concrete, and rock. Celia can also *shift* a limited number of beings. Disadvantages include not being able to breathe or see until she surfaces.

solis natus magicae The proper term for sunlight born of magic, created by a wielder of spells. Considered "pure" light. Capable of destroying non-master vampires and demons. In large quantities may also kill shape-shifters. Renders the wielder helpless once fired.

Superior Witch A witch of tremendous power and magic who assumes a leadership role among the coven. Wears a talisman around her neck or carries staff with a precious stone at its center to help amplify her magic.

Surface Celia's ability to reemerge from a shift.

susceptor animae A being capable of taking one's soul, such as a vampire.

Trudhilde Radinka (aka *Destiny*) A female born once every century from the union of two witches who possesses rare talents and the aptitude to predict the future. Considered among the elite of the mystical world.

turn To transform a human into a werebeast or vampire. Werebeasts *turn* by piercing the heart of a human with their fangs and transferring a part of their essence. Vampires pierce through the skull and into the brain to transfer a taste of their magic. Werebeasts risk their lives during the *turning* process, as they are gifting a part of their souls. Should the transfer fail, both the werebeast and human die. Vampires risk nothing since they're not losing their souls, but rather taking another's and releasing it from the human's body.

vampire A being who consumes the blood of mortals to survive. Beautiful and alluring, vampires will never appear to age past thirty years. Vampires are immune to sunlight unless it is created by magic. They are also immune to objects of faith such as crucifixes. Vampires may be killed by the destruction of their hearts, decapitation, or fire. Master vampires or vampires several centuries old must have both their hearts and heads removed or their bodies completely destroyed.

vampire clans Families of vampires led by master vampires. Masters can control, communicate, and punish their keep through mental telepathy.

velum A veil conjured by magic.

virtutem lucis "The power of light." The goodness found within each mortal. That which combats the darkness.

Warrior A werebeast possessing profound skill or fighting ability. Only the elite among *weres* are granted the title of Warrior. Warriors are duty-bound to protect their Leaders and their Leaders' mates at all costs.

werebeast A supernatural predator with the ability to *change* from human to beast. Werebeasts are considered the Guardians of the Earth against mystical evil. Werebeasts will achieve their first *change* within six months to a year following birth. The younger they are when they first *change,* the more powerful they will be. Werebeasts also possess the ability to heal their wounds. They can live until the first full moon following their one hundredth birthday. Werebeasts may be killed by destruction of their hearts, decapitation, or if their bodies are completely destroyed. The only time a *were* can partially *change* is when he or she attempts to *turn* a human. A *turned* human will achieve his or her first *change* by the next full moon.

witch A being born with the power to wield magic. They worship the earth and nature. Pure witches will not take part in blood sacrifices. They cultivate the land to grow plants for their potions and use staffs and talismans to amplify their magic. To cross a witch is to feel the collective wrath of her coven.

witch fire Orange flames encased by magic, used to assassinate an enemy. Witch fire explodes like multiple grenades when the intended victim nears the spell. Flames will continue to burn until the target has been eliminated.

zombie Typically human bodies raised from the dead by a necromancer witch. It's illegal to raise or keep a zombie and is among the deadliest sins in the supernatural world. Their diet consists of other dead things such as roadkill and decaying animals.

This book contains an excerpt from Sealed with a Curse, the first full-length novel in The Weird Girls Urban Fantasy Romance series by Cecy Robson. The excerpt has been set for this edition only and may not reflect the final content of the final novel.

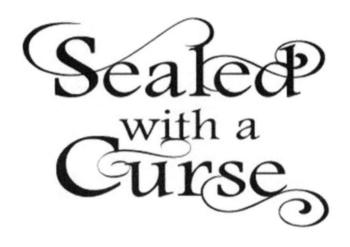

A Weird Girls Novel

Cecy Robson

Chapter One

Sacramento, California

The courthouse doors crashed open as I led my three sisters into the large foyer. I didn't mean to push so hard, but hell, I was mad and worried about being eaten. The cool spring breeze slapped at my back as I stepped inside, yet it did little to cool my temper or my nerves.

My nose scented the vampires before my eyes caught them emerging from the shadows. There were six of them, wearing dark suits, Ray-Bans, and obnoxious little grins. Two bolted the doors tight behind us, while the others frisked us for weapons.

I can't believe we we're in vampire court. So much for avoiding the perilous world of the supernatural.

Emme trembled beside me. She had every right to be scared. We were strong, but our combined abilities couldn't trump a roomful of bloodsucking beasts. "Celia," she whispered, her voice shaking. "Maybe we shouldn't have come."

Like we had a choice. "Just stay close to me, Emme." My muscles tensed as the vampire's hands swept the length of my body and through my long curls. I didn't like him touching me, and neither did my inner tigress. My fingers itched with the need to protrude my claws.

When he finally released me, I stepped closer to Emme while I scanned the foyer for a possible escape route. Next to me, the vampire searching Taran got a little daring with his pat-down. But he was messing with the wrong sister.

"If you touch my ass one more time, fang boy, I swear to God I'll light you on fire." The vampire quickly removed his hands when a spark of blue flame ignited from Taran's fingertips.

Shayna, conversely, flashed a lively smile when the vampire searching her found her toothpicks. Her grin widened when he returned her seemingly harmless little sticks, unaware of how deadly they were in her hands. "Thanks, dude." She shoved the box back into the pocket of her slacks.

"They're clear." The guard grinned at Emme and licked his lips. "This way." He motioned her to follow. Emme cowered. Taran showed no fear and plowed ahead. She tossed her dark, wavy hair and strutted into the courtroom like the diva she was, wearing a tiny white mini dress that contrasted with her deep olive skin. I didn't fail to notice the guards' gazes glued to Taran's shapely figure. Nor did I miss when their incisors lengthened, ready to bite.

I urged Emme and Shayna forward. "Go. I'll watch your backs." I whipped around to snarl at the guards. The vampires' smiles faltered when they saw *my* fangs protrude. Like most beings, they probably didn't know what I was, but they seemed to recognize that I was potentially lethal, despite my petite frame.

I followed my sisters into the large courtroom. The place reminded me of a picture I'd seen of the Salem witch trials. Rows of dark wood pews lined the center aisle, and wide rustic planks comprised the floor. Unlike the photo I recalled, every window was boarded shut, and paintings of vampires hung on every inch of available wall space. One particular image epitomized the vampire stereotype perfectly. It showed a male vampire entwined with two naked women on a bed of roses and jewels. The women appeared completely enamored of the vampire, even while blood dripped from their necks.

The vampire spectators scrutinized us as we approached along the center aisle. Many had accessorized their expensive attire with diamond jewelry and watches that probably cost more than my car. Their glares told me they didn't appreciate my cotton T-shirt, peasant skirt, and flip-flops. I was twenty-five years old; it's not like I didn't know how to dress. But, hell, other fabrics and shoes were way more expensive to replace when I *changed* into my other form.

I spotted our accuser as we stalked our way to the front of the assembly. Even in a courtroom crammed with young and sexy vampires, Misha Aleksandr stood out. His tall, muscular frame filled his fitted suit, and his long blond hair brushed against his shoulders. Death, it seemed, looked damn good. Yet it wasn't his height or his wealth or even his striking features that captivated me. He possessed a fierce presence that commanded the room. Misha Aleksandr was a force to be reckoned with, but, strangely enough, so was I.

Misha had "requested" our presence in Sacramento after charging us with the murder of one of his family members. We had two choices: appear in court or be hunted for the rest of our lives. The whole situation sucked. We'd stayed hidden from the supernatural world for so long. Now not only had we been forced into the limelight, but we also faced the possibility of dying some twisted, Rob Zombie–inspired death.

Of course, God forbid that would make Taran shut her trap. She leaned in close to me. "Celia, how about I gather some magic-borne sunlight and fry these assholes?" she whispered in Spanish.

A few of the vampires behind us muttered and hissed, causing uproar among the rest. If they didn't like us before, they sure as hell hated us then.

Shayna laughed nervously, but maintained her perky demeanor. "I think some of them understand the lingo, dude."

I recognized Taran's desire to burn the vamps to blood and ash, but I didn't agree with it. Conjuring such power would leave her drained and vulnerable, easy prey for the master vampires, who would be immune to her sunlight. Besides, we were already in trouble with one master for killing his keep. We didn't need to be hunted by the entire leeching species.

The procession halted in a strangely wide-open area

before a raised dais. There were no chairs or tables, nothing we could use as weapons against the judges or the angry mob amassed behind us.

My eyes focused on one of the boarded windows. The light honey-colored wood frame didn't match the darker boards. I guessed the last defendant had tried to escape. Judging from the claw marks running from beneath the frame to where I stood, he, she, or *it* hadn't made it.

I looked up from the deeply scratched floor to find Misha's intense gaze on me. We locked eyes, predator to predator, neither of us the type to back down. *You're trying to intimidate the wrong gal, pretty boy. I don't scare easily.*

Shayna slapped her hand over her face and shook her head, her long black ponytail waving behind her. "For Pete's sake, Celia, can't you be a little friendlier?" She flashed Misha a grin that made her blue eyes sparkle. "How's it going, dude?"

Shayna said "dude" a lot, ever since dating some idiot claiming to be a professional surfer. The term fit her sunny personality and eventually grew on us.

Misha didn't appear taken by her charm. He eyed her as if she'd asked him to make her a garlic pizza in the shape of a cross. I laughed; I couldn't help it. *Leave it to Shayna to try to befriend the guy who'll probably suck us dry by sundown.*

At the sound of my chuckle, Misha regarded me slowly. His head tilted slightly as his full lips curved into a sensual smile. I would have preferred a vicious stare—I knew how to deal with those. For a moment, I thought he'd somehow made my clothes disappear and I was standing there like the bleeding hoochies in that awful painting.

The judges' sudden arrival gave me an excuse to glance away. There were four, each wearing a formal robe of red velvet with an elaborate powdered wig. They were probably several centuries old, but like all vampires, they didn't appear a day over thirty. Their splendor easily surpassed the beauty of any mere mortal. I guessed the whole "sucky, sucky, me love you all night" lifestyle paid off for them.

The judges regally assumed their places on the raised

dais. Behind them hung a giant plasma screen, which appeared out of place in this century-old building. Did they plan to watch a movie while they decided how best to disembowel us?

A female judge motioned Misha forward with a Queen Elizabeth hand wave. A long, thick scar angled from the corner of her left jaw across her throat. Someone had tried to behead her. To scar a vampire like that, the culprit had likely used a gold blade reinforced with lethal magic. Apparently, even that blade hadn't been enough. I gathered she commanded the fang-fest Parliament, since her marble nameplate read, CHIEF JUSTICE ANTOINETTE MALIKA. Judge Malika didn't strike me as the warm and cuddly sort. Her lips were pursed into a tight line and her elongating fangs locked over her lower lip. I only hoped she'd snacked before her arrival.

At a nod from Judge Malika, Misha began. "Members of the High Court, I thank you for your audience." A Russian accent underscored his deep voice. "I hereby charge Celia, Taran, Shayna, and Emme Wird with the murder of my family member, David Geller."

"Wird? More like *Weird*," a vamp in the audience mumbled. The smaller vamp next to him adjusted his bow tie nervously when I snarled.

Oh, yeah, like we've never heard that before, jerk.

The sole male judge slapped a heavy leather-bound book on the long table and whipped out a feather quill. "Celia Wird. State your position."

Position?

I exchanged glances with my sisters; they didn't seem to know what Captain Pointy Teeth meant either. Taran shrugged. "Who gives a shit? Just say something."

I waved a hand. "Um. Registered nurse?"

Judging by his "please don't make me eat you before the proceedings" scowl, and the snickering behind us, I hadn't provided him with the appropriate response.

He enunciated every word carefully and slowly so as to not further confuse my obviously feeble and inferior mind.

"Position in the supernatural world."

"We've tried to avoid your world." I gave Taran the evil eye. "For the most part. But if you must know, I'm a tigress."

"Weretigress," he said as he wrote.

"I'm not a *were*," I interjected defensively.

He huffed. "Can you *change* into a tigress or not?"

"Well, yes. But that doesn't make me a *were*."

The vamps behind us buzzed with feverish whispers while the judges' eyes narrowed suspiciously. Not knowing what we were made them nervous. A nervous vamp was a dangerous vamp. And the room was bursting with them.

"What I mean is, unlike a *were*, I can *change* parts of my body without turning into my beast completely." And unlike anything else on earth, I could also *shift*—disappear under and across solid ground and resurface unscathed. But they didn't need to know that little tidbit. Nor did they need to know I couldn't heal my injuries. If it weren't for Emme's unique ability to heal herself and others, my sisters and I would have died long ago.

"Fascinating," he said in a way that clearly meant I wasn't. The feather quill didn't come with an eraser. And the judge obviously didn't appreciate my making him mess up his book. He dipped his pen into his little inkwell and scribbled out what he'd just written before addressing Taran. "Taran Wird, position?"

"I can release magic into the forms of fire and lightning—"

"Very well, witch." The vamp scrawled.

"I'm not a witch, asshole."

The judge threw his plume on the table, agitated. Judge Malika fixed her frown on Taran. "What did you say?"

Nobody flashed a vixen grin better than Taran. "I said, 'I'm not a witch. Ass. Hole.'"

Emme whimpered, ready to hurl from the stress. Shayna giggled and threw an arm around Taran. "She's just kidding, dude!"

No. Taran didn't kid. Hell, she didn't even know any knock-knock jokes. She shrugged off Shayna, unwilling to back down. She wouldn't listen to Shayna. But she would listen to me.

"Just answer the question, Taran."

The muscles on Taran's jaw tightened, but she did as I asked. "I make fire, light—"

"Fire-breather." Captain Personality wrote quickly.

"I'm not a—"

He cut her off. "Shayna Wird?"

"Well, dude, I throw knives—"

"Knife thrower," he said, ready to get this little meet-and-greet over and done with.

Shayna did throw knives. That was true. She could also transform pieces of wood into razor-sharp weapons and manipulate alloys. All she needed was metal somewhere on her body and a little focus. For her safety, though, "knife thrower" seemed less threatening.

"And you, Emme Wird?"

"Um. Ah. I can move things with my mind—"

"Gypsy," the half-wit interpreted.

I supposed "telekinetic" was too big a word for this idiot. Then again, unlike typical telekinetics, Emme could do more than bend a few forks. I sighed. *Tigress, fire-breather, knife thrower, and Gypsy.* We sounded like the headliners for a freak show. All we needed was a bearded lady. I sighed. *That's what happens when you're the bizarre products of a back-fired curse.*

Misha glanced at us quickly before stepping forward once more. "I will present Mr. Hank Miller and Mr. Timothy Brown as witnesses—" Taran exhaled dramatically and twirled her hair like she was bored. Misha glared at her before finishing. "I do not doubt justice will be served."

Judge Zhahara Nadim, who resembled more of an Egyptian queen than someone who should be stuffed into a powdered wig, surprised me by leering at Misha like she wanted his head for a lawn ornament. I didn't know what he'd done to piss her off; yet knowing we weren't the only ones hated brought me a strange sense of comfort. She narrowed her eyes at Misha, like all predators do before they strike, and called forward someone named "Destiny." I didn't know Destiny, but I knew she was no vampire the moment she strutted onto the dais.

I tried to remain impassive. However, I really wanted to run away screaming. Short of sporting a few tails and some extra digits, Destiny was the freakiest thing I'd ever seen. Not only did she lack the allure all vampires possessed, but her fashion sense bordered on disastrous. She wore black patterned tights, white strappy sandals, and a hideous black-and-white polka-dot turtleneck. I guessed she sought to draw attention from her lime green zebra-print miniskirt. And, my God, her makeup was abominable. Black kohl outlined her bright fuchsia lips, and mint green shadow ringed her eyes.

"This is a perfect example of why I don't wear makeup," I told Taran.

Taran stepped forward with her hands on her hips. "How the hell is *she* a witness? I didn't see her at the club that night! And Lord knows she would've stuck out."

Emme trembled beside me. "Taran, please don't get us killed!"

I gave my youngest sister's hand a squeeze. "Steady, Emme."

Judge Malika called Misha's two witnesses forward. "Mr. Miller and Mr. Brown, which of you gentlemen would like to go first?"

Both "gentlemen" took one gander at Destiny and scrambled away from her. It was never a good sign when something scared a vampire. Hank, the bigger of the two vamps, shoved Tim forward.

"You may begin," Judge Malika commanded. "Just concentrate on what you saw that night. Destiny?"

The four judges swiftly donned protective ear wear, like construction workers used, just as a guard flipped a switch next to the flat-screen. At first I thought the judges toyed with us. Even with heightened senses, how could they hear the testimony through those ridiculous ear guards? Before I could protest, Destiny enthusiastically approached Tim and grabbed his head. Tim's immediate bloodcurdling screams caused the rest of us to cover our ears. Every hair on my body stood at attention. What freaked me out was that he wasn't the one on trial.

Emme's fair freckled skin blanched so severely, I feared she'd pass out. Shayna stood frozen with her jaw open while Taran and I exchanged "oh, shit" glances. I was about to start the "let's get the hell out of here" ball rolling when images from Tim's mind appeared on the screen. I couldn't believe my eyes. Complete with sound effects, we relived the night of David's murder. Misha straightened when he saw David soar out of Taran's window in flames, but otherwise he did not react. Nor did Misha blink when what remained of David burst into ashes on our lawn. Still, I sensed his fury. The image moved to a close-up of Hank's shocked face and finished with the four of us scowling down at the blood and ash.

Destiny abruptly released the sobbing Tim, who collapsed on the floor. Mucus oozed from his nose and mouth. I didn't even know vamps were capable of such body fluids.

At last, Taran finally seemed to understand the deep shittiness of our situation. "Son of a bitch," she whispered.

Hank gawked at Tim before addressing the judges. "If it pleases the court, I swear on my honor I witnessed exactly what Tim Brown did about David Geller's murder. My version would be of no further benefit."

Malika shrugged indifferently. "Very well, you're excused." She turned toward us while Hank hurried back to his seat. "As you just saw, we have ways to expose the truth. Destiny is able to extract memories, but she cannot alter them. Likewise, during Destiny's time with you, you will be unable to change what you saw. You'll only review what has already come to pass."

I frowned. "How do we know you're telling us the truth?"

Malika peered down her nose at me. "What choice do you have? Now, which of you is first?"

CECY ROBSON is an author of contemporary romance, young adult adventure, and award-winning urban fantasy. A double RITA® 2016 finalist for Once Pure and Once Kissed, and a published author of more than sixteen titles, you can typically find her on her laptop writing her stories or stumbling blindly in search of caffeine.

www.cecyrobson.com

Facebook.com/Cecy.Robson.Author

instagram.com/cecyrobsonauthor

twitter.com/cecyrobson

www.goodreads.com/CecyRobsonAuthor